# Sinning AND SANCTIFIED

## Amy Patterson

# G

### STREET CHRONICLES

Published by:
G Street Chronicles
P.O. Box 1822
Jonesboro, GA 30237-1822

www.gstreetchronicles.com
fans@gstreetchronicles.com

Cover design:
Hot Book Covers
www.hotbookcovers.com

ISBN: 978-1-9384425-3-7
LCCN: 2012956476

Join us on our social networks
Like us on Facebook
G Street Chronicles Fan Page
G Street Chronicles CEO Exclusive Readers Group

Follow us on Twitter
@GStreetChronicl

# Sinning
## AND Winning
# SANCTIFIED

## *Acknowledgements*

I first want to thank you God. You have loved and accepted me, despite all of my flaws. I ask that you mold me into a masterpiece that only you can create. I take pride in praising your name every day of my life, and you always cut it close, blessing me at the 59th second. Thank you, for a second chance. This is my debut book. I pray that my new readers will enjoy. I thank you Lord for technology.

To my friends, family, and supporters, I ask that you check your emails. I am sending you the original version of my acknowledgements. My love, respect, and appreciation cannot be stifled.

Andy, Andrea, niece Brenda Justice, author, Cordelia Alexander, Autrella, Rainell, Lottie, Dionnie Bolar, Michele Calhoun, Jessie, Lisa, Mary, Teresa, David, Andre, Ms. Groom, Michele, Janice, Michael, Richard, Mike, Jerome, Mother Glover, Mother Edge, LaKeesha, Steve Harvey, Tyler Perry, Foody, Pastor Creflo Dollar, Kage, Plugg, Kevin, Kelvin, R.J., Bishop Huriah Boynton, and H.T.

To those who have departed, I know you're with God; and you're cheering me on. Rest in Peace.

Thank you, G Street Chronicles, George Sherman Hudson, Shawna A., Mz. Robinson, and Ms. Randolph. If I'm forgetting anyone, I ask your forgiveness.

This is dedicated to anyone who has ever attended a church, but had no idea what took place after the preacher's sermon ended.

# Chapter 1

*Detroit, Michigan*

"Thank God, it's Friday," I said, as I exited my deep blue, 2011 PT Cruiser and headed up the walkway to the door of the church. It was 9:55 am. I was due at work at 10:00. *Four hours of work and I will be free for the weekend,* I mouthed. My name is Natalie Jenelle Champion, daughter of DeAndre and Natalie Jenelle Champion. I am single, 25 years old, no children, and living in Lathrup Village. I stand at 5'9", weighing 135 pounds. I never knew my mother although I was named after her; she walked away from her marriage to my father when I was two years old. Six months later, she was murdered by one of her clients. I am the exact shade of brown as an old school paper bag. No drama…at least, not at this moment.

\* \* \* \* \*

I am currently the part-time administrative assistant to Reverend Doctor Terrell Lamar Hunter of The Journey Toward Christ Missionary Baptist Church in Detroit, Michigan. The building I work and worship in is an art dome-shaped, mega-church with elevators, escalators, media centers, an onsite daycare facility, two computer learning centers, bookstore, sky box offices, four stadium type bathrooms, an underground escape tunnel built into the pulpit, and another one in the baptismal pool. It had a tri-level sanctuary that seated 10,000 people. The building also had several thick, glass doors that were unbreakable, except for one that was located on the north side of the church. I found out about that door and the escape tunnels when I overheard some men talking about them while they were doing some minor renovations on the sanctuary.

\* \* \* \* \*

Since unemployment is at a staggering rate in Michigan now, this is the only position I have at this time. I am also the youngest person on the church Trustee board. I currently hold a Bachelor's Degree in Human Resources Management and a Bachelor's Degree in Business Administration from Eastern Michigan University in Ypsilanti, MI. Due to several prior investments, carefully organized financial planning, and my "seize the opportunity presented and get paid from it" attitude, I can live somewhat comfortably for now, but, I am seeking long-term financial stability and am in the process of investigating how I can increase and stabilize my financial situation for the future. My philosophy is to never say no to money.

I am not your ordinary female. Players, pimps, and hookers raised me. I love my money, I love my freedom, and I am determined to have both-by any means necessary. I would often tell men who would try to talk to me, "If you are not man enough to hold my attention, keep my pockets filled with cash, buy me jewelry, sex me fiercely, and expand my mind by teaching me something to benefit me financially, I will quickly lose interest and disappear." I am not arrogant, but I will not deny myself anything I want. I am definitely my father's daughter. I am argumentative, opinionated, short-tempered and will shoot at someone at the drop of a hat. I also love things that come in threes.

* * * * *

Looking around the parking lot, I see Pastor's vehicle. *Pastor really needs to get one of the deacons or that freeloading, crack head son of his to wash that car; it doesn't make sense for a vehicle that luxurious* (a white, 2011 Bentley Rolls Royce) *to be dirty like that,* I thought. Blessed with such a nice ride and he really doesn't give a damn about it. That's because he didn't pay for it, the members did. Yes, I was privy to church financial information. I knew where the money went and how the money was spent. I knew about the secrets, lies, betrayals, indiscretions, infirmities, murders, and all the other dysfunctional activities of Pastor and his flock.

* * * * *

As I unlocked the entrance door to the church, I could hear in the distance the sounds of Pastor's B.B. and C.C. Winans CD playing. It was coming from his office. As I looked in that direction, I could see that the door was slightly ajar, yet the light was not on.

*I better not bother Pastor right now, seems like he is in the zone. He's getting his by himself time on; I thought to myself. I will call him from my office and speak to him later.*

\* \* \* \* \*

I entered my office, flicked on the overhead light, proceeded to turn my computer on and adjust my chair. I grabbed my day planner from my desk drawer and scanned it for Friday's tasks to be completed. At that very moment, my office phone rang, "Good morning, Journey Toward Christ Missionary Baptist Church, how may I be of service to you?" I said.

"Good morning, Natalie," replied the melodious, baritone voice on the other end, "how long have you been in?"

I paused, exhaled, (from lustful thinking) and then replied, "I just walked in the door, Pastor; how are you today? I heard your music and did not want to disturb you, which is why I did not come down or call you."

"Well, I need to see you in my office, come on down; I'll turn on the light," he replied.

*I really wish you wouldn't,* I lustfully thought, *I might have enough nerve to start something if it was dark. Something like rub my body up against you.*

I walked to the slightly opened door and was greeted by the Reverend Doctor Terrell Lamar Hunter. Pastor Hunter was extremely tall, 6'5", 200 pounds, handsome, semi-dark, age 44, with a melodious, baritone voice, well-built, and possessed a smile that would melt the coldest of hearts and moisten the driest of coochies. In addition, he had a swagger in his walk that would make women ask for forgiveness even though they hadn't committed any infraction. He was married to his high school sweetheart, Charisse Kelly, with two adult children, Dominique and Terrell, Jr. Today, he was dressed in a dark grey, linen suit with a light grey shirt, a two-toned, black and grey tie with grey alligator shoes. Around his neck was a gold cross, encrusted with enough diamonds to feed a third world country and on his wrist, a matching diamond studded watch. Judging from the imprint under his suit jacket, Reverend was blessed by God in more ways than one. As I gazed upon the Pastor, I knew he had to have been some type of hustler, pimp, or street king before he became a man of God, by the way he was dressed. I knew he dealt with all types of people, including politicians, judges, lawyers, drug dealers, pimps, prostitutes, street gangs, murderers, arms dealers, number runners, and every other unsavory character one could mention. He had no fear of going anywhere. Moreover, he never turned his nose up at anybody. He made everyone feel as if they were someone special, even if they were not. You might see him at a $2500 a plate dinner and then look up and see him coming out of a crack house. A graduate of the number one Theological Seminary and Theatrical school, he was the real deal. He was never at a loss for words and if you were not careful in the way you approached him, you may wind up getting your feelings hurt. He was a master at the gift of gab and he possessed a vocabulary that would make Webster run and hide. He could smile at you while cussing you out and still have you lusting after him. Everybody, especially the females, love Pastor Hunter.

\* \* \* \* \*

"Natalie, I have finally made up my mind for my sermon Sunday. I will preach on "Staying on Top while the Bottom Falls Out." He handed me a large, yellow sticky with those words written on it.

"Good choice, Pastor," I said, "we all need some type of spiritual instruction in this economy. Funds are tight; people you thought you would never see struggling are now on the front line with the rest of us. President Obama better do something quick. If you need me, I will be in my office putting the finishing touches on Sunday's bulletins. It should take about three hours and after that, I will be heading out."

I hear the song ringing in my head, *Hush, Hush, Casino is Calling My Name.* I chuckled, but before I could begin the journey back to my office, I stopped when I heard the words, "Now, Natalie you shouldn't even be thinking about going to a casino. That is no place for church members."

"I know, Pastor," I said, replying to his comment, "God gives blessings to people in different arenas, so don't go getting sanctimonious on me. You do some things around here and out in them streets that are not on the straight and narrow, too, now. Trust me; I have seen you, but you did not see me. Just because I don't comment on certain things, doesn't mean I don't know about them happening. I just believe in discretion, that's all; but, I can be tempted to expose some extracurricular activities if the need arises. You better recognize. Let me remind you, every week I pay tithes just like some of those old, rich women you have in your congregation. I never let your collection plate pass me without putting something in. Every week, you get four, new from the bank, one hundred dollar bills from me. It's been over three years now and I have not missed a Sunday; NOW HAVE I?" I covered my mouth with the yellow sticky Pastor had handed me with the sermon topic on it when I realized I had raised my voice. "Pastor, I apologize for raising my voice in God's house, but you know when I'm provoked, even just a little, I go into my volcano erupting episodes. Now, back to what I was saying, you know those are my c-notes because I always leave a Fashion Fair makeup thumbprint on them. The trustees always complain that they have to wash their hands after handling them. Oh yeah, I've overheard them talking about me, especially that Jeanette Porterfield and her husband, Leon, along with Shavonne Swanson's sidekick, DeJuana Edwards. Do the math, Pastor, for these three days, four hours a day that I work as your administrative assistant, the money you pay me each week doesn't even compare to what I am putting in that collection plate on Sunday. If I were working in corporate America, I would be making a lot more. I will continue to work my show and get my money on by any means necessary. So, pump your brakes, Pastor, and back the hell up." I rolled my eyes at him and walked out of his office.

* * * * *

Two hours and 45 minutes into editing bulletins for Sunday service, the church phone rang. I answered it on the second ring. "Good morning, Journey Toward Christ Missionary Baptist Church; how may I be of service to you?" I said.

"Listen here, you bitch, why wasn't my name and donation amount in last Sunday's bulletin? I put in $15,000 out of my change purse and I don't see my name," yelled the enraged female on the other end of the telephone.

"Calm down, please; hello? Who is this?" I asked.

"You know who the fuck this is, bitch; I am the illustrious Frenchee B. Henderson, wife of Claude N. Henderson; Henderson Realty. Your sorry ass is probably renting one of our properties; most of you bums in the church are. I am landlady to basically all of Detroit. I am the black Leona Helmsley, the African Queen of Mean I am filthy rich and can afford to have whatever attitude I choose. People fall at and under my feet. New York belonged to Leona; Detroit belongs to Frenchee B. Do you hear me?" She screamed.

"I hear you, Frenchee B.; but truthfully, I really, really need for you to calm down. And, to answer your statement, NO, I don't rent any of your properties; I live in Lathrup Village, MI. I own my condo, free and clear."

*Boy, oh boy, if I wasn't in this church building, I would give this wannabe diva a royal beat down verbally, talking to me like that. She forgets I know what kind of car she drives. I know where she lives, too.*

"Mrs. Henderson, can you please be civil and respectful on the phone?" I pleaded. "I know that you put $15,000 in church last Sunday; but all large donations are recognized on the last Sunday of the month, therefore, your name and donation amount will be in this week's bulletin since it will be fifth Sunday. As a matter of fact, your name will appear several times due to the fact you also gave something for the Children's Ministry as well as your Usher Board, The Frenchee B. Henderson Usher Board #1." I said that because I figured hearing her name spoken aloud, along with her auxiliary, would diffuse some of her anger. It didn't work.

"Yeah, well, I better see my name in print Sunday or I will tell Pastor to get rid of your triflin' ass. I have clout like that," she yelled.

"Okay, then, Frenchee B., I will see you on Sunday. Have a nice day," I replied. I hung up and thought to myself, *One day, that old bitch is gonna get what she deserves; Lord, please just let me be near to witness it. All that money and just evil; she should be thanking God for her blessings.*

\* \* \* \* \*

Francesca Belize Henderson, also known as Frenchee B. Henderson, a self-proclaimed diva. Frenchee B. was a semi-brown skinned woman who stood about 5'7". She was around 44 and had the body frame and facial features like the actress Jenifer Lewis. She possessed a Bachelor's Degree in Business Management from Florida State University, but was not working now. She thought she was larger than life. Every Sunday, she would come strutting down the center aisle of the church so everyone would have to look at her. She craved and demanded attention. Frenchee B. had been married to Claude for 20 years after having a drunken one-night stand with him and getting pregnant. She went to Chicago to terminate the pregnancy, but just could not go through with it, so, when she returned to Detroit, she and Claude got married.

\* \* \* \* \*

Claude was a fast walking, 46 year old, tall, stocky, dark-skinned man. He had a speech impediment that caused him to stutter. Claude promised Frenchee that he would do whatever he had to do to make her happy. He was just glad that she showed mercy toward the baby. He took a job at a real estate company, furthered his education, and received a Bachelor's Degree in Real Estate, along with an Associate's Degree in Business Law. He then opened his own real estate company. Frenchee had some money from before they were married and loaned Claude some of it to help start the business. After two years, Claude paid her back with interest, but she never let him forget it. He acquired a ton of properties (residential and commercial) in the Detroit Metropolitan Area. He put Frenchee's name on the business with his and the business skyrocketed. Tragedy came when their only daughter, Chynna Lynn, was killed in a drive-by shooting. A single gunshot hit her in the head as she exited her school bus on the way to a class field trip. The loss of his daughter drove Claude to work twice as hard. Profits soared.

\* \* \* \* \*

When I raised my head from the short, silent prayer regarding the phone call I'd received from Frenchee Henderson, I looked into the face of Pastor Hunter who was now leaning on the wall of my office entrance.

"Is everything okay, Natalie? Who was that on the phone?"

"That was Frenchee Henderson trippin' out because she thought I left her name off the bulletin," I replied.

"Pastor, why do people with a little money sometimes act so nutty? I wish you could have heard her mouth on the phone. I wonder if she ever kissed her mother with that mouth."

He then said, "I heard her, Natalie, let it go. You did the right thing by staying calm. I'm proud of you, kiddo."

*"I figure Brother Henderson has to keep sanitizer well stocked, so after he kisses her, he can cleanse himself.* Oops! Did I say that out loud?" I asked.

Pastor Hunter tilted his head to the side and answered, "Well, Natalie, some people who have never had anything and get the privilege of getting something just do things like that. You never know, they might have a reason for acting that way, maybe some childhood issues or just issues, period."

"Yes, Pastor, you are probably right," I replied. *That woman has issues all right and I am gonna find out what they are if it is the last thing I do,* I thought to myself. At that point, I just sat there, thinking about what he said, while trying to get a sneak peek of him from head to toe without being too obvious. *Oh, Lord, this man was soooo damn fine.*

*Lord, please relieve me of the thoughts I'm having inside. Lord, I know I can't work here much longer because, if I do, I am gonna be asking you for forgiveness. I am telling you now, if the door of temptation cracks open even a centimeter, I am gonna be rushing in. Lord, help me,* I silently prayed. *Keep me near the cross. I have to step up my game and get up out of here before I get in trouble.*

\* \* \* \* \*

"Natalie, Natalie," Pastor called, interrupting my lustful thoughts and mini prayer. He touched my shoulder, making me melt inside as if I were a piece of chocolate that had been left in the sun. He said, "I will be leaving in about 30 minutes. If my wife calls, tell her I am gonna stop at Farmers' Market, go by The Broadway to get one of those suits I saw Steve Harvey wearing. After that, I'm going to get my grandson, Little Tee, a suit and some shoes. My daughter, Dominique, is coming home from college this weekend and I want her son to be looking good Sunday when she comes."

"Oh, yeah, Pastor, I forgot about Dominique, seeing as she only makes an appearance on special occasions. How is she doing at Spelman?"

"Dominique is doing great, Natalie," stated Pastor Hunter, sporting that smile that made me want to find his shoes under my bed and him in it. "Dominique is carrying a 4.0 average right now. Another year and she will have her Bachelor's in Media Communications, with an Associate's Degree in Language Arts. I just wish she would join a church, not necessarily mine, but join somewhere. I just cannot understand where I went wrong with her; she has no type of belief in God or participating in anything where the church is concerned. I literally had to bribe her to come to church this coming Sunday for the anniversary celebration."

"You are joking, huh, Pastor? How much do you have to give her, Pastor? Don't answer that; I'm just kidding," I said. I interrupted before he could speak, "Just be thankful that she's in school and that she only had the one child; it could be worse, you know, she could be out there on drugs or dealing drugs, stealing, robbing, the lady of a drug lord, prostituting, or doing God knows what. Sometimes, we have to be appreciative of the small things," I replied.

"Yeah, Natalie, you're right about that," he said. "Let me go make a phone call and then I will be leaving shortly after." As he walked back down to his office, I thought to myself, *Farmers' Market, The Broadway, my foot. I know he's going to see Lady Monica Davenport. It's time for him to pull some "Maintenance Man" duty.*

\* \* \* \* \*

*Friday, 1:00 p.m.*

Lady Monica Christine Davenport's husband, Anthony, is out of town on radio business and won't be back until Monday. I overheard him speak about it to one of the trustees last Sunday as I was walking past. Anthony was usually out of town three of four weekends a month. Pastor would have access to Anthony's house this weekend. He'd get an extra thousand, too. Lady Monica wouldn't have to pay for the luxurious hotel villa they'd use when they would have their weekly Friday afternoon sexual rendezvous. Anthony Davenport was the second husband of Lady Monica. She married him after her first husband, Luther Hutchinson, passed away as a result of complications from surgery to remove his legs because of diabetes.

Lady Monica was still a very beautiful lady, even though she was now in her mid-40s. She was around 6'1", 145 pounds, with an extremely light complexion. She had shapely legs that went on forever and only pursued men who had financial stability. Her first husband, Luther, was originally from Ohio and met her while attending Eastern Michigan University where he was studying Mortuary Science. Lady Monica was pursuing her Master's Degree in Music Appreciation. Luther had two children, a son, Luther III, and a daughter, Melissa. He also had a brother named Lawrence who everyone called L.H. When Luther and Lady Monica got married, Luther sent both children to boarding schools and ran a lucrative funeral business, which had been passed down to him by his late father. For years, their clientele consisted of African American politicians from Ohio, Michigan, Alabama, Chicago, Georgia, Louisiana, Philadelphia, and several other states. All of the African American sororities, fraternities, and lodges used his services. Their funeral business was number one in Detroit until his death. After Luther's death, Lady Monica sold the business to Julius K. Fitzpatrick who was an up and coming Funeral Director and a member of Journey Toward Christ for a large, undisclosed amount. She banked some of the monies after giving a large donation to the church and giving me 55 grand because I gave her a stock tip that paid off.

Lady Monica said I was like the daughter that she always wanted. She loved me like a daughter and I loved her back, like the mother I never had. Lady Monica was wealthy money wise, but she was richer with character, wisdom, insight, a genuine love for humanity, and a multitude of friends. Rumors floated around that Lady Monica had a grown daughter somewhere in Southern California. It was also rumored that they had become estranged because her daughter wanted to become an actress. They had a big fight and the daughter took off. She never spoke on it and if you inquired, she would quickly change the subject or just walk away from you. The Hutchinsons were instrumental in the startup of Journey Toward Christ Missionary Baptist Church.

\* \* \* \* \*

Several years later, Anthony Reynard Davenport, a widower, moved to Detroit from Huntsville, Alabama, looking to expand his thriving radio consulting practice, which was already on the Fortune 500 list of African American owned businesses. He walked into Journey Toward Christ one Sunday as a visitor. He saw Lady Monica, and fell in love with her at first glance. They dated about six months and married thereafter. Truthfully, I believe she only married him for his money. Anthony's looks paled in comparison to the lovely Lady Monica. Anthony was the same height as Lady Monica, but had a pudgy body, almost pear-shaped. His facial features were what one would normally say was okay. Having money, one would have thought that he would have taken better care of his body by at least working out. He did dress well, along with his weekly visit to the barbershop to maintain his beard and perfectly low-cut, waved hairstyle.

\* \* \* \* \*

Lady Monica had Anthony's nose open so wide, he granted her total access to all his business and personal monies. He was grateful to have her as his wife. In his eyes, Lady Monica could do no wrong; so the more money Anthony made, the more Lady Monica spent, especially when it came to giving at Journey Toward Christ. Anthony took on a second job as a part-time radio talk show host for a couple of years just to cover her extravagant lifestyle. He even carried caskets on the weekends he was in town for Julius K. Fitzpatrick, who now held the position of in-house Funeral Director for Journey Toward Christ. Therefore, Lady Monica Davenport would be considered one of Journey's largest contributors financially, next to Frenchee B. Henderson and she, in return, demanded (as many women in the church did) special attention from the handsome Pastor Terrell L. Hunter.

\* \* \* \* \*

The electronic folding machine completed the fold on the last of the Sunday bulletins. I began to count them to make sure that I had enough to distribute. Eight-thousand should be enough. The Sunday coming up is the fifth Sunday of the month and required more bulletins because The Arch Angel Choir sang on the fifth Sunday and Assistant Minister Marvin Cunningham usually preached the sermon. This combination always drew a large crowd because of the type of songs the choir sang and the way Minister Cunningham preached and turned the pulpit into a dance floor. In addition, the bulletins listed the names and donation amounts of the members. It's funny how people like to see their name in print. I knew people who would write checks that would bounce just so they could see their name in the bulletin. I would then have to send a letter to the member letting him or her know that the check they submitted had come back NSF (non-sufficient funds). Journey Toward Christ banked at the same branch in which Shavonne Swanson worked. Huntington Bank in Novi, Michigan. I'm sure she was also aware of this, but she never said anything; at least, it never got back to my desk where most of the church gossip ended.

\* \* \* \* \*

The Arch Angel Choir was the only choir that had extra musicians (drummer, Shawn Griffin, guitarist Ronald Black and a wild keyboard player, Leon Ballard). When The Arch Angel Choir sang, you were guaranteed to be joy filled when you left Journey Toward Christ. This choir was widely recognized and was always being invited to sing at other churches. They were even invited out of state to sing, which is how Sharondelle wound up in Texas. When The Arch Angel Choir performed, people would dance as if they were in the nightclub. Even the children and older members enjoyed this choir. The majority of the members of Journey were lively and loved to dance and praise. If you were one for that sad hymnbook singing and those old, sad, slow songs that made people cry, this would not be the church for you. This was a church filled with fire and I mean that in more ways than one.

\* \* \* \* \*

*Fifteen more minutes and I am out of here*, I silently rejoiced, looking at the clock in my office. I picked up the box with the bulletins in it, placed the thank you note on top of it addressed to the ushers, which expressed my appreciation to them for making sure each member received a bulletin when they entered the sanctuary. I took the escalator down to the ushers' quarters, unlocked the door and went inside. Two minutes later, the telephone began to ring. I placed the box on the table and picked up the phone that was in their office.

"Good afternoon, Journey Toward Christ, Missionary Baptist Church; how may I be of service to you?"

"Good afternoon, Natalie; this is first lady, Charisse Hunter, how are you this afternoon?"

"I am truly blessed, Mrs. Hunter, and you?"

"I don't know yet, Natalie. Is my husband there?"

"No, Mrs. Hunter," I answered. "He left about 1:00. He said he was going to run some errands and pick up a suit and shoes for Little Tee."

"That's what he said, huh?" She replied, in a monotone. I could tell by her tone that she was not buying my story. "Natalie, I realize that it's almost time for you to leave, but, I am on my way down there. I need to speak with you face to face. I will be there in 15 minutes. This is not a request, Natalie." Before I could respond, she hung up.

\* \* \* \* \*

*Oh, well, I guess my Friday will be starting later than I expected,* I thought, as I paced the floor of my office wondering what this was about. First Lady Hunter was a classy lady. She held a job at the City of Detroit Election Commission as Director of Voter Operations. She was beautiful and smart, but she sometimes acted as if she was naive. She held a Master's Degree in Business Operations. She was 43, petite, 5'4', 135 pounds, and a brown complexion. Looking at her shape, it was hard to believe that she was the mother of two children, Terrell Jr., and Dominique, who were now adults. First Lady Hunter was one of the nicest people you would ever want to meet. I once saw her empty one of her designer purses of all of her personal belongings and give it to a homeless lady who had been standing at the back door of the church. All that was left in the purse was $1,000 and a Kleenex. That lady was blown away and so was I.

* * * * *

Ten minutes later, I smelled the fragrance of Vera Wang perfume. I knew it was First Lady Charisse. "Hello, there," I said, as she came into my office. She had a look on her face that I had never seen in all the time I'd known her.

"Sit down, Natalie, we have to talk," she said. "What's wrong, first lady?" I asked, sincerely.

"Let's cut right to the chase, Natalie. I suspect my husband is cheating on me with several females in the congregation. Would you happen to have seen or heard anything about this? You are Pastor's administrative assistant and I know you are privy to a lot of things that go on around here. I am really concerned with mainly two females. One by the name of Shavonne Swanson and the other one is Lady Monica Davenport. Lately, I've been watching her and Shavonne, and the way those two look and react every time my husband is in the vicinity. I've been noticing that he leaves the house smelling one way and returns smelling altogether different. Weekend before last, he left the house smelling like The Eddie Bauer Cologne Collection I had purchased for him, but when he returned that night, well, really, I should say the next day because it was 5:00 in the morning, he smelled like The Armani Black Cologne Collection."

"Now, first lady," I said, without looking at her. "You know I love both you and Pastor. I enjoy working here and I enjoy my membership here at Journey. I am not one to come between a husband and wife. Pastor is the one you should be speaking to. I beg of you, please leave me out of this. I really am not qualified to be answering these questions. Once again, I reiterate, talk to your husband."

"Natalie? Did you see the gaudy diamond and ruby bracelet that

Shavonne had on last Sunday?" First Lady asked.

"I thought it was nice," I answered. "Women like gaudy things; well, some of us do. First Lady, I really have to leave now. I have an appointment downtown." *I used that as an excuse to escape her interrogation.* "Everything is ready for Sunday. Don't forget to lock up when you leave. Pray, First Lady. See you Sunday." I grabbed my car keys, made a beeline to my car, jumped in, cranked up, and pulled away. I thought to myself. *Pastor, you better watch out. Your game is falling off and your shirt tail is showing.*

\* \* \* \* \*

I entered Northbound Chrysler I-75 freeway. I would take this to Walter Ruther 696 West toward Lathrup Village. As I reached over to turn on the radio in my vehicle, I got a glimpse of my passenger seat and realized I'd left my coat and purse, along with my drivers' license, on my desk, at the church. *Son of a bitch!* I mouthed, and looked up to see exactly where I was. I was approaching exit 55 Holbrook-Caniff.

"I better get off here and go back," I said. "I hope First Lady is gone. I really don't want to talk to her right now." My mind drifted back toward Pastor Hunter. Right about now he should be showering and getting ready to leave Lady Monica's house. That man is going to face doom before it's over. I foresee trouble coming and its right over the horizon. I can almost taste it.

\* \* \* \* \*

I arrived back at the church about seven minutes later. No cars or people were in sight. *Thank you, God,* I mouthed, and rushed to open the door. I walked into my office, grabbed my purse, and started to leave. The ringing of the church telephone startled me. I looked up at the clock; it was 3:05 pm.

"I am not answering that," I said aloud. "I am officially off duty." Just as the telephone stopped ringing, my cell began to play a special ring tone, indicating I had a text message. "What the hell? What now?" I reached for my phone, which was in my pocket, flipped it open, and pushed several keys on the pad to reveal the message.

The message read: "Natalie, I need you to hit me up on my cell right now, I mean right now; Pastor." *Uh, oh,* I thought. *I'm gonna ignore this,* but before I could, the message ringtone sounded again. This time, the message read: "Natalie, I'm serious, call me now, 911, Pastor." I deleted both messages and proceeded to gather my belongings and exit the building.

\* \* \* \* \*

As I opened the door to my vehicle, a different ringtone sounded, indicating I had an actual voice message. "I foresee trouble coming," I said aloud, as I fastened my seatbelt. I entered my code and a baritone voice began to speak.

"Natalie, Natalie, call me, I need to hear from you, call now, 911."

"Let me call this man back; I know he is not gonna stop until he hears from me." I pushed received calls on my phone, hit dial, and was immediately connected to Pastor's number. He answered on the first ring.

"Natalie, business ran long for me. Have you heard from my wife yet? You know, I think I saw her car ride down the street I was on earlier."

"Oh, really, Pastor? And where was this?" I inquired.

He answered, "I was at Lady Monica's house. Don't judge me, Natalie; just answer me. Have you heard from my wife today?"

I answered, "Yes. I told her what you told me to tell her; she's not buying it. My suggestion to you-have some bags of clothing, some fruits or vegetables and your game in order when you get home because it's about to get "extra" at your spot. That's all I have to say. Peace." I hung up my cell phone, turned it off completely, and drove away. I thought to myself, *I really don't want to get caught up in nobody's drama. Something major is gonna happen soon and I don't want to be a part of it. I've got to get me a game plan and disappear before disaster strikes.*

# Chapter 2

*Lathrup Village, Michigan*

I pulled into the attached garage of my condominium and began to sing, "It's the weekend and it's Natalie's time to shine." In the gated community of Lathrup Estates, I owned a tri-level, 4500 square foot abode of bachelorette comfort and ecstasy. There was plush carpeting throughout, a spiral staircase, three extra-large bedrooms, with a stripper pole in my master bedroom. One of the bedrooms was a loft on the top level with attached bathroom, along with a built in Jacuzzi that could accommodate eight or more. All bedrooms had walk-in cedar chest closets and fireplaces. There was also an 800 square foot kitchen with stainless steel appliances, rectangular island with marble counters, and a breakfast nook. My laundry room housed a built in Laundromat-sized washer and dryer. There were also fireplaces in the living room and dining room. A glass enclosed soundproof office with computer and state-of-the-art office accessories (printer, fax, copier, and shelves), and stereo system was located on the second level of the condo, with a spectacular view of a wooded area. My game room was equipped with state of the art stereo system, casino-sized slot machine, vintage jukebox, an eight-foot pool table, wet bar with mini fridge, and a 72-inch plasma TV. In my main bathroom, three separate pulsating showerheads in a separate standup shower, white porcelain toilet bidet, and garden tub adorned with gold plated faucets. In the living room, there was expensive artwork and other numerous amenities. Yes, my condo was fabulous and completely paid for. I only had to pay taxes once a year and due to the generosity of a set of twin gentlemen, I was paid up in taxes until the year 2014. I exited my vehicle and jogged up the stairs of my luxurious abode.

I opened the door and yelled, "Lucy, I'm home!" Making a joke to remind myself of my freedom and independence of not having to answer to a single soul and loving every minute of it because having your own is PRICELESS.

I threw my coat and purse on the leather sectional and raced to the refrigerator to retrieve the pitcher of apple martinis. I grabbed a glass, poured a glassful, and took a long sip. I proceeded to the shower, turned it on, and watched as steam began to rise. I finished my drink and began to disrobe in anticipation of a long, hot, relaxing shower. I entered the shower and began to bathe myself with the vanilla scented body wash. The hot water soothed my tension with each spray of pulsating water. I rejoiced in the fact that later tonight I would be at the casino, letting my hair down and letting the troubles of the world disappear from my mind and body. I exited my shower, dried myself off, and slipped into my plush, terrycloth robe and slippers.

\* \* \* \* \*

As I proceeded to my bedroom, I heard my house phone ringing. I walked over, checked the caller ID, and realized that it was the infamous Shavonne Swanson. "Hey, Natalie, girl; what's going on? I've been calling around looking for you; what's up with your cell phone?"

"Hello, Shavonne," I replied. "What can I do for you? Why are you calling me at home?"

"I need a big favor," she stated.

"Oh, really, and what would that be?" I asked.

She replied, "I need you to call Pastor and have him meet me at Hawthorne Villas on Evergreen and 696 tonight, 8:00 p.m. I can't get through to his cell or house phone. I believe his wife has blocked my numbers from both phones and he doesn't know it yet. Do me this favor and there will be something in it for you."

*Hmmm,* I thought. *This woman has long paper and so does her sidekick, DeJuana. Why not make me something? This loot will replenish some of the loot I'm gonna spend tonight and help with my weekly donation.*

"Hello, hello, Natalie? Are you still there?"

"Yeah, Shavonne, I'm here, so where is your sidekick, DeJuana? And what would she have to say about you doing this?" I asked, knowing that she was on the line, too. Being Shavonne's sidekick meant they were like two peas in a pod; wherever Shavonne was, DeJuana was there or not far behind.

"What would I say?" DeJuana huffed through the receiver. "I would say that's my girl and I support whatever she does."

"Well, hello to you, too, DeJuana," I replied, arrogantly. I did not like that bitch, but I tolerated her like everyone else who liked Shavonne. "Shavonne, tell DeJuana to hang up," I requested.

"Hang up, bitch," I heard Shavonne say with a nasty tone. Then I heard a click and Shavonne say, "She's off."

"I tell you what I'm gonna do," I said, while rubbing my palms together. "I want $1500 from you and $800 from your girl. Y'all are getting off cheap 'cause I know you already have four or five times that amount on hand right now; that's why you are looking for Pastor Hunter."

Shavonne laughed and replied, "Girl, you are so crazy." "Yeah, whatever," I said. "I'm getting dressed now and I will be on West Outer Drive in 30 minutes. Leave my loot in your plant box. Don't fuck with me, Shavonne."

\* \* \* \* \*

I geared up in weekend clothes, a black Baby Phat top, dark Apple Bottom jeans, and black, low-cut boots. I grabbed my phone, purse, and keys, topped off my outfit with a matching cap and left. Twenty or so minutes later, I was at Shavonne's residence on West Outer Drive. It was a large, 6500 square foot brick home with stained glass windows and a three-car garage. All I will say is that the inside of her house was decorated like a palace.

\* \* \* \* \*

Shavonne's Chrysler 300 SRT8 was parked in the driveway along with DeJuana's matching Chrysler 300 SRT8. There was also a red 2011 Cadillac Escalade. I noticed the license plate was from out of state, Texas, and immediately knew it belonged to Sharondelle. Sharondelle was Shavonne's daughter. I parked on the street and walked up to the plant box. Inside the green envelope was a note instructing me what to say to Pastor and my funds. I went back to my vehicle and sat down, locked my door, and proceeded to count my money. It was in two separate piles with a rubber band around each one. I counted the first pile. It consisted of eight crisp one hundred dollar bills. I replaced the rubber band and counted the second. There were 10 crisp one hundred dollar bills and 10 crisp 50-dollar bills. I replaced the rubber band, secured the money on my person, re-read the note with the instructions, and made my call.

"Hello, T. L. Hunter here," stated the melodious voice. "It's me, Natalie. You solo right now?"

"Yes, I am," he replied.

"Shavonne Swanson. Tonight, 8:00. Hawthorne Villas. 11 Mile/696. Call cell when you are five minutes away. Get your phone straight. The word is 'delete'. Peace." I hung up, hit previous number and Shavonne answered. I said, "Handle your business." Then, I disconnected the call.

\* \* \* \* \*

Shavonne Swanson. (5'9", brown complexion, body frame and facial features resembling Actress /Comedienne, Niecy Nash). Shavonne was 39 years old, somewhat thick, with a flat stomach, but her jiggles were all in the right places. A bona fide thoroughbred, with the heart and mentality of a hustler, Shavonne was classified as a money hungry, high-class call girl, who only dated men with large amounts of cash money. She was divorced and had a son who had changed his name to Sharondelle. Actually, Sharondelle was born a male named Regis. However, at age 18, he decided to have a complete sex change and now was an anatomically correct female, who was now 21, and a renowned musician/choir director at New Mt. Herald Church of the Covenant in Houston, Texas. Sharondelle looked like a younger version of Shavonne.

\* \* \* \* \*

Shavonne was not dating anyone exclusively, but from time to time, she and Pastor Hunter would disappear at the same time. They would be MIA for days at times. I can imagine this was eating away at First Lady; I think that's why she would always go to Cincinnati to visit with her sister. Pastor would send Shavonne and a few other female members to sleep with other men, married and unmarried, to "get money for the church." Being the thoroughbred she was, she did not seem to mind. She would do anything for Pastor. She would take it in stride and follow his instructions to the letter. I never saw or heard about any dissention between Pastor and Shavonne concerning money or anything else.

\* \* \* \* \*

Shavonne was always draped in the finest clothes, shoes, minks, diamonds, and perfume. She drove a vanilla cream 2011 Chrysler 300 SRT8. She ate at the finest restaurants, attended the best concerts, plays, and parties. Once a year, she would get a fully paid vacation to the destination of her choice paid for by Pastor Hunter, via member donations. You never saw Shavonne without her makeup and hair done. She was considered a VIP at Diva's Doorstep, Detroit's finest hair salon. There were only two things I never understood about Shavonne. She had never gotten her nails or toes done professionally and why did she hang around that unattractive DeJuana Edwards? Personally, I liked Shavonne Swanson.

\* \* \* \* \*

We started on a bad note when I first arrived at Journey Toward Christ. She thought I was an airhead and she looked down her nose at me. That quickly changed, however, when Shavonne had to come off her high horse at a Journey Toward Christ Church's congregation meeting. One of her secrets was revealed and she had to admit that her son, Regis was now her daughter, Sharondelle. I came to her rescue verbally in front of the entire church administration and congregation when they tried to verbally and physically beat her down. I also negotiated so that she would not be kicked out of the church. I was sort of her defensive mouthpiece without a law license. DeJuana was at a hotel FINALLY having sex, giving Leon Porterfield a blowjob, which I had set up, and did not attend the church meeting that night. I had experienced several times being ganged up on and no one having my back; so that night, I made it my business to have Shavonne's.

\* \* \* \* \*

Shavonne was so impressed by my vocabulary and me having her back, she apologized for attempting to stereotype me. After that, we began talking and found out that we had a lot in common and we knew some of the same people. We became good friends. Shavonne used her connects to help me secure a seasonal job with the United States Post Office, which helped put some extra monies into my accounts. She was sassy and considered a questionable woman by a few individuals, but she was all right with me. I liked her style. She was beautiful, smart, scandalous, down for whatever presented itself, didn't take no shit, and she was going to get her monies by any means necessary. Last, but not least, she had an aura that drew men to her like moths to a flame; and most of them did not have a problem emptying their wallets and bank accounts and giving her their cash.

\* \* \* \* \*

DeJuana Edwards was a different story. She was also 39, 5'9", extra dark complexion, large, pink lips, and medium framed. I have to admit she had a nice figure, but her facial features were extremely unattractive. She could pass for Flavor Flav in a dress. She also had a flirtatious walk. She lived on the Westside of Detroit in the Ewald Circle area, a neighborhood that once was known for its elegance, glitz, and glamour. She drove the same type of vehicle as Shavonne. She also had the same type of clothes, jewelry, shoes, and furs, which she would mismatch on the colors, like wearing green and orange. As for her hair, she wore these reddish and sometimes, brownish, wigs. She had a multitude of them, but regardless of their style, she still looked like Flavor Flav unleashed. She actually thought she was the shit and would sometimes try to talk down to people, which only led to getting her feelings hurt the majority of the time.

She tried it on me when I first came to Journey and I fired three .9mm rounds from my Glock at her. I missed on purpose because I had just been baptized and vowed that I was going to try to do better with my life and calm my hair-triggered temper. My gunfire ceased her bullshit indefinitely. That was why I didn't like her. She had a brother and several sisters who were also members; they all looked like crack addicts.

\* \* \* \* \*

She also served on the same auxiliaries as Shavonne. Although she didn't have the men on lock like Shavonne, some did sleep with her once or twice. A few claimed they were drugged out or drunk and only let her give them a blowjob just so they could have a gateway to Shavonne. DeJuana worked at a Drug and Alcohol Rehabilitation Center in Cass Corridor. I heard her complaining about drunks and junkies one Wednesday at choir rehearsal. Even though Shavonne treated DeJuana like shit and would sometimes talk to her as if she walked on four legs, DeJuana always remained faithful toward Shavonne. When Shavonne Swanson did something, DeJuana Edwards attempted to do the same thing. They both even went to the same school for Travel Agent, but not at the same time. Diva Shavonne Swanson graduated first.

\* \* \* \* \*

When I pulled up to the Credit Union, my car clock blinked 5:15 pm. "Ooh, let me hurry and deposit the majority of this money," I said. "I believe they close at six. I'm looking forward to tonight, but I'm no fool, I am putting something up for a later date." I exited my vehicle and headed for the front door. *I hope it's' not crowded in there; maybe I can get in and out,* I thought. Once through the door, I secured a place in line behind two people. As I got closer, I realized that I knew the man and woman who were waiting for the teller. It was Leon Porterfield and his wife, Jeanette. Both were trustees at Journey Toward Christ.

Leon also sang in the male choir and served on Frenchee B. Henderson's Usher Board. Leon was a man of small stature, 135 pounds and stood about 5'3", mid 30's. He wore these hideous black rimmed eyeglasses. Lately, he was beginning to look like a crack head in training. Leon was losing weight, hair falling out, skin ashy and looking old. Leon was the manager of a neighborhood supermarket which was in walking distance of his house on North Martindale. Leon had held that job since high school and never tried to do anything else. Leon could be considered quiet and meek. He was satisfied with life just as it was. How he ended up with that wildcat Jeanette? I will never know.

\* \* \* \* \*

Jeanette Porterfield, on the other hand, was the total opposite. She was loud, wild, and extremely violent toward Leon. Jeanette was on her way to becoming a millionaire. She was an investor in the stock market and always made stock trades, which would usually pay off. Jeanette controlled Leon because she had the money in their marriage and they had no children. Jeanette worked at the downtown branch of UPS. Jeanette was selfish and never shared her stock tips with anyone, not even her church members. I obtained one of her stock tips because I picked her pocket at a Saturday night choir rehearsal because she made a remark toward me that I didn't particularly care for. Jeanette was much taller than Leon, 6'0", same age, brown skinned, and was an extremely large woman, weighing about 300 pounds. To top it off, she drank a lot and was always loud talking and hitting Leon. There was no place sacred when it came to embarrassing him. Not even church. Jeanette would go from zero to 60 in 10 seconds using her mouth and was subject to backhand him like he was a child. She hit him one Saturday night at choir rehearsal; he tried to run and wound up falling into the baptismal pool, which was filled with water. Choir rehearsal ended early that night.

\* \* \* \* \*

I approached Jeanette and Leon. I spoke and Jeanette spoke; Leon mumbled something That sounded like, "Please help me." I asked them if they were coming to the anniversary celebration on Sunday. Leon looked at Jeanette as if he had to get permission to speak, but said nothing. I shook my head. Jeanette said she would be there and then she grabbed and drug poor Leon off, holding him by the back of his shirt collar to the next available teller window. I thought to myself, *He needs to find him a backbone.*

\* \* \* \* \*

My turn came quicker than I thought. "Hello, Ms. Champion, how may I help you today?" The teller asked.

"Hello," I replied, "deposit of $2,000 cash."

"May I have your account number?" I pointed to it on my deposit slip and counted out all of the money. I took six of the 50 dollar bills and put them in my pocket. I handed the remainder to the teller. I took the slip from the teller and verified she had made my deposit. I then looked at my balance. I now had in this one account almost 100-thousand. *Soon, I would have to move this money elsewhere,* I thought.

\* \* \* \* \*

Walking back to my car, I spotted Leon and Jeanette leaving and I waved to them. Jeanette waved back and then she did the strangest thing. Without saying a word, she hauled off and slapped the shit out of Leon. She hit him so hard that it sounded like a gunshot. He fell to the ground and his feet went over his head. I thought to myself, *What was that for? Oh, well, love is strange.* I looked at Leon and felt sorry for him, but my money hungry demon had other ideas brewing. I had to get home and call Shavonne. We definitely would have to do lunch. I wouldn't even get mad if she brought "The Creature from the Black Lagoon," DeJuana Edwards.

\* \* \* \* \*

After stopping at the gas station, I arrived back at the condo around 7:00. "I am going out tonight, despite all these interruptions. I am going and that is final," I spoke aloud, trying to convince myself. I looked in the refrigerator and in the cabinets. I had enough food to last for another week, but decided I would go grocery shopping tomorrow. I poured myself another glass of apple martini and sat on the side of my bed. "I am gonna take a power nap, get up, shower, get dressed, and be out," I stated softly. I swallowed the last of the martini and drifted off to dreamland.

\* \* \* \* \*

I was awakened from my sleep by the sound my cell phone ringing. When I answered, I heard a very sexy male voice. He asked for a name. I did not recognize and I told him that he had the wrong number. He apologized and hung up. I usually dismiss things like that, but for some strange reason, that voice stuck in my head. I got up, showered, put on my makeup, and began to put the finishing touches on my hair. I had a sexy, low-cut jacket and skirt outfit from Lover's Lane that I had never worn before and decided I would wear that. I checked my makeup, hair, and outfit. "You look fabulous," I said, looking in the mirror.

Twenty minutes later, I was at my destination, Aces High Hotel/Casino. People were dancing, drinking, gambling, and having a good time. Motown music was playing through the speaker system, bells and whistles were ringing, indicating winners on slot machines and table games. I walked to the bar, ordered an apple martini, and lit a cigarette.

I felt the presence of someone standing behind me. I turned to investigate and looked into the face of one of the finest men in Detroit. He was 6'1", 185 pounds; his skin color was the equivalent of smooth caramel. He had the sexiest beard and moustache. He was wearing all black, a platinum chain, and matching wristwatch.

"Excuse me, dear lady," he said. "If I was standing too close, I truly apologize. I did not mean to invade your space."

"That's okay," I replied, "but, thank you for being a gentleman and acknowledging the fact."

"My name is Monticello Strickland," he said. "And you are?" As he spoke, his voice seemed familiar. I knew that I had heard it before, yet I could not remember where.

"Hello, Monticello, my name is Natalie Champion," I replied.

"And you definitely look like a champion," he replied. "Your outfit is stunning and so are you. May I buy you a drink, Natalie?" He asked.

"That would be nice," I replied.

He ordered an apple martini for me and a Hennessey for himself. We conducted small talk for a while, had a couple more drinks, and then he told me he had to leave for work. I found out he was a homicide detective for the Detroit Police Department, single, no kids, living the bachelor life, and he had no fear of money or spending it. He was filling in for a co-worker who had to leave town for an emergency.

He handed me his card and told me, "Tonight will be your night. We will meet again." He hugged me, took my cell number, and walked away. As I watched him walk away, I thought to myself, *Yes, we will.*

\* \* \* \* \*

I proceeded to find my favorite dollar slot machine. When I did, I inserted my player's card and two 20-dollar bills, pushed the "play maximum" a few times, and nothing major happened. I decided I would spin a couple more times and get up. I pushed the button again and this time, all three sevens with the fire under them came up. I looked up at the marquee and realized that I had won a total of $5,000. Bells and whistles began to ring and the machine lit up, indicating that I had won the jackpot. A casino attendant approached me and asked for ID. She returned shortly with another lady and had me sign a form. She then counted out $5,000 in one hundred dollar increments. Monticello was right; tonight did wind up being my night. I looked at my watch; it was now 1:30 am. "Well, I am outta here," I said. "I can make it to the store in my neighborhood and get home by 2:15." I left the casino and looked around to make sure I was not being followed.

\* \* \* \* \*

I arrived at the party store near my residence. I purchased several bottles of champagne, Hennessey, Belvedere, and Remy to stock my bar. By 2:10 a.m., I was in front of my condo. I exited my vehicle, took my things into the house, and poured myself another martini. I still had some money left from what I had taken with me to the casino (thanks to Monticello buying my drinks) and the $5,000cash that I had won. As I sipped on my drink, I thought about everything that had happened tonight. As I remembered the conversation between Monticello and myself, the sound of his voice came into play. That was he with the wrong number earlier. Could this be a coincidence or was something going on?

\* \* \* \* \*

Saturday morning, I awoke to the sound of my alarm clock radio. It was playing an old school tune by The O'Jays, *Living for the Weekend.* I checked the time; it was 10:00am. "Oh, damn," I shouted. "I gotta get going; the credit union closes at noon. I need to make a deposit, go grocery shopping, to the cleaners, clean my condo, plus, I have to call Shavonne." I jumped out of bed, stripped it down, took all the linen to the laundry room, entered my bathroom, and turned on the shower. I entered the shower, lathered up and took a quick shower. As I exited the shower, I heard the last ring of my cell phone. I dried off, put on slippers, and robe. I checked the number, but did not recognize it, so I proceeded to brush my teeth, get dressed, and touchup my hair. After getting myself a breakfast bar and a glass of milk, I grabbed my shopping list, cleaner's receipt, keys, purse, money and phone and I left the house.

\* \* \* \* \*

I stopped at the cleaners and gave the receipt to the clerk. She returned with my three outfits, which were paid for in advance. I put the clothes in the trunk and headed toward the credit union. When I arrived on Livernois, it was 11:40 am.

"Thank you, God; I made it!" I said, softly. An EMS unit and a Detroit Police cruiser were parked in the lot, but I thought nothing of it until I got inside. I entered the credit union, got in line, and, once again, looked up to see Jeanette and Leon Porterfield. Jeanette was in a shouting match with the security guard. He was attempting to calm her down. From the conversations of others in line, it appeared that Jeanette had followed Leon and caught him trying to withdraw money from the account.

At that point, she assaulted Leon by beating him in the head with her purse. Leon was sitting on the other side of the credit union being treated by an EMS tech. He was holding his head with a bloody towel as the EMS tech attempted to stop the bleeding and bandage him.

I heard a woman in line ahead of me say, "Boy, she really fucked him up with that purse. Mike Tyson ain't got shit on her. I hope ol' boy hid a couple of dollars so he can get himself a baseball bat. That's what he will need to tame that wild beast."

I shook my head and said to myself, "She's going to kill that man. Please, God, help him; nobody deserves that." As the EMS tech attempted to lead Leon to the truck, Jeanette broke free from the grip that the security guard had on her and attempted to strike Leon as he walked by. She was intercepted by a large police officer that grabbed her and handcuffed her. He then led her to an awaiting police cruiser. I could only stand there in amazement.

* * * * *

"Next in line," yelled the teller. I approached the window.

"Hello, Ms. Champion, did you see what that lady did to that man?" She asked.

"No, I came in on the tail end," I replied. "How can I help you?" She asked.

"Deposit of $4,000 cash," I replied. I counted out the money, took 10 one hundred dollar bills from the stack, and handed her the rest with my deposit slip. She made the transaction and handed me a receipt. I thanked her and left. Outside, everything was now calm. The police cruiser and EMS truck were gone and things seemed back to normal.

* * * * *

I reached Kroger on West 8 Mile and Wyoming at 12:55 p.m. I grabbed my shopping list, coupons from the glove compartment, and a shopping cart. I began to browse each aisle, selecting produce, meats, wines, champagne, and all the other items I needed. I sensed a presence near me, but when I turned to look, I didn't see anybody. As I made my final selections, I began to organize my coupons and made my way to the checkout line. I had spent more than I had planned.

I attempted to leave the line to put a few items back, but was interrupted by someone saying, "That is not necessary; I got you covered." I turned to see who it was and there stood Detective Monticello Strickland, in his work gear.

"Hello again, Natalie," he said. "Put your things on the counter." I quickly obeyed his command. I watched as the cashier rang up the items.

After deducting the coupons, she stated, "Your total is $980.87." Monticello placed his hand on mine and proceeded to go into his pocket. He retrieved a large wad of bills and peeled off nine one hundred dollar bills, four 20-dollar bills, and then handed the bills and change to the cashier. She counted everything, handed the receipt to Monticello, and began to assist the store bagger in loading the bags into my cart.

* * * * *

"Thank you, Monticello. To what do I owe this?" I inquired.

"I just like to make sure a lady has the things she needs," he answered.

"Do you do this for a lot of ladies?" I stated, inquisitively.

"No, only for special ones," he answered.

"Oh! So, you think I'm special? Well, thank you."

"Like I said last night, we would meet again, and I am a man of my word," he replied. *Hmmm, evasive, kinda sexy*, I thought to myself. At that point, he flashed that sexy smile at me and I almost lost control of the cart as I was pushing it toward my vehicle.

I smiled back and asked, "So, what's up? Are you stalking me?"

He laughed and answered, "No, I live in Southfield; I always shop here."

I guess he noticed me looking at the five grocery bags he had and he then said, "It's only me at the townhouse; I really don't need much. I'm single, no kids, and no baby mama drama; don't believe in wasting time and life like that."

"I feel you, baby," I replied.

"What are your plans for tonight?" He asked.

"I'm going home and clean my condo, put these groceries away, probably watch a movie, chill, and get ready for church tomorrow."

"May I call you later?" He asked.

"If you wish," I replied.

He then said, "I have to work the latter part of the afternoon shift and part of the midnight shift; I will call you on my lunch."

"Fantastic," I said.

Monticello then hugged me tightly, smiled, and walked away. I sat in my car waiting to see what he was driving. I watched as he approached and opened the door to a 2011 Black Cadillac Escalade. *Hmm*, I thought, *good looks, living in a townhouse in Southfield, driving a nice vehicle, single, no kids, willing to spend money, a definite possibility.*

\* \* \* \* \*

When I arrived at my condo, I unloaded the groceries and hung my three outfits in the hall closet. I headed for the laundry room, loaded the washer, added detergent, and turned it on. For the next few hours, I performed my condo cleaning regime of mopping, dusting, vacuuming, laundry, replacing bed linens, bathroom attire, and restocking my bar. As I folded the last of the laundry, I checked my phone and deleted the call I didn't recognize. I made a new pitcher of martinis and placed it in the fridge. My phone began to ring. I looked at the caller ID; it was Shavonne.

"Hey, my diva," I answered, "I was just about to call you." Before she could say anything, my other line beeped. "Hold on a second," I said, and pushed the button.

"Natalie, T.L. Hunter here, I have temporarily moved out of my house. I will be staying at Caesar's Palace Hotel in Windsor, room 2404. I will go into detail about this later. See you tomorrow. Peace."

"Okay," I replied. My mind was racing at 100 miles per hour. I clicked back over, "Shavonne, you there?"

"Yeah, I'm still here."

"Diva! I got something for you. Girl, I need two grand from you and two from DeJuana; she still owes me from the Leon deal. I will be at your spot in 30 minutes. I guarantee after you hear what I have to say, you won't mind giving it to me. You won't be disappointed, I promise. Have my money ready."

"Yeah, okay, we'll see," she groaned.

\* \* \* \* \*

I washed, changed into a pair of jeans, white Tee, and my Nike sneakers and cap. Twenty-five minutes later, I pulled into Shavonne's driveway. There were no visible cars. "All right now," I said, beginning to get irritated. However, before I could start to curse, I spotted Sharondelle's Escalade coming down West Outer Drive. She pulled into the driveway and got out, along with Shavonne. When she saw me, she waved for me to come into the house.

As I entered, Sharondelle hugged me and offered me a Hennessey and Coke. I accepted and thanked her for her hospitality. "How long are you in town for?" I asked Sharondelle.

"Just until this anniversary thing is over. I can't wait to get back to Houston. I do want to see Raphael while I'm here, but Momma is tripping. She doesn't want him over here."

"Be cool, Sharondelle. After I talk to Shavonne, she won't be home this evening, you'll have the house to yourself. Okay? Get lost for a minute so I can holler at Shavonne," I said. Sharondelle handed me my drink and left the room.

\* \* \* \* \*

Shavonne came in as she was leaving. "My diva, my diva," I said. "Why are you riding with Sharondelle? Where's the 300?"

"Oh, it's at the car wash with DeJuana and her car."

"Well, pack your sexiest shit and your condoms; T.L. has moved out of his spot temporarily," I informed her. "He will be staying in room 2404 at Caesar's Palace in Windsor. You know what to do. Make your move before someone else finds out."

"Good looking out, baby girl," Shavonne said, giving me a high-five. "Come in my room while I pack. I'm waiting on DeJuana to call about my car. Here, take this." She handed me a wad of bills that she pulled from her bra. "Natalie, have you ever performed the scarf striptease for anyone?" She asked.

"Yeah; a long, long, long time ago when I entertained as The Platinum Princess."

"What do you think of this one?" She held up a long, silk, multi-colored scarf that reached the floor.

"A couple of those, some fishnet stockings, and stilettos should definitely take him over the top."

"Yeah, I'm gonna fuck around and have that man sucking his thumb tonight," she giggled. "Sharondelle, Sharondelle! Call DeJuana and see if my car is ready. I'm leaving the country overnight, so you will have the house to yourself. I don't care what you do; you just better be at church to play tomorrow. Come get my suitcase and put it in the truck. I will transfer it to the car when you take me to get it," Shavonne yelled to her and smiled as she locked the suitcase.

"Okay, diva, I'm gone; I'll walk out with Sharondelle, have fun," I replied. We hugged and Sharondelle grabbed the suitcase and opened the door so I could follow her outside.

"What did you say to get my mother to leave overnight?" Sharondelle inquired.

"It's all good," I replied. "You better call Raphael quick before your mother comes out here; you know how nosey she is."

\* \* \* \* \*

Sharondelle put the suitcase in the Escalade and walked me to the curb. She hugged me and placed two one hundred dollar bills in my hand. "Have fun, baby diva," I said, and blew her a kiss. I started my car and drove off. It was now 5:47 p.m. "Well, that was some quick and easy cash made," I laughed. "Chase Bank closes at six and there's one on Grand River and West Outer Drive. Let me go put something in that account."

Three minutes later, I arrived at the drive-through. There was only one car ahead of me, so I quickly wrote a deposit slip and waited. When the car moved, I pulled forward and took the tube from its housing, placed my deposit slip and $3300 inside. I then put the tube back into the housing and watched as it traveled up the slide to the teller. Two minutes later, I heard through the speaker, "Thank you, Ms. Champion, the bank is now closed; have a good night." I retrieved my receipt from the tube and checked my balance. My Chase Bank account was now at 84-thousand. "Looking good, Lucy," I replied, and drove off.

\* \* \* \* \*

It was 6:40 after I stopped to pay my hairstylist $175 to do my hair on Sunday morning and getting my nails done. I had a carton of cigarettes and $840 cash in my pocket. "Well, I'm in for the night," I said, as I entered my abode. I put the packs of cigarettes in the fridge and took the semi-filled garbage bag to the dumpster. I replaced the bag with a new one, turned on my Jacuzzi tub, put a previously wrapped and seasoned lamb chop and a potato in the slow cooker, and headed off for a long awaited, relaxing soak. I disrobed, entered the tub, and made two calls.

The first was to Shavonne's house phone where Sharondelle answered. "Hey, baby diva, you good?"

"Yeah, Natalie. Raphael is in the shower and I am about to join him."

"Okay, have fun. I'm out, love you." I disconnected. The second call was to Shavonne's cell. When she answered, I inquired. "Diva, you good?"

"Yeah, Natalie; I'm pulling up to the entrance now," she replied.

"Okay, have a great night. See you in church tomorrow." I ended the call. I poured myself a glass of champagne, lit the candles surrounding the Jacuzzi, made a toast to myself and my money collecting divas, and began to enjoy my time of relaxation.

\* \* \* \* \*

*Ding dong! Ding dong!*

Sounded the door chimes in room 2404 at the Caesar's Palace Hotel. Pastor Terrell Lamar Hunter, dressed in a navy blue, silk pajama bottom and matching robe, slowly peeped through the gold plated door hole and a smile instantly appeared on his face. Standing on the opposite side of the door was the one and only Shavonne Swanson with suitcase in hand. Pastor Hunter opened the door and she entered. They embraced and shared a long, sensual kiss.

Pastor Hunter backed up a couple of feet and said, "Baby, I am soooo happy to see you; I really need you right now." He watched as she disrobed from her full-length grey and white chinchilla with a mink collar, revealing only a red skirt with a split up to her thigh and a red matching bra. Her 44DD breasts were feverishly attempting to make their escape. She also had on red fishnet stockings, six-inch stilettos, encrusted with clear rhinestones, a clear heel, and a furry ball in the center. On her wrist was a five-carat diamond and ruby bracelet, previously given to her by Pastor, when she tricked some fool out of 25 grand and padded his pockets. "Damn, girl, you are definitely fucking with a brother's head," he replied, attempting to reach for her.

"Whoa, whoa, slow down, big daddy," she said playfully, in her little girl voice. "You are gonna get what you want, but you are gonna have to let me be in charge tonight. When I move, then you move," she said, with authority. "Where's the stereo system? I have a surprise for you." Pastor Hunter pointed to the bar that also housed a state of the art stereo system, complete with CD changer. "Fix your sexy self a drink and put this on." She handed him a CD she had made. "Sit down on the sofa and get comfy; I'll be back in two minutes," she said, making her way to the bathroom with her bag in hand, closing the door.

\* \* \* \* \*

Pastor followed her instructions and poured two glasses of champagne. Looking at the still closed bathroom door, he quickly poured a glass of Hennessey on the rocks, took a long sip, and placed the CD in the player. He sat down on the long, caramel-colored sofa, took another sip, and lit a blunt. As the music began to play, Pastor Hunter could feel his manhood rising as Shavonne exited the bathroom covered in sheer, multicolored scarves. Starting at the top of her head, Shavonne began to peel off one scarf at a time, gyrating sexually to the sound of the music, Terrence Trent-D'Arby's *Sign Your Name*. With each movement she made, Pastor's 10-

inch long penis grew harder. Shavonne moaned sexually as she danced and Pastor begged her to come closer and let him touch her. The more he begged, the more Shavonne toyed with him.

* * * * *

As the song began to wind down, Shavonne peeled off the last scarf. Dropping to her knees, wearing only a red thong, Shavonne took Pastor's penis into her mouth and began sucking and licking like it was the last penis in existence. "Ooh! Ooh, aaah! Oh, Jesus; please, baby, ooh," he moaned and stood to his feet, holding Shavonne's head close to his body. "Damn, girl! This shit is soooo good; don't stop, baby; please don't stop. Oh, shit, girl. Girl, damn. You are fucking with my mind, girl; damn, girl! Ooh, yeah, shit, ooh." Just as he was about to climax, Shavonne snatched his pajama bottoms down to his ankles and stuck her thumb inside his asshole. "Aaaah, shit, damn," he screamed and squirted cum all over Shavonne's face, mouth, and hair. Being the thoroughbred diva Shavonne was, she held her head back and swallowed Pastor's gift. Pastor Hunter went wild seeing this.

He grabbed Shavonne, playfully wrestled her down on her back, ripped off her thong, threw her legs over his shoulders, and began to devour her pussy like a man who hadn't tasted a meal in a month. "Terrell Lamar, Terrell Lamar, ooh, big daddy, suck me, daddy! Suck me; shit," she screamed, as he licked and twirled his tongue in and out, up and down, like a maestro conducting a symphony. "Ooh, daddy, ooh daddy," she moaned, as his hands teased and tantalized her 44DD breasts. "Ooh, daddy, ooh, daddy," she continued to moan, as she moved her hips to meet his every movement. Pastor worked his magic spell with precision. "Yes, baby, yes, aaah, ooh," she cried. "This pussy is yours; it's yours, daddy. I'll do whatever you say, yes, yes, yes." Pastor stopped mid-lick, grabbed Shavonne by her hair, and flung her onto the king-sized bed. Before she could regroup, he grabbed her legs, pulled them apart, and thrust his hard, 10-inch, unprotected penis inside of her pussy. "Terrell Lamar, Terrell Lamar, please, daddy," she screamed again and again as each thrust of his hard dick hit her back wall. "Please, please, yes, baby, yes," Shavonne continued to moan as each thrust took her closer to ecstasy. "Tell me what you want, daddy; tell me, daddy. I'll get it for you; just tell me," Shavonne moaned.

Pastor grabbed Shavonne again, rolled over, and placed her on top of him. He leaned upward and began to suck on her 44DD breasts. "Ride this dick, bitch," he commanded. "Ride it, bitch; ride daddy's dick, bitch."

\* \* \* \* \*

Shavonne handcuffed one of Pastor's hands to the headboard of the king-sized bed, arched her back and began to move up and down, tightening her pussy walls, making Pastor Hunter groan like Lurch from the Addams Family. "I want, I want, ooh, ooh, I need, I need," Pastor stuttered. "Shavonne, I need, ugh, ugh, ride it, baby, ride it; damn, girl, damn, girl, ride, shit, ride this dick, shit, ooh damn." Shavonne was riding Pastor hard and heavy, like a jockey riding the winning horse in the Kentucky Derby. Pastor had his own thumb in his mouth sucking it like a newborn. After a few seconds, Pastor stuck his thumb and forefinger inside Shavonne's asshole and she came, squirting cum on his dick and stomach. Pastor climaxed a couple of seconds later, took a deep breath, and went limp. Shavonne dismounted, laid next to him, rubbing his forehead, kissed and cuddled his body.

"Damn, girl, you are the shit! You definitely have skills. You definitely have skills. I see why the brothers don't mind emptying their wallets. You better not be fucking those other motherfuckers like that," he stated. "Fucking like that is exclusively for me, you understand? Do you understand?" He repeated, his voice now showing authority.

"I understand, big daddy; I understand," she replied, like a child who had just been chastised. They hugged and kissed, then showered together, toasted with the bottle of champagne, and ordered room service. After eating steak and lobster with baked potato and salad, they stood out on the balcony of the villa overlooking the river, had a couple more drinks, made love again, and drifted to sleep in each other's arms.

\* \* \* \* \*

Back at the condo, I'd dozed off in the heated Jacuzzi tub. The sound of the slow cooker's timer awakened me. I exited, dried off, lotioned my body, and put on a sexy, black nightie. I retrieved my food, ate, put in a movie (The Fighting Temptations), and got comfortable in my bed. Half way into the movie, my cell phone rang. I answered and a sexy male voice greeted me.

"Hey, sexy lady, what are you doing, love?"

"Well, hello," I replied. Are you at work?"

"Yeah, doll, I'm on lunch now. I was thinking about you," he replied.

"I was just watching a movie," I said.

"Oh, yeah; which one?" He inquired.

"Beyoncé and Cuba Gooding, Jr., The Fighting Temptations. Since I'm going to church tomorrow, I wanted to go to sleep with some gospel music in my head," I replied.

"I feel you, baby; I saw that movie once and I agree; they have some good gospel songs. The O'Jays are my favorite," he said. "Speaking of church, which one do you attend?"

"Journey Toward Christ Missionary Baptist in Detroit," I answered.

"I've passed that church, yeah; they really get live up in there, or so I've heard. I'm gonna have to visit one Sunday when I'm not working," he stated.

"That would be nice; let me know when."

"I will," he replied, "and it will be soon, I promise. You'll see; I always keep my promises."

"Ooh, sounds intriguing," I answered.

"I'm glad we ran into each other earlier today," he said.

"Yeah, me, too," I replied. I heard his cell line click.

"Hold on, babe," he asked and then clicked over. While on hold, I pictured his face, his body and remembered his swagger as he walked toward his truck. Yep, brother was definitely packing. I pictured his sexy lips, his smile, his voice, and my temperature began to rise.

"Slow down, girl," I said to myself. "Slow down."

At that point, I heard the phone click back over. "Natalie, I gotta go, baby; a body has been found in an abandoned house on the eastside. Call me tomorrow after you get out of church. Call my cell or my house phone," he said. "Can't wait to hold and kiss you. Sleep peacefully, boo; talk to you tomorrow."

"Okay, baby, be careful. Good night," I said.

"Good night, doll," he responded, then the line disconnected. I smiled, sighed, and looked at the clock. It was midnight. I re-wound the movie back to the place it was when my phone rang, got comfortably situated in my bed again, told God thank you for the day's events, began watching, and soon, drifted sleep.

\* \* \* \* \*

Sunday morning, I woke up with a strange feeling. Trina, my stylist, came by at 8:30, did my hair, and left at 9:45. "This is going to be a day that will go down in history," I said to myself. I showered and got dressed. I pulled up in the parking lot of the church at 10:40 a.m. There was a velvet rope and an actual red carpet. There were also people with cameras and the local black TV station had reporters and a camera crew posted just outside of the entrance of the church. Limousines and other luxury vehicles lined the streets for at least three blocks. People were dressed in their finest outfits and the array of church hats being worn by ladies reminded me of Easter. Pastor arrived shortly thereafter with First Lady. They were being chauffeured in a white on white stretch Bentley Rolls Royce limousine. Both were dressed in purple and white silk matching outfits, trimmed in gold. As they walked the red carpet, camera lights flashed and people reached out in an attempt to shake their hands or just to get a touch of them as they passed by. They were like royalty. Once inside, you could tell that today was all about Pastor and his family.

The pulpit where he preached had been transformed into a throne with a Roman theme, adorned with huge gold and white pleated drapes, 10-foot white and gold pillars, two plush gold and purple high back chairs inscribed with the words King and Queen. There were pictures of Pastor, with and without his family, displayed, along with several fabulous flower arrangements, gold statues and two female harpists. The service was also going to be televised.

\* \* \* \* \*

As I entered the sanctuary, I was summoned by Frenchee B. Henderson. *What does this bitch want now?* I thought to myself.

"Hello, Natalie, baby, you look soooo nice in your white and gold outfit. That suit is unique. I have never seen anything like it. I can tell that it was tailor made and is from New York. Natalie, I am very proud of you and all that you do for this church; I want you to be Mistress of Ceremonies for the anniversary service. Please say you will accept. I thought about this all night and I couldn't think of no one more worthy of this than you. Would you do me the honor of accepting this task please? I would be eternally grateful. I won't take no for an answer."

"Yes, I would be honored, Frenchee B.," I replied. All the while, I was thinking, *What's up with this?* She handed me a document detailing the order in which the events would take place. It was in the shape of a Roman Scroll. I looked over it for a couple of minutes and began to make my way to the podium, walking down the aisle with Frenchee B. "Where's Claude?" I asked.

"He will be here shortly; he's in Pastor's office. He will escort First Lady Hunter to her throne and Shavonne will be escorting Pastor Hunter to his throne."

*Uh oh,* I thought, *here we go.* At that point, Frenchee B. showed me where I would be standing, gave me thumbs up, and walked away.

\* \* \* \* \*

As I stood on stage at the podium, I saw Frenchee B. wave her hand, indicating that it was time to begin the festivities. I gazed out into the congregation and held my hands up. At that moment, trumpets sounded and through the smoked filled floor, musicians Sharondelle Swanson and Lady Monica Davenport came down the center aisle, escorted by men on both sides of them dressed as Roman soldiers. Sharondelle and Lady Monica were dressed in white, sequined, long evening gowns with gold trimmings. Behind them was Pastor's family, his mother and father, brothers, daughter, Dominique, Terrell, Jr. and little Tee. After that, came First Lady's family, her mother and father, sister from Ohio, and a host of other family members. After they were all seated in the front rows of the sanctuary, the trumpets sounded again.

A man appeared next to me, dressed as a Roman messenger, and I handed him the microphone. He asked that everyone stand to his or her feet. He then announced, "Presenting the King and Queen of Journey Toward Christ Missionary Baptist Church. King Terrell Lamar Hunter and Queen First Lady Charisse Hunter."

\* \* \* \* \*

The sanctuary entrance door opened and there stood Pastor Hunter and Shavonne Swanson, behind them were Claude N. Henderson and First Lady Charisse. Claude and Shavonne were dressed in all white. Pastor Hunter was now wearing a crown and cape to match his outfit and First Lady was wearing a tiara and cape that matched her outfit. From the look on First Lady Hunter's face, she was not too happy to have Shavonne holding her husband by the arm walking him down the aisle. I don't think many people noticed, but I certainly did.

\* \* \* \* \*

The sanctuary entrance door opened and standing in the middle of Shavonne Swanson and DeJuana Edwards was Leon Porterfield. The trio was dressed in all white. Shavonne and DeJuana had on matching, white, two-piece, double-breasted skirt suits from Dolce and Gabbana and white Manolo Blahniks. Leon was wearing a white designer suit from Stacy Adams and white crocodile shoes. You could still see the knot on his head from the assault, even though he had tried to cover it with a thin layer of cheap makeup. The trio came down to the front of the sanctuary as Sharondelle Swanson, on the organ, and Lady Monica Davenport, on the piano, began playing the intro to the song. I saw Jeanette Porterfield look out from the trustees' office, which was in the skybox overlooking the main sanctuary, and I knew then something was going to happen before program's end. For five minutes, Shavonne, Leon, and DeJuana sang. The trio had marched down center aisle holding hands. Leon and DeJuana continued to hold hands during the entire song. After the song ended, the trio took a bow and walked away, hand in hand.

\* \* \* \* \*

I approached the podium and announced that a second offering would be taking place. This offering would be exclusively for the anniversary celebration. All members were asked to give a minimum of $500. Before I could say anything else, Frenchee B. Henderson and Lady Monica Davenport rushed the stage, both holding an envelope filled with cash. Lady Monica took the microphone from me and announced that she was giving $75,000. Before she could finish, Frenchee B. Henderson snatched the microphone and announced she was giving $90,000.

A combination of applause, whispers, and other forms of expressions overtook the congregation and visitors. Things were getting out of control. Some of the congregation began to rush the stage with wads of cash. *This was a church that had no shame when it came to competition.* I grabbed the microphone from Frenchee B. and quickly thanked both women for their generous donations and invited them to serve as honorary ushers. I handed each of them a large wicker basket and separated them by escorting them to opposite ends of the stage, where the harpists were positioned. I asked the ushers to come down and waved for Julius K. Fitzpatrick, head trustee, to come and pray the offering prayer. He obliged and everything was once again back in control.

\* \* \* \* \*

As the children were performing, Pastor tapped me on the shoulder and requested that I meet him in his office immediately. Once inside his office, he told me that he came home at 4:30 a.m. He had clothes for Little Tee and some groceries in the trunk, but was greeted with a locked door and a suitcase sitting in the foyer of their house. First Lady had followed him and saw him coming out of Lady Monica's. He also told me that he decided it just wasn't worth arguing about, so he left the groceries and Little Tee's outfit and went to the hotel in Windsor. First Lady let him stand in the foyer of their house until the limousine showed up to bring them to the church this morning. He asked me to pray with him for a minute so he could get through the rest of this day. I obliged. I heard the children's praise team dance ending. I returned to the podium, thanked the children as the crowd applauded, and gave them a standing ovation. All of a sudden, I heard a series of loud noises. At first, I thought it was thunder, but glancing at the window, I definitely saw sunshine and quickly dismissed that thought. I looked up and saw Leon Porterfield hanging from the railing of the balcony where the trustees had their office. Standing over him was his wife, Jeanette.

I couldn't hear what she was saying to him because of the distance; but, looking at her, I could tell that she was enraged. Julius, Shavonne, and a few other trustees were trying to reason with Jeanette and, at the same time, rescue Leon before he fell. Some of the nurses located in the rear of the church also saw what was taking place and rushed to get mattresses out of the room where they had an emergency bed, just in case. The congregation that was sitting under the balcony quickly moved as the mattresses were put in place. About 10 seconds later, Leon lost his grip and spiraled downward. He fell about three stories down. The mattresses broke his fall. Trustee Fitzpatrick called 911. Leon seemed dazed, but not hurt. However, the nurses told him to lie still so that he could be checked out by the EMS techs. Most of the trustees, not including Jeanette, had made their way to the main floor where Leon was lying on the mattresses. The church was in total chaos once again. People were running around but, for some strange reason, both Pastor and First Lady remained calm and sat on their thrones as if nothing had happened.

* * * * *

I noticed that Dominique and Terrell Jr. were not in their seats. They had disappeared. I waved for Sharondelle, Lady Monica and the harpists to play something. As they began to play, the crowd began to calm down and return to their seats. By this time, EMS had arrived and was attending to Leon. I received a written statement from the church nurses stating that Leon would be transported to the hospital for a full examination. I made the announcement to the audience and asked that everyone stand to their feet to pray for Leon.

I motioned for Pastor to come forward and lead the prayer. After the prayer was over, Pastor stated that he would not be preaching his sermon and that he wanted everyone to adjourn to the dining area located in the building next door, so that dinner could be served. I looked at Frenchee B, placed the microphone on its housing, and approached Lady Monica, who was leaving the piano.

"Well, this was a disaster, wasn't it? And to think, it was caught on live broadcasting," I said to her.

"Yes, it was Natalie," she replied. "You look really beautiful today; who did your hair?"

"A friend of mine named Trina came by early this morning," I replied. "If you're going next door and get some food, I will meet you there. I need to go to my car for a minute."

\* \* \* \* \*

When I reached my vehicle, there was an envelope taped to my windshield. "What the hell?" I shouted. I snatched the envelope from under the windshield wiper and opened it. There was $900 inside and a note reading, "This is for your weekly donation and for your anniversary donation. Love you, call me later, Monticello." As I smoked my cigarette, I saw a vehicle, which looked like an unmarked police cruiser, pass by. At that point, I started to call Monticello. However, after looking at my watch, I decided to put that on hold and go to the annex to get a dinner. I began to wonder how he knew about the $500 anniversary donation and how he knew about my regular donation of $400 a week. This shit was getting freaky and I was going to get to the bottom of it quickly.

\* \* \* \* \*

I returned to the annex and found a place in line behind Lady Monica and Sharondelle. People were already talking about what had happened at the service. After getting a plate of food, I proceeded to follow Lady Monica to the table reserved for the musicians and all of those who participated in the program. As I gazed around the room, I saw Shavonne and DeJuana, now dressed as Roman serving girls, taking food to Pastor, First Lady, and their families. Shavonne was outright flirting with Pastor as First Lady sat, looking at her with a scowl on her face. Dominique and Terrell Jr. were nowhere in sight. I began to converse with Lady Monica.

"This has been a weird day. I hope the worst is over now."

"Yeah, me, too," she replied.

"After we eat, let's slip off and go get a drink," she suggested. "I know a nice place up on Woodward; it won't take long to get there and we can be back before anyone notices that we were gone."

"No problem," I replied, "I will drive."

"Good, my eyes are bothering me; but after that drink, I know I'll be okay."

Before I could say anything, I heard a loud bang and glass breaking. First Lady had grabbed the serving tray from DeJuana and had attempted to hit Shavonne with it, but wound up missing her because she ducked.

The tray hit DeJuana in the shoulder and crashed to the floor. DeJuana did not seem to be hurt, just startled. Claude N. Henderson and several other members were attempting to restrain First Lady. Pastor was still seated and was acting as if nothing had happened.

"Come on, Lady Monica, let's get out of here. I need two drinks to your one. This is getting bizarre," I said.

\* \* \* \* \*

When we entered the lounge, it was filled with older gentlemen and four or five females. All eyes were on Lady Monica. She ordered a Cosmopolitan and told the bartender to bring me whatever I wanted. I held up two fingers so that he would bring two. One of the men approached the bar and told the bartender to bring a bottle of champagne, too. He looked to be in his late 40s, six feet, extremely light-skinned with salt and pepper hair and dressed in a burgundy Armani Suit and matching alligator shoes. He looked at Lady Monica and told her, "You are so beautiful; you and your friend only deserve the best."

The bartender returned with the champagne, glasses and the other two drinks. The man sat down next to Lady Monica and she winked at me. "I am gonna see what music they have on the jukebox; I'll be right back," I said.

The man said, "You don't have to leave; I am proud to be seen with two lovely ladies. I won't be here that long." He introduced himself as Lawrence R. Hutchinson. He looked familiar, but I couldn't put my finger on it. He paid the bartender for all the drinks, whispered something into Lady Monica's ear, slipped her a wad of cash, and then he walked away. Lady Monica then disappeared for about 15 minutes.

\* \* \* \* \*

I remained at the bar watching some TV program until she returned. When she did, we continued drinking at the bar. I waited for her to say something about what had just happened, but she didn't, so I left it alone. I knew she would tell me in due time.

"Lady M, I met this man a couple of days ago and I have a strange feeling about him; I don't want to seem paranoid, but I think I might have a potential stalker on my hands. He is a Detroit Police Detective and his name is Monticello Strickland. He lives in Southfield, drives a black Escalade, and looks similar to R. Kelly. He's spent almost two grand on me already. It seems like he's following me around town. I just found an envelope from him on my windshield when I went to the car to smoke.

He's supposed to be at home sleep or getting ready for his evening shift."

"Baby, I want you to be careful, but don't write him off yet. Get what funds you can out of him; go slow and do not be far from your money. Make sure everything is listed by your PO Box so he can't track you because he could use your license plate to find out your personal information. Re-do your internet also because you can be tracked through that, too. I know you may not understand yet, but you will. I got your back if you ever need to disappear for a while. Drink up and let's get out of here."

When we arrived back at the church parking lot, people were leaving because the evening program had been cancelled. At that point, I drove Lady Monica to her vehicle. After making sure she had gotten in safely, I pulled off, debating where I would go. It was 2:30 in the afternoon and I had planned to be at church at least until 6:00; but now, I had time on my hands. I decided to go home and change clothes. After that, I would decide what I would do. At that very moment, my cell rang. It was Lady Monica.

"Hello, Lady M," I replied.

"Natalie, I need you to be discreet about what took place in the lounge; no one is to know of this and I need you to come by tomorrow after you leave your office and take some papers to my lawyer and accountant for me. It will be worth your while if you do."

"Lady M, I will be more than happy to. I will call you tomorrow then. Love you," I replied and hung up.

\* \* \* \* \*

After arriving home, I wondered what to do. I decided to stay near the house. After changing clothes, I walked around to my cousin, Debonair's, who had a condo in the same subdivision. Debonair was my first cousin and we were as thick as thieves. People would often mistake us for girlfriend and boyfriend instead of relatives. Debonair was born DeAngelo, Jr. His father nicknamed him 'Debonair' when his mother left and it stuck. The Champion brothers, DeArthur, DeAngelo (Debonair's father) and DeAndre' (my father) were pimps and players from back in the day. They were born two years apart and Uncle DeArthur was the oldest. Each of them was 6'5" around 205 pounds.

The three of them, along with a few of their handpicked women, raised Debonair and me. My father was the youngest and meanest of the brothers. The smallest thing would set him off and send him into a violent rage. Although he didn't smile much, when he did, his smile had the power to melt an iceberg. He pulled many of his women that way. If he saw you about to fuck up, he would warn you; after that, you either got a beat down or shot. Either way, you were history. DeAndre Champion would knock a female down in a heartbeat about his money, looking at him the wrong way, or if speaking in a way that he didn't approve. He also didn't mind shooting at someone for the same reasons.

\* \* \* \* \*

DeArthur Champion was the charmer. He was also the best dressed of the three. He was into unique colors regarding his cars his clothes and shoes. My family dressed their asses off, all the time. Uncle DeArthur really didn't have to speak. His body language spoke volumes. The way he walked and moved were key. He was quick and catlike, yet sometimes, slow and methodical. The straight razor was his signature weapon and he was a master at using it. He would try to reason with you, but didn't play when it came to his money. He had a long temper, but if you were unfortunate enough to make him angry, you might wind up dead. Women loved the ground he walked on and he switched women frequently.

\* \* \* \* \*

DeAngelo Champion was the smooth talker of the three and the middle son. Like Pastor Hunter, he possessed the gift of gab. He could talk anyone into anything. As a child, I once saw him talk a woman out of her clothes, while hiding under his bed, playing hide-and-seek with Debonair. After not liking what he saw, he told her to put her clothes back on and leave. She was devastated.

Uncle DeAngelo switched women frequently, too. You only got one chance with him. If you fucked up, you were history. He didn't accept lies, attitude, jealousy, ultimatums, controlling women, or attempts at trying to change him. He was DeAngelo Champion and was going to remain DeAngelo Champion.

\* \* \* \* \*

Debonair's mother, Phyllis Janae, and my mother, Natalie Jenelle, were exotic dancers and both left when we were young. We were told that the pressure of competition with other women in Uncle DeAngelo's and my father's stable got to them. Uncle DeArthur, Uncle DeAngelo, and my father started pimping women the day they each turned 17. They were now all retired and joint owners of a men and boys clothing store named *Dress like a Champion.*

Uncle DeArthur was sterilized from a childhood car accident, therefore, he never married and had no children; but, like I said earlier, he was loved by many women. He now lived in Farmington Hills around the corner from three of his women, Chanterelle, Trixie, and Rochelle. My father lived in Sterling Heights and three of his women, identical triplets, Charlene, Darlene and Marlene, lived together in a subdivision called Shoal Creek, three miles away. Uncle DeAngelo lived in Troy. His women lived in a high-rise apartment in downtown Detroit.

\* \* \* \* \*

Uncle DeArthur's bottom women Chanterelle and Rochelle taught me how to conduct myself as a female regarding dressing, makeup, exotic dancing, sexing men, using straight razors, and lifting (being a pickpocket). Chanterelle, along with my father's women, Darlene and Marlene, made sure I dressed in the finest clothes so that I could attend school every day and get the best grades in the class. If I messed up in school, Chanterelle and Rochelle both would kick my butt and get me back on track. They made sure my head stayed in the books. Trixie taught me how to be observant and how to avoid a lot of drama. I was a loner.

I hung out with the males. They would give me money and buy me things. All of them knew the reputations of my father and uncles, so the majority of them never tried to get me to do anything with them. If they did try, there were several not so attractive females who I knew that would do anything to get attention from guys. I would send them to sleep with the guys, give them blowjobs, or let them feel them up and they'd be satisfied. They would then give me money or jewelry for hooking them up.

\* \* \* \* \*

I finally lost my virginity at age 16 to a pretty boy named Bobby Carter. I had been told by my father and uncles to never have sex with anyone I couldn't stand to look at up close, so pretty boys became my thing. Bobby was 19 and fine as hell. His father was a bookie and loan shark and his mother had died from a heart attack. He had an older brother named Jade who was doing life in Jackson Prison for murder. Bobby was tall; caramel-colored, and had black, wavy hair. He was a burglar who broke into jewelry and fur stores and stole only top-notch merchandise. Bobby could bypass any security system. He stayed draped in diamonds and sold diamonds and furs to make money. He'd even sold diamonds to my family on occasions. He gave me my first full-length mink with matching hat and muff one month after we started seeing each other. He dressed uniquely like Debonair and Uncle DeArthur, and drove a black Cadillac. He was in the process of teaching me his trade and had bought me my own tools.

After a year of being his girlfriend and partner in crime, we were caught and almost got in trouble, but got out of it on a technicality. Two years later, Bobby and his father moved to Florida because his father got a real job. I went back to school and quickly dismissed that vocation.

\* \* \* \* \*

My cousin Debonair had been raised to believe that he was too good for any woman and that women owed him. He graduated from several schools. He had women doing everything for him, including his schoolwork. He held a Bachelor's Degree in Broadcasting, along with a degree from ITT Technical Institute. Since age eight, he had been groomed to be smooth and seductive. In elementary school, the girls would buy his lunch and give him their dollar bills. His being fine as hell didn't help, either. Debonair looked like a younger version of his father. He always dressed in the finest clothes and drove the finest sports cars. I admired the fact that he sometimes worked for what he wanted, but he mainly lived off women.

When he did work, it was only to recruit more women who would take care of him. If you were a female and wanted to be with Debonair, your pockets needed to be fat and you better not have a problem spending, have jealousy, or control issues. Because, if you did, you were not going to be around for long. Most of the women Debonair dealt with had extremely high paying jobs. He also had several women who were professional boosters who did not mind buying or stealing whatever he wanted. Debonair's condo was laid out beyond belief.

\* \* \* \* \*

Debonair did not like trucks or SUVs. He drove several different pimped out sports cars, one being a 2012 Chevrolet Corvette that would make you want to slap your own mother. Debonair was three years older than me. When I turned 16, Debonair secured a red Ford Mustang convertible for me. I loved Debonair unconditionally; there was nothing I wouldn't do for him. He helped keep my pockets full as a child and he even made his booster girlfriends give me clothes and jewelry. He also taught me a lot about hustling, sexual skills, guns and the overall game.

\* \* \* \* \*

After arriving at Debonair's crib, we played pool for a while, (which I was great at and always beat whomever I played), had a few drinks, talked shit, and played video games. Also that evening, Debonair introduced me to one of his girlfriends, Alessandra Marlowe, who worked at a Mercedes-Benz dealership, and to his road dogs, identical triplets, Brandon, Braxton, and Broxton Sullivan, who were visiting from Las Vegas. I had forgotten about calling Monticello after meeting the triplets, especially after they promised me an all-expense paid trip to Vegas for three weeks of shopping, gambling, partying, and sexual escapades. We finalized the plans and I was scheduled to leave Saturday morning. I fell asleep fantasizing about a foursome with the triplets. The Sullivan brothers were extremely gorgeous and each of them had heavy pockets.

* * * * *

Monday morning came quickly. I woke up at 7:30 a.m. I did some minor cleaning, showered, ate breakfast, and prepared myself to leave for my four-hour workday at the church. I arrived at 9:45 a.m. When I entered my office, the telephone was already ringing. *Who could this be?* I thought to myself. Everybody knows that the office doesn't open until 10. I decided to answer out of nosiness.

"Good morning, Journey Toward Christ Missionary Baptist Church, how may I be of service to you?" I asked.

"Natalie, Natalie. This is Terrell Jr." By the tone of his voice, I could tell he was high as hell from smoking crack. "You know what? They're trying to kill me. I owe them massive money," stated the frantic voice on the other end. "I am on the east side in this empty building. I am not paying them shit. I was born getting high; I will die getting high. Fuck them motherfuckers," he said, rushing his words.

Before I could say anything, he hung up. I pushed *69 on the phone, but only received a busy signal. I tried again, same results. I had previously dealt with Terrell Jr., especially when he was high. He had a bad habit of playing on the telephone like a kid. Terrell Jr. was a bona fide crack head and in his warped mind, thought he was a real player. According to the talk on the streets, he owed several drug dealers massive amounts of money. They would often let him run up large tabs because he would pay them with church money from his father and because of whom his father was and what he had. They knew that he was good for the money, but that was becoming a thing of the past seeing as how Pastor had cut him off. I once made the mistake of giving him my cell number. Every time he got high, he would call me, regardless of the time, talking crazy or crying like a baby into the receiver. I finally had to get my number changed. I never made that mistake again.

\* \* \* \* \*

I decided that I would proceed to record the donations from Sunday's service into the computer database and send out thank you letters. As I was entering data from the envelopes and reports left by the trustees, I sensed something wasn't quite right. The numbers were not adding up. There was money missing. I re-checked several times and still came up with the same total. There was $100,000 missing. Trustee Julius K. Fitzpatrick had to be notified.

I called Julius, told him of my findings, and told him to come down right away. I attempted to contact Pastor, but could only reach his two voicemails. I left a message for him to contact me ASAP. After about an hour, Trustee Fitzpatrick arrived. I escorted him to my office and we both re-checked the numbers and reports. Julius contacted the rest of the trustees and within the hour, everyone except Jeanette, who was in court, and Shavonne, who had Mondays off and was out making money for Pastor, had made it to my office. Julius continuously attempted to contact Pastor. When he finally reached Pastor, he was given the authority to "handle it."

I thought it was odd that Pastor, knowing money was missing, did not really seem to care, but that was on him. After Julius finished questioning all of the trustees, I asked Julius to retrace yesterday's events and asked him if there was any way that anyone other than the trustees could have gained access to their offices during the commotion. Julius said, "I don't think so." There was a key card associated with the elevator to that floor and office entrance door. The only people, besides Julius K. Fitzpatrick, that had key cards were Pastor, First Lady, and Frenchee B. Henderson.

\* \* \* \* \*

After the meeting ended, DeJuana Edwards and Leon Porterfield left the church together first. After everyone else left, surrounded by quiet, my thoughts began to turn to Dominique and Terrell Jr. When Dominique came to town, she would always make it her business to say hello to me and we would sometimes go out for drinks. This time was different. She never came near me; she didn't even wave when the family entered the sanctuary on Sunday morning. She and Terrell, Jr. were not at the annex during dinnertime. I decided to give her a call on her cell; the message said that her phone was "out of range."

I called the limousine service in Atlanta pretending to be her and was told that my driver would meet me at Hartsfield-Jackson Airport, Atlanta at 3:00 p.m. when my flight from Detroit landed. It was adding up now. Dominique had taken the money and given it to Terrell Jr. I decided not to say anything just in case I was wrong, but my theory was that Terrell Jr. had access to the key cards because he lived at home. Dominique loved her brother and would do anything for him. Dominique had spent the night at home, therefore, she and Terrell Jr. had time to search the house since Pastor was away and First Lady had taken Little Tee to Chuck E. Cheese's and the Detroit Zoo that Saturday. In addition, I remembered that when the security company set up the security system and keypad entries for the trustees' office, Dominique was at the church flirting with the installation tech. No telling what she'd found out.

* * * * *

Two o'clock came and I left. I decided to make a trip through the 'hood to visit an old friend and purchased another handgun and silencer. After making my purchase of a .45 caliber automatic handgun along with a silencer, I drove down E. Forest, approaching Chene. I spotted the Detroit Police Crime Scene Investigation van, the medical examiner's van, and several investigators leaving an abandoned building. A body was being carried out in a black body bag. A yellow crime scene tape surrounded the building. I decided I was going to be nosey and see what was going on. By the time I had circled the block, everyone was gone. This was a desolate area with this building being one of a few already vacant or burned out structures for about a mile. I parked on a side street, made my way to the back of the building, and found an opening. I entered the dark building being careful not to step in the blood that was on the floor or touch anything that would indicate that I'd been there.

Even though the building was dark inside, there was a beam of light coming from a small window located over the door. As I looked around, something caught my attention. I approached it and saw that it was a black notebook. I wondered how the evidence techs had missed it; but, then again, the Detroit Police were some of the most incompetent individuals you'd ever want to know. I approached the book and retrieved it with a black handkerchief I had in my pocket. It felt heavy. I looked around again and when I saw the chalk outline of a body, it sent chills up my spine, so I decided to take off.

* * * * *

I pulled away from where I'd parked and drove several streets over. I carefully opened the black book using the handkerchief. Some of the pages were cut out in the middle where something could be concealed. Inside the cut pages were four bundles of cash with rubber bands around them. I counted the first one and discovered that it contained 25 thousand dollars. My heart began to race and I thought I had better get somewhere safe. Instead of driving home, I slowly drove to Debonair's subdivision, taking the side streets, parked in a remote corner of the property and counted the remainder of the money. In total, there was 88 thousand dollars inside. I examined the book and discovered that it belonged to none other than Pastor's daughter, Dominique. I then realized she had given it to Terrell Jr. and that's whose corpse the medical examiner was taking to the morgue. As badly as I wanted to call Pastor, I knew I couldn't get involved. I just had to be patient and leave things to the authorities. I know no one saw me in the vicinity, but the book had to be destroyed. I just couldn't risk the DNA thing or anything else.

\* \* \* \* \*

I saw Debonair coming back, waited until he parked and went inside his condo, and then I walked up to his door and rang the doorbell. He invited me in and I told him I'd won money at the casino and gave him 15 grand. He tried to make me tell him the exact amount I'd won, but I refused.

"I'm getting ready to barbeque, Natalie, wanna help me?" Debonair asked.

"Yeah, kiddo, I'll get the fire started in the grill," I stated, knowing that it would be the perfect way to get rid of the book. As I emptied the charcoal briquettes into the king-sized grill. I ripped the pages from the notebook, mixed them in with the coals, and added lighter fluid and wood chips. As the flames took flight and soared upward, I dropped in the notebook cover and the handkerchief. The flames became my refuge and my nervousness began to subside. At that very moment, my cell rang; it was Lady Monica.

"Hello, Lady M," I answered.

"Natalie, I can't talk long, do not come, I repeat, do not come. Anthony just walked in. I hid the papers just in time. We'll have to get together some other time. I've got to go." She hung up.

*Good*, I thought to myself. *I'm glad I don't have to make that trip*, because Lady Monica lived in a mansion on Arden Park, in the middle of the city. I needed to be near the crib today. Debonair came out with a tray filled with ribs and steaks.

"Is the fire ready?"

"Almost, let it burn for a few more minutes, then you can start. I need to borrow your car for a minute; I will back in 10 minutes. I'm going to the house; I need to be inconspicuous."

"Baby doll, what's wrong?" He inquired.

"Nothing, Dee, I just want to go put up this money in my safe."

"Uh, no way, doll face; I'm not letting you leave here by yourself with cash. I'm putting this food on the grill, then I will escort you home. Let me make a call; they'll be here in 10 minutes."

"Okay, but I want you to drive, Dee."

"That's cool, my boy will let me drive his shit and I will go inside with you to make sure everything is all right. Are you sure you only won money at the casino? You are acting real brand new; is there something wrong? Is there something else I should know?" He asked.

"Nah, Dee, I'm good. I love you," I said, sheepishly.

\* \* \* \* \*

Eight minutes later, three men showed up driving a 2011 black Yukon Denali. Debonair instructed the driver to remain behind and watch the grill. He then took possession of the steering wheel. We arrived at my subdivision, parked on the corner, and the other two men remained in the vehicle while Debonair and I entered my condo from the rear entrance so no one could see exactly where I lived. Debonair checked the condo after I'd disarmed the security system. I made my way to my bedroom safe, which was hidden in the closet floor, and placed $60,000 inside. I decided that I would give the church $4,000 and have Debonair and the guys take me to Chase Bank and make a $4,000 deposit. When we got back to the truck, we did just that. My Chase Bank account was now eighty-eight grand. I knew eventually that I would have to make some investments and move money around again. I had to figure out a way. Also, something was tugging at me. I felt I needed to change vehicles, so I had to concoct a story if needed.

\* \* \* \* \*

I sat on the condo deck with Debonair, one of his many girlfriends, Alessandra Marlowe, Nate, and the other two guys, *Desmond Anderson and Jerome Kendricks*. We discussed me trading my car for a cute, two-seater convertible. I made my list of what I was going to do on Tuesday. I'd change my internet, get another PO Box, and dispose of everything associated with Monday, (clothes, shoes, etc.), and secure myself another vehicle. I would be dealing with Alessandra via Debonair. She could get me a cute two-seater convertible and take my other vehicle on a trade in. One of her associates in Arizona needed my car for a client of his. The car would be shipped to Arizona as soon as I could turn it in.

# Chapter 3

As Tuesday morning daybreak surfaced, Leon Porterfield awoke to find himself lying in the front yard of his residence naked as the day he was born. He reached to cover himself but could barely move his arms without feeling intense pain. He tried to stand up but couldn't. As he looked down, he felt something attached to his manhood. At first, he thought he was hallucinating. As his blurred vision become clearer, he realized that something was actually there. After a closer look, he saw that it was a large dead rat. He tried to dislodge it from his private parts, but soon discovered that it had been super glued in place. He began to scream uncontrollably. Several of his neighbors rushed out to assist him and called 911. In a matter of minutes, Leon had been transported to Detroit Medical Center and was receiving medical attention for his injuries and bizarre situation.

\* \* \* \* \*

It started Monday night when he arrived home from work. Jeanette was already in a drunken rage. She started accusing Leon of having an affair with DeJuana Edwards and stealing money from their joint savings account. She claimed that six grand was missing and she claimed to have seen him with DeJuana on Monday. Moreover, she claimed to have heard rumors about him giving money to Shavonne. Even though Leon did not drink, he took six or seven drinks in an attempt to block out her arguing, not knowing that Jeanette had drugged the liquor bottle he was drinking from. After he had passed out, Jeanette attacked and brutally beat him with a baseball bat, stripped him naked, super glued a dead rat to his testicles and threw him out on the front lawn.

As Leon lay in the hospital room recuperating, he made up his mind-this was the straw that broke the camel's back. He picked up the phone, which was on the table next to the bed and dialed a number. When the phone was answered, Leon stated. "I want that bitch dead by any means necessary. I will stop giving money to Journey Toward Christ. I will be getting out of the hospital tomorrow. When I open the door to my house, I wish to find no one there. Make it happen."

\* \* \* \* \*

### 3:15 p.m.

A cell phone sounded indicating a text message. The message read "I have an assignment for you." 30 minutes later instructions were found on the front seat of a vehicle detailing duties to be carried out along with an envelope filled with currency. 5:52 p.m. An unknown female, dressed in all black, carrying a .357 magnum pistol with silencer, made her way down the dark, seldom used corridor of the downtown branch of UPS. She waited for her victim to approach. Jeanette Porterfield, carrying several boxes began her journey through the corridor toward the freight elevator. Sensing a presence, she began to walk faster. Reaching the elevator, she pushed the call button and waited. At that very moment, she felt cold steel pressed against her neck. She dropped the boxes, attempted to turn around only to be punched repeatedly in the face. Jeanette re-grouped and somehow managed to retaliate against her attacker, snatching an object from the attacker's body. As the struggle grew more intense between the two, the elevator door opened, only the cables were visible, the attacker attempted to push Jeanette into the empty shaft but did not have enough strength. Jeanette was getting the best of her attacker.

At that very moment, a shadow appeared out of the darkness and said, "I had hoped you would be able to take care of this; but, I guess I was wrong." The accomplice grabbed Jeanette, threw her against the wall, took the gun from the female attacker, and emptied two rounds into Jeanette's head and two into her chest. Jeanette was then pushed into the empty elevator shaft where she fell six floors down.

"Get out of here now," the accomplice instructed the female attacker. At that moment, both disappeared into the night, neither being seen nor heard by anyone.

\* \* \* \* \*

### 8:30 p.m.

I was the last customer leaving the Mercedes-Benz dealership. I was now the proud owner of a Black 2011 Mercedes SLK350 convertible. If anybody asked, I'd say my car was hit, totaled, and this is what I wound up with. I hugged Alessandra and gave her a $15,000 cashier's check from my credit union. The actual price of the car was around $55,000, but with my trade in and Alessandra hooking up the paperwork, and the $15,000 given; the car was mine, insurance included and a zero balance. To be safe, I cancelled my old license plate and ordered a new one. I set up everything using my new P.O. Box.

The money I gave Alessandra I knew would somehow wind up in the pocket of Debonair and I'd get some of it back later. I stopped by his house to show him the vehicle. He told me he'd treat me to a $1,000 gas card. We parked in my condo's garage, walked back around to his condo, and waited for Alessandra. She was going to prepare lamb for Debonair. I had not cooked, so I decided I'd eat with them, have a few drinks, and go home. When Alessandra arrived, she didn't seem too happy to see me. I decided I wouldn't stay long; so, after eating, I left. Debonair didn't want me to leave, he wanted to shoot pool; but I thought it would be best if I just went home. I knew then that their relationship wasn't going to last long. I decided I'd call Alessandra and calm her down when she went back to work.

\* \* \* \* \*

*10:30 p.m.*

I arrived at home; the chill of the night air gave me a reason to start a fire in my fireplace. After gathering all of the clothing and the shoes that I had worn on Monday, I placed them in the now raging fire along with some powdered incense to cover the smell. As I watched everything burn and turn to ashes, relief once again overtook my being. I smiled, knowing that I now had a reason to go shopping again. I also thought it would be a good way to connect with Alessandra and ease her mind concerning Debonair and me. My thoughts soon faded as my cell phone began to ring. I answered and to my surprise, on the other end was DeJuana Edwards.

"Natalie, this is DeJuana."

"What do you want?" I spat into the receiver.

"I was calling to find out if you had heard about Jeanette Porterfield?"

"What about her?" I inquired.

"She was found in an elevator shaft at her job, dead with four bullets in her body."

"Oh, really?" I said.

"Yeah, Leon is in the hospital and will be getting out tomorrow. I will be going to pick him up and take him home," she bragged.

"Well, good for you," I said.

DeJuana then said, "With Jeanette dead, Leon will be coming into a lot of money, and he will be sharing it with me. We just might wind up getting married."

I repeated, "Well, good for you."

"I need to see you at prayer meeting tomorrow night, I have some monies for you," she replied.

"Yeah, okay. Anything else?" I asked.

"No, that's it," she replied. I then disconnected the call. I carefully swept all the burned ashes from my fireplace, put them in a paper funnel, and took them outside onto the deck. The wind had picked up so I emptied the ashes and let the wind take possession of them and blow them into the unknown. I then flushed the paper funnel and destroyed the small broom I'd used, placing it in the wood chipper that the Forestry Company used for the trees they were cutting. Now all evidence connected to me no longer existed.

* * * * *

## *10:00 a.m.*

Wednesday morning, Pastor woke up and hugged his plush king sized pillow. He was glad to be back at home in his own bed until he heard the words, "I knew I shouldn't have let you back into this house; get all of your belongings and get the fuck out for good. You will be hearing from my attorney as soon as I can find him," yelled Pastor's wife, Charisse.

"Crazy woman, what are you talking about?" He asked, as he leaped out of bed.

"I'm talking about this." She held up a five-carat diamond and ruby bracelet. "You had her at the hotel in Windsor didn't you? Don't lie; I know this belongs to her. That's right; you're busted. FedEx just brought it. Seems the housekeeping staff at the hotel in Windsor found it and turned it in. The hotel was under the impression that it belonged to Mrs. Hunter so they sent it here addressed to me," she screamed. "This is Shavonne Swanson's bracelet. She may or may not get it back, but if she does, it will be on my terms. Now get your shit and get the fuck out." First Lady screamed again.

Pastor stood there looking dumbfounded not knowing what to say, but at that very moment, their house telephone began to ring. "Hello, Hunter residence, T. L. speaking," he answered.

"Are you Terrell Lamar Hunter Sr.?"

"Yes," he answered.

"This is the Detroit Police Homicide Division calling. We are requesting that you meet Officer Marcellus Robinson and his partner Officer Monticello Strickland at the Wayne County Morgue as soon as possible to identify the body of your son Terrell Jr. He was found dead in an abandoned building on the eastside of Detroit. It appears that he was murdered. It also appears to be drug related. We currently are investigating. We will send a car for you and your family." When Pastor heard this, he dropped the telephone and fainted.

"Terrell, Terrell are you still there?" asked First Lady as she listened in on the extension. She told the man on the telephone, "Please send a car right away, and EMS also, my husband just passed out." She ran to Pastor, swept him up into her arms, and began to scream, "Oh, my God; oh, my God, my baby. What have they done to my baby?"

\* \* \* \* \*

*4:00 p.m.*

Wednesday evening, as I walked into my kitchen area, my house telephone began to ring. I checked the caller ID and saw Shavonne's number. "Hello, my diva," I answered.

"Natalie, what are you doing? I really need someone to talk to right now. I am around the corner from your subdivision; can I come over? You aren't real busy are you?" She asked.

"Nah, not really, come on by, I'll be waiting for you, I'll pour you a drink."

About 5 minutes later, I watched from the kitchen window as Shavonne pulled into my driveway and honked her horn. I then walked outside. "I thought you had left, I didn't see your car."

"Come on in; let me get you that drink. Diva, what's wrong? You don't look good at all." (She looked like she was losing weight and her skin color was off somehow). She also seemed sickly and nervous. I handed her the drink and as she sat on the sofa, she began to cry. "Hey, hey now Shavonne, what's wrong? This is definitely not you. You are like a Tigress; even I draw strength from you. Talk to me Shavonne," I said.

"Natalie, I know Terrell deals with a lot of other women but I always thought that I was his number one outside piece, but now I think I'm losing my position. I think there is someone else. I sense that there is a new female competing for my spot. You know that I have prided myself on doing anything for that man, but now it looks as if I'm falling out of favor with him. Natalie, anytime we are together, it's all about me, and no one can interrupt. But, lately, he's been getting calls from an unknown female and when she calls, he makes me be quiet or he will go into another room to talk. Monday, he got a call and he actually got up and left me. He put his clothes on and left. He said he would call, but I haven't heard from him since. Now when I call him, all I get is his voicemail."

"Shavonne, now don't go getting paranoid, you know how Pastor is. He's always into something." I said, trying to comfort her.

"Oh, and another thing, Natalie, I lost my ruby and diamond bracelet."

"Damn, girl," I replied, "I hope you had insurance on it. I am so sorry. Did you call the hotel?" I asked.

"Yeah, but they wouldn't give me any information," she replied.

"Damn, Shavonne, I pray that it will turn up; it's a really nice piece of jewelry," I said, as I handed her a Kleenex and prepared her another drink. As she wiped the tears from her eyes, I told her, "Stay focused, Shavonne; everything is gonna be okay." Little did I know, those words were lurking around waiting to slap me in the face, then circle around, and bite me in the ass.

\* \* \* \* \*

*6:00 p.m.*

I started getting ready for prayer meeting. I didn't want the new car seen yet so I decided I'd take a taxi to the church. I would use some of the money I was to get from DeJuana to pay the fare. As I watched Channel 7 News, they did a segment on the death of Terrell Jr. and one on Jeanette Porterfield. When I arrived at the church and exited the taxicab, the first person I encountered was DeJuana.

"Natalie, where is your car? Why are you riding in a cab?" She asked.

"Somebody hit my car and totaled it. From the looks of it, I believe it was an 18 wheeler," I lied.

She then said, "I'm sorry. I'm glad you weren't hurt. Take this." She handed me an envelope. "Maybe you can put some more with it and get yourself another ride."

"Yeah, that's the plan," I said to her.

She then said, "Leon is at home resting, I picked him up this afternoon. Once the insurance money kicks in, we are going to be doing some things."

I then asked, (pretending to care) "How much do the police know? Any suspects yet?"

DeJuana answered, "No suspects as of yet. All they know is that she was shot twice in the head and twice in the chest." She then asked, "Did you hear about Terrell Jr.?"

"Yes I did, I saw it on the news. Pastor and First Lady must be devastated. Julius K. Fitzpatrick will have his work cut out for him next week. He will need a vacation after this," I replied.

"Well, Natalie, I'm gonna go call Leon. See you later." When she walked away, I headed straight to the ladies' room. I counted the contents of the envelope. Inside was five thousand dollars cash.

\* \* \* \* \*

Prayer meeting was called to order by Deacon Claude Henderson. As the singing began, I put $5600 in an envelope, along with a note explaining what it was for. That would cover my donation for the weeks I'd be in Las Vegas with the triplets and it covered the four grand I had promised to give out of the "recently acquired" money. I felt someone sit next to me. I looked over and there was Lady Monica. Shavonne was right behind her. We hugged and she asked, "Honey, are you okay? I heard you came to church in a taxicab."

"Yeah, my car got totaled; I will have something by tomorrow morning. I won't be at church for a couple of weeks, I'm going on vacation for three weeks, and everything is paid for by several generous gentlemen." As Trustee Julius K. Fitzpatrick walked down the aisle, I stopped him and gave him the envelope. He shook my hand and proceeded to the podium. He then read an announcement regarding the deaths of Jeanette Porterfield and Terrell Jr. Everyone stood to their feet and the prayer sessions began.

At the end of the prayer, Pastor and First Lady entered the sanctuary. First Lady's eyes were red as tomatoes; you could tell she had definitely been crying. Pastor had a blank expression on his face. Another round of prayer took place and Lady Monica started to sing. At that point, the sanctuary doors opened and a female walked in accompanied by a teenage male. She looked to be around 30 and the boy looked to be 12 or 13. She was about 5'5 medium complexion, 130lbs. She looked like singer Rihanna. She was dressed in a designer jean outfit with high boots. There were plenty of open seats, but for some strange reason she came over and sat right next to me. Lady Monica and Shavonne looked at me and I looked at them.

When things got quiet, the lady said to me, "Hello, my name is Denise Bellman. This is my son, Lance, and we wish to join this church." Lady Monica shook her hand and asked her if she would consider joining an auxiliary. A few seconds later Claude Henderson asked all visitors to stand. Denise stood up, introduced herself and her son, and made her request to join the church known. She then began to sing a song without music. I must say she had a beautiful voice. She sounded similar to Whitney Houston. After she finished singing, she looked at Lady Monica and told her she would be happy to join the choir.

Shavonne didn't say anything; she just rolled her eyes at Denise. I saw Pastor staring at her and his eyes remained fixed on her while Julius K. Fitzpatrick had her fill out a registration card. After prayer meeting ended, I watched as Pastor hugged her tightly and held on as if he'd previously had dealings with her. Shavonne noticed it too. I started walking toward the lobby to call a taxi for my return ride home, but heard Pastor say that Homicide Detectives from the Detroit Police Department were here and wanted to address the church with a progress report regarding the death of Terrell Jr. Pastor asked everyone to remain seated.

When Pastor mentioned Terrell Jr., First Lady fell out of her chair and began to scream and cry uncontrollably. Several of the church nurses rushed to comfort her. Pastor thanked everyone for their prayers and then (holding back tears) introduced Homicide Detectives, Monticello Strickland and his partner Marcellus Robinson. When I heard the name Monticello, I eased my way from the audience and called a cab from the church lobby. I just wanted to get out of there before he saw me or got a chance to say something to me.

I felt a presence behind me and turned around to find Shavonne and DeJuana. DeJuana was on her cell talking to Leon. She was rocking back and forth, holding her stomach. Shavonne asked me what I was doing in the lobby and I told her that I was waiting on a taxi. She offered to take me home, but I told her I didn't want her to go out of her way. She insisted and told me that she "owed me that" for being so understanding earlier. I called back and cancelled the taxi. Shavonne waved goodbye to DeJuana, (who was still on her cell phone) and we left the church.

* * * * *

On the ride home, we began to talk about Denise. Shavonne asked me, "Did you see how Pastor was hugging her?"

"I certainly did," I answered.

"Something tells me that this was not a first encounter between those two," Shavonne said accusingly.

"I agree, and now we have a mission to find out who she is and what her agenda is. I'll invite her to my office in the morning for a new member interview and find out what I can because I never want to see you like you were this afternoon. You know you are my "Diva." Seeing you like that hurt my heart. Oh, yeah by the way, DeJuana is in seventh heaven isn't she?" I asked.

"She definitely is. That's going to be an ugly couple," Shavonne laughed. "A crack head lookalike and Shabba Ranks in a dress."

"Shavonne, why do you talk like that about your girl? And wasn't Leon giving you money?"

"Yeah, Natalie, about 10 grand in total; but the truth is the truth and DeJuana- I will let her stay around as long as she's useful to me."

"Damn, Shavonne you are one cold piece of work at times," I replied.

"Yes, I am Natalie, yes, I am." She gave me a high five and we both laughed.

* * * * *

As I opened the door to my condo, my cell phone rang and so did my house phone. I answered my house phone and Lady Monica was on the other end. "Natalie, it's me, I am glad you are getting a much needed vacation, but I will miss you. Will you have your car by tomorrow?" She asked.

"I sure will," I answered, hating to lie to her.

"Anthony has to go to a conference at Cobo Hall in the morning. Do you think you could come by before you go to the office and get these papers? My attorney and accountant are in the Ford Building, but on different floors."

"Lady Monica, no problem, I will be happy to do that for you."

She then asked, "Do you have any monies you might want to invest? If you do, my attorney can move up to $100,000."

"Great," I said. "I will make sure to bring my funds."

"Well, I have some monies I'm gonna invest for you, too," she stated.

"Lady M, that's not necessary, I can handle it."

"No, baby this is a gift from me to you. Am I gonna have to give you money lessons again? Haven't I told you time and time again, never say "no" to money?" She asked.

"Yes, you did." I chuckled.

"Oh, by the way, what did the detectives say about Terrell Jr.?" I inquired.

"They said that they think he died of gunshot wounds. Someone supposedly shot him, execution style, and left him with a crack pipe near his feet."

"Wow, Lady M, that is so sad. I really feel bad for First Lady. I know I need to call her, but I don't know what to say."

"Well, just pray on it, something will come to you," she replied. "Okay, Natalie, got to go. See you tomorrow."

\* \* \* \* \*

After I hung up from Lady M, I checked my cell phone and there were over 20 messages from Monticello. As I listened, each additional message seemed to become more filled with anger and accusations. The first few had started out as simple as "sorry I missed you call me back." Now they were beginning to get more demanding. One implied that I was his only girlfriend. A few wanted to know where I was and whom I was with. Some wanted to know why I didn't call back. A few questioned my knowledge of telephone usage. A few threatened to track me down by running my license plate. The very last one was why did I leave the church so fast this evening? I then thought, if this is happening and we haven't slept together yet, I could imagine what would happen if we did. I loved Lady Monica and was now beginning to realize some of the things she'd told me previously, but as far as her advice to "get what funds you can out of him." I was truly considering writing him off. I'd talk to Debonair about it. I decided I'd call First Lady and offer up some words of sympathy. I took a deep breath and dialed. The phone went straight to voicemail. I left my name and spoke a few words of comfort. After hanging up, I took the money DeJuana had given me, and put it in my safe. The safe now held a little over $45,000. I decided to invest $40,000 with Lady Monica's people in the morning.

\* \* \* \* \*

Thursday morning, I got up extra early, made a trip to the credit union, and made a withdrawal of $45,000. 9:30 a.m. I pulled into Lady Monica's driveway. I had my $40G's in a black briefcase and was dressed very plainly in a white Donna Karan blouse and a black skirt, with my hair in a bun so I would not draw attention to myself. Lady Monica had her coat on because she was on her way out. She complimented me on the car and told me to call her later. She handed me four envelopes. She told me to give the three white envelopes to her lawyer and the one blue one to her accountant. She had called ahead and both of them would be in the lawyer's office on the 14th floor. She also told me to give my money to the lawyer if I was investing. When I got to the Ford Building, I was escorted into the lawyer's office and I realized that I knew both the lawyer and the accountant. I had dealt with them before, so I felt comfortable giving up my money. After 45 minutes, all business had been transacted and all papers signed.

\* \* \* \* \*

I arrived at the church at 11:00. Julius K. Fitzpatrick had left the registration cards for Denise Bellman and her son on my desk. I proceeded to enter their information into the church computer database. I called the number on the card but no one answered. I then call the cell number and Denise answered. She told me she was at work and would be getting off at noon. I invited her to come by and have lunch. She agreed to meet me at 1:00. I then called Lady Monica and told her everything had gone well at the Ford Building. I noticed that as I was talking to her a male voice could be heard in the background. As I focused on the voice, I realized that it belonged to Julius K. Fitzpatrick. I then heard a knock and someone say, "Housekeeping, here are the extra towels you requested."

It clicked in again, what Lady Monica had told me. "Don't be far from your money." She had sold the funeral home to Julius K. Fitzpatrick. In addition, she was sleeping with him and getting funds from him. He was going to be in charge of two funerals next week and Lady Monica was going to get a cut from both. No wonder she was investing again. I called the Sullivan triplets and told them that I needed to leave for Las Vegas later than what we had planned because I had to be at the funeral of Pastors son, seeing how I was his Administrative Assistant. They were disappointed, but understood. While I was on the telephone with them, I revised my flight plans and received a new confirmation number.

\* \* \* \* \*

I heard the church doorbell ring; it was 12:55. Denise Bellman was retrieving bags of food from the trunk of her 2005 Honda Civic. She was dressed in a cute denim outfit consisting of a short jacket and long skirt with split.

"Hello Natalie, it is Natalie, isn't it?"

"Yes it is," I answered as I escorted her into my office.

"I hope you like soul food. I stopped by Bert's Smokehouse on the way here," she said, as she removed the food from the large bag. "

"Thank you," I replied. She sat down and we began to dine on baked chicken, candied yams, sweet tea, and salad. "Tell me about Denise," I inquired.

She told me that she had just moved here 11 months ago from Chicago. She had a son Lance, and they did not know who, or where his father was. She was working part time at AAA Insurance Agency in Dearborn and she had recently met this guy that she was really feeling and that she'd do anything for. She knew of his situation (he was married) but she was okay with it. She also said she called him on Monday and he met with her, stayed until midnight, and helped her get out of a sticky situation. I waited for her to tell me his name, but she said that she had to figure out whom she could trust. She also told me that she loved money and would do whatever she needed to do to get it. She told me that she was confronted by DeJuana last night. She did not go into detail on it; but she did tell me that she did not appreciate it and let it be known by cussing DeJuana out. She told me she was very discreet and if she were your friend, it would be for life. She said she was drawn to me, and felt that we would be friends for a long time. She then told me she was misunderstood a lot. I was beginning to see that she might be useful in the long run. She sounded a lot like me in my beginning; but I realized that she was loose with the lips. I thanked her for lunch and escorted her to the door after telling her of certain ones in the congregation to watch out for. She then told me her sister worked the bar at Aces High Casino/Hotel, and she would treat us to drinks if we came down. We arranged to meet Friday night.

\* \* \* \* \*

After Denise left, I decided I'd call Alessandra. I called the Mercedes-Benz dealership and they paged her. When she came to the phone, I asked if she was okay. She apologized for the other night and told me that she was in pain after she left work. She said she did not mean to be nasty toward me but she was scared. She explained that she was still waiting on some medical test results regarding a mammogram. I dismissed the idea of discussing Debonair and asked her if there was anything I could do. She asked me if I could go with her on Monday afternoon to find out the results, because she had no one and she didn't want to be by herself when she found out. I told her I would be happy to and that I would take her shopping for an outfit afterwards. I began to pray at that very moment for Alessandra. I had heard about breast cancer and was hoping that Alessandra would be okay. I knew all of Debonair' girlfriends but I only connected with two or three of them. Alessandra was one.

\* \* \* \* \*

I finished my prayer and my cell phone began to ring. I answered and heard the words "And where have you been?"

"Excuse me," I said as politely as I possibly could.

"I've been busy, and I am not very appreciative of the messages that you left me. Monticello, I am concerned about your attitude because of the messages. When we first met, I remember telling you that I did not approve of questioning and that I would extend the same courtesy to you. I also told you that I was independent and answered to no one. I cannot and will not condone jealousy or control issues from anyone. Therefore, I think we should take a breather from one another for a while and see how things play out," I suggested.

"Natalie, that's why I am calling, I wish to apologize for my outbursts over the phone. I just got nervous when I didn't hear from you and I over-reacted. I promise it won't happen again. I am off on Friday, let me take you to dinner," he begged.

"Monticello, I have plans already, but I'd be up for lunch if you could," I replied. "Okay, lunch will be fine, what time do you want me to pick you up?"

"Let's say 1:00 at the Greek restaurant downtown; I will meet you there. I'll be dressed in a black denim outfit." I did this because I did not want him to know where I lived or see the new car, which I was going to have parked by the valet at the casino across the street.

"Thank you, Natalie," he said.

"Well, I've got to go; see you tomorrow," I said, and hung up.

* * * * *

I still had a bad feeling about meeting with Monticello. I just couldn't shake off some of the words he'd used in those telephone messages. I decided right then I'd go talk to Debonair and have him take a date to the restaurant and watch my back. I dialed Debonair's number and he answered the phone coughing like crazy.

"Hey, are you all right?" I asked.

He answered, "I don't know, seems like I'm coming down with something. I've been feeling strange ever since I ate that lamb yesterday."

"Damn," I replied. "I'm on my way. "I'll stop at CVS and get you something, sit tight; I'll be there soon."

When I arrived, one of his girlfriends, Molina Saunders, the booster, was there. It had been a while since we'd seen each other. She thought I was one of his other girlfriends and started to get ghetto fabulous until Debonair told her who I was and showed her an old picture of all of us at one of boxing promoter, Emanuel Stewart's, birthday parties in Southfield. She quickly apologized and asked me why I had let my hair grow out, because she thought it was cuter when it was short and spiked. She then asked if I knew what to do to help Debonair. She said that he had been vomiting and running back and forth to the bathroom all day. I gave him some Kaopectate and had him drink some warm Vernor's Ginger Ale, which he bitched about for 30 minutes. Molina had him lie down on the sofa while I explained my situation regarding Monticello to the both of them. Molina said that she would make sure that Debonair would get some rest and when he felt better tomorrow that they would be at the restaurant to have my back. She then took me out to her Hummer and gave me a beautiful black party dress from Gucci and black Manolo Blahnik peep-toe heels. I hugged her and told her I might call later to see if Debonair was feeling better. She said okay, because she would be spending the night.

\* \* \* \* \*

It was now 6:00 and I decided I'd call Lady Monica. She answered her cell and told me that she was on 696 West and Evergreen at Michigan First Credit Union. I told her to wait in the car and I would be there shortly to bring her paperwork. She agreed and within minutes, I was there. As I pulled into the parking lot, I observed Julius K. Fitzpatrick's' vintage white hearse entering Walter Ruther Freeway 696 Eastbound. I looked at Lady Monica and smiled because The Hawthorne Inn was right across the freeway.

She winked at me and said, "I told you, don't be far from your money."

I said, "Lady M, you are something special."

She then said, "Baby, if anyone asks, I was at the Ford Building with you."

I answered, "Yes you were." I handed her the paperwork that was inside the envelopes she'd given me this morning. She gave me one back. It had a star drawn on it.

"This one belongs to you. It's the gift I told you about. Put it in your safe." She then yawned, stretched and said, "I'm going home and go to sleep. Julius and I have two funerals to do next week."

I watched as she drove away. Lady Monica was my hero. She was married to Anthony, sleeping with Julius and Pastor, and collecting large cash from both of them. She even had the two of them (Anthony and Julius) working together on occasion. I thought about the conversation I'd had with Denise. I couldn't expose her to Shavonne yet. I decided I would hold off until after I returned from Las Vegas. Denise might just be beneficial to me later.

\* \* \* \* \*

My phone rang and it was DeJuana Edwards. "Natalie, I just called to tell you that the morgue has released Jeanette's body to Julius K. Fitzpatrick. I am going to take some clothes over to the funeral home tomorrow. The detectives said that the Medical Examiner found a piece of jewelry lodged underneath one of Jeanette's breast. They will be DNA testing it on Wednesday."

"Really, that's interesting," I said. "So they should have a suspect soon, huh?"

"I hope so," she answered. I heard Leon moaning in the background.

"How is Leon doing?" I then asked.

"He's healing slowly, he has two cracked ribs. The funeral is scheduled for Tuesday. Jeanette's family will be coming in on Saturday," she replied.

"Is that it?" I inquired.

"Yes," she replied, I then hung up.

* * * * *

At the Phoenix Apartments on the east side of Detroit, the inside of Unit 2662 looked like a tornado had touched down. Everything was in disarray, especially Denise Bellman's bedroom.

"Lance did you find it yet?" Denise yelled.

"No, Mama, not yet," he yelled back.

"Dammit, that was my favorite piece. It cost me a grip. Now I can't find it. This is fucked up. Not only do I have to return some of this money, I have lost my favorite piece of jewelry. I really fucked up this time. Lance, keep looking, baby," Denise yelled as she tossed around everything in sight frantically searching for her missing jewelry. As her mind wandered back to the last time she had it on, she began to get a sick feeling in the pit of her stomach accompanied by a headache. She now remembered. She knew where it was. She had to retrieve and destroy it. But, how was that going to happen? That was the 64-thousand dollar question.

# Chapter 4

*Atlanta, Georgia*

In the dormitory of Spelman College, Atlanta Georgia, Dominique Hunter was preparing a slideshow for an upcoming presentation to be shown in her Media Communications class. There was a knock at the door.

"Dominique? Are you in there? You are wanted in the Dean's office right away. It's an emergency," screamed her roommate Snowy Bell.

"I'll be right there," she answered. Five minutes later, she entered the office of the Dean.

"Dominique, I sent for you because there is an emergency with your family back in Detroit. We're sorry to inform you that due to the death of your brother, your family needs you to come home right away. All arrangements have been made; your flight will leave at midnight. All of your professors have been notified and your assignments have been postponed until further notice. Ms. Hunter, we are sorry for your loss; if there is anything we can do to be of assistance to you, please do not hesitate to let us know."

"Thank you," replied Dominique as she ran from the office in tears. When she returned to the dormitory, she fell across her bed and cried herself to sleep.

\* \* \* \* \*

Several hours later as Dominique packed her bags, she thought about what she had done, stealing the hundred thousand on anniversary Sunday and giving it to Terrell Jr. "Why didn't he just pay them? Now he's dead, killed by drug dealers, but which ones?" She just couldn't bring herself to believe that Terrell Jr. was a crack head out of control. He was her brother, the one she loved unconditionally. "What am I gonna do now? I have no one left now. Well, at least no one knows I stole the money, or do they? I'll have to go to the funeral and get back to Atlanta before I become suspect,"

She continued thinking. Her thoughts were interrupted by her roommate Snowy Bell barging into the dorm.

"Dominique, your ride is downstairs," she said. Dominique grabbed her bags and headed down the hall, to the awaiting limousine. She was dreading her flight back to Detroit. She didn't know who or what might be lurking around the corner waiting on her.

# Chapter 5

*Detroit, Michigan*

I arrived at my office at 8:00 a.m. I decided that I would work until 12:30 today and head downtown. I arranged for Pastor's favorite visiting minister Rev. Samuel Glastonbury because I knew Pastor wouldn't be in shape to preach on Sunday. I completed the bulletins and called Frenchee B. Henderson to take my place for the weeks I would be out of town. Around noon, my cell phone rang.

"Natalie, hey girl, this is Molina. I just called to tell you that Debonair is doing much better; we will see you at 1:00. Oh, by the way, did you want us to acknowledge you or just lay low?" She asked.

"Molina, just lay low, I will come by and speak at the appropriate time," I replied.

"Cool, see you there," she said. Then she disconnected the phone. The next call I got was from Denise Bellman.

"Natalie, are we still on for tonight?"

"Yes we are," I answered. "I think I am going to get a hotel villa with my comps and get a party going."

"That would be great; I need a place to release some tension. I have to tell you something in person; I think I might have a real big problem," she replied.

"Hope I can help, see you tonight," I said.

I called Monticello and told him I was on my way. I then called Lady Monica and told her of my plans, seeing as she would not be meeting Pastor for their Friday afternoon tryst. Pastor and First Lady were with Julius Fitzpatrick making funeral arrangements.

\* \* \* \* \*

I left my car with the valet at the casino because I was going to go over and book a hotel villa for the weekend after I'd had lunch. When I arrived at the restaurant, Monticello was sitting at the bar. He almost knocked over a waitress in an attempt to greet me. He had a special table set up for me with flowers, balloons and other decorations. He'd also ordered a bottle of Cristal and had it chilling on ice. I looked around the restaurant and did not see Debonair or Molina. I began to get an uneasy feeling until I felt someone bump me from behind and say, "Excuse me."

When I turned around to see who was apologizing, it was Molina. Debonair walked behind her as if he didn't know her or me. Monticello ordered a lamb dish for the both of us along with salad. He apologized all through lunch stating that Detroit was dangerous and by me being in Detroit as much as I was; he was just worried that something may have happened to me when he didn't hear from me. I thanked him for his concern, and told him that I would be fine. I still wasn't happy about those messages, but I thought I might be able to use him to help Denise. I had put two and two together and knew that she was in trouble and why. Monticello begged and pleaded for me to spend the entire day with him. I told him I had late afternoon appointments. We talked about his job and I found out that he knew someone at the crime lab.

Before lunch ended, I knew everything I needed to know about gaining entrance to the crime lab and how evidence would sometimes disappear and all staff schedules and personnel. When lunch was over, I walked by the table where Molina and Debonair were seated.

I spoke and asked Molina, "Hello, isn't your name Phyllis and didn't we go to school together? My name is Natalie."

"I believe we did and this is my boyfriend Javier," she replied. I told her I was going to the ladies' room and she followed me. Debonair got up and went to summon a waitress, leaving Monticello standing alone.

\* \* \* \* \*

While we were in the bathroom, I told Molina that I was booking a villa at the casino/hotel to have a party for the weekend and to ask for me at the desk. When we got back to the table, Debonair was walking back with a waitress who had a bottle of Moet and four glasses. He then asked Monticello and me to join them for a drink. As we sat and drank champagne, Debonair stayed quiet as Molina and I made small talk. Monticello refused to drink or talk to Debonair or Molina and he had a look of anger and jealousy on his face. He also kept looking and pointing at his watch. I spoke on my appointment and said goodbye. As Monticello escorted me to the front door of the restaurant, a gorgeous older lady (Lady Monica) approached me and asked me to help her locate her car. I agreed to help her and told Monticello I'd call him later. Monticello objected at first, and then he stormed off leaving us standing there.

* * * * *

Lady Monica and I walked through the tunnel to the casino/hotel parking structure. I booked villa 2650 using my casino comps. I picked up the keycards and had the valet recover my vehicle. I took the suitcase from the trunk and had the valet re-park my car in the casino/hotel VIP parking structure. I called Molina on her cell and requested that she and Debonair meet me at 6:00. I also told her to make sure she and Debonair were not being followed. Then I called Shavonne.

"How have you been?" I asked.

"Not good Natalie, I have been feeling extremely exhausted lately and I still haven't heard from T.L. I know he has problems right now, but he won't even answer his phone."

"Girl, just be patient," I said, "you know he's going through right now. Oh, I did get a chance to meet Denise, she's new in town, there's nothing going on with her that I could see. She's just trying to be a mother to her kid and keep a few dollars in her pockets." I felt somewhat bad lying to my girl, but I was looking for future allies. "Well, Shavonne, it's the weekend and I'm going to hang out. See you Sunday; if you need me, call my cell. Peace."

* * * * *

My hotel telephone rang as I was retrieving a frozen daiquiri from the mini-fridge. "Ms. Champion, you have a visitor by the name of Denise Bellman," stated the woman at the hotel front desk.

"Thank you, I replied, send her up please." Five minutes later, I heard a knock at the door. As Denise entered, I offered her a daiquiri from the mini-fridge. I told her that my cousin and his lady friend would be joining us later and that I had the villa for a party weekend.

She smiled and said, "Let's go to the casino bar and have my sister fix us some drinks." We traveled downstairs and I was introduced to her sister Renee. Her sister looked like a watered down version of Rihanna, but with long hair; and she was not stingy with the liquor, so I made sure I left her a generous tip. A few hours later, after having several drinks, Denise began to show signs of being intoxicated.

She said, "I better tell you my problem." She explained what I already knew. She had lost her jewelry at a crime scene and it had to be at the crime lab by now. She was sure that they were going to do a DNA test on it. She also told me who her new man was and how he came to her rescue. I had a feeling from the beginning that I knew who it was and I was right.

"Well, Denise, I think I might know a way we can get your jewelry back. But, you're gonna have to destroy it for good. I said. I just hope it's not too late."

"You'd do that for me?" She asked.

"Maybe, we'll talk about it tomorrow," I answered. I put an end to the conversation when I saw Debonair and Alessandra walking through the casino. He saw us sitting at the bar and came over with Alessandra following behind him.

"What happened here, baby Moses?" I asked, as I spoke to Alessandra and introduced her to Denise.

"Too much mouth and too much attitude, so I had to put two cab drivers to work," he quickly replied. I knew what he meant so I left it alone. Alessandra saw some of her co-workers walking by and called them over. Introductions were made and I asked everyone to join me in my villa so we could start the party. Debonair called several of his partners. I also ordered several trays of food. An hour later, after Debonair's partners showed up with liquor, beer, music, and other party favors, I had a full-fledged party going on in my villa. There were gorgeous men everywhere, and even though Denise had gotten drunk, she was flirting, dancing with several of the men, and seemed to be having a good time. Monticello kept calling my phone and Molina kept calling Debonair; but with all of the partying going on, we both refused to answer our phones. It was going to be tripped out when Molina and Monticello caught up to us.

\* \* \* \* \*

The party was a blessing in disguise and just what I needed. I even got a chance to get my sex on and practice my fellatio skills with one of my former sex buddies Lorenzo Franklin (who could pass for the actor, Brian White). I'd run into Lorenzo at the bar. Lorenzo gave me the best oral sex session that a female could ever want. A sex session was long overdue for me. I passed out twice from the pleasure. Lorenzo and I had lost contact when he moved out of state but I was glad he was back and that we'd run into each other again. The sex would hold me until I could get with the Sullivan triplets.

\* \* \* \* \*

Around 8:00 a.m. Saturday morning, the hotel lobby called and told me an older female who said she was my mother was looking for me. I knew then that it was Lady Monica. She came up and attempted to put the last of the partygoers out of my villa. All I could do was laugh because it reminded me of the times when Debonair and I were teenagers and Uncle DeArthur would try to break up our money making basement parties or outside pool parties. After I promised her that I would come to church on Sunday, she left. Denise was in one of the other bedrooms with one of Debonair's partners Desmond Anderson. They were still knocked out. I was glad she had a good time and relieved some of her stress. I was going to have to speak to her regarding her holding her liquor along with her tongue. She talked a bit too much after having a couple of drinks. I knew then to only disclose certain information to her. I decided to let her sleep until 10:00. I rehearsed in my head what I would tell Denise so that she could retrieve her jewelry from the crime lab. She had to get it before Wednesday.

* * * * *

Denise woke up at 9:30 and took a shower with her new friend Desmond. He gave me $500.00 and apologized for using one of the extra bedrooms. He claimed that he was too drunk to go to the front desk and book a room. After he left, Denise and I discussed a plan for her and her sister Renee to enter the crime lab and retrieve her jewelry. She then called her sister. Saturday was a good day to do it because there would not be many staff on duty. After going over the plan several times, Denise prepared to leave and told me that she would call after everything was taken care of. She also called her new man and actually got through. He told her he couldn't see her until next week. As she was leaving, I wished her well in recovering her property and told her the party would be back on later tonight and to come back if she could get a babysitter. She thanked me for my hospitality and left.

* * * * *

I took a shower with Lorenzo, changed clothes, and went down to the gaming floor so that housekeeping could clean my villa. Lorenzo and I stopped at the casino restaurant and he bought breakfast for us. He asked me if he could hang out with me until lunchtime and I agreed. Lorenzo gave me $2500 to gamble with and I played a machine close to the crap table where he was positioned. Lorenzo had the sexiest ass a woman ever wanted to see. It was hard for me to play my machine because I was continually watching his ass as he moved around leaning over the table throwing the dice to the end of the crap table. Around 1:30, I began to get sleepy from partying all night, so I told Lorenzo I would be going back to the villa. He bought carry out lunch for the both of us and walked me back to the villa. He promised to return around 7:00 and asked what I needed for the party tonight. I gave him a list and entered my villa. I fell asleep as soon as my head hit the pillow.

\* \* \* \* \*

At Fitzpatrick's funeral home, Pastor and First Lady were finalizing the arrangements for Terrell Jr. First Lady had brought an Armani suit for him to be buried in. Pastor was on the phone with the insurance company attempting to explain what happened to Terrell Jr.

"It's your fault he's dead," First Lady stated, as Julius Fitzpatrick excused himself and left his office to answer the funeral home door. "You were so busy with your church, collecting money and dealing with your whores. You turned your back on him when he needed you most. You should have done whatever it took to get him treated and don't you dare give me that "he was a grown man" shit. He was a "sick man" and you stopped helping him. Now he's dead. I will deal with you in due time, but for now, this funeral is my top priority," she continued.

Pastor ignored his wife and continued to talk to the insurance agent; but deep down inside he knew his wife was right. He had to find a way to make her forgive him. He wondered if he'd made a mistake by cutting off funds to Terrell Jr. Pastor knew that his journey back into First Lady's good graces would be a long one.

\* \* \* \* \*

Julius K. Fitzpatrick opened the funeral home door and DeJuana Edwards walked in carrying a large bag filled with clothing. "These are the things for Jeanette to be buried in, she replied. When will the body be ready for viewing?" She asked.

"Monday evening," Julius answered.

"Why are you in such a rush for Jeanette to be buried? What's going on between you and Leon?" Julius inquired.

"Don't get beside yourself DeJuana; you may wind up being disappointed. Just be careful," he said. He then escorted DeJuana to her vehicle and returned to finish up with Pastor and First Lady. "Everything will be ready by Thursday. We can have the viewing on Friday night and the funeral will be next Saturday at noon if that's okay with the two of you. I have also scheduled three limousines."

"That will be fine," answered First Lady. "Dominique is already in town and everyone else will be in on Thursday. I will also have Natalie to announce it this Sunday so that everyone will know."

"Okay then, if you need me give me a call," Julius said. He hugged First Lady, shook Pastor's hand, and escorted them to the front door of the funeral home.

* * * * *

As Julius' limo driver was returning Pastor and First Lady back to their residence, Pastor's cell rang. "Answer it dammit; it's probably another one of your hookers calling. I will give you five minutes to get whatever clothing you can out of the house because you will not be staying there tonight. Go back to Windsor or wherever," First Lady spat out like fire.

"I'll get a room in town this time," he said. "I will see you at church tomorrow. I'll be back early so we can ride to church together; we still have to keep up appearances you know."

"Whatever," First Lady replied. The rest of the drive home was in silence. When they arrived home, Pastor went upstairs, kissed little Tee, packed a suitcase; he then opened his wife's jewelry box and grabbed the bracelet he'd previously given Shavonne. He retrieved his vehicle and left the house. He called Shavonne and told her he needed money and that she needed to meet him downtown. She told him she wasn't feeling well, but agreed to meet him anyway.

* * * * *

*4:30 p.m.*

I awoke from my mid-morning nap, took a shower, and dressed in a Gucci outfit. As I headed back down to the gaming floor, my cell phone began to vibrate indicating I had a text message. The message read: "Natalie, funeral next Saturday at 12:00 noon for Terrell Jr. I moved out of the house again. I will be staying at Aces High Casino/Hotel downtown. I have booked room number 2550."

"Oh shit," I said aloud as I made my way to the roulette table. "Pastor is gonna be one floor beneath me." Shavonne called me and told me she was meeting Pastor. She said she was feeling queasy, but was going anyway; and that she hoped he would take it easy on the sex.

"See, didn't I tell you everything would be okay?" I said, attempting to cheer her on. "Just try to relax and enjoy yourself." I then hung up and proceeded to the high limit area to play roulette. Before I could buy any chips, Denise called and said everything had gone well at the crime lab. She and her sister Renee retrieved her jewelry and were sure that DNA testing had not taken place. She said she used a fake name and took the piece of jewelry to one of those places where they melt it down and pay you for it. She also said she was going to show her appreciation to me for helping her tonight when she came back for night two of the party.

I said, "Okay" and told her I was on the gaming floor and I would see her later. After I hung up from Denise, my cell phone vibrated and showed that I had 15 messages from Monticello. "Not today, I am in too good of a mood for his bullshit. Maybe tomorrow," I said to myself.

\* \* \* \* \*

For the next few hours, I played roulette, won $800, and around 6:30 headed back upstairs to change into a jean outfit and my dancing shoes. Upon entering the elevator, I smelled Cool Water Cologne and knew that Pastor was in the vicinity. I ran into Debonair, Jerome, and Lorenzo on the elevator, who had bags of liquor, beer, and food trays. Debonair brought Donna Buchanan, another one of his girlfriends, with him. Donna had a bag that contained a gallon of Hennessey. Denise, who was buzzed already, and Desmond arrived about 15 minutes later with six magnums of Moet. Denise told me "thank you" and handed me $1,000 cash. I decided I would give it back to her later. I figured she could use it for her kid. Debonair's other partners came to the villa about 30 minutes after that. About 20 people from the floor I was on came by bearing party goods and asked if they could come in. I told them "no problem." The party was on and popping once again. I began to harbor a funny feeling so I appointed Desmond to answer the door and to tell people that this was his villa and his party. I would end the party around 6:00 a.m. because I'd planned on going to church in the morning, but I knew I was going to be late. I wondered if Lady Monica was still downtown, so I stepped out into the hallway and called her. She was at home and told me that she was getting her outfit together for Sunday. I thanked her for the investment she'd made on my behalf and told her I might be late for church. I returned to the party in anticipation of another fun night of drinking, dancing and a second sex session with Lorenzo.

\* \* \* \* \*

Around midnight, someone knocked on the door complaining about the music. When Desmond answered the door to see who it was, I realized that it was Pastor. He stated that his room was directly underneath this one and that he had to get up early. Desmond told him that he would take care of it. I was happy that he did not see me, Denise, or a few other members of his congregation that were in the villa. My sixth sense had paid off. It would have been awkward if I'd been the one to answer the door.

* * * * *

## Sunday morning. 6:00 a.m.

Desmond announced the party had to end. Debonair and Donna were in one of the bedrooms asleep. Denise had been knocked out since around 3:00 and Desmond was on the prowl. He'd been dancing and flirting with some female who came in with the crowd from down the hall. They left the party, had sex, and came back while Denise was sleeping. Lorenzo and I had sexed each other up so fiercely that we could barely get out of bed. I was hurting good from head to toe. All I wanted to do was to go home and get in my own bed. I woke everybody up, showered, dressed, and was at home by 9:00. I now had over 50 messages from Monticello. I wondered how many Debonair had from Molina. Lady Monica called me at 10:30 and said morning services had been postponed until 4:00. She said she'd heard it on the radio and it had been sent by text message and email to all members that had internet connections and cell phones. I checked my cell and she was right. She also said that Pastor Glastonbury had been informed and was okay with it. I thanked her and decided I'd get some more sleep so that I could attend.

* * * * *

I woke up again at 3:00 with a slight hangover. I bathed and dressed in Oscar de la Renta from head to toe. When I arrived at church, I saw Frenchee B. and asked her to take over the announcements for me, seeing how I was feeling woozy and didn't want to stand up in front of the congregation and be seen on the Jumbo Tran, giant screen TV.

She agreed to take over and said to me, "You better tone down that partying; you're gonna pay for it in the long run."

I took a seat in the rear of the sanctuary, put on my Cartier shades, and draped a scarf over my head. Denise came in by herself about 15 minutes after I did. She sat in front of me. I could tell that she was hungover, too, and she was sporting Cartier shades and a scarf. To my surprise, Pastor and First Lady were sitting on pulpit. They both looked drained. Shavonne was in the choir stand. When she saw me, she shot me a strange look and did the same thing to Denise. After that, she kept her eyes glued to Pastor all during the service. Every now and then, I would glance at Denise. She looked sickly from something other than a hangover. She was staring at Pastor and smiling like someone who had won the lottery. When the congregation headed up front for altar prayer, Denise and I remained behind and started a conversation.

I handed her the thousand back and told her, "Use it for your kid or yourself, because I know you had to return some of your assignment money; and you lost out having to destroy your favorite jewelry. You can get at me some other time. You need to be going shopping. We'll go Monday, me, you and Alessandra."

Denise thanked me and said, "You are a good person, Natalie." She then told me she had something lined up with an old man and she would be coming into a large piece of money in the near future. I warned her about her loose tongue and alcohol and told her about Desmond. She thanked me again and agreed to be more careful. She also said she wasn't fazed about Desmond; she just needed to get laid because she was horny and that Desmond did give her some money. I told her not to stop demanding respect though.

\* \* \* \* \*

Pastor Samuel L. Glastonbury did his best to get the church revved up, but seemed like the entire congregation was in a blue funk. I guess everyone was thinking about the upcoming funerals of Terrell Jr. and Jeanette Porterfield. Pastor Samuel Glastonbury danced in the pulpit like M.C. Hammer and Michael Jackson and he preached with gusto while the choir attempted to sing uplifting songs but nothing seemed to work. The spirit just wasn't there. The fire was definitely out on this particular Sunday. After church ended, I decided I was going to leave quickly, but that idea was derailed when Pastor requested to see Shavonne and me in his office. Shavonne's attitude changed immediately. I watched her as she walked toward his office. She moved slower than usual, you could tell that she was not operating at full capacity.

I made it into Pastor's office before she did. He quickly handed me a note with a name on it and told me to deliver it ASAP. I looked at the name and prepared to do as he requested. I made a call on my cell phone and told the person who the note was for to meet me in the lobby. I delivered the note and watched as the recipient read it and smiled.

"Girl, I gotta go home, change, and get myself together. I hope I can convince him to let me stay overnight," she said.

"Good luck, See you later," I replied. I then spoke to several people, including Lady Monica and made my way to the parking lot and left.

\* \* \* \* \*

When I entered my vehicle, my cell phone began to ring. I checked and it was Shavonne. She asked, "Girl, are you okay? And what is up with that Denise? Why is she trying to copy your style?"

I answered, "I partied too much over the weekend. I'm just glad church was this afternoon, 'cause I didn't get home until this morning. And as far as Denise, I don't know why she's imitating me; maybe it was just a coincidence. I'm going home and go back to bed."

"Well, Pastor wants me to meet him in an hour; we spent the night together last night, I gave my baby big money, too. Natalie, I feel weird; it's like I'm not a hundred percent. These symptoms started a couple of months ago. Well, I gotta go. I'll talk to you whenever," Shavonne said.

"See girl, I told you everything would be all right. You know you're his top side piece," I replied in an attempt to boost her ego. I made it home, attempted to eat but couldn't; so I got me a "hair of the dog" (drink of Moet) and got in bed. I turned my cell off because I now had 75 messages from Monticello. I decided that I would start fresh on Monday and deal with his bullshit then.

\* \* \* \* \*

*10:00 Sunday night*

Pastor left his hotel room, retrieved his vehicle, and pulled over on Grand River and W. Warren. He made a call from his cell phone.

"Hey lovely, I need to see you; can you get away? I want you to stay with me tonight."

"Yes, I can," was the answer he received.

"I need to get some sex from you. I need you to come to room 2550 at Aces High Casino/Hotel."

"I'll be there in 30 minutes," replied the female voice. About 25 minutes later, Pastor received a call from the front desk of the hotel letting him know that he had a visitor. Five minutes later, a sexy woman dressed in black and silver entered his room. No words were spoken, only a hug was given, and the lovemaking between the two of them took place. The only thing you could hear was sexual moaning from the both of them. After they both climaxed, Pastor smiled and drifted to sleep with her still lying beneath him and his unprotected manhood still inside of her.

\* \* \* \* \*

Monday morning came faster than I wanted it to. I made my way to my office and entered at 9:55. Luckily, there weren't many envelopes or reports that had to be recorded, so around one o'clock, I was down to my last few. Lady Monica called and asked me to contact Maurice Williams and the cleaning crew so that the church would be clean for Jeanette's funeral. I thought about DeJuana, she was hanging tough with Leon. She didn't even show up for church yesterday. I called Alessandra, who had taken the day off, and she asked me to meet her at 2:30 at The Karmanos Women's Center, which was five minutes from the church. I arrived at 2:35 and we held hands and prayed. About 45 minutes later, her doctor came in with her test results and gave her a clean bill of health. We jumped for joy, hugged each other, and thanked God. I told her that we were going shopping. She said she only had $100.00 and a credit card with a grand on it. I told her the shopping trip was on me. I then called Denise who was at home and told her to be ready because Alessandra and I were on our way.

* * * * *

After picking her up, we went to Somerset Mall. She was bragging about spending the night with her new man. However, every now and then, she'd drift off as if she was suffering from a loss of her thoughts. When we arrived at the mall, we all went to Gucci. Several times, we had to stop to let Denise catch up with us. She walked as if she was in total pain. I told Alessandra to get an outfit so she picked out a cute black and white Gucci skirt set, a scarf, and peep toed shoes to match. We went into Cartier where the three of us purchased sanglasses and a few other items. After that, we went to Tiffany's where Denise bought a diamond set—necklace, earrings, and bracelet—and stated that it was going to be her favorite from now on. I only bought a pair of earrings. I didn't buy much because I knew the triplets were going to let me shop until I dropped when I got to Las Vegas.

* * * * *

We left the mall and headed to Red Lobster to eat. While we were eating lobster, Debonair called Alessandra and told her about one of his partners, Leonardo DeGraffenreid, who was having a party on Wednesday night and wanted three females to dance. Most of his crew were ballers and were going to spend big money because it was Leonardo's 30th birthday. They were booking the entire top floor at Royal Flush Casino/Hotel for a party, along with a stretch Hummer limo. Alessandra asked me if I wanted to participate and I said yes. Denise quickly asked if she could be included also. Alessandra told Debonair that we were interested and he told her he'd give us the details when we got to his place. We stopped by Lovers Lane in Madison Heights and each of us purchased two outfits and shoes to dance in. I found the perfect silver ensemble; I would revise my "Platinum Princess" act from back in the day. Debonair told Alessandra that we were guaranteed a minimum of $10,000 each if we did this party. We only had to dance for four hours. I was hyped because I knew that money would come in handy and I wanted to take at least five grand with me to Las Vegas. I knew the triplets were going to do right by me, but I still wanted to have some funds, just in case.

* * * * *

As we headed back to Denise's apartment, darkness was beginning to set in. As I looked around the neighborhood, I become concerned about her and Lance's safety because the area she lived in was a haven for drugs and other unsavory activities. I asked her if she would consider moving into Shelbourne Townhouses. I told her I could get her an appointment to see the place and she agreed. I called Gabrielle Parker, the manager and she told me she'd wait if I could come right away. We all rode over and looked. The apartment was larger, less expensive, and more modern. It came with carpeting and all appliances, which included a washer and dryer; also, Lance would have his own bathroom. Gabrielle told Denise that she could move in on Saturday if she wanted to. The place was closer to the freeway and closer to Lance's school, which meant he could walk to school if he chose to. Denise said she wanted the place and gave Gabrielle the deposit and first month's rent; but she needed $300 for her movers. She said she was going to pick up Lance from his grandmother and get some boxes so that she could start packing, and contact the utility and cable companies. I dropped her off and Alessandra and I headed back toward Lathrup Village.

* * * * *

When I entered 696 West, my cell phone rang. I answered it only because I was wearing my Bluetooth. Shavonne was on the other end and she was furious. "Natalie, I am really getting fed up with T.L. Why is he hurting me like this? What am I doing wrong? I gave him almost 20 grand Saturday night. I got with him after church at the hotel yesterday evening and we were having a good time. Last night around 9:30, he told me to get out because I told him I wasn't feeling my best. I hung around for a minute and he came down, got in his car and left," she said. I already knew why, but I pretended to be dumb.

"Girl, you know that this week coming up is the funeral; he's probably just freaking out about the funeral. Shavonne, stop tripping, after this funeral ordeal he will be all yours again. And your hot ass probably need to cool out a bit," I said.

"Oh yeah, Natalie; I got my bracelet back. The hotel sent it to his house and Charisse got a hold of it. He stole it back and brought it to me."

"Damn girl, are you serious?" I replied.

"Yep, I tried to go back Sunday night but was told he was not accepting visitors. If I was a betting woman, I'd say he had someone else up there," she implied.

"Shavonne, stop it now! Pastor just needed some by himself time." I knew exactly why he'd put her out. "The word is funeral, Shavonne. The man has lost his only son. F-U-N-E-R-A-L," I spelled the word out to her. "I'm driving right now; I'll call you when I get settled."

Alessandra looked at me and I said, "Complicated, drama to the one hundredth power." She laughed and shook her head. When we got to Debonair's crib, he had flowers, champagne, candy, and a giant card for Alessandra. I got the party information from him, had a drink and left. I insisted that he and Alessandra be alone to celebrate her news about the medical tests.

* * * * *

When I got home, I picked out luggage and began to pre-pack for my Vegas trip. I didn't want to wait until the last minute. I knew before the week was over, I'd pack and re-pack again. I decided to listen to my messages from Monticello. To my surprise, the messages sounded more like Marvin Gaye or Smokey Robinson pleading forgiveness. "Baby please" was in every one of them. Monticello moaned, groaned, begged, and pleaded. Before I reached the last of the messages, I was hot and horny as hell. I was ready to fall into his bed with the quickness. For a split second, I lost my damn mind. I started to call him on the phone, but I was brought back to reality when my cell phone rang and Debonair said, "I'm in jail for assault and battery, come get me."

"What the fuck?" I yelled. "I'll be right there."

I grabbed three grand out of my safe and headed to the Lathrup Village Police Department. When I arrived, Debonair had been released and was sitting on a bench in the lobby.

"What happened?" I inquired.

"Molina came over unannounced and got up in my face about what I was doing in *my* house and about *my* telephone. Alessandra was in the bedroom and came out. Molina tried to fight me so I had to tag her in order to get her off me. My neighbors called the police regarding the noise. I don't believe in hitting women Nat, but it got out of hand. She was not respecting me, my lady, or my house. After I got here, they ran Molina's name, too, and found out about her violent history. Then, they told me I could leave. Alessandra is at my house, she is so shook up I didn't want to chance her driving so I called you. Molina is a thing of the past; she is dead to me."

"Is there any money that has to be paid?" I asked.

"No," he replied. "I just need to get back home to Alessandra."

"Let's go," I said. After dropping Debonair off, I returned home to do some more packing and lay out an outfit for tomorrow's funeral. I proceeded to clear all messages, dialed and received calls and texts from my cell phone, after that I did some practice dancing on my stripper pole so that I would be limber for the party on Wednesday.

\* \* \* \* \*

At the Hunter residence, Dominique was playing video games with little Tee. Little Tee laid his head on Dominique's chest and said.

"Mama, is Uncle Terrell in heaven? Why did God take him? I'm sorry, Mama; I should have been a better nephew to him, huh?"

Upon hearing this, Dominique replied, "Yes, baby, Uncle Terrell is in heaven with the rest of the angels; God took him because it was his time. And baby, you were a good nephew, so don't be sad, Uncle Terrell will always be with you right here." She put her hand on his chest.

At that moment, First Lady Charisse screamed loudly, startling them. "Mama, what's wrong?" Dominique asked.

"It's gone; that son of a bitch took it. He's probably with her now giving it back to her."

"Giving what back, Mama; what did he take?" Dominique inquired.

When First Lady Charisse realized that Little Tee was looking at her, she said, "We'll talk about it later." She then walked out of the room and retreated to her husband's study where she broke down and cried. As she cried, she began to pray.

"Lord, I know that everything you do is for a reason and you will not give me more than I can bear, but Lord, I am tired and frustrated. I am trying to be a good wife, but my patience is truly being tested here. My husband is running around, you've taken my baby from me, and I am having difficulties in other areas. There is a major decision I need to make. Lord, I ask that you come and comfort me and show me what I need to do. I need to hear from you, Lord."

\* \* \* \* \*

As Julius K. Fitzpatrick put the finishing touches on Jeanette Porterfield's body, he looked at his reflection in the mirror and realized that it was later than he thought. "Where is she? I got a funeral in the morning. I can't keep burning the candle on both ends like I'm doing. I'm getting older by the minute. I'll call over there and see what the holdup is," he said aloud.

He dialed several numbers but no one answered the telephone. He dialed again, same result. He closed the lid on Jeanette's casket and rolled it over to the conveyor belt where it would be loaded into the hearse for transport to the church. About 5 minutes later, he heard the doorbell to the funeral home ring. He answered and said, "It's late although I'm glad you came, what took you so long? You know I have that funeral in the morning; are you gonna stay overnight?"

"I'll do whatever you want me to do; just tell me what you want. You know he's out of town and won't be back until Wednesday," she stated. Julius stood back and waited for her to walk into his awaiting arms. They hugged and shared a long, passionate kiss. She looked at him and said, "I really love you, Mr. Julius K. Fitzpatrick."

"My exact sentiments," he replied. "I love you, too, Frenchee B. Henderson." They caught the elevator from the basement to Julius' third floor apartment over the funeral home. They began undressing one another and made love in the luxurious bedroom filled with scented candles and roses that Julius had prepared for Frenchee's visit.

* * * * *

At the Porterfield residence, Leon who had just gotten out of the shower was now looking in the bathroom mirror shaving in preparation for Jeanette's memorial service in the morning. DeJuana was in the kitchen washing the last of the dinner dishes. Since Jeanette's death, DeJuana had locked up her own house, taken a leave of absence from her job; and moved in with Leon. She quickly stepped into the position of lady of the house, cooking, cleaning, and sexing Leon in anticipation of sharing the insurance money. DeJuana even had some of her mail coming to the house.

"Leon, I'm almost finished with the dishes, meet me in the bedroom when you're done," DeJuana yelled from the kitchen. Leon shook his head and responded under his breath.

"I just got out of a marriage; I'm not going into another one. She can think what she wants to think but I have other plans. She is too bossy, having the nerve to tell Jeanette's family that they had to go to a hotel. When I get this check, I am gonna be long gone. To hell with everybody, DeJuana included. My house has been rented furnishings and all. I'm going to get a deposit and rent for 6 months on Monday, all I have to do is walk away, and I will be free." He smiled and entered his bedroom. DeJuana was in bed waiting on him.

"Baby, are you okay?" She asked.

"Yes, I'm good," he answered. DeJuana proceeded to position herself so that he could enter her doggy style. "Not yet baby, I want you to suck me off right now."

DeJuana complied with his request. As Leon laid there getting oral sex, his mind wandered regarding starting his new life, without DeJuana. Ten minutes later, he climaxed, pushed DeJuana off him, told her goodnight, turned over, and fell asleep with her sitting on the side of the bed looking down at him. At that moment, she felt a slight pain in her stomach. She took several pain pills and finally drifted off into a coma-like sleep.

\* \* \* \* \*

Thunder, lightning, wind, and rain over took this dreary Tuesday morning. I found a black Giorgio Armani pinstripe suit and a matching trench coat to wear. I left the condo around 9:15 am. When I arrived at the church, Maurice Williams was overseeing the cleaning team who were vacuuming the sanctuary and placing the delivered flowers on the pulpit. There were flowers from Jeanette's job, the credit union, merchants where she shopped, her hairstylists, her doctor's office, the Trustee board, the Sunday school class, her accountant and from friends. Maurice proceeded to open and stabilize the center sanctuary door so that the casket could be easily transported down center aisle. At 9:55, Julius K. Fitzpatrick arrived with the body. Along with him were Anthony Davenport and several others of Julius' staff. They proceeded to unload the casket and roll it down center aisle to the front of the sanctuary. Even though I would see Julius Fitzpatrick at church, I never really paid any attention to him. However, today, at age 50, he was looking extremely handsome. I guess having money and nice clothes do make people look better. He was dressed in a black Versace double-breasted suit with white shirt, black tie, and black alligator shoes. His salt and pepper hair was cut short. Julius was a high yellow man, with the body structure and facial features of U.S. Attorney General, Eric Holder. Today, he had a swagger in his walk that somewhat reminded me of my uncle, DeAngelo.

\* \* \* \* \*

The phone in my office had begun to ring and I was in the process of answering questions regarding Jeanette's funeral. Julius came into my office, spoke, and handed me the funeral programs that contained Jeanette's obituary and the order of events to take place. Jeanette's childhood pastor would be performing the eulogy, a request by her grandmother. I was happy about that because I knew Pastor Hunter was in no shape to do anything right now, and Assistant Pastor Marvin Cunningham was not in town. I sat in my office waiting for the Ushers to come down and retrieve the programs. In honor of Jeanette, The Trustees would be acting as pallbearers. I began to get an eerie feeling in the pit of my stomach. Funerals always gave me the heebie-jeebies. I retreated to my vehicle and attempted to lose myself in anticipation of my trip to Las Vegas. After 30 minutes of meditation, my thoughts were interrupted as people began to pass my car entering the church for the services.

\* \* \* \* \*

I returned to my office and ran into Frenchee B. Henderson. She was glowing and smiling like someone who had gotten some great sex. She giggled and hugged me as if she hadn't seen me in five years. I watched her blush and grin from ear to ear, as Julius passed by us as he continued his undertaker duties. Lady Monica entered with music book in hand and a few choir members in tow. They quickly disappeared and returned dressed in their dark burgundy funeral robes and headed for the choir stand. Before long, I heard music. Julius Fitzpatrick and Anthony Davenport began escorting Jeanette's childhood pastor, a Reverend Joshua R. Caldwell from New Orleans, Louisiana, Jeanette's family, Leon's family, and Leon into the sanctuary. DeJuana Edwards walked behind him and chose to sit behind him in the second row. Shavonne came down from the choir stand to sit with DeJuana for support, because she was receiving the evil eye from most of the funeral goers. After the families were seated, the congregation, and others entered.

\* \* \* \* \*

Reverend Caldwell took the podium. He recited a prayer and a scripture. The choir sang two songs. Jeanette's supervisor from work and several of her co-workers gave two-minute speeches. A few more songs were sang, sympathy cards along with the obituary, were read by Frenchee Henderson. As Reverend Caldwell prepared to give the eulogy, Pastor Hunter and First Lady were escorted in and seated on the stage. When Reverend Caldwell opened his book to begin the eulogy, First Lady started shaking and began to cry uncontrollably. Not only did the church nurses have to comfort and console Jeanette's family, they also had to comfort and console First Lady. Reverend Caldwell's topic was "Living an Unselfish Life." I thought, *How ironic.* Jeanette Porterfield was one of the most selfish people I'd ever known.

\* \* \* \* \*

After the eulogy was completed, everyone prepared to take the final view of Jeanette's body. Surprisingly, DeJuana had brought a nice dark purple outfit for her to be buried in. Julius had done a magnificent job on Jeanette's hair, it was done like songstress Anita Baker used to wear hers back in the day. Julius had also reconstructed her face. She looked like she was asleep. I had to give it to Julius; he was a master in his vocation. All through the services, I had noticed that Leon just sat there with a blank expression on his face. He never showed any type of emotion or cried. As the service ended, I saw Leon enter Pastor Hunter's office. Julius and his crew loaded the casket into the hearse and proceeded to place flags on the cars that were going to the cemetery. About 10 minutes later, Pastor and Leon exited the church. Leon got into the first limousine with DeJuana, Shavonne, his brother Ray-Nathan and his sister Jeannie. Reverend Caldwell rode in the hearse with Julius. Pastor and First Lady rode with Jeanette's family in the second limousine and Anthony Davenport drove the flower car. I decided I was not going to the cemetery until Lady Monica asked me to drive her Cadillac. I asked her if we could stop for a drink on the way back to the church, and she agreed.

\* \* \* \* \*

The drive to Forest Lawn cemetery on Van Dyke took about 55 minutes. I was glad we were driving slowly because my nerves were totally shot; and me driving someone else's car was not helping my situation either. As they lowered Jeanette's casket into the ground, I grabbed Lady Monica and practically drug her back to the car. I peeled rubber leaving the cemetery. I had taken the flag off the car and put it in her back seat. She could return it to Julius later. I needed that drink and time was of the essence. We decided to go back to the same lounge that we went to on Anniversary Sunday. I walked in ordering. Within 10 minutes, I'd swallowed three shots of Hennessey.

"What is the problem? Who's on your last nerve? I've never seen you act like this," Lady Monica stated.

"I hate funerals; they give me the heebie-jeebies. I'm also freaked because Monticello called and left some more messages. These weren't that bad but I am still leery of him. I can't wait until Saturday is over so I can get the hell out of here and go to Vegas." I replied.

"I did notice how he was acting at the restaurant Friday, but I think you can get around that," she stated.

\* \* \* \* \*

When we arrived back at the church annex, for the after funeral dinner, Leon and DeJuana were standing in the corner. They were engaged in deep conversation. DeJuana looked as if she was about to cry at any given moment. Pastor saw what was happening and went over to intervene. I stopped Frenchee B. and reminded her that I would need her to take over the office beginning Monday. I handed Lady Monica her car keys, hugged her, and left. By the time I got home I had calmed down. It was now 4:00 so I packed some more clothes. I called Monticello, there was no answer; so I called the Sullivan triplets and we laughed and talked until midnight. I could hardly wait to see them on Saturday night.

\* \* \* \* \*

I woke up feeling a lot better than I'd felt yesterday. I packed my dance outfits, shoes, and other miscellaneous items in my mini-suitcase for the party and placed it in my trunk. When I arrived at the church, I saw a strange car in the parking lot. When I reached the front door, I checked it but it was locked. Once inside I called Alessandra and Denise to see how we would be traveling this evening. Since Alessandra lived on the other end of Lathrup Village, I would leave my car at her place and ride with her. She would pick up Denise on the way downtown. Around noon, after I got off the phone with them, I decided to take a walk around the church grounds then take the escalator and go to the ladies' room on the lower level. I needed to kill some time because 2:00 o'clock was taking forever to come. As I was returning to my office, I overheard noises coming from Pastors office. I knew no one was supposed to be inside of the building but me; so I quickly made it back to my office and retrieved my .9mm from my purse. I put the silencer on it and proceeded to tiptoe back to Pastor's office. The door was slightly ajar.

As I eased closer to the door, I heard a voice whisper "let me taste it, let me taste it." I heard a series of moans, slurps, slaps and other sexual sounds.

Then I heard Pastors voice say, "Do it, dammit; I said do it now. Suck this, big baby, now."

I figured Pastor must have come in through one of the alternate entrances of the building and had some female hemmed up in his office recruiting her by having sex with her. He'd do stupid shit like that every occasionally; I knew about it, but would ignore it.

\* \* \* \* \*

I started to walk away this time too, but nosiness got the best of me because of the door being ajar, so I eased up to the door and pushed it open a little further. They could be seen, but couldn't see me. I damn near passed out, damn near dropped my weapon, and damn near threw up at the sight of what I saw next. Pastor was totally nude and standing up with his right arm holding on to his six-foot wooden reference library shelf.

On his knees in front of Pastor, also completely nude and in the process of sucking Pastor's dick was the one and only Leon Porterfield. I could only stand there in shock and amazement as Leon performed a blowjob on Pastor, who moaned and twisted his body to match Leon's every movement. Leon was sucking him off better than any female could ever do. Leon sucked, licked, and massaged Pastor's dick for about 10 minutes. Then Pastor climaxed in Leon's mouth and squirted cum all over Leon's face. Pastor snatched Leon up, kissed him in the mouth (tongue included), turned him around, bent him over, entered him raw, and proceeded to perform anal sex. Leon begged for mercy with every thrust Pastor gave him. Every now and then Pastor would slap Leon on the ass. Leon would make a whimpering sound that seemed to turn Pastor on and Pastor would slap him harder. I prayed that the phone would not ring and interrupt them, and it didn't.

\* \* \* \* \*

Pastor fucked Leon for another 10 minutes, then climaxed again inside of Leon; pulled out and squirted his leftover cum all over Leon's back. Both of them groaned simultaneously in a sick and sadistic tone. I felt myself losing consciousness, so I leaned against the wall to keep from passing out. I watched as Leon wiped his mouth with the back of his hand and look up at Pastor who pointed him toward his office bathroom walking behind him. I took that opportunity to retreat to my office. I had a bottle of water in my office refrigerator, which I grabbed and proceeded to take small sips to keep myself from throwing up everything that I had eaten for breakfast. I was so fucked up I knew I wouldn't be able to drive. I just kept pacing back and forth in my office. I somehow managed to call Debonair, his girlfriend Donna answered and gave him the phone.

"Debonair, I need you to come get me right now! I'm at the church and bring Donna with you so one of you can drive my car back home." I yelled.

"What's wrong, Nat?" Debonair asked.

"I'm at the church come get me now, dammit I expect you here in 20 minutes; this ain't no goddamn request," I yelled and slammed the phone down. Debonair knew that I only used profanity when something was totally fucked up.

\* \* \* \* \*

I was surprised that he didn't get a ticket, but he made it from Lathrup Village to the Medical Center area in 14 minutes. I must have had a look on my face that put the fear of God in Debonair, because when he looked at me he didn't say shit. He took my keys and my weapon. He handed them to Donna; helped me inside of his Corvette and fastened my seatbelt.

All I could say as Debonair drove me back to Lathrup Village was, "I can't believe what I just saw; that was some fucked up shit." I repeated that statement about 500 times.

\* \* \* \* \*

Donna got back to Debonair's first. When we arrived, she was in the process of making a large pitcher of Remy, Coke and ice. When we entered the condominium, she handed me a large glass. I poured and began to drink myself into oblivion. She and Debonair both put their arms around me and said. "We're here for you, we know you will tell us what happened in due time." Debonair received a call from Leonardo. The party for tonight had been cancelled because Leonardo's little sister, Latreese, (who was now 16), had been critically injured in a drive-by shooting on Plymouth and Greenfield. Debonair said that Leonardo and his crew were on their way to Sinai Grace Hospital. I knew then that it was going to be some bloodshed in Detroit before the weekend was over. I made my way to the kitchen and managed to send a text to Alessandra and Denise. I knew they would be disappointed, but after what I'd witnessed today, my head would not have been in the game for dancing anyway. Denise returned my text and said that she had been throwing up all day and would not have been able to make it anyway.

\* \* \* \* \*

An hour later, I'd polished off the pitcher of Remy and started working on pitcher number two. Debonair took me upstairs to one of his guest bedrooms and made me lie down. "Can you talk about it yet?" He asked. I shook my head back and forth indicating that I wasn't ready yet. I kept trying to get up and come back downstairs. Each time I would make it to the bottom of the stairs, Debonair would stop me, take me back into the bedroom, and make me lie down again. I was afraid to go to sleep because every time I closed my eyes, I saw the image of Leon sucking Pastor's dick. Now I'd seen shit like this in the movies, but to actually walk up on it in person had really fucked my head up. I thought about everybody that I knew Pastor was having sex with. I was hoping that they were not letting him enter them in the raw. Bile formed in the pit of my stomach and I felt the urge to throw up. I ran into the bathroom, which was attached to the bedroom and puked my guts out, over and over and over again. After that, I fell into a deep sleep.

\* \* \* \* \*

When I finally woke up, darkness had set in and Donna was gone. Debonair heard me moving around and came upstairs with Shanita Alford, another one of his girlfriends, trailing behind him. Shanita had a bag from Fredrick's of Hollywood, which she handed to me. I excused myself, took a shower, put on the outfit that was in the bag, put on one of Debonair's robes, and came down to the living room. A plate consisting of fried shrimp, French fries and coleslaw had been placed on the cocktail table for me. I thanked Debonair and Shanita but I couldn't eat right then. I asked for a glass of champagne (which Shanita retrieved for me) and told the both of them what I had walked up on earlier.

"Damn, Nat, please tell me that you didn't fuck with that nasty beast," Shanita spat out like fire.

"I wanted to at one time, but when I saw all the motherfuckers he was dealing with I changed my mind," I replied.

"I'm glad you changed your mind because you definitely dodged a bullet on that one," she said. "He's probably gonna wind up having AIDS; he might have it already. Being fine don't mean shit if you're fucked up medically."

\* \* \* \* \*

Debonair came over and hugged me. Talking to them about what I saw made me feel a lot better. As I thought about it further, my sanity began to return to me because I started laughing about it. After about 30 minutes, I was making jokes about it and had Debonair and Shanita cracking up as if they were at a comedy show. I heated up the food in the microwave and ate. After watching the 11:00 news with the two of them, I decided I'd go home. I felt that I would be able to sleep without any problem now. I changed clothes and left.

\* \* \* \* \*

Soon after I'd arrived home, Monticello called me on his last break. I decided to talk for a minute so that he'd leave me alone once and for all. I told him I had been busy with the funeral and would be attending another one on Saturday. I also told him that it I was having family problems and it might be a minute before we would see each other again. I expressed my concern about his behavior at the restaurant last week. I let him know that I was one who interacted with many people and if he couldn't accept it that, there was going to be a major problem with us. This time I insisted that we take a breather. I told him I would call him in a couple of days. I hung up before he could respond. I knew that I was slipping because usually in a situation like that, I would have already dismissed the person and moved on to someone else. My house phone started ringing. When I answered, DeJuana was on the phone whining.

"Natalie, Leon told me to move back home until Tuesday," she whimpered into the phone.

I said to her, "Well, he probably wants to grieve, clean house and get rid of Jeanette's stuff by himself. She was his wife and he did love her at one time. Give him a little time, damn, don't crowd him right now. He just came from a funeral; it's not all about you. Let the man have some by himself time for a minute. Go to the spa, go shopping; go back to fucking work; let the man breathe, shit." I paused for a minute, then said, "You know what, DeJuana? Disregard everything I just said. That's your man, do what you do best, do you. I'm sorry, leave me out of your drama and stop calling my phone. Why are you calling me anyway? Where's your girl Shavonne?"

"Yeah, you're right, Natalie," she replied and hung up on me.

I really wanted to hurt that bitch by telling her what I'd witnessed but I knew if I did that; karma would kick my ass later on, so I just kept quiet. She'd find out soon enough. I went to bed thinking, *Let Saturday come and go so I can leave for Vegas. If I had my way, I'd be on the plane now.*

\* \* \* \* \*

*8:00 a.m.*

Leon Porterfield sneezed loudly and crawled out of bed when he saw the sunshine peeking through the bedroom window of his home on N. Martindale. He rejoiced for making it through the second night by doing the twist at the foot of his bed. He opened the door to the attached screened in porch located at the rear of his bedroom and proceeded to bring in several large boxes. He began to snatch all of the female apparel from the bedroom closet and fill the boxes. He then gathered all of the shoes, undergarments, beauty products, perfumes and everything else that had belonged to Jeanette.

After filling the last box, he grabbed his cell phone, dialed a number, and inquired, "How long before you get here?"

The voice on the other end responded by saying, "Sir, the driver just left our facility and should be in your neighborhood in the next hour and a half."

"That's great; replied Leon; that will give me time to shower and get dressed. Everything will be ready and the boxes will be on the front porch." Leon quickly made his bed, disrobed, jumped in the shower, and bathed himself. After exiting the shower, he was dressed and proceeded to devour a microwave breakfast he'd prepared. At that moment, his house phone rang.

"Leon Porterfield here," he answered.

"Meet me at Palmer Park at 11 o'clock. Take a cab; I will drop you back off after we're finished. I have a surprise for you; don't stand me up now. I will be expecting you."

"No problem, but why can't I take my car?" Leon inquired.

"Please just do as I asked, all of your questions will be answered when I see you," the voice stated. The caller then disconnected.

\* \* \* \* \*

Around 9:15, Leon heard the roar of a truck engine followed by a horn repeatedly blaring. He looked through the living room curtain to see the red and white Salvation Army truck in front of his house. He quickly opened the door as two men approached.

"Good morning, gentlemen," Leon said, "the quicker you take this shit the better." He pointed to the dozen or so boxes positioned neatly on the front porch. After the men had loaded the last box, one of the men handed Leon a form.

"Fill this out and turn it in when you do your taxes, you may be able to earn yourself a few dollars."

"Thanks," replied Leon. "Have a great day; I know I'm gonna have one." Leon then retreated into his house and prepared for his 11 o'clock appointment.

\* \* \* \* \*

*10:30 a.m.*

Leon dialed and requested a cab. Within 15 minutes, United Cab number 8223 was in front of his residence. Leon hopped in and instructed the driver where to drop him off. As Leon exited the taxi, he saw a familiar face sitting behind the wheel of a vehicle. He walked over and was told to get in. He entered the vehicle and the driver sped off. 15 minutes later the driver pulled up in the alley behind Leon's house.

"I need something out of your garage," the driver said to Leon. "Open it up I'll show you what it is." Leon followed instructions, lifted the door and they entered. "So, you just thought that you were gonna rent the house, go to closing on Monday, get your check, collect your insurance check, disappear, and start over huh?" The driver angrily spoke. "You have something on someone that I love and that could destroy the both of us and I don't like it." The driver then proceeded to attach the silencer to the .45 caliber pistol that was being concealed under the newspaper that was taken from the back seat of the vehicle. "The real estate agent contacted me. Shows just how dumb you are; you used the wrong name and number as a reference."

"What? What are you talking about?" Leon asked, with a look of surprise in his eyes. The gun was then handed off to an accomplice who had made their way out of the trunk of the vehicle. Leon was then grabbed by his shirt collar, spun around and received two bullets into his head. As Leon's body fell toward the floor, the accomplice emptied the remainder of the clip into Leon's stomach. The driver and accomplice walked out, returned to the vehicle, and drove away, leaving Leon's dead body in a bloody heap on the concrete floor next to his vehicle.

\* \* \* \* \*

As I was watching afternoon TV, doing the laundry and selecting more clothes for my Vegas trip. My cell phone rang.

"Hello, Natalie, TL Hunter here, how are you?"

"I'm good Pastor, how are you?" I asked.

"Could be better, but that's irrelevant at this point. I need you to get in touch with someone for me. I need to hear from them right away." He gave the name and cell number.

"Will do Pastor," I replied in an attempt to get him off my phone quickly. I really at that moment wanted to expose Pastors' unsavory behavior but I didn't. I dialed the cell number and when it was answered, I relayed the message.

"Thanks, Natalie," the recipient replied. I then disconnected the call and cleared my phone log.

* * * * *

I had stopped to prepare myself a snack when my house phone started ringing. When I answered, DeJuana Edwards was on the line again.

"What do you want now?" I spat into the receiver.

"I can't locate Leon, I've tried calling both his house phone and his cell, and I don't get an answer from either one. He didn't report for work, either. Natalie, I know we don't really get along, but you are smart and speak the truth, that's why I keep calling," she added.

"Well, call your girl Shavonne and make a trip over there then. I gotta go; I'm in the middle of packing." I hung up and decided to pause on the packing and clean my entire house. I knew that would take up a couple of hours and would help to tire me out. I put dinner on and wound up doing just that. I kind of felt bad about the way I'd talked to DeJuana. I just didn't like her, but I made a mental note to myself to try to be a little nicer to her. The operative word being, "Try."

* * * * *

Shavonne Swanson took her 4:30 break alone in the employee lounge at Huntington Bank of Novi, and called Pastor Hunter's cell phone from the lounge.

When he answered, she said, "I am getting off work soon, can we meet somewhere? I miss you."

"Not today, I have a last minute meeting with Julius Fitzpatrick. I'll call you when everything settles down. Be patient with me," he said and disconnected the call. Shavonne then called Julius Fitzpatrick in an attempt to verify what she'd been told by Pastor. Julius sat up and looked over at the telephone. When he saw her number, he let the voicemail answer.

"You have reached the Fitzpatrick Funeral Home, I will be in meetings throughout the day; I will be checking my messages every two hours; please leave your name and number and I will call you back." He then laid back and re-positioned himself beside the sleeping Lady Monica Davenport.

"Damn," Shavonne replied as she disconnected. "I know Terrell is up to something and I am gonna catch him, I swear," she promised herself.

\* \* \* \* \*

5:00 o'clock Wednesday evening, Pastor was being entertained by a female in room 411 of the Comfort Inn Suites at 696 East and Dequindre. He had instructed her to say that they had been in each other's company since last night. She said it would be okay because she had taken the day off work. She worked as a Pediatric Nurse at Children's Hospital.

"Do you have something for me?" Pastor asked. The female handed him an envelope containing $13,000 cash and a small jewelry box containing a platinum and diamond bracelet.

"Shavonne is getting old and played out, I want her spot," the female stated. Pastor smiled upon receiving the gifts.

He then said. "This definitely puts you in the running for the number one spot. I had someone else under consideration, but now it is mandatory that I have to take into account what just happened here. But don't get it twisted; I don't like demands or ultimatums." The female smiled as he hugged her and stroked her back. "Yes, Ms. Marion Stevenson, this definitely gives me something to think about."

They drank champagne, ate shrimp cocktails, made love, watched TV, played a sexual board game, and soaked in the queen-sized Jacuzzi. Pastor even got a private strip show. They both turned off their cell phones and agreed that they wouldn't leave each other's company until the next day. At that point, she proceeded to give Pastor an unprotected blowjob in hopes of gaining the position of top sidepiece.

\* \* \* \* \*

*7:00 p.m.*

Shavonne Swanson's Chrysler 300 pulled up on Davison and Ewald Circle. DeJuana Edwards came out got in.

"How much gas money do you want? I only have a 50 dollar bill," she said.

"Don't worry about that now, where are we headed?" Shavonne asked.

"We're going over to Leon's," DeJuana answered.

"Didn't he tell you he'd get back with you on Tuesday?" Shavonne said as she rolled her eyes.

"Yes, he did, but I didn't get an answer when I called; I am worried about him and I have a strange feeling," DeJuana replied.

Fifteen minutes later, Shavonne parked in the driveway of Leon's residence on N. Martindale. DeJuana still had the key to Leon's house, so she opened the front door and began to call his name. She then proceeded to search the house and the basement. As she entered the bedroom with the enclosed porch attached, she looked out of the side window and noticed that the garage door was opened slightly. She then yelled to Shavonne who was standing in the dining room. "I think he's in the garage."

\* \* \* \* \*

DeJuana locked the front door and followed by Shavonne, made her way outside to the garage. She could see the tires of Leon's car from under the door. She called out his name as she lifted the garage door. She took a few steps and felt a wet sticky substance under her feet. She looked down and saw that the concrete floor was covered in blood. She and Shavonne began to scream as they discovered Leon lying next to his vehicle. He was not breathing, covered in blood and part of the back of his head was missing. DeJuana fainted and Shavonne ran out into the alley. Some of Leon's neighbors heard the screams and came outside to find Shavonne still screaming and running around in circles. One of the neighbors called the police and EMS. Another neighbor got DeJuana out of the garage, wrapped her in a blanket, and sat her down on a milk crate in the alley until the police arrived.

\* \* \* \* \*

Homicide Detectives Monticello Strickland and Marcellus Robinson were the first to arrive on the scene along with the Medical Examiners Van and the Crime Scene Investigators. A couple of hours later, a yellow police tape surrounded Leon's garage and back alley areas. The body had been removed and all evidence collected. It was going to be a busy night at the crime lab.

"This is gonna be an easy case since we found all those shell casings," Monticello told Marcellus.

He answered, "yeah and those fibers on the victim's vehicle came from the perpetrator's clothes."

\* \* \* \* \*

By the time I'd finished cleaning, it was 10:30. I showered, put on lingerie; made myself a plate of food and plopped down in front of the TV. Channel 7 News preview came on and I watched as they announced

"Man found murdered in garage, Teenagers shot in drive by 2 fatal, 2 critical Story at 11."

I thought about Debonair's friend Leonardo. I was hoping that his little sister Latreese wasn't one of the fatalities. As the news began, I grew impatient waiting for them to get to the main stories. Then it aired.

"This is Michelle Gregory Reporting for Channel 7 Action News The body of Mr. Leon Porterfield was discovered in the garage of his residence on the west side of Detroit. He had been shot multiple times. He was found by two of his church members after not reporting to work and not answering his phones. It does not appear to be drug related or a case of robbery. Mr. Porterfield had just buried his wife on Tuesday. A DeJuana Edwards is being held for questioning, she is considered a person of interest. Mr. Porterfield was the manager at Westside Supermarket."

I almost fell off the couch when I saw Shavonne and DeJuana standing with the news reporter. They were explaining how they had went looking for Leon at his house and walked up on his body in the garage. I thought to myself, *Damn they just buried Jeanette the other day, now he's dead, damn.* While they were still on camera, the police came and took DeJuana with them. The next story was about the teenagers.

"Yesterday, four teenagers ranging in ages from 14 to 16 were shot in a drive by on Greenfield and Plymouth. There were two survivors: Latreese DeGraffenreid, age 16 and Benjamin Holyfield, age 15. Radiance Davis age 14 died at the scene, and Joanna Holt age 14 died in the emergency room at Sinai Grace Hospital. All parents and family members have been notified. There were two male shooters. They were last seen driving a Black 2008 Ford Explorer with no license plate and are still at large. They are considered to be armed and dangerous. The two survivors have now been upgraded to stable condition. "This is Michelle Gregory reporting for Channel 7 Action News."

I was glad Latreese was going to be okay. I was also glad that I was leaving town, because I knew that Leonardo and his crew were going to turn Detroit upside down and inside out; until he found out who'd shot his little sister. Debonair called at 11:30 and asked me if I'd seen the news and if that was Shavonne on TV. I told him yes and suggested that he and one of his girlfriends come to Las Vegas because it was getting ready to be off the hook in Detroit. He agreed and said he was booking a flight as we were speaking. His flight was leaving Friday afternoon. He was going to be traveling solo because he wanted to meet a few Las Vegas females and get his freak on. He told me if any of his girls called me to say I didn't know where he was. I laughed and told him to make sure that the first thing he packed was some condoms. He made a smart comment to me and we both laughed. As soon as I got into bed Lady Monica called.

"Natalie, I caught the tail end of the news, was that Shavonne and DeJuana on Channel 7 News?"

"It sure was, Leon Porterfield has been murdered and they are questioning DeJuana. I really don't think she's a suspect though; she was in love with Leon. I don't think she would have or could have done anything to hurt him," I replied.

"Does Julius know about this?" I inquired.

"I'm not sure," she answered. I heard her phone beep. She said, "Natalie, that's Julius now."

"Okay Lady M, call me tomorrow and give him his funeral flag back; it's in the back seat of your car," I said to her.

"He has it already; I gave it to him this morning," she replied.

"Good, talk to you soon," I said as I ended the call.

* * * * *

When I got to the church, Friday morning, Frenchee B. was already there. She had everything set up for me and had even brought breakfast. "I know I was not supposed to come in until Monday, but I was going stir crazy sitting in the house. I hope you like this." She held up a cute strapless black and gold sequined party dress that had a $4,000 price tag on it. I held it up to my body and knew right away that it would fit perfectly. She also handed me a certificate to Lord and Taylor.

"I did not know what size shoe to buy, so I got you a gift card, the shoes that match the dress will be located on the second floor. This outfit is for you to wear in Vegas, so go and get the shoes after you leave today."

"Thank you, Frenchee B.," I replied.

"I just want you looking good when you get to Vegas." She then changed the subject and said. "What the hell is going on with Journey's members? They are dying off, dropping like flies. And all of them are young. Terrell Jr., Jeanette, now Leon. You're leaving town for a while might just turn out to be a blessing in disguise. If you want me to, I'll pay for an extra week for you. I'm coming down for a real estate conference in a couple of weeks and we can hang out."

"Thank you again, Frenchee B., I would be honored."

"Good, call me in a couple of weeks and I will wire you the money Western Union, then we can really have some fun. But you must promise me that what happens in Vegas will stay in Vegas."

"I promise," I replied.

* * * * *

At that moment, the church phone began to ring and she answered it, along with assisting me with the bulletins. As I watched her work, I knew

I'd made the right decision asking her to hold the office down. I retrieved a tithe/offering envelope and put $400 and a note in it. This would cover my obligation for the extra week I would be gone. I handed it to her and asked her to turn it in for me on Sunday. Debonair called and asked if I would take him to Metro Airport. He needed to be there by 3:00. I told him I would. I would stop and get my shoes on the way back. At 1:00 Frenchee B. put the bulletins in the Ushers room, called Maurice Williams and the cleaning team and we left.

\* \* \* \* \*

Debonair was waiting in the courtyard when I arrived. After loading his luggage into the trunk we headed out. We arrived at Metro Airport at 2:50. I hugged him and told him not to break the bank in Vegas until I arrived. I picked up my shoes from Lord and Taylor and purchased a matching purse with the remaining money on the gift card. I stopped in Oak Park and got my nails and toes done. I called Trina my stylist and asked if she could meet me at 6:00 and do my hair. She arrived at 6:15; she relaxed, shampooed, trimmed and styled me. I gave her an extra fifty dollars for coming on such short notice. I finished the last of my packing, got my money, travelers' checks, credit cards and other documents together and got ready for bed. When the 11:00 news came on, they updated the story on Leon's murder. DeJuana had been released and they had no suspects, but Detectives Robinson and Strickland stated with the evidence that was found at the scene, they were close to making an arrest.

\* \* \* \* \*

The next update was about the teenagers. Latreese was doing better, but would need a great deal of therapy. Benjamin was now awake from the coma he'd been in. There was also going to be a fundraiser at Bert's Warehouse on Sunday night to raise money for burial expenses for the teenagers that didn't survive. I called FedEx and wrote two checks for $100.00 each. I left the envelope where the FedEx driver could get it and deliver it to Bert's. They announced that the services for Terrell Jr. would be held at Journey tomorrow at noon. They still didn't have any suspects in that murder. I packed another suitcase containing only sequined outfits, which included the dress and shoes given to me by Frenchee B. I discarded food that might spoil from my refrigerator and put in a new box of baking soda.

\* \* \* \* \*

After paying bills online; (that couldn't wait for my return) I called the Sullivan triplets and we talked until 1:00 a.m. Broxton sounded extremely stressed. I told him to hang in there. I would be there to relieve his stress soon. I called my father and talked with him a couple of hours, and reminisced about my grandfather. (Who had also been a pimp in his day). I asked my father if he wanted any type of souvenir from Vegas. He said just send money if I won. I told him that was guaranteed either way. I decided that I would bring him some tie pins and cuff links and a chain; seeing as he still dressed up every time he left the house.

\* \* \* \* \*

I awoke at 8:00, took out the garbage, showered, double-checked my condo, secured my money and documents in my purse, dressed myself in a black DaVinci outfit, loaded my luggage into the car and arrived at Journey around 10:30. I wondered why there was no security in place; seeing as how there was going to be thousands of people in attendance. 10:55 a.m. Julius K. Fitzpatrick and his team arrived with the body of Terrell Jr. He looked tired but was still managing to do his funeral directing duties. Frenchee B. was running around in an attempt to help Julius by instructing the cleaning team on how to arrange the flowers that were being delivered. She was beginning to aggravate Maurice Williams by re-arranging the flowers after his team members had put them in place on the altar. I could see by the look on Maurice's face that he was about to physically attack Frenchee so I invited her to join me in my office.

When Julius delivered the funeral programs for Terrell Jr., Frenchee B. could hardly contain herself; she started giggling like a schoolgirl. I asked Julius to give her a hug before she started hyperventilating and he obliged me; which made her calm down. I was now beginning to see a different side of Frenchee B. As Julius left my office, I looked at the funeral program to see who would be doing the eulogy for Terrell Jr. Reverend Maxwell Solomon was listed.

"Damn, this is gonna be a long service," I said aloud.

"Why do you say that?" Frenchee B. inquired.

"Old man Solomon is doing the eulogy, you know he loves to talk and he goes on forever. I hope I won't have to slip out in the middle of the service, you know I've got a plane to catch today." We began to hear music from the organ.

"Well here we go again. Watch me work," she said.

She made a phone call; then sent a note to Lady Monica who was on the organ. Fifteen minutes later, Minister Marvin Cunningham, the Assistant Pastor at Journey Toward Christ and Terrell Jr.'s favorite pastor, walked into the office dressed in black, carrying his funeral book, and his black and gold funeral robe. Minister Cunningham was a hip-hop Pastor. The children and younger members of Journey Toward Christ loved him. He was around 22 years old. He spoke to the both of us; hugged Frenchee B. and the three of us took the escalator down to the main the floor. I took a seat in the back of sanctuary and Denise came in and sat next to me.

"I couldn't find my man Wednesday, but I met with him early this morning and he gave me food and moving money. My whole body is aching, and it's not from sex. I think I'm coming down with something. I am moving tonight; thanks for letting me know about the townhouse," she said.

"No problem," I replied.

As I looked toward the front of the church, I could see Pastor, First Lady Charisse, Dominique and Little Tee sitting in the front row. Frenchee B. made her way to the pulpit with Minister Cunningham following behind her. Frenchee B. whispered something to Reverend Solomon who stood up and followed her as she made her way to the back of the sanctuary. He then left the building. At that point, Minister Cunningham took a seat on the pulpit.

\* \* \* \* \*

The usual funeral activities took place. Cards and obituary were read; the choir sang several songs, friends of Terrell Jr. made speeches; including one of his former supervisors. I was surprised to see that because I never knew that Terrell Jr. had a job. He'd always lived off of his parents as long as I'd known him. First Lady and Dominique took the death of Terrell Jr. extremely hard. They screamed, fainted and rolled around on the sanctuary floor. The church nurses, who were being directed by senior nurses, Estelle Farr, Mildred Calloway, and Charlotte Hudson, consoled and comforted Dominique and First Lady and First Lady's sister Chrystale and members of the congregation. Little Tee (now age 4) had to be made to sit down on several occasions. He kept breaking away from his mother and attempting to crawl under the casket. For some strange reason, Pastor didn't seem to be aware of what was happening around him. He had an expression on his face that showed he was somewhere else and had something major on his mind. I just kept staring at him. If karma were to rear its head, Pastor would have burst into flames at any given moment. But as luck would have it, karma was on coffee break.

* * * * *

Minister Cunningham's eulogy was "*If you're Gonna Live Life in the Fast Lane; You'd Better Let God Do the Driving*" and it lasted about 30 minutes. As he ended, he referred to "what you put out comes back in." As soon as he spoke the words "comes back in," four or five young thugs all dressed in black hooded silk jogging suits wearing light brown timberlands with scarves covering their mouths, rushed the sanctuary. They were armed with tech nines and machine guns. They headed straight to the casket and began firing. Almost 10,000 people hit the floor in unison in an attempt to take cover.

The thugs didn't care about the family, the police, or anybody else; they shot up the casket, the flowers, and the pulpit. They engaged in gunfire for about three to five minutes before they turned around and exited the church via center aisle. By the time the smoke had cleared, the casket was in pieces, Terrell's body was sprawled out on the steps of the altar, and the suit he had on was in shreds. The church was in total chaos. People were pushing and shoving, screaming, running and trampling one another. When I arose from the floor, I looked around and saw Frenchee B. scrambling to reach Julius Fitzpatrick who had been hiding behind the baby grand piano. Lady Monica's organ acted as a shield for her and husband Anthony Davenport. Minister Cunningham had escaped gunfire by diving into the baptismal pool which was filled with water. Pastor and First Lady were inside of the office. I saw that all of them were okay, so I grabbed my purse and made my way out of the church. There still was no security in sight. I was determined to leave town right away. I would sit at the airport for hours if I had to. I heard sirens in the distance and decided that if the police were going to interview me, it would be a month from now. Surprisingly, I made my way through the crowd with no problems. I located my car, got in, and took off. I entered I75 going north and when I reached I94 west, I took the exit and headed straight toward Romulus.

* * * * *

I arrived at Metro Airport it was 2:15. I checked in, made it through security and decided that I would go have a couple of drinks and calm my nerves at the lounge located near where I would eventually board the plane. I was happy that I only had two hours to wait. As I drank Hennessey and ice at the bar, the overhead TV began broadcasting a breaking news story.

"Today unknown suspects engaged in gunfire at the funeral of Terrell Hunter Jr. which was being held at Journey Toward Christ Missionary

Baptist Church on the eastside of Detroit. Witnesses state that five armed men entered the sanctuary and opened fire; destroying the casket, pulpit and flowers. No one was injured from the gunfire, but several funeral goers sustained minor cuts and bruises as a result of the stampede that took place. The shooting appears to be a message to the family of the deceased. It was rumored that the deceased owed huge amounts of money to several neighborhood drug dealers. The gunmen are still at large; and are considered to be armed and dangerous. This is Michelle Gregory reporting for Channel 7 Action News."

The newscaster interviewed Julius who stated he was going to provide another coffin free of charge to the family. He also told the newscaster that he couldn't understand why there was no security at the church. Julius also said that he had no police escort to the cemetery. I knew then that somebody was about to be out of a job before long. As I continued to watch the newscast, I felt a presence next to me. I looked over and into the face of one of the most gorgeous white men on the face of the earth. He was 6'2, 29 years old, medium build, tanned and had the facial features of the movie star Tom Cruise. He spoke and introduced himself as Michael Cavelleto. He was dressed in a steel gray Calvin Klein suit with matching alligator shoes. He was Italian, but it was clear that he had some black blood inside of him somewhere. You could tell it by his mannerism and his speech. He insisted that I let him buy me a drink. I agreed and we began to talk. He was from Las Vegas' Caesar's Palace Casino/Resort and held a position as Assistant CEO. He was returning home from visiting his brother who lived in New York. He had stopped in Michigan to see his other brothers produce company in the Eastern Market. As we talked and watched the newscast; I told him I was at the funeral earlier.

"Detroit is a dangerous place," he stated. "If you ever consider moving to Las Vegas, I think I could be of service to you." He then handed me his card and said, "I have a connection to some investors, if you invest correctly, it could turn out to be lucrative." I smiled took his card and placed it in my purse. He then said, "Oh, by the way if you want to have some fun, give me a call. I am single, no kids, deep pockets and I am freakish. No disrespect, but I know I could make you smile in more ways than one." He smiled, winked at me, and walked away.

\* \* \* \* \*

I finally heard the announcement I'd been waiting for.

"We are now boarding first class passengers for flight 410 to Las Vegas, please approach door number 4C to prepare for boarding."

"Thank you Jesus, this is it." I said. I grabbed my carryon bag and I began walking slowly because I was now tipsy. I decided that I would sleep on the plane, because the flight would take at least 7 hours. That idea was quickly dismissed when I made it to my seat in first class. Seated directly next to me was the one and only Michael Cavelleto. At that point, we began to talk again and wound up drinking a bottle of Dom Perignon that he purchased. After talking for a few more hours, Michael and I were feeling each other fiercely, the champagne probably was a contributing factor. So we wound up joining the mile high club. I must say his sexual skills and his package were on point; and I honestly had to give him a score of 9.5. My whole body was tingling with pleasure. I knew I'd done my duties because Michael was smiling like an actor standing in front of the paparazzi. After our entry into the mile high club, we cleaned up and changed clothes in the bathroom. We returned to our seats and both slept for the remainder of the flight.

# Chapter 6

*Las Vegas, Nevada*

I was awakened by the pilot announcing: "Ladies and Gentlemen Welcome to Las Vegas, the temperature is now 75 degrees, with a slight breeze entering from the west. We will be landing momentarily. We hope you enjoyed your flight. Thank you for flying Northwest Airlines."

As we were leaving the plane, I kissed Michael and told him that I would text him in a couple of weeks. I lagged behind because I did not want him to see me when I met the triplets. As I retrieved my luggage from baggage claim, my cell phone began to ring.

"Natalie, welcome to Las Vegas, we hope you had a good flight, we are just outside of the glass door, we see you."

I walked through the glass door and standing there were the Sullivan triplets Brandon, Braxton and Broxton. The only way that you could tell them apart was by the small moles on their faces. Brandon's mole was above his left eye, Braxton's was on the left side of his face under his eye; and Broxton's was on the right side of his face under his eye. All of them were dressed in white Hugo Boss shirts and pants. They then proceeded to load my luggage into a white stretch Hummer limousine. We hugged and kissed and I was assisted into the vehicle by the limo driver. As the driver pulled off each of them handed me a small box from Tiffany's. Inside of each box was a 3 carat diamond ring with matching earrings, necklace and ankle bracelet. I was so glad I'd gotten my nails done as I slipped each ring on different fingers. To my surprise, they all fit perfectly.

We pulled up to the VIP parking area of The Bellagio Casino/Resort. I was escorted to the top floor and entered a villa that was half the size of my whole condo. The villa was exquisite. It had a Jacuzzi, a super king-sized bed which looked like it could accommodate at least 10 people, a full sized bar; a state of the art stereo system, a TV that covered an entire wall, and many other amenities too numerous to list. The bed had been moved upon a platform near the window and the view of all the Vegas lights was breathtaking. I realized then that these three brothers were clocking major dollars. The triplets drank champagne while I took a quick shower and changed clothes. I also found two grand cash from Michael in my makeup bag.

\* \* \* \* \*

After I got dressed, we then headed to the casino and were escorted to the high limit gaming area. Each of the triplets gave me five grand to gamble with as they made their way to the high stakes crap table. I decided that I would play roulette next to where they were. After losing $2,000 I stopped and walked over to the crap table and starting betting with the triplets. A hostess came by and asked if I wanted a drink. I thanked her and ordered an apple martini. I did not want to drink heavily until after I'd gotten some food in me. After a few hours the triplets walked away from the crap table with $15,000 and some change each. I'd won about $7,000 by betting with the triplets. I was highly impressed with their gambling skills.

\* \* \* \* \*

Around 4:00 a.m., Brandon stated that he was tired of gambling and wanted to go drinking. We found a revolving bar and were seated in a circular booth overlooking the gambling floor. We all dined on Lobster, baked potato and salad and ordered a magnum of Moet. I felt like a celebrity with my own entourage. I had put my hair in an up do with a long cascade curl hanging. I had on a black, sequined cat suit that hugged my curvaceous body, accompanied by my black Manolo Blahnik peep toed heels. I was iced out wearing a diamond necklace from Braxton, a diamond ankle bracelet from Broxton, and diamond earrings from Brandon plus several diamond rings. The Sullivan brothers were in all black Hugo Boss trimmed in silver. And all of them were iced out with matching Rolex watches and diamond chains that would make Pastors chain look like something from the "Mr. T." starter kit.

\* \* \* \* \*

All eyes were on me especially from the females who walked by hating and doing double-takes. I was sitting in between Brandon's legs; Braxton was on my left and Broxton was on my right. Seeing me sitting there hugged up with three gorgeous black men, you could smell the hatred in the air. Several times that night females approached and ask if they could join us; but they were turned away by at least one of the triplets. Some of them even went as far as returning with their girls coming over trying to get in, but they wound up walking away disappointed too. One female had the nerve to sit down anyway. Braxton politely took her hand, escorted her away from the table; handed her a one-dollar bill and told her that she had been given her exactly what she was worth. She walked away in tears. I didn't have to say a word, all I had to do was sit there, smile, drink and look fly. Around 6:30 a.m., the triplets and I went back to the villa to continue our drinking escapades. We all got into the super king sized bed; drank champagne and smoked blunts until we all passed out.

\* \* \* \* \*

Sunday afternoon we all arose and showered together, as room service brought up brunch which consisted of fresh fruit, scrambled eggs, hash browns, Canadian bacon, toast, orange juice, more champagne and other items. Brandon demanded that my first week in Vegas be all about what he wanted to do. We all agreed as we watched the local and national news on TV preparing to leave for the day. I wrote out a form for Western Union and wired $5,000 back to my Chase bank account, and $3,000 to my father; so that he could give both of my uncles' a grand and have one for himself. I turned it in as we began our day of spa treatments. Brandon had everything planned for his week. Sunday was dedicated to spa treatments. The four of us experienced mud baths, massages, aroma therapy sessions, manicures, pedicures and all other treatments associated with the care and purification of the body. I even got a Brazilian bikini wax. I had never had one before and it hurt somewhat, but it would be worth it in the long run. After being pampered for the majority of the day, we all returned to the villa, changed clothes, gambled, and took pictures as we traveled from casino to casino.

\* \* \* \* \*

Monday afternoon began with a shopping trip to Cartier's, Tiffany's and Gucci. Brandon picked out three Badgley Mischka outfits, two furs, one being a full-length grey and white chinchilla, similar to Shavonne's, and one being a waist length, black jacket. I also received several Dolce and Gabbana outfits, shoes from Manolo Blahnik, purses from Judith Leiber and Michael Kors and six diamond sets consisting of necklace, bracelet, ring, earrings and ankle bracelet. I knew then that I would have to purchase some luggage or a trunk to transport my belongings once the shopping spree with the triplets was completed. That evening we all went for a helicopter ride, and completed the night with a midnight walk on the strip and several hours of gambling and fine dining. We partied until sunrise then returned to the villa.

\* \* \* \* \*

I had ideas of my own for Tuesday, and decided that Brandon would be the main star in my sexual escapade. Before the triplets got up, I set up my video cam, showered and dressed myself in a provocative outfit so that I could do a strip show for the three of them. I had recorded a CD to use for my dance but all of my plans quickly came to an end; because when I exited the bathroom the triplets were up and dressed like male dancers. Brandon was dressed like Denzel Washington from "Training Day" Braxton was dressed like Samuel L. Jackson from "Shaft" and Broxton was dressed like Wesley Snipes from "Blade." The sight of those men in those long black coats made my whole body shiver. I was told to grab a drink and a blunt, have a seat and enjoy the show. And that is just what I did. The three of them gyrated and teased me like the male dancers from "Venus Entertainment." If you didn't know better, you would have thought that this was their profession. I boosted their egos by making it rain several times (throwing hundred dollar bills at them). I thought I would pass out from excitement and anticipation. I knew from watching the packages on the triplets that I was not going to be disappointed come sex time.

Since I was already dressed, I joined the triplets by doing my strip show and took the spotlight as the center of attention; especially when I played my sexy CD and entertained them as "The Platinum Princess" seeing as how I didn't get to dance in Detroit. After that, we stayed inside and I finally fulfilled my long awaited fantasy by having sex with all of the triplets. I had Brandon on top, Braxton on the bottom and Broxton giving my body a tongue twirling that was second to none. Every so often, we switched positions so that each of the gentlemen got a chance to be on top for a while. The triplets were all packing 10 inches, each possessed superb skills and they each gave me a helluva run for my money; especially Broxton, but I represented with a vengeance; and worked my show with precision and dignity. My divas would have been proud. Yet, many others would have hated. Wednesday, Thursday and Friday, consisted of more shopping at shops like Louis Vuitton, Gucci and Tiffany again, more sexual escapades, a limousine tour of some of Las Vegas's historical sites, more spa treatments, and photographs, more furs, gambling, dancing, and drinking.

\* \* \* \* \*

Saturday, Brandon informed all of us that this would be show night. He asked me if I had any sequined outfits. I showed him my suitcase full of glittery clothing but he insisted that he dress me for the first show so we went to the designer store again. Brandon bought me a sequin dress similar to the one Frenchee B. had given me but it was much sluttier. When I put it on, I was glad I had three men with me. This dress was sleazy-backless, an opening in the front which exposed much of my cleavage; super short, tight fitting; with practically everything else showing. There wasn't much that could be left to the imagination with this one. That night we saw three old school shows, Chaka Khan, along with the Contours, Charlie Wilson, and Mary J. Blige. Steve Harvey, and Cedric the Entertainer. We all changed clothes several times that night.

During one of the shows, Brandon and I slipped off and had a private sex session which left me mesmerized. After that, we rejoined Braxton and Broxton, ate, drank, danced, and partied the night away. Again, women tried to join our entourage; but were turned away. Angry and disappointed they had to seek pleasure in other venues. Again, as daybreak set in, we retired to the villa for some more sexual enjoyment. Next week would be Broxton's week. He said it was going to be all about Circus Circus and Treasure Island. I could tell he wanted to let his hair down, get wild and just be a big kid in charge.

\* \* \* \* \*

Sunday morning, as the triplets slept, I stepped out into the hallway and made several calls to Detroit. I hadn't spoken to anyone since the shooting at the funeral. I didn't know what type of reception I'd get, but I decided to call anyway. I called Alessandra first. She told me that she heard Detroit was off the chain. She had seen it on the news. She said she couldn't find Debonair. She also asked me to bring her a souvenir back. I called Shavonne next. She said she was spending time once again with Pastor; but she was feeling sickly. I had an idea why. I called Lady Monica but she was not at home, I figured that she had left for church. I spoke briefly to Frenchee B. who told me that First Lady was "MIA." She figured that she'd gone to Ohio to see her sister. I called my father but got no answer. I figured he was out somewhere having breakfast. I heard the triplets moving around in the villa so I dismissed calling anyone else and returned inside to be with them. Since it was Sunday, we stayed in the villa drinking, smoking, watching sports and the triplets sexing me up like porn stars.

\* \* \* \* \*

The new week came quickly and Broxton stepped in. We moved out of the villa of the Bellagio, to a high rollers villa at Paris Casino/Resort. That night we went shopping again, this time all the clothing purchased for me was casual. I was treated to several pairs of open toed shoes and sandals by Jimmy Choo, purses from Prada, Louis Vuitton, Michael Kors and Coach. I received another full length mink and a short mink vest—this one had no sleeves—so I guess it could be called a vest, several casual outfits, some skirt sets, pantsuits and several toe rings and ankle bracelets from Van Cleef and Arpels jewelers. Luckily I'd put my phone on vibrate, because just as we were leaving Van Cleef and Arpels, I got a text from Debonair. He was doing his thing and having fun with the ladies of Vegas and had won over $75,000 since he'd been there. He said he'd wired ten thousand of it to my Credit Union account, and sent some to his father and both uncles. I sent a text back and thanked him for the money, I told him we had moved to the Paris Casino/Hotel and that I was having the time of my life. I reminded him to send some of the money back home for a rainy day.

\* \* \* \* \*

The triplets and I acted like a bunch of little children, riding the circus rides, playing the midway games, watching the shows, eating ice cream, popcorn, cotton candy, hotdogs, taffy and other goodies I hadn't had since I was a kid. We also went to Treasure Island Casino Resort and played pirates. The triplets even participated in a magic show and fooled the magician who didn't know that there were three of them. When they revealed their identities, the audience went wild. I had everybody's attention again as I carried around several life sized stuffed animals won for me by the triplets.

\* \* \* \* \*

By the time daybreak approached we were all wiped out just like kids, so we did exactly as kids would do. We went back to the villa, showered and went to bed with a bottle. A bottle of champagne each that is. Broxton woke up before the others so he and I got a chance to have a one on one sex session in the bathroom Jacuzzi tub bubbles included. I could tell by his sexual movements that he was still harboring a lot of pinned up issues. But by the time we were finished, he seemed to be a lot more relaxed. He made me promise not to tell because the triplets usually shared everything on an equal basis. Little did he know; I had already done the same thing with Brandon a few days ago.

# Chapter 7

*Cincinnati, Ohio*

Cincinnati, Ohio was the place of rejuvenation for First Lady Hunter since the funeral. She'd sent Little Tee to his other grandmother and boarded a flight on Southwest Airlines on a mission of grieving and cleansing herself spiritually so that she could begin the healing process. Since Pastor was still living downtown, First Lady decided to take a trip to Ohio. For the first few days she stayed with her sister Chrystale, but after Chrystale's boyfriend came back for a pit stop; First Lady moved into a downtown hotel. Every night since moving, she had been entertaining a gentleman by the name of L.H. They had dinner every night, went to the movies or a Jazz Club and enjoyed each other as dessert in the wee hours of the morning. L.H. and First Lady had maintained a long distance relationship ever since she first found out about Pastors' cheating which was in the first year of their marriage. L.H. was her refuge when things with Pastor became unbearable.

\* \* \* \* \*

They grew up together in Ohio and never lost contact, even when First Lady married and moved out of state. "Again let me tell you how sorry I am about Terrell's death. You have no idea how this is tearing me apart. It feels like someone has taken a razor and sliced me into confetti. I really wish I could have been there to support you; but I didn't want to cause any problems," L.H. said to First Lady as they entered the hotel lobby. "Have you been getting my packages?" He asked. "I know it doesn't make up for what I should have done. I really should have manned up, but you know back then I didn't have my act in order. But now I am the second partner in Ohio's most prestigious law firm," he said continuing the conversation.

"I understand, but things are going to change soon. Everything will soon be the way it is supposed to be. Karma is lurking around the corner. I see the universe making everything right; we just have to be patient a little while longer," stated First Lady.

"I can't wait, but I must say that I know it will be worth it." L.H. said as he took the keycard, opened the hotel door and ushered First Lady inside. They shared a passionate kiss, stripped each other's clothes off drank champagne, ate strawberries and chocolate, relaxed in the Jacuzzi and made love until sunlight from the next day filled the room.

# Chapter 8

*Detroit, Michigan*

The streets of Detroit were running red with blood. It started the following week after his sister got shot. Leonardo DeGraffenreid and his crew were gunning down everything in sight. Leonardo's take of the situation was "*Keep knocking on the devil's door and sooner or later someone will answer.*" Homicide Detectives Monticello Strickland and Marcellus Robinson were working double time in an attempt to solve the multiple shootings that were taking place in Detroit. From the eastside to the westside, bodies were falling like dominoes. Leonardo DeGraffenreid had lost his mind. There were shootings at schools, gas stations, bus stops, Coney Island restaurants, recreation centers, rap concerts, anywhere young people were gathered was not off limits to Leonardo and his crew. I got a text message from Donna that Detroit was practically a war zone. She stated that she had not seen Debonair in a couple of weeks, but watched Detectives Robinson and Strickland on Channel 7 News practically every night. Donna lived in Westland, but often would visit Detroit. I told her to be careful if she decided to go downtown and that I had to get going. I never made reference to Debonair or his whereabouts; but I knew he was staying on the strip between New York, New York and the Venetian.

\* \* \* \* \*

DeJuana Edwards was finishing up her shift at the Drug, and Alcohol Center in the Cass Corridor. As she proceeded to lock her desk and gather her belongs, she felt a sharp pain in her body which caused her to shake violently, throw up and scream out. Before her supervisor could reach her, she had fallen to the floor and was now unconscious. Her supervisor called 911 and requested a unit. Five minutes later, an EMS unit arrived on Peterboro Street.

"What happened here?" the EMS Tech asked.

The supervisor answered, "I heard a scream and when I came to investigate, I found her passed out on the floor." Her supervisor called her family and informed them of what had taken place and asked that they meet DeJuana at the hospital. After stabilizing DeJuana, the EMS Techs questioned her then transported her to Detroit Medical Center for further treatment.

* * * * *

In room 2550 at the Aces High Casino/Hotel in Detroit, Shavonne was once again enjoying her time with Pastor. She had given him 17-grand and another Rolex watch. "It's time for you to go," he said looking at the new watch. I want you to stop and get yourself some vitamins and orange juice, go home and go straight to bed. I will call you later, I can't guarantee it, but I will try to stop by," Pastor told Shavonne as he handed her coat and purse to her. She looked at him, ran out the door toward the elevator and burst into tears. Before she could get down the hall to the elevator, Pastor was on the phone to the housekeeping staff.

"I need you to send someone to clean room 2550. I am going down to the restaurant and will be back in 45 minutes." After receiving a confirmation that it would be done, he dialed a number and a female answered.

"Hey, lovely, I need to see you in one hour," he said.

"I'll be right there," she answered. Fifty-five minutes later, a female entered room 2550 of the Aces High Casino/Hotel. Cell phones were turned off and the female handed Pastor an envelope containing nine grand in cash, and a box containing a brand new black preaching robe trimmed in dark purple with gold piping with a $2,000 price tag attached.

"Not bad, but we are going to try to be in the two-digit region next time, like 10 or 11, isn't that right, dear heart?" He asked lovingly.

"I promise I will try to do better. I'm off my square right now, I'm kind of tired. I have been feeling extremely ill lately, but I did make a doctor's appointment. No excuses, I will make you proud," she said.

"Well baby, I am looking to upgrade, I want you to be my number one side piece, but you are going to have to show me that I am not making a mistake. I'm counting on you, no excuses okay?" Pastor stated. He then hugged her tightly; tongue kissed her, slapped her on her behind and said, "Now get in that bed and give me what I have been waiting on."

"You got it, daddy," she replied.

That night they drank champagne, smoked blunts, and enjoyed each other sexually. Pastor counted his money and smiled at his new up and coming number one sidepiece. He then requested that she stay with him until the next day. For a brief moment, Pastor though about Marion Stevenson and was appalled by her demanding character; so he officially gave his visiting lady the promotion to number one sidepiece. She accepted and celebrated her new promotion by giving Pastor a special lap dance which led to a long awaited unprotected blow job and more sexual episodes.

# Chapter 9

*Atlanta, Georgia*

In Atlanta GA, Dominique Hunter was back in the swing of things regarding her school assignments. She was happy to have made it back to Georgia without incident. Little Tee was now staying with his other grandmother. Dominique was putting the finishing touches on her Media Communications presentation, and would be showing it midweek. For a split second her mind drifted back to the funeral. She hated that her mother and father were estranged and that he'd temporarily moved out, but she also knew her mother was going to Ohio for a while and wouldn't be alone; so returning to school and the house being empty gave her an excuse to get back to Atlanta. In addition, while she was in Detroit she had noticed Detective Marcellus Robinson eyeing her at the cemetery the day of Terrell's burial, but since he never said anything to her, she chalked it up as a harmless momentary flirtation on his part.

# Chapter 10

*Detroit, Michigan*
*1:15 a.m.*

Shavonne Swanson turned over in her bed and glanced at her clock radio which was sitting on her nightstand. "He said he was going to call me later, now it's after midnight and I still haven't heard from him," she said aloud. She then reached over and dialed his cell number but it went straight to voicemail. "That's it; I am going down to the hotel and confront him. I have given him too much money; he should not be treating me this way."

As she attempted to get out of bed, she became very lightheaded. She doubled up from the pain she felt inside of her. The room began to spin and her vision became blurry, as her body released an odor that was foreign to her. She fell backward, her king-sized bed breaking her fall. "I am going to the doctor in the morning," she said, as she regrouped and dialed her supervisor's number.

When the phone went to voicemail, Shavonne left a message indicating that she would be taking a sick day. Shavonne then called her physician's emergency line and after explaining her symptoms from the last few months, she was instructed to meet him at the hospital within seventy two hours. Nervous and unable to fall asleep, Shavonne took several sleeping pills with a glass full of champagne. After about 30 minutes, she was sleeping like a newborn.

\* \* \* \* \*

Friday evening Claude Henderson entered his mansion on Lodge Drive and yelled out for his wife Frenchee B. Frenchee could tell by the tone of his voice that another argument was on the horizon.

"What do you want now Claude?" Frenchee asked, as she stood in the doorway of their master bedroom entrance.

"I want to know why you have been in such a good mood lately. Are you fucking around on me? Are you getting dick somewhere else, because you are definitely keeping me at bay. You haven't let me touch you in months. I heard a rumor that you are running around town with one of our church members; is that true? After everything I've done for you and everything I had to put up with from you; I know that you shouldn't even be thinking about cheating on me," he replied. "If I find out that you have been unfaithful, I swear that I will take everything you have and leave you homeless, you low down tramp."

"Oh really, well let me tell you something you spineless bastard, you weren't much of nothing when I met you and I just stayed with you because of the social status we obtained, but now I really don't give a damn anymore." At that point, he slapped Frenchee and she landed on the bed.

"I have everything I need now and don't you forget that we have a pre-nuptial agreement in place. If you want to split everything and go that is fine with me. I really am tired of arguing with you all the time and I would be happier by myself. Every few months for years now, we've had this same argument. I will not answer your question even though you keep asking it. If you want to leave, then do so." Frenchee began to snatch Claude's clothing from the closets and proceeded to load them into several large suitcases.

"I don't know what you think you are doing, this is my house and I refuse to leave," he said.

"Well, fine, then I'll go," Frenchee countered. "I've prayed and agonized over this, but I am stronger now and know I will be all right," she said with confidence. She dumped the clothes from the suitcases and replaced them with hers. "My attorney will contact you."

She proceeded to gather her remaining belongings, and along with the suitcases, she loaded them into her vehicle. As she drove away, she dialed several numbers and reached a voicemail. She left a message that requested she be contacted immediately. Thirty minutes later, as she was entering Royal Flush Casino/Hotel VIP parking her cell phone rang.

When she answered, she told the caller, "I have left, Claude. He is threatening to take everything, despite the pre-nup; and if this happens, you will also be affected. Do what you have to do to secure your future." As she hung up, she was approached by the hotel valet.

"Are you checking in ma'am, and how long will you be staying?"

Frenchee answered, "I am not sure, but let's start with five days for now."

After receiving her keycard, Frenchee B. entered room 2477 and began making calls canceling the house utilities, cable services, security systems, water and property maintenance. She then called the bank and transferred all of the monies into a new individual account. She also called her attorney and somehow got the ball rolling on removing Claude's name from their real estate empire. After completing her calls, she showered, unpacked a few suitcases, laid across the queen sized bed and exhaled. She kept making a gesture with her index finger and her thumb by holding them an inch apart. She giggled lightly and said aloud; "well I won't have to worry much longer; soon I will be in possession of a love I can feel."

\* \* \* \* \*

After Frenchee left the house, Claude poured himself a shot of bourbon. He stood in the living room, looking around the house, noticing all Frenchee's belongs gone. "This is crazy, he said aloud. She'll be back, she can't give up all of this luxury; I just know it." Before he knew it, he'd finished the whole bottle. "I am drunk, I better lie down." He said. Grabbing a blanket, he positioned himself on the couch and turned to ESPN on the TV. Within 10 minutes, he was sound asleep.

Around 2:00 a.m. Claude's private line began to ring. "I need you to go and check on the church, someone is trying to break in. I have already contacted the police and they are going to meet you there," stated the female voice on the other line.

Still groggy from the liquor, thinking it was First Lady calling, Claude responded. "I am on my way, I will be there in 20 minutes," He grabbed his black jogging suit top, his wallet, and his keys and left the house. Fifteen minutes later, he pulled into the driveway of Journey Toward Christ. Not thinking rationally, he decided to exit his vehicle and look around while waiting on the police to arrive. A shadow appeared out of the darkness and several silenced shots rang out. Claude never got a chance to see, hear or say anything. He was dead before his body hit the ground.

# Chapter 11

*Las Vegas, Nevada*

Back in Vegas, Broxton's week was winding down. I had really enjoyed this week. Acting like a kid and eating stuff I had forgotten about reminded me of some of the better times of my life. I hated to see its completion. Braxton had made plans for his week and his theme was going to be romance. The last day of Broxton's week was spent buying extra luggage and several trunks to ship all of the clothes, shoes, furs, jewelry and stuffed animals back to Michigan. We all made a trip to UPS. I shipped everything to my father's house; and made a call to let him know that the stuff was on its way. He told me to stay in Vegas because Detroit was 'out of control.' I asked what did he mean by that and he told me to watch the National News. He said that there had been over 25 shootings since I'd left town. He said that he hadn't seen Officer Monticello Strickland at the bowling alley or pool hall in several weeks. He also told me that my Uncle DeAngelo was looking for Debonair; and if I hear from him to have him call. I said if I saw him I'd deliver the message.

\* \* \* \* \*

The triplets and I packed and moved to a villa at the Venetian Casino/ Hotel. When I got a look at the Venetian, I could have sworn that I was in Rome, Italy. Day one, Braxton took me to several specialty shops that catered to evening wear. I was treated to gowns by Givenchy, Jean Paul Gaultier, and Valentino, along with matching shoes and handbags, several mink wraps and a mink muff. Jewelry followed, along with a new hairstyle and hair color. That evening the triplets and I went to several shows, drank, gambled, and danced. Braxton and I managed to slip away from the others while they were at the crap table, and take a romantic gondola ride. Braxton held me in his arms and he serenaded me as we floated down the canal. Braxton had a very deep baritone/bass voice. He sounded just like the late Barry White. I started to fall in love with him at that instant. When we rejoined the others, Braxton and I couldn't keep our hands off each other, so when Brandon and Broxton disappeared again to play another crap table, Braxton and I went back to the villa and made love on the balcony overlooking the Vegas lights. Later that night we joined Brandon and Broxton once again and decided to eat and gamble until daybreak.

\* \* \* \* \*

Braxton was definitely all about romance. For the remainder of the week, he and I made love in some of the most extraordinary locations without the other two. We went on carriage rides, he serenaded me by moonlight on several bridges and balconies, we dined on Italian food and wines, and we danced the tango in the wee hours of the morning. I was falling deeply for Braxton and I could now identify with what Denise was saying about being open. I knew I had to shake the feeling because of the other two. After eating all of that rich food, I knew that I would have to make a trip to the gym as soon as I could get some me time.

\* \* \* \* \*

Early the next morning, as the triplets slept, I called Michael Cavelleto. Michael was extremely happy to hear from me and asked me if we could get together at the beginning of next week. I thanked him for the money and the sex. I told him I would give him an answer on Sunday night.

He responded by saying, "Please don't make me wait, I need to taste you again."

I knew then that I also had to taste him again. Michael would be a pleasant diversion and help me to get over Braxton. I heard movement inside of the room and re-entered. I then joined the triplets in the shower. As the triplets and I exited the shower, my cell phone was vibrating indicating that I had messages. As I checked it, I realized that there were over 100 messages. Frenchee B had left the most recent one. I checked the latest one, and it read: "Natalie, "I will be headed to Vegas soon. I will call you when my plane touches down. I have left Claude for good."

"Damn, what is it with me?" I questioned. Drama was beginning to chomp at my heels. I decided not to answer and after the last day with the triplets, I would get with Michael Cavelleto and hide out.

# Chapter 12

*Detroit, Michigan*

Frenchee B. Henderson was awakened by the sound of the hotel television as it began to broadcast the mid-morning news.

"This is Michelle Gregory reporting for Channel 7 Action News at 10. We here at Channel 7 Action News are sad to report that *yesterday around 3:00 a.m. the body of Detroit Real Estate Mogul Claude Henderson of Henderson Realty was found next to his car, in the parking lot of Journey Toward Christ Missionary Baptist Church on the eastside of Detroit. He had been shot numerous times. There was no sign of struggle or robbery. It does appear that Mr. Henderson had been drinking. This is the same site of recent gunplay that erupted at the funeral of Terrell Lamar Hunter Jr. several weeks ago. The death count for members of this church now stands at four. The suspects are still at large. Mr. Henderson was a long time member and head Deacon of this church. Many of us here at Channel 7 personally knew Mr. Henderson. He provided housing for many of our interns and co-workers who relocated from other states. He will be sadly missed. Our sympathy goes out to his family. This is Michelle Gregory reporting,* for *Channel 7 Action News."*

"Oh shit, screamed Frenchee B. I better make plans to get out of here; they are gonna be looking for me soon." She grabbed her day planner and began dialing Shavonne to make travel arrangements to Las Vegas. She was unsuccessful in reaching Shavonne so she then decided to contact DeJuana. Not having any luck once again; she called the lobby and asked the concierge to aid her in her quest. After 2 hours she was packed and on her way to Metropolitan Airport in Romulus.

\* \* \* \* \*

DeJuana Edwards entered the Detroit Medical Center approximately 10 minutes after being picked up by EMS unit 3120. After once again explaining to the doctor the symptoms she'd been experiencing, DeJuana was told that an AIDS test had to be performed and for her to list all of her sexual partners within the past 2 years. Upon hearing this DeJuana began to scream uncontrollably and once again passed out. After she was revived, she was then sedated and transferred to a private room. Shavonne Swanson had been given the same instructions and she was feeling quite uncomfortable and scared as she sat in her private physician's waiting room. She called Sharondelle, but only reached her voicemail. She called DeJuana, but DeJuana had turned her phone off. As Shavonne sat waiting for the nurse to call her name for testing she began to pray.

"Lord, I need you now, I know that you are already aware of my situation, so I will not put on a front with you. After all I have done for that man, now here I am faced with the possibility of being infected with a disease that could end my life and may have affected the lives of so many others. I know that I am smarter than this. I should have known better and taken precautions. I ask that you have mercy on me and let me be okay. I ask that you forgive me for my indiscretions and if I hurt anyone, I ask for forgiveness about that too. I guarantee that I will change my ways immediately. Amen."

\* \* \* \* \*

Lance Bellman arrived home from school, to find his mother on the floor of their apartment. She was lying in the fetal position, sweating profusely, crying, and shaking. He felt her head and it felt like she was on fire.

"Mama, mama, what's wrong?" He asked.

"Can you speak to me mama?"

When she didn't answer, he grabbed his cell phone from his pocket and dialed 911. "Something is wrong with my mother; she appears to be in great pain," he told the operator. "Yes, she is conscious, but she is hurting so bad that she is unable to speak; I also see blood coming from under her. Please send someone to help her. My address is 6100 Mt. Elliott, The Shelbourne Townhouses, Unit 3880. Please hurry; I don't want my mother to die," he pleaded. He then found a sheet and wrapped it around his mother. He went to the kitchen and retrieved a cup of ice chips.

"Here mama, chew on these ice chips, 911 is on the way."

He prayed to himself, "God, please don't let my mother die. I know that she does some bad things and sometimes she hangs around the wrong type of people; but she does make sure that I have the things I need. But regardless of her faults; she is a good mother. She just joined the church and said that she was gonna try to do better. She deserves the chance to try, give that to her I ask of you. Lord please, do not take my mother from me."

As Lance finished his prayer, the EMS Truck pulled up to the townhouse. People began to gather outside. Seeing this, Lance went into protective mode as the EMS Techs carried his mother to the truck on the gurney.

"Okay, there is nothing to see here. Go back to your apartments and take your noses out of this business. Where were you when she needed help? All of you can go to hell with your nosy asses."

Hearing this, Denise yelled out. "Lance, stop it now and get in this truck." Lance obeyed, hopped in the truck; and the EMS driver took off in route to The Detroit Medical Center.

# Chapter 13

*Las Vegas, Nevada*

The last two days of my week with Braxton was spent at the actual residence of the triplets. After shipping a second round of my belongings to my father's house, I was only left with a few items of clothing and carry-on bag for the plane ride back to Detroit. Braxton wanted me to see where the triplets lived. After checking out of the Venetian, we were escorted to an awaiting limo that whisked us to a subdivision of condos in an upscale neighborhood of North Las Vegas. The condo had been reconstructed to accommodate 3 separate residents, along with separate entrances and exits. It looked like something out of *"Lifestyles of the Rich and Famous"* it was indescribable.

It showcased each one of the triplets individually. Each unit was adorned with some of the most expensive electronics, sports memorabilia, artwork, and other amenities and yet it showed the individual characteristic of each triplet. Each of the triplets owned their own 2011 H3 Hummer and also each had a Ferrari and a Jaguar. I knew that these brothers were clocking major dollars being in the import/export business and dabbling in transportation and other avenues; but, after seeing how they were rolling, I knew that I was going to have to change my game. Debonair met us at their condo the first night, where I was introduced to many of their friends and business associates and we held a leaving town party.

By the time the party ended, I had a multitude of business cards and contact numbers in my possession, and a minute curiosity of how it might be to reside in Las Vegas. During the party Debonair said he'd talked to his father. It was about Molina attempting to get back into his good graces. He also told me he would be staying in Vegas another week. He was thinking about seeking a career with one of the local radio stations, since his degree in broadcasting was still active.

\* \* \* \* \*

While the party was in full bloom, Braxton and I went back to Van Cleef and Arpels and purchased items for my father, Alessandra and Donna. We also stopped at UPS and had them shipped. The triplets and I spent the very last night in the condo and said our goodbyes by once again drinking Moet, eating Lobster, smoking blunts and a sexual encounter with all of the triplets; this time in their Olympic sized swimming pool. Braxton kept telling me that he had fallen in love with me and asked me to sell my condo and move to Las Vegas. I wound up crying in his arms, and admitting that I had feelings for him also; but knew it would not work because of Brandon and Broxton. I told him I would come back in 3 months and if he still felt the same; we would figure something out then.

\* \* \* \* \*

The next morning I was escorted via limo to McCarran Airport, where each of the triplets presented me with $5,000 cash as I prepared to board flight number 346. Before I actually boarded, I was approached by the ticket agent at the desk. She informed me that my flight number and time had been changed, and if I were to accept the change, I would be reimbursed several hundred dollars for the inconvenience. I then asked the triplets to say goodbye; because I didn't want to break down and cry in front of the three of them. I agreed to the change and really wasn't too concerned, because I only had to wait another hour. My original flight was for noon. After boarding, I did notice that there weren't many people on this particular plane, and it looked more private than commercial.

\* \* \* \* \*

About an hour into the flight, the pilot announced that the plane had to return to Las Vegas due to some mechanical difficulties. When we landed back at McCarran Airport and exited the plane, I looked out on the tarmac and saw a man dressed in a white tuxedo complete with top hat and tails. He was standing in front of a super stretch white Rolls Royce Phantom limo holding a picture and a sign that had my name on it.

When he saw me, he approached me and said, "Welcome back, Ms. Champion, there wasn't anything wrong with the flight, my boss decided that it wasn't time for you to leave Las Vegas right now. The people that were on the plane with you are part of his staff. Follow me, please."

I walked behind him to the awaiting limo. He then opened the door to the limo and sitting inside holding two glasses and a bottle of Dom Perignon, dressed in white from head to toe; was the one and only Michael

Cavelleto. I was so touched until all I could do was cry. Michael jumped out of the car, grabbed me, hugged and kissed me as if I was about to leave for war.

"You did all of this for me?" I asked, as I wiped the remaining tears away.

"Yes I did, and would do it again in a heartbeat," he said.

As the limo driver pulled away, Michael said, "That is one of the company jets. I had my Administrative Assistant cancel your other flight, I have your refund at the villa and you can get it when you check in."

\* \* \* \* \*

We pulled up to Caesar's Hotel Casino and I was escorted to the top floor and presented with the keycard to another high rollers villa. As I gazed out of the window I realized that I was seeing another spectacular view of Vegas.

Michael then said, "Your refund money is in the drawer underneath the bar; I have to take care of something; make yourself comfortable and I will be back soon. We will go on a shopping spree when I get back, so if you want to make a list do so."

He left and I decided to call Frenchee B. and Debonair. Both phones went straight to voicemail so I left a message on Frenchee B's. After an hour, I received a call from Debonair. I told him where I was and got him caught up to speed about what was going on. He playfully scolded me for making Braxton fall in love with me. I told him that was a two way feeling, but knew it was impossible for me to follow through on it. Debonair also told me he had a funny feeling after talking to both my father and his father; and he told me not to leave Las Vegas without standing face to face with him. I agreed, and told him about Frenchee B. coming to town. Debonair told me to steer clear of Frenchee B. We then agreed to meet at the end of the week at MGM Grand Mirage to decide what we would do next.

\* \* \* \* \*

After Debonair's call, I decided to listen to a few of my messages since I was by myself. Monticello had left quite a few. He and Marcellus had been working on the majority of the shootings taking place in Detroit, and they had both been given a special team of officers that they were supervisors to. He also was angry that he had not heard from me and wanted to know if I was all right, and where I was; seeing as how several of Journey's members were now dead. He let me know that it was the Freeman brothers who shot up the funeral because Terrell Jr. owed the oldest brother Nathaniel twenty five grand. The Freeman brothers were in custody, but could only be held on charges of destruction of property and firearms possession and discharging for now, since no one actually got hurt. Nathaniel was untouchable because he didn't participate in the shooting. There was still no proof of who actually murdered Terrell Jr. Monticello also said that he knew who had murdered Leon and Jeanette but had not arrested them yet. He was letting them think they had gotten away; but arrests would be made in the coming weeks. He was now working on solving the case of who had murdered Claude Henderson and he could not find Claude's wife. And last but not least that he missed me; and he had a surprise waiting for me. "Damn," I said aloud, finding out that Claude was now dead.

\* \* \* \* \*

I knew that Frenchee had left Claude and was on her way to Las Vegas; but his death came as a complete shock. After listening to a few more messages I decided I'd had enough and deleted all of them. I showered and changed into a Jimmy Choo casual outfit and began to touchup my hair. At that moment, Michael walked into the villa, dressed in a light beige Sean John shirt with matching pants and wearing a diamond and platinum watch and chain.

"Have you made your list baby? Are you ready to go shopping?" he asked. I looked at him and he returned to me the same look. Five minutes later, we were both completely naked and making love in the super king sized bed. After making love for hours, we finally drifted off to sleep in each other's arms as daybreak introduced Las Vegas to a new day.

\* \* \* \* \*

Around 10:00 a.m. the next morning, Michael shook me and said, "Baby, your cell is vibrating." I looked over and checked the caller I.D. I hesitated for a minute and Michael asked, "Is everything all right? Aren't you going to answer it?" I picked it up and let him read the display. "Who is Frenchee B.?" he inquired.

"She is one of my church members who's coming out here for a Real Estate conference. She has left her husband, and I recently heard he was murdered back in Detroit," I answered.

"Natalie, I must say that you know an interesting group of people. What are you gonna do?" He inquired.

"I don't know Michael. Any suggestions?" I asked.

"Well, like they say in Vegas, let it ride. I think you should avoid it for now; could be trouble in the long run; but baby I will leave that decision up to you," he responded. We got up, showered together, Michael ordered breakfast and after we ate, he said, "Get dressed, beautiful baby, and let's go shopping; I saw something special that I want you to have."

Two hours later, I again was the proud owner of several minks, a matching mink hat and muff, numerous outfits, lingerie, purses, shoes and jewelry and a large trunk. The something special was a five-carat marquee cut diamond ring surrounded by emeralds with matching bracelet, necklace and earrings. When we arrived back at the villa, Michael explained how he wanted me to look and dress for the next nights midnight dinner. We then went out to eat and gamble. Frenchee B. kept blowing up my cell phone and Michael noticed how it kept vibrating so he asked me politely to turn it off completely because he wanted my undivided attention; and I honored his request immediately.

* * * * *

While walking back to the villa with Michael the next morning at daybreak, I had a momentary surge of fear invade my body; which usually meant that something was about to go haywire if I wasn't careful. I thought about what both Debonair and Michael had said regarding avoiding Frenchee B. I also thought about what I'd been told about not returning to Detroit, and I was also thinking about Monticello. He had never before exposed anything major to me about his job except for the crime lab information. He had mentioned in one of his messages of "playing with the murderer's head" and letting them believe things were just the opposite of what they actually were. I figured he might be doing the same thing with me; because he was once again angry with me. At that moment Michael interrupted my train of thought by asking me where I wished to have midnight dinner. I then told him that I wanted him to surprise me. He once again explained how he wanted me to be dressed and I promised him that he would not be disappointed. That afternoon while Michael was doing his thing, I pampered myself at the spa, got a makeover including a new hairstyle and color, manicure/pedicure and massage. That evening I was dressed just as he asked in a red evening gown by Kay Unger New York with matching shoes and evening bag and my white fur muff on my right hand. I was called upon at the villa by Michael's valet around 11:45p.m; and escorted to the top of the Paris Casino's Eiffel Tower replica. Michael's staff had created a very romantic atmosphere. There was a harpist, a candlelit table which held dinner for two consisting of champagne and strawberries, and a lobster meal. There were also flowers everywhere.

After we had dinner, we took a midnight stroll on the strip; (with the limo not far behind; following us). We walked and talked about me moving to Las Vegas and the possibility of me making several investments guided by Michael. As the night wound down, Michael and I ended up drinking champagne and making love in the back of the limo as we were being taken back to the villa at Caesar's. We entered the villa, showered changed clothes and took off again. We ended up at New York, New York Casino. We gambled until dawn; with me winning $10,000 on slots and Michael winning a cool $50,000 at the crap table. I wired three grand to my father; and another fifteen hundred to my bank account. Michael and I re-entered the villa and made love again as I gazed upon the several new full length mink coats that Michael had his staff leave on the bed while we were out gambling.

# Chapter 14

*Detroit, Michigan*

**B**ack in Detroit at Detroit Medical Center, Denise awaited the results of her medical tests. It was not what she wanted to hear. She had the HIV virus. She was going to have to take several different medications and would not be able to have any more children. She was told to abstain from sexual encounters. She also found out that even though she'd recently acquired the disease, it was rapidly destroying her body. She called her mother and told her the news, but instead of receiving sympathy; she received a tongue lashing and a threat to have Lance taken away from her for being such a whore with her body. She knew then that she had to do something quick to get some money to fight with in court. She attempted to call Pastor but got no answer. She wanted to get angry, but realized that she had business to handle; so she put contacting Pastor on the back burner. She knew that Felix Watson, the 65 year old man she had been tricking with, was dying of prostate cancer, but at this point she decided that she would have to do something to expedite his demise. She began to devise a plan to have him gone by weeks end. She reached in her wallet and looked at the credit card that he'd previously given her for emergency purposes. She then smiled deviously as she dialed his number. As the phone rang, she pondered what she would say. "Felix, we need to take this evening to have a mini get away. I want us to go to Toledo and have a couple days of alone time; I got a babysitter for the weekend," she stated. "I thought you'd forgotten about me. I'll need you to drive and I will pay for all the gas." He said. The call then disconnected.

\* \* \* \* \*

Two hours later, after Denise had spoken with her sister, Lance was dropped off at Renee's house to spend the weekend with his cousin Louis. Denise left her car at Renee's; then caught a cab to Enterprise Rental and requested a car for the weekend. She made a trip to her house then headed to Felix's. Denise pulled up to Felix Watson's house on Melbourne Street in the rental car from Enterprise Rental. She had packed several vials of liquid medication, a syringe, a few pieces of clothing, a large thermos for Felix's liquor and her .380 automatic handgun. "Where is your car? Why are you driving a rental?" Felix asked. "I wanted us to be comfortable." She replied. After stopping at the gas station and the liquor store to get Felix a fifth of vodka, some grapefruit juice and cigarettes, Denise poured the liquor and juice into the thermos so that Felix could drink undetected while riding. Denise proceeded to take I75 South, headed to Ohio. After an hour and some minutes of driving, and small talk, Felix and Denise pulled up to the Comfort Inn located in Downtown Toledo. Denise requested that Felix get a room in a secluded area. She let Felix check them in using his name and credit card while she remained in the vehicle so that no one would see her face. When they entered the room, Denise was careful not to touch anything. As Felix entered the bathroom, Denise carefully removed several vials of liquid medication from her travel bag and quickly mixed them together. Felix stated that he was somewhat intoxicated and tired from the drive, and after using the bathroom; Felix undressed and laid across the king sized bed. Ten minutes later he was fast asleep. As Felix snored loudly, Denise filled the syringe with the mixture, eased over to Felix and injected it into the fleshy part of Felix's buttocks. Felix was a hard sleeper which Denise already knew and at that point he just moaned and made an attempt to turn over, but the drugs quickly took effect and rendered him helpless temporarily. Several minutes later, he opened his eyes extra wide, clutched his chest and attempted to scream out; but all he could do was roll over and fall from the bed to his death.

\* \* \* \* \*

Denise emptied his wallet of all of his cash and remaining credit cards. She then checked his wrist and his heart. Not feeling a pulse or heartbeat she blew him a kiss, rubbed her palms together, gathered her belongings, and again careful not to touch anything; retreated to the rental car and began her trip back to Detroit. After stopping at several ATM machines and withdrawing all of the cash on Felix's' cards, Denise returned to Detroit, destroyed all the cards, discarded the syringe and medication, wiped down the vehicle and turned it in. She caught a cab back to Renee's, retrieved her vehicle and was now back at her apartment waiting for word of Felix's death, so that she could began making plans to collect on the two hundred fifty thousand dollar insurance policy that he had promised her when he died. Denise was in possession of eleven thousand dollars. After arriving back at her apartment; she showered, changed clothes, took all the clothing and shoes she'd worn and dropped them in the Salvation Army drop box on the corner. She returned home and called Desmond Anderson. She invited him over for a night of drinking and wild sexual escapades; seeing as how Lance would be spending the weekend with his cousin. By 3:30 a.m. Denise was completely intoxicated, and on her third round of unprotected sexual enjoyment with Desmond.

\* \* \* \* \*

The next morning after Desmond left, Denise cleaned her townhouse and went to the liquor store to purchase liquor, wine and beer to restock her bar using a portion of the five hundred dollars Desmond had given her. While in the checkout line, she was approached by a young, sexy thug who introduced himself as Leonardo DeGraffenreid. He resembled the singer/actor Andre Benjamin—*aka Andre 3000*. They talked for about fifteen minutes, while waiting on the cashier. Realizing that she had her house to herself for several more days, Denise went into her *I just wanna get high and have sex all night long* mode. She exchanged numbers with Leonardo and promised him a night of wild sexual escapades and drinking, if he would come over later that night. They made plans to meet at midnight. Denise promised him right then that if he spent the night he wouldn't be disappointed. Leonardo, needing a place to lay low for a while agreed immediately. He then called his crew and told them that the weekend was theirs to do whatever they wished, but to be ready to resume business on Monday; not knowing that he and the members of his crew were under surveillance by Detectives Monticello Strickland, Marcellus Robinson, and their new task force.

\* \* \* \* \*

In the office of her private physician, Shavonne was told that she now had full blown AIDS and was in the final stage of the disease. She was also told that hopefully medication could keep her as comfortable as possible and she probably only had another year and a half to live. "This is messed up. All I have done for that man and this is what I am reduced to. I do have to take responsibility for a lot of what has happened but I was not alone in this." She shouted out. She attempted to contact her daughter, Sharondelle, again, but got no answer. She then called Pastors' cell and it went straight to voicemail. "He will be dealt with," she replied. "What am I gonna do now? This is gonna interfere with my money making if anyone finds out. I refuse to go down by myself. If I am gonna be punished, I am taking as many as I can. I'm gonna play this as long as I can." She angrily shouted. After leaving the pharmacy with her prescriptions, she began to call all of her high roller clients and make plans to meet with them. She decided that every dollar she received this time would not be shared with Pastor. It was now her turn to reap the benefits.

# Chapter 15

*Cincinnati, Ohio*

"I really hate to see you go," L.H. told First Lady Charisse as she prepared for check in at the airport. "Baby, don't do this, I promise it won't be much longer, I don't want to cry so stop it okay. I love you so much and I swear after the loose ends are tied up; we will be together forever. Hold on to that thought and we will be back in each others arms before you know we were ever apart." She said. She then boarded flight 801 for her return trip back to Detroit. The past few weeks had been just what she needed to renew herself. She was now a new woman, stronger, more self-assured, and definitely ready to sever old ties and embark upon new horizons. She now had a new man waiting in the wings. Before boarding she'd left a message on Dominique's phone that Little Tee would have to stay with his other grandmother because she was moving out of town. She would give herself two weeks to disassociate herself from her marriage and all possessions held by her and Terrell Sr.

\* \* \* \* \*

An hour later as flight 801 touched down at City Airport, First Lady Hunter felt a twinge of pain overcome her body and a tingling sensation from her head. She shook it off and attributed it to just being nervous. She stroked her hair and to her surprise a hand full of it came out and became lodged in between her fingers. "What the hell is going on here?" she screamed aloud as she looked around for the baggage claim. She recovered her luggage, retrieved her vehicle and called her private doctor from her cell phone. She was instructed to meet him at his Southfield office within the hour. After dropping off her bags, showering and changing clothes, First Lady headed to the office of Dr. Jaheem Mathis.

# Chapter 16

*Detroit, Michigan*

Marion Stevenson entered room 2550 of Pastor Hunter once again, and presented him with a large envelope filled with cash. He counted it and it totaled ten grand. "I've been waiting to hear from you regarding our last conversation. Have you made your decision yet?" She inquired. "I am still thinking about it. He replied. I have to say that I was really turned off by your demanding personality. You stepped out of line when you attempted to give me an ultimatum. That is not the way a lady acts, especially a lady of mine. I am really considering dismissing you altogether." Marion dropped to her knees in front of him and said. "Please Terrell, Please big daddy, I'm sorry daddy; I didn't mean to come off like that, it's just my rough upbringing; please forgive me and give me another chance; I love you and I am willing to do anything for you; I promise I am going to control my attitude. I know my place, believe me." As she spoke, Pastor Hunter thought about his new side piece and smiled, unknowingly giving Marion the impression that he was smiling at her. He then hugged her and proceeded to undress her. "I'm gonna give you another chance; don't make me regret it. Oh, and I will need another five grand by the end of tomorrow. Having the wrong attitude costs," he said to her. "I'll have it for you daddy, just don't throw me away; I'll make it up to you, I swear. Please forgive me." She whined into his ear. Ten minutes later they were engaged in unprotected lovemaking for the remainder of the day. Pastor never did let on that someone else now held the position of number one side piece.

\* \* \* \* \*

"Charisse K. Hunter, the doctor will see you now," stated the medical receptionist as she held the door for First Lady to enter. After changing into the gown that was left on the examining table, First Lady sat on the edge of the table and looked up into the seductive, hazel eyes of Dr. Jaheem Mathis. Dr. Mathis was a tall, thin, light-skinned man in his mid-40s. "I made notes on the symptoms you told me you were experiencing, and I want to run several tests. I believe that I already know what the problem is; but I want to be a hundred percent sure. Relax for a minute; the lab tech will be with you shortly." He then exited the room. While waiting, First Lady began to engage in prayer.

*"Lord, I need you right now. I got a chance to grieve over the death of Terrell Jr. and now I have a chance to be happy and at peace. Lord I have tried to be a good wife, but my husband and I have run our course. It is time that I move on. Lord let me be all right; let this just be stress that I am experiencing and not anything major. Lord I will always love you and know that you feel the same about me. I ask that you forgive me and my indiscretions, but I've got to move on. I am ready to move on. Please let me have this. These things I ask in the name of Jesus."* Amen.

"Mrs. Hunter, my name is Forrest, and I will be conducting your testing," stated the husky brown skinned male who wore a white lab coat, carrying a clipboard. First Lady followed him to another area; and after several hours of probing, prodding, and giving hair, blood and urine samples, First Lady was ushered back to the exam room and told to get dressed. After about five minutes, Dr. Mathis entered once again and said. "Mrs. Hunter, your tests are being sent to the lab, and I will contact you on Monday with the results."

"Thank you doctor, I will wait for your call. I ask that you call me on my cell phone."

"No problem, I'll do that," he stated. First Lady headed home in preparation of calling Terrell and having him come home to discuss the finalization of their divorce.

\* \* \* \* \*

4:00 p.m. Saturday afternoon, Marion Stevenson was entering her vehicle to leave as Pastor Hunters cell phone began to ring. He waved for Marion to drive off as he answered. "I see you have not been home, stated First Lady. Well I am back from Ohio, and I need you to come home so that we can finalize things. I will be moving out in two weeks. I want us to be adult about this. I've spoken to my attorney. We cannot prolong this any longer. I expect you here within the hour." "I'll be there soon. Tomorrow is Sunday and everyone will be looking for us at church. I'm bringing all my clothes home. I know you are still angry, so I will sleep in the guest room." He stated. "Do as you wish; I really don't care anymore." She replied. The call then disconnected. Two hours later, Pastor Hunter entered the side door of his residence with several suitcases. First Lady met him as he proceeded to climb the stairs. "I see you finally broke away from your whores. I just came back from my doctor; my hair is falling out, and I am in pain. For your sake, I hope you haven't given me anything you nasty beast, because if you have; I will take everything you've got." Pastor looked at First Lady and answered her by saying, "Well like you said earlier; do as you wish; I still love you and wanted to fight for this marriage, but I've decided to throw in the towel. You said that you wanted out, well so do I now." Pastor then walked down the hallway to his study and called Minister Marvin Cunningham to verify that he would still be delivering the sermon tomorrow. After concluding his phone call, Pastor sat at his desk staring into space. Around ten o'clock Pastor decided it was time to get some much needed sleep so he undressed and retired to the guest bedroom located on the other of the house.

* * * * *

At exactly twelve midnight, the doorbell rang at Denise Bellman's townhouse. Looking out of her bedroom window, Denise witnessed a man closing the trunk to a 2011 Black Chevrolet Trailblazer. She slowly opened her door and standing there was Leonardo DeGraffenreid with a large white plastic bag. "Come in, welcome to the eastside." Denise giggled.

"I hope you like Hennessey, I brought two fifths," Leonardo said.

"Yes, it will go good with these blunts that I have," stated Denise.

As Leonardo sat the bag on the counter, Denise stepped back, opened the white terry cloth robe to expose the all black ensemble that she had on; which consisted of a bra and thong along with black fishnet stockings. Denise walked back and forth, and then posed like a magazine cover model. "Do you like what you see?" She inquired.

"Most definitely, but I hope you are not a tease; and I wind up having to kick your ass for wasting my time."

Looking at Leonardo standing there, Denise could feel herself becoming wet with excitement. "Don't worry baby, like I told you earlier; you won't be disappointed."

She then offered Leonardo some fried chicken wings, coleslaw and French fries. After Leonardo finished eating Denise loaded several discs in her CD player and proceeded to do a dance for Leonardo.

"This will make up for the party. I was supposed to be one of the dancers at your birthday party. Oh, by the way, how is your little sister doing?" Denise inquired.

"How do you know my family?" he asked.

Denise explained that she'd heard about the party and his sister through an acquaintance. She then insisted that he turn off his cell phone, so that there wouldn't be any distractions.

\* \* \* \* \*

Several hours later after smoking blunts and drinking, Denise and Leonardo were totally nude, unprotected and sexing each other up like two porno stars. Denise sexed Leonardo up so fiercely, that he secretly got scared. He had never been sexed like that before. She sucked him so good that he almost cried from the pleasure. He then decided he wasn't leaving until Monday morning. He folded up ten one hundred dollar bills and left them in her medicine cabinet. He checked her bar and realized that she had enough liquor and beer to last, because they had already went through the two fifths and the sun was just beginning to rise.

\* \* \* \* \*

Sunday, mid-morning, Leonardo awoke to a full course breakfast consisting of grits, eggs, bacon, ham, cinnamon toast, and orange juice. They showered together, and Denise changed the linen and dressed herself in another sexy ensemble; and for the remainder of the day, they smoked more blunts, listened to music, and this time drank Denise's liquor, sexed each other up orally, and every other way one could have sex. Denise had unplugged her house phone and parked her car down the street so that people would think she wasn't home; not knowing Leonardo's vehicle was under surveillance by Strickland and Robinson.

# Chapter 17

*Las Vegas, Nevada*

While lying next to Michael, who was asleep; I received a phone call from Lady Monica. She said she missed me and wanted to catch me up to speed on what was happening at the church. She told me that Sunday services at Journey were once again somber. Assistant Minister Marvin Cunningham attempted to preach to the few members that did show up. The mayhem at the funeral of Terrell Jr. had caused attendance for Sunday services to drastically decrease, and a lot of members were sending letters and others were calling; stating that they were leaving Journey and joining other churches. Journey Toward Christ was falling apart. Realizing that he was fighting a losing battle, Minister Cunningham dismissed the congregation at noon instead of the usual 1:30. There was going to be a major announcement next Sunday from Pastor and from First Lady. Shavonne and DeJuana were asked to come in on Monday and help the young lady from the temp agency to contact as many members as possible. Lady Monica also told me that DeJuana was pregnant by Leon and had been keeping it a secret until now. She had known for a minute but would have to abort the fetus because she had HIV. She said that Shavonne seemed to be angry at Pastor, but she did not know why. She also told me that Frenchee B. was MIA and that the funeral for Claude was on hold. I was glad to hear from Lady Monica. She asked when I was coming back to Detroit. I told her I didn't know; and at that moment I made a mental note to buy her a gift and ship it to her when Michael and I went shopping again.

# Chapter 18

*Detroit, Michigan*

Monday morning, 8:00 a.m. Denise awoke to the alarm of her clock radio. She shook Leonardo and said. "Good morning baby, time to get up; I have to go to work soon, so you need to get a shower and get dressed. I'll make you a quick breakfast and you can take it with you."

Leonardo moaned, stretched, hopped out of bed and entered the bathroom. He quickly bathed, got dressed and took the Styrofoam container of bacon, eggs and toast. He kissed Denise and told her he'd call her later. He left her apartment, entered his vehicle and drove toward I94 expressway. He entered I96 and came up at Greenfield. An unmarked police cruiser pulled up behind him and flashed their lights. At that point he was approached by two males who showed him badges and identified themselves as the police. The officers read him his rights and told him that he was being detained regarding several shootings that had taken place in the previous weeks. He was immediately arrested. His vehicle was towed and he was transported to Wayne County Jail. He was allowed to eat his breakfast in the police car while being driven downtown.

\* \* \* \* \*

Around 9:45 a.m. First Lady Hunters' cell phone vibrated indicating that she had an incoming call. She answered and was told by her private physician that her medical tests had revealed that she was eight weeks pregnant, and that she had been experiencing a massive amount of stress which was the cause of her hair falling out. She knew right away that the baby belonged to L.H. because she hadn't had sex with Terrell Sr. in over 6 months. She was instructed to not be involved in anything that would cause her to become too excitable and was also instructed to pick up several prescriptions at her neighborhood pharmacy, which would include prenatal vitamins. She was also told to be prepared for testing for STD's when she returned for her next appointment. First Lady Hunter thanked her physician for all of the information, and then requested that he transfer her medical case and history to a doctor that was located in Cincinnati, Ohio. She did agree to come in to see Dr. Mathis before she left town. She then called L.H. and told him that she had some extra great news for him and to be prepared to have an extravagant celebration.

\* \* \* \* \*

Desmond Anderson was awakened by the sun beaming through his bedroom window. He entered his bathroom, raised the toilet seat and as he proceeded to urinate he felt a burning sensation which caused his body to shake as each stream of water sent shockwaves of pain throughout his entire body. "What the fuck?" he shouted. "I should have known better. That skank bitch has fucked around and gave me something; I'm gonna fuck her ass up." He grabbed his cell phone and dialed Denise's number but it went straight to voicemail, so he left a message. "Yeah, bitch, this is Desmond; I'm gonna fuck you up when I see you, bitch, and don't act like you didn't know something was wrong with you in the first place. This was our third time, I thought you were straight. My shit is burning over here, but don't worry, when I'm finished with you you'll think twice about trying to be slick and I want the money back that I gave you, you skank bitch." He then called his physician and made an appointment to come in and get some medication. He showered, dressed and headed down to Herman Keifer Hospital, with the intention of waiting around the area and retaliating against Denise.

\* \* \* \* \*

At the Wayne County Jail, after Leonardo DeGraffenreid had been fingerprinted, photographed and processed. He was lead to the shower area and instructed to shower and change into the jumpsuit issued to him. As he stood alone he relieved himself in the shower. A sharp burning sensation overtook his manhood and he screamed out in pain which resulted in the guard entering the area. "Are you all right?" the guard asked.

"Hell no man, I'm not all right, I need to go to the infirmary; my shit is on fire."

"Dry off and I will take you," replied the guard.

As they walked down the hallway, Leonardo told the guard. "Man, I don't believe in hitting women, but if I ever see that bitch again, I'm gonna do something to her."

"What's her name?" The guard asked.

"That bitches name is Denise, Denise Bellman. I met her the other day;

we knew a lot of the same people. She was immaculate in her appearance and a dime piece. She was freaky as hell, but she didn't tell me that she was fucked up. I was with her for the last two days. I should have known better than to fuck with her; but she seemed like she was legit so I hung out with her. I wish I could take the last two days back. I'll never do that shit again. I don't care how fine a bitch is, I'm gonna act like I got some sense from now on." Leonardo replied.

The guard laughed heartily and said, "Yeah, I feel you man. A lot of these bitches out here are burnt and they are passing out sex like handbills; and they are burning as many brothers as possible, so you definitely have to be careful now."

\* \* \* \* \*

The doctor entered and the guard stepped outside of the door. "What can I do for you Mr. DeGraffenreid?" the doctor asked. Leonardo answered. "Man I did something stupid and sexed up this female unprotected and I caught something; my shit is on fire every time I pee."

"I'll give you a shot and take some tests. You know you will have to be quarantined until we find out what it is exactly." the doctor said. At that point, Leonardo was given several tests, administered medication and a mild sedative. "Hop up on the table and get some sleep, I will send your specimens to the lab and I'll wake you when I have the answers."

Leonardo positioned himself on the examining table and was handed a blanket by the guard who had been posted outside of the door. He covered himself and within 15 minutes was sound asleep; not realizing that he was going to have a lot on his plate, being charged with multiple shootings and gun possession. Several hours later, he was told by the jail physician that he had been infected with Gonorrhea.

\* \* \* \* \*

Desmond Anderson entered the clinic at Herman Keifer Hospital on John C. Lodge Freeway, signed in, and was immediately called for treatment. After receiving treatment, and being told he had Gonorrhea, he drove to the liquor store that was a block from Denise's house and purchased a fifth of Hennessey. He parked in the store parking lot and drank the whole fifth. After a few hours he was passed out drunk in his vehicle. As the sun went down he awoke to see Denise's vehicle turning into her apartment driveway. Desmond started his vehicle and followed Denise. He pulled up into a parking space several cars away. When she exited her vehicle, Desmond exited his vehicle and approached her. Striking in a catlike manner; he surprised her with a barrage of closed fist punches to her head, face and chest area. As she fell to the ground, Desmond kicked her several times in her stomach, pulled his .45 pistol and began to pistol whip her fiercely. "That will teach you to burn a nigga, you filthy, rotten skank bitch. And this is for all the other nigga's you've burned bitch. The streets talk, and I heard you were with another nigga, Saturday and Sunday night." He angrily yelled.

As Denise laid on the ground shaking, bleeding and her hands still covering herself to ward off any more blows from the gun; Desmond grabbed her purse and emptied it onto the hood of her vehicle. He then retrieved all the cash she had—nine thousand dollars that she'd forgotten to deposit into her account—and threw her purse to the other side of the parking lot. He entered his vehicle and drove away.

Several of her neighbors had witnessed the attack from their townhouse windows; but none attempted to come to her rescue. After about thirty minutes, Denise found the strength to get up. Bloody and bruised, she entered her apartment and passed out on her living room floor.

* * * * *

A few hours later Denise awoke. Seeing herself bloody and battered, she replayed the attack in her mind. She looked around the apartment and when she realized her purse was missing she panicked and began to cry uncontrollably now knowing that all of the efforts she had taken to obtain money was now in vain. She did not know where Desmond lived so she tried calling his cell phone only to be told that the number had been disconnected; or that the party had chosen another cellular provider. A few hours later, the insurance company called her regarding Felix's death. He'd been found by the motel maid. The insurance agent told Denise that his death was under investigation and that they would not be paying the policy off, because the premiums had become delinquent and the policy was now null and void. Denise threw the telephone receiver across the room.

"All that work for nothing," she cried.

She knew karma had truly kicked her in the ass, for her dirty deeds, and she wanted to kick herself for not depositing the other money in her account on her lunch break.

# Chapter 19

*Las Vegas, Nevada*

B ack in Las Vegas, Michael, Debonair and I met at MGM Mirage. I introduced Debonair to Michael and they hit it off right away. Debonair's interview with the radio station had fallen through and he was going to leave for Detroit on Friday. I had decided to spend a couple of days with Frenchee B. but that fell through too because she had met and was hanging out with two men, one looked like Terry Crews, *Damon from 'Next Friday'* and one who looked like Michael Clarke Duncan, *from the movie, 'The Green Mile'*.

Debonair, Michael and I ran into them in the restaurant of MGM Grand. Frenchee definitely was not acting like a grieving widow. It was like so what Claude is dead; that's his problem not mine. She told me that she would ditch her new friends, but I told her to hang with them and have fun. We did get to talk for a minute and she explained that she and Claude had been unhappy for a long time and her leaving was something that she should have done years ago. She also said that the reason she acted so mean sometimes was because Claude would actually fight her, pin her down and force her to have sex with him; and she was not satisfied seeing how his package had shrunk to the size of a tootsie roll; but all of that was now going to change, seeing as how he was now dead. She also told me that she had a man waiting in the wings in Detroit and she would reveal his identity on Sunday.

As Frenchee B. walked away; Michael and Debonair looked at each other, then looked at me and simultaneously said; "Natalie, your church member Frenchee B. is a real piece of work."

I told them both to back off, and not to judge me by the people I came in contact with.

\* \* \* \* \*

I decided that I would fly back on Friday with Debonair so that we could ride back from the airport together. Michael kept telling me he had a bad feeling about me leaving Las Vegas and insisted that I stay. I figured he wanted me to invest money so that he could get a 'finder's fee' although I didn't disclose my feelings about it. Michael went back to work on Thursday after giving me ten grand cash.

Debonair and I hung out the remainder of the day. I stopped and bought a diamond broach and earrings for Lady Monica. I would give them to her Sunday when I when I attended church. That evening Debonair and I both packed and went gambling until midnight. I checked out of my villa and spent the last night in Debonair's guest bedroom; so that we could leave for the airport together. Friday afternoon at 3:30 p.m.; Debonair and I boarded Northwest flight number 426 first class headed back to Detroit. That weird feeling that had I previously had while in Vegas once again invaded my body for several seconds, then it disappeared as quickly as it came. I must have subconsciously made a face, because I caught Debonair staring at me but he didn't say anything.

# Chapter 20

*Lathrup Village, Michigan*

We touched down at Metro Airport at 11:00 p.m. I called my father and asked him to bring my belongings. He told me he'd see me in the morning. After dropping Debonair at his condo, I drove home, unpacked my suitcases, separated clothes to be taken to the cleaners, did a load of laundry, took a shower, made a pitcher of appletinis, drank one and by 3:00 a.m. was asleep in my comfortable bed that I had been missing for over a month. Saturday, around 12:30, I awoke when I heard my father ringing my doorbell and talking loudly. I answered the door and he said, "Get your tail up and put some clothes on; the day is halfway over, you gonna lay in the bed all day? I went by Debonair's and he was in the bed too. I don't know what's wrong with you twentieth century Champions, when the weekend came, your uncles and I would be up as soon as the sun appeared." "Yeah and what would y'all do when it was cloudy, dark, cold and raining?" I replied, trying to be flip. I shouldn't have said that because my father gave me a look like the back in the day pimp who had been told that his bitch didn't have his money. I backed up several feet away from him. "I'm sorry daddy, I was just playing; I know I'm grown but you are still my father. I'll always be your little girl won't I?" I asked in my little child voice. "Let me throw something on and I will help you get my belongings from your car." "No need to bother, I got that lazy ass cousin of yours Debonair in the car, just tell us where to put the stuff." He answered. "Oh, and another thing, the next time you want to play comedienne and shoot your mouth off, be prepared to get laid out. I brought you up; but I will take you down."

\* \* \* \* \*

Debonair overhearing what had just taken place laughed as he entered the condo carrying several boxes. "You are a punkette, Natalie," he said, as I directed him to put the boxes in the guest bedroom. My father then turned and looked at Debonair and said to him. "You shouldn't be saying anything to anybody, damn grown ass man still in the bed at noon. You should be up chasing paper." Both of us simultaneously said; "We've been in Las Vegas partying for a month, we are tired and jet lagged." My father looked at both of us and said. "See that's what I'm talking about; fools give you reasons; where wise people never try to explain." My father flexed his body and started walking toward Debonair who turned tail and ran toward my guest room dropping one of the three boxes he was carrying. I giggled and headed to the kitchen to prepare a late lunch for the both of them. That was one thing about us younger Champions; although we were grown and we would talk shit from time to time; we respected our older family members.

* * * * *

After all my stuff was brought in, I served lunch to my father and Debonair. In the middle of lunch, Uncle DeAngelo and Uncle DeArthur showed up on my doorstep. I was glad that I made extra food because they joined my father and Debonair and also ate. Now that my father had an audience, he started in on his brothers about me and Debonair. Uncle DeArthur attempted to defend us, but gave up after about 10 minutes of my father's ranting. Debonair, still tired from the flight home, took his plate of remaining food upstairs and fell asleep in my guest bedroom. After my father and his brothers left my house; I made a trip to the cleaners, dropped off several bundles of clothes, came back home, put dinner on for Debonair and myself in the slow cooker and went back to bed. I decided that I was not going to get up until the next day, but that was quickly derailed because around nine o'clock that evening, I woke up. I called Michael but the call went straight to voicemail. I then called Lady Monica and told her that I was at home and had something for her. I told her I would bring it to church. I overheard Debonair in my guest room talking to Alessandra on his cell phone; telling her that he would see her tomorrow. He kept telling her that where he had disappeared to was none of her business. I laughed and thought about how females could sometimes be so insecure.

* * * * *

I then called Monticello, when he first heard my voice, he had an attitude, but after we talked for a while he seemed to calm down. I agreed to go out to lunch with him the next time he was off. I found out that he would be off on Monday. He told me about the arrests of Leonardo and some of his crew. I asked him about the surprise he had for me and he told me he would present me with it on Monday. Debonair went home around 11:30 after having dinner with me and watching the news. I tried calling Michael again but the message stated that his phone was "out of range." I fell asleep around 1:00 a.m. in anticipation of attending church in the morning.

* * * * *

Sunday morning, I woke up at 9:00, showered, dressed in a Dolce and Gabbana ensemble and left the house around 10:15. When I arrived at Journey, the parking lot was packed. Inside of the church was almost filled to capacity. I guess everyone wanted to see what the big announcement from Pastor was going to be about. I ran into Lady Monica and presented her with her gifts. She hugged me and thanked me like I'd given her a million dollars. She asked me about Vegas, I smiled and told her that I had a really good time. She tried to make me elaborate; but I told her that what happened in Vegas needed to stay in Vegas. I found a seat near the rear of the church and got comfortable. As I looked around the sanctuary, I saw Shavonne and DeJuana sitting in the choir stand. Both of them looked extremely sickly. Five minutes later, I felt a presence behind me. Denise was making her way to a seat. She was dressed in all navy blue with sanglasses and a large scarf covering her head. She did not look well at all. When she removed her glasses; I could see that she had two black eyes. Her lips and cheeks were also swollen. I asked her what happened and when she told me about her disease and getting her ass whipped I almost passed out. I asked her if she filed a police report and when she answered no; I decided to leave it alone.

* * * * *

When she stopped speaking, I closed my eyes for a split second and that eerie feeling I had in Las Vegas and on the plane ride home, crept into my body for the third time. This time it lasted for over two minutes. I opened my eyes because I heard music beginning to play indicating service was about to start. Pastor and First Lady were sitting on stage along with Minister Cunningham and several others. Frenchee B. was sitting in the middle section on the third row, near the rear of the sanctuary. Seated next to her was Julius Fitzpatrick. When she saw me she came over with Julius and hugged me. "This is going to be my new man," she announced. Julius smiled, looked at her, and kissed her on the cheek. Frenchee B. started giggling and took off running toward the rear of the sanctuary.

\* \* \* \* \*

As I continued to look around, I saw faces I hadn't seen in a while. Marion Stevenson was in the audience. First Lady's sister Chrystale was in the audience, along with Dominique; who seemed really nervous and kept looking toward the exit. When I looked to see what she was looking at; I saw several men holding large chains with locks attached to them. Through the glass window; I saw a small 15 passenger van with the Detroit Police logo on it. I also saw several uniformed police officers standing in the wings of the pulpit area. Detectives Monticello Strickland and Marcellus Robinson were also standing near the altar. I began to get that eerie feeling once again. Before I could re-act Pastor stood up (dressed in a purple and black preaching robe trimmed in gold). He grabbed the microphone and thanked everyone for coming. He then started his announcement. "Church, I will not be preaching today; I will just be clearing my conscious today." He began by confessing his deepest, darkest secrets, and asking for forgiveness. "Church," he said. "What I tell you today, I guarantee that you will take to your graves. Church, I have sinned against God in many ways. I've been unfaithful to my wife, Charisse; I have slept with many men and women in the congregation (he started dropping names) including, the biggest whore in Detroit, Shavonne Swanson. I've slept with Frenchee B. Henderson, Lady Monica Davenport, Denise Bellman, Marion Stevenson, Leon Porterfield, and Mother Charlotte Hudson's nephew Frank the homosexual. To me; it was all about the almighty dollar. But the money means nothing to me now because; I have full blown AIDS. I've known for over a year now; and those I've been with are probably infected too, because I refused to use protection." He continued by saying. "I told the Freeman brothers where Terrell Jr. was and sent Pastor Marvin Cunningham to do bodily harm to him because I found out that he was not my son. Marvin Cunningham is my son; his mother is Frenchee B. Henderson. We sent him to private schools and Theological school years ago. We also gave him the last name Cunningham because that was the last name of the nurse in the delivery room with Frenchee B."

\* \* \* \* \*

The church became totally quiet. Basically everyone was in shock. Minister Cunningham hearing his name; stood up, and called Pastor a "low down dirty snitch." He was then handcuffed and led to the side of the sanctuary. Pastor Hunter continued to speak adding. "Yes, my wife cheated on me too, and I refused to continue supporting Terrell Jr. or his drug habit. The father of Terrell Jr. was not me; his father is Lawrence Hutchinson of Ohio; those of you who know him; call him "L. H." My wife kept going to Ohio, claiming to be visiting her sister, but I knew she was with Lawrence Hutchinson. But Charisse; while you were in Ohio with L.H.; during the first years of our marriage; I was here with Frenchee B. putting Marvin inside of her. Claude thought she was just picking up weight, and when it came time for her to deliver, I arranged a business trip for Claude so that he would be gone for a week. Lady Monica, you betrayed me; acting as go between for L.H. and my wife. Yes church, Lady Monica was once married to his brother Luther." It hit me right then; when Pastor mentioned Luther; I thought back to the time Lady Monica and I were in the bar. I remembered that I had met Lawrence years ago. So Lawrence and Luther were brothers; I knew I'd seen him before. "I know about the money "L.H." was sending and you collecting it and giving it to my wife." Pastor continued. Lady Monica almost fell off of the organ bench when he mentioned her name. "I know that my daughter Dominique stole from me and she is gonna pay, too." He continued. "What a waste. You gave Terrell Jr. that hundred grand you stole on Anniversary Sunday and it wound up being spent on drugs anyway. Natalie Champion, I thank you for not exposing me. You knew about a lot of my unsavory activities; and could have blown me out of the water at any given moment; but you didn't." I looked at Dominique, who now had a look of sheer terror on her face. At this point the church was in total chaos, people were whispering, pointing fingers, jeering, and some could be heard swearing. First Lady Charisse rolled her eyes at me then she lunged at Pastor and began clawing him with her three inch fingernails. Two of the policemen approached and attempted to restrain her. They managed to calm her down and she resumed her place on the stage. Shavonne and Denise then charged the stage in pursuit of Pastor in an attempt to do bodily harm for being exposed. They were stopped and detained by several other policemen. I was glad Denise didn't pull her pistol; that is if she had it. My cell phone started vibrating as Pastor continued to unload his indiscretions to the congregation. I made my way to the lobby, sat down on one of the couches and answered. "Natalie, are you at the church?" Debonair asked. "Yes," I replied. "Come outside now before it's too late, don't ask any questions; come out now." Debonair yelled through the telephone. "I'll be out soon, service is going on right now" I replied. "No, Bitch right now, you fucking hear me? Come out now." Debonair yelled again. I sensed something was wrong; so I got up and headed toward the exit. Some of the ushers motioned for me to sit down; but I ignored them and continued walking. One of them grabbed me and tried to restrain me but when I showed him my pistol, he quickly moved away from me. "Come outside now," Debonair yelled once again. At that moment I heard Pastor through the loud speakers instruct the men I'd seen earlier to lock all doors. "Lock all the doors; no one is leaving here today." Pastor screamed over the loud speaker. Upon hearing this I made my way to one of the side entrances only to find it already locked.

* * * * *

"I'm locked inside," I screamed through the receiver. "Where are you?" Debonair asked. "I'm at the side entrance, on the north side of the church. This is the only door that is not unbreakable." I replied. Debonair drove quickly to the entrance jumped out of the car and told me to stand back. He retrieved his Uzi machine gun from his already opened trunk and fired, emptying the clip into the glass door shattering it completely. He threw the gun into the trunk and slammed it shut. "Come on dammit" he yelled, as he grabbed me and shoved me inside of his car. "Give me your car keys; we don't have much time," He then drove around the church to my vehicle. When we reached my car, Alessandra was standing there with the one and only Michael Cavelleto. Debonair threw my keys to Michael and yelled; "Go, Go, Go." Michael and Alessandra jumped in my vehicle and took off; driving in front of Debonair. Both cars entered I75 going north. Michael sped up and was out of sight before Debonair and I came to the second exit.

* * * * *

As we continued driving, Debonair turned on the radio and I began to hear Pastor's broadcast. You could hear people screaming, crying, and begging for the church doors to be opened so that they could get out. I then heard Pastor say. "No one leaves this church. For all of you that thought you could just walk away, its' not gonna happen. We are family, and family stays together until death. I am the one who murdered Jeanette Porterfield; she was planning to stop giving money to this church. I am the one who murdered Leon Porterfield; he wanted to take his money and leave, so he had to die too. I am the one who murdered Claude Henderson. He was about to divorce Frenchee B. and take their fortune with him. Like I said before; no one leaves Journey Toward Christ. We will all die together first. And so you all will know; my accomplices were Marion Stevenson and Denise Bellman. Denise was with me when Jeanette was murdered; she was supposed to handle it but I wound up completing the job. Marion was the one who lured Claude to the church; and Terrell Jr. to that vacant building. Marion also lured Leon to me. And as for you Miss

DeJuana; I was having sex with Leon that's why you have HIV and your baby will never be born." Once again you could hear the crowd reacting in the background. "Denise became my number one side piece a few weeks ago. Shavonne, you are finished being number one. You are old and played out." Pastor yelled. When I heard that I almost passed out again. I wondered how Shavonne must have been feeling right about now. The eerie feeling returned once again and I began to tremble. Then I heard a loud explosion causing Debonair's car to shake violently. You could see buildings shaking and debris falling. It felt like an earthquake. I witnessed other drivers on the freeway swerving, trying to maintain control of their vehicles due to the intensity of the explosion.

\* \* \* \* \*

As Debonair tried to maintain control of his car; we both looked out of the rear window and witnessed a large fireball. It was extremely huge and rose about a hundred feet into the air, then disbursed like a firework. "Oh shit, Oh shit" yelled Debonair. I said nothing, I'd become frozen with delayed fear and couldn't speak. I couldn't believe that I had been in the same building 5 minutes ago. A few seconds later we heard sirens in the distance. I began to cry uncontrollably; knowing that from the size of the fireball that there probably were no survivors. I knew where it came from because the broadcast on the radio in the car stopped. It was now dead air, and then a buzzing sound took over. Debonair pulled the vehicle over to the freeway shoulder at the East McNichols exit and attempted to comfort me. After a few minutes he handed me three sedatives and a small bottle of water. "Take these, he said. I'll explain everything later." Debonair's cell phone began to ring; he answered and put it on speaker. "Hey Dee, man this is Desmond, where you at?" Debonair answered. "Desmond just come to the crib, I have a situation right now and can't talk. Meet me at the crib." He then hung up and continued to drive.

\* \* \* \* \*

When we arrived at Debonair's the sedatives had kicked in. I was so groggy, I could hardly walk. Debonair put me in the guest bedroom and I heard him tell Michael to stay with me until I woke up. I heard Michael answer by saying, he wouldn't dream of being anywhere else. After that I fell into a coma like sleep. I had several nightmares about actually being in the explosion. I heard the noise and I could feel my skin burning from the flames. I would try to run but couldn't move. Each time I shook myself I could feel someone rubbing me and whispering "it's okay, you're safe" so

I could calm down and sleep again. When I finally woke up, I felt someone lying next to me. I looked over and there was Michael Cavelleto, he was wearing vanilla colored silk pajamas with the long night shirt and someone (probably Alessandra) had me dressed in a beautiful vanilla colored long gown. The matching peignoir was lying at the foot of the bed on the floor. When I saw Michael I pinched my forearm because I thought I was dreaming. He hugged me and said to me. "You are not dreaming Natalie, it's me. I'm here for you; I'm gonna take care of you now." Just hearing the sound of his voice, made me melt inside. I pulled him toward me, and hugged him like my life depended upon it.

\* \* \* \* \*

I felt myself shaking inside and tried to conceal it but my nerves won the victory and I trembled on the outside. Michael rubbed my arms and shoulders and whispered in my ear. "It's over, baby. You're gonna be fine, I promise, you are gonna be fine; Michael is here." After about a half hour, I began to feel at ease, so I got up, locked the guest room door, walked back over to the bed where Michael was, pushed him backward, positioned myself on top of him and gave him one of the best sexual sessions that a man could ever dream of. I guess our moans of ecstasy drifted downstairs because just as we climaxed together, we heard a knock at the door and voices telling us to "tone it down." We both smiled like two giddy teenagers as we proceeded into the bathroom to shower together.

\* \* \* \* \*

Alessandra or Debonair had bought me a cute red and white outfit from Baby Phat and left it inside of the bedroom door. I dressed myself in it and headed downstairs. When Michael and I reached the living room, Alessandra was in the dining room, and had the table set up like a business meeting was about to take place. There was a large bowl of fruit, cheese and crackers, small plates, champagne glasses, several bottles of champagne, napkins, small forks, notebooks, and pens. Debonair's wall hung flat screen TV was positioned where everyone would be able to see it. "We all are gonna talk about moving to Las Vegas." Michael replied. But at that moment, the doorbell rang and at the same time so did my cell phone.

\* \* \* \* \*

I walked away from Michael, answered and all I could hear in the background was "Oh my Lord, Oh God; Thank you Jesus, she's okay."

I realized that it was Sullivan triplets. "Natalie, oh baby, I love you so much," stated Braxton. "What happened up there? It's all on the news that your church was blown to bits." "We've been nervous all day," Brandon intervened. Before I could say anything, Broxton said. "Natalie we want you back in Las Vegas. You know we don't mind paying the airfare." I then answered. "Gentlemen thanks for your concern, yes I am okay. I really am not sure about what happened but as soon as I find out everything I'll call you back, it will be later on tonight, I promise." I hung up just as Michael walked up to me and put his arm around me in a protective manner. "Who was that on the phone?" He asked. "It was just some friends that had seen the news and they were concerned about me." I answered. "Were they male or female?" he inquired. I turned my body into his and kissed him passionately, hoping he would stop asking questions. "You're not getting off that easy," he replied. "You are gonna be mine." He took my hand and I closed my eyes, as he slipped something on my ring finger.

\* \* \* \* \*

I looked down to discover a 7 carat princess cut diamond ring surrounded by twenty four smaller diamonds on my hand. I automatically panicked, but was also mesmerized by this exquisite piece of jewelry. "I'm not rushing you, I know we will have to discuss this, but you will wear this from now on." He stated. I held him tightly and kissed him passionately once again as Debonair asked us to join everybody in the dining room. When we reached the dining room table, Desmond Anderson was sitting on the far side of the room. He spoke, and was introduced to Michael by Debonair. He then asked me if I was okay and explained that he'd found out about the church explosion on the news. He also told Debonair that Denise had burned him and he had kicked her ass the other day. He turned to me and asked if I'd seen her recently. I answered that she had been at church earlier; but I did not know if she made it out or not, seeing as how the doors were locked. I explained that I had made it out only because I had been rescued. Desmond said he was still angry with Denise but was hoping she wasn't one of the fatalities. He discreetly handed several blunts to Debonair, excused himself from the table and told Debonair he would get with him later.

\* \* \* \* \*

In the day room at the Wayne County Jail, Leonardo DeGraffenreid and several others were seated on benches with their mouths wide open and in a state of sheer amazement after hearing the radio broadcast from The

Journey Toward Christ Ministry. "Damn man; sounded like that Pastor had some major shit going on huh?" replied a dark, heavy built brother; named Larry Newkirk; who was in the process of lighting a cigarette. "Yeah; that was some wild shit; and to top it off, I was just with a bitch that attends that church, she fucked around and burned a brother." Leonardo said. "I wonder if she was inside, when the explosion happened? It would serve her right for what she did." He added. "Yeah, man that's why I don't fuck with them church going girls, some of them can be more whorish than the ones on the street." Larry replied; as he puffed on his cigarette. The security guard came in and turned on the TV and used the remote to tune in to Channel 7 Action News. The news preview announced: *"Update to this morning's news story in 2 minutes."* Everyone in the day room became silent as they waited for the news report to begin.

* * * * *

Back at Debonair's house, we all sat at the dining room table eating cheese, crackers, and fruit waiting for the news report to start. Michael held my hand, and put his other arm around me as the 6:00 o'clock news began to air. Standing several feet away from the rubble was Channel 7 news reporter, Vincent Arbetello.

*"Good evening, this is Vincent Arbetello reporting for Channel 7 Action News. There was more tragedy at Journey Toward Christ Missionary Baptist Church. Today around noon, there was a massive explosion that actually leveled the entire structure. Police, Fire and EMS were on the scene within minutes; but due to the extreme heat and intense flames they were unable to get close to the situation for several hours. We have confirmed that there were over 6,000 people inside of the church at the time of the explosion. People in the surrounding area state that the aftershock from the blast could be felt for several miles, and several vehicles on the freeway almost lost control; as the fireball rose to more than one hundred feet. The Detroit Police Bomb squad and several other agencies, including the ATF, and FBI are currently investigating. They are saying that the explosives used had enough power to level 5 city blocks; but was only rigged to implode this particular building. There were massive casualties, and there does not appear to be any survivors that we know of. Rescue squads from several counties and tracking dogs are now sifting through the rubble in hopes of finding any survivors. We will be following this story and will bring you updates as they become available."*

A lady who was interviewed stated that the fire ball reminded her of an "atomic bomb." She also said that the heat was so hot that she almost lost her ability to breathe and she lived several blocks away. Reporter Arbetello then spoke with a man who said that he was on I75 near 8 mile and he almost lost control of his vehicle while driving. He thought that it was an earthquake too. In the background you could still see smoke rising from the rubble and several damaged unrecognizable vehicles. The fire department was still on the scene spraying water. You could also see investigators with dogs attempting to access the damages from the blast. While Vincent was talking to one of the investigators, he was interrupted by Michelle Gregory back at the studio who said that a video had been sent to them by someone who lived nearby. Whoever sent the video had been sitting in their window and captured the entire event on camera. When they showed the church exploding, it was like it was in slow motion. First the church was standing there and the next minute bricks and debris were falling, the fireball appeared then fire was everywhere. As I watched, I became lightheaded and felt myself losing consciousness. Michael wrapped both of his arms around me and said. "It's okay, baby, you are safe. Don't worry; I got you." I clung to him like a drowning person to a life raft. As I continued to watch, I was comfortable in the fact that I had parked and exited where I did, that way none of us were on camera. I knew if we had been seen; it would have taken us twenty years to explain that we had nothing to do with what had happened. I felt my cell phone vibrating so I told Michael I was going to put some water on my face and excused myself from everyone and entered the bathroom on the other side of the condo. When I answered, it was Monticello. "Natalie baby, are you okay, where are you? I saw you get up, but lost track of you when I transported Minister Cunningham to the van. I decided to smoke a cigarette, so Marcellus and I drove off with him in the back handcuffed and went up to Woodward. On our way back we heard the blast and saw the fireball." I began to question him about several people, including Shavonne, Lady Monica, Frenchee B. and Denise. He told me that Lady Monica and Frenchee B. followed him outside trying to find out if they could post Minister Marvin's bail, but those were the only people he remembered seeing outside. They actually followed the van up to Woodward begging us to let them make bail for the prisoner. Monticello asked me to hold on while he called one of his investigators. When he came back to the phone he told me that his partner told me that a lady named Shavonne had found a door where the glass was completely shattered at the north side entrance and got out through it along with three other ladies. I asked him to describe the ladies and when he did I realized it was First Lady, Chrystale and Dominique. I was happy about their being safe. Monticello asked if I was still going to meet him tomorrow and I said yes. We agreed to meet at The Foxy Lady in Greektown for lunch.

I figured that Michael would get a hotel room; but I still had to find a way to slip away to meet Monticello. I decided I would have Debonair keep him company and I would tell him that I had to go visit with Uncle DeArthur, one on one, to discuss a private business venture. That should cover me for a couple of hours and have Uncle DeArthur watch my back at the restaurant. I didn't realize that I'd been on the phone that long until I heard Michael knocking at the bathroom door. "You haven't fallen in, have you?" He shouted through the door. "I'll be right out," I answered quickly. "Who was that?" Monticello asked. "Oh that's my uncle looking for his girlfriend. I'll call you in the morning." I opened the bathroom door and Michael was still standing there. I then rejoined everyone in the dining room and as we resumed watching TV; Michael decided to reveal what I'd been waiting all day to hear. How he knew that I was in danger.

* * * * *

Michael asked everyone to move to the living room. Alessandra and Debonair sat on the couch and Michael and I sat on the loveseat. Michael sat so close to me and hugged me so tight I could have sworn he was my second skin. He began by saying that he overheard some guy talking on his cell phone while in one of the casino restrooms about coming to Detroit to set up some explosives. The guy was leaving in the next couple of hours. He was explaining to whomever he was talking to that he was feeling apprehensive about wiring a church using C4. Michael said that the guy kept questioning the fact that whoever was ordering this didn't want there to be any survivors. Michael said he was in the next stall, and he continued to listen to the conversation. The guy then negotiated triple the amount that he was to originally get paid, what time he was supposed to leave Las Vegas, and repeated the name of the church and the time and day the bomb was to be detonated. Michael then said that he realized that it was the same church I attended. After the guy left the bathroom, Michael immediately headed to Detroit on one of the company jets; contacted Debonair, brought him up to speed, had him pick him up from the airport and immediately came to rescue me. Michael and Debonair both told me they felt remorse for not being able to help anyone else; but my safety was their top priority. I asked Michael why he didn't contact the police, and he once again said that my safety was his top priority and that was all he could think about. At that point, Debonair and Alessandra both got up and came over to the loveseat. Michael and I stood up and the four of us hugged for about 10 minutes, all the while I was crying like a baby.

\* \* \* \* \*

When we finally entered the dining room again, Debonair noticed my hand and said, "Natalie, cousin is there something I should know about? I know you have a lot of jewelry, but that ring could feed several third world countries." Michael smiled and looked at Debonair. "Man, is that you?" Debonair asked. Michael smiled and shook his head. "You are the man, Michael Cavelleto. I may have to re-name you Casanova Cavelleto-Champion. Man, let me be the first to pre-welcome you to the Champion family." Michael smiled and said. "Well, I am definitely working on it, nothing is set in stone yet but I am working on it." Debonair then gave Michael a fist pound and a manly hug. Upon witnessing this I smiled and began to giggle. Michael turned to me and said. "Did I keep my word or not? Did I or did I not say that I knew how to make you smile in more ways than one?" I answered. "Yes you did baby, yes you did." We then opened the bottles of champagne and toasted until it was all gone. Darkness was beginning to set in and Michael stated that he was going to get a hotel room nearby and that I would be coming with him because he was not letting me out of his sight. I was tired of hotel rooms and wanted to sleep in my own bed; and be with my own things. I knew I was about to fuck up; but I asked Michael if he would consider staying with Debonair; and Alessandra could stay with me around the corner at my condo. Before I could finish I got an answer of "no." "Big N, Big O." Michael said quickly. Debonair started laughing because he knew what was about to happen next, and out of my mouth it came. "Michael I want you to stay with me at the condo." "That is why you are going to be my wife. You have brains, beauty and most of all common sense." Michael said. We all laughed as we retrieved his suitcases and prepared to take them to my condo. I was still nervous so I told Michael that I needed Debonair and Alessandra to spend the night in my condo with us. Michael and I got in my car and drove around to my house. Alessandra drove Debonair in her SUV. After seeing the layout of my condo, Michael agreed because the loft bedroom (with the attached bathroom) was on the other side of the house on a different level and we wouldn't be disturbed.

\* \* \* \* \*

Alessandra left to go get a few pieces of clothing, so I turned the overhead lights and put some music on so that Debonair and Michael could shoot a few games of pool and have drinks. I entered the kitchen and began to prepare a light dinner for the four of us. I knew before long my telephone was going to start ringing. I needed to devise a plan to get

Michael out of the house for a minute. I texted Alessandra and told her to hurry up and get back over here. She rang the doorbell just as I pushed send. I let her in and asked Debonair to go to the store and get some beer, wine, Remy and Hennessey. I told him to take Michael with him while Alessandra and I put the final touches on the dinner. Michael overheard me and immediately said. "Oh you think I changed my mind. Like I said earlier, I am not letting you out of my sight. I almost lost you once; that is not going to happen again." "Michael I'll be all right, Alessandra is here and the store is just a two miles away. Let us have some girl talk and finish this dinner. You will be back before you realize that you were gone." I replied. Michael looked at Debonair who put his hand on his back and ushered him to the door. When they left I called Lady Monica who answered on the first ring. "Are you okay?" I asked. She replied. "That was the scariest thing I've seen in my life. I've been thanking God ever since I got home. I am so glad that Anthony was out of town. I called him and told him what happened; he is on his way back as we speak. I had to call and thank Frenchee B. also because if it hadn't been for her asking me to go in on the bail and us following those policemen begging to pay Marvin's bail; I would have still been sitting at that organ. I'm still trying to wrap my head around what Pastor said; and the fact that Marvin was his and Frenchee's son. Since Journey no longer exists, I think Anthony and I are gonna sell this house, move south and retire. What are you planning?" I answered. "I don't know, I am seriously thinking about Las Vegas and settling down. I don't know. Lady Monica, please go get tested before Anthony comes back. Oh, by the way I'm glad that you are okay and that Anthony is too. What about Julius?" "He's fine; he'd left right after talking to you. He told Frenchee he had to go back and lock up the funeral home. She's probably glad he didn't hear what Pastor said." "He more than likely heard it over the radio broadcast while driving." She replied. "Damn, I forgot about that, he probably did hear it. And oh, I got tested last week; the doctor gave me a clean bill of health. I will have to test again in 6 months. I used condoms and he couldn't object, all the money I was giving him." At that moment; my phone beeped and I told Lady Monica I had to go. She hung up and I handed the phone to Alessandra. She looked at the phone, said "hello" and handed it back to me. "I was just calling to make sure you were all right; we are pulling into the cul-de-sac now." It was Michael. I decided to tease him and said. "Come on in big daddy, little mama has something special waiting on you." When they entered the house, they were loaded down with bags. They had bought enough to serve a party of about twenty people. I looked at Debonair and he said. "He called ahead; it was ready and waiting for us when we got there. Looks like you have a definite big baller kid."

* * * * *

After we all dined on Lamb, rice, salad, garlic bread and iced tea, Alessandra and I cleaned up. We had drinks, and played several games of guys versus girls' billiards. Alessandra and I won every game distracting both Debonair and Michael by purposely bending over the table in seductive sexual poses. We then watched the 11:00 p.m. news and I began to cry again as they showed more bodies being removed from the rubble. They'd found several children that were in Frenchee's Sunday school class. They found Mother Evelyn Montgomery (who was head of the Mothers Board) and her husband Deacon David Montgomery. Those two had been married over 50 years. Deacon David was still holding on to their 5 year old great-grandson David IV. They found church nurses Estelle Farr, Alberta Wright and Mildred Calloway. They found Denise Bellman and her son Lance. Lance was in the media center filming a video. They found the body of DeJuana on the escalator. Along with them they found what was thought to be Pastors body. They had also found numerous bodies that would never be identifiable because they had been burned beyond recognition. They'd also found about a thousand bodies in the church dining hall including the Gallagher family who always attended church. The Gallagher's had about 30 people in their family. The rescue squads were definitely earning their paychecks today. I thought about Pastor and all the lives he'd destroyed and for a minute I was glad that he would eternally burn in hell. I said under my breath "Karma finally came off coffee break."

* * * * *

Michael must have heard me and whispered in my ear. "The first step to recovery is forgiveness; and you must continually pray baby." I broke down and started to cry again. As Michael wiped the tears from my eyes; I gained massive respect for him, due to his words of wisdom and his tenderness. Debonair saw what was going on and told Alessandra to go pick out some movies from my office. They both said goodnight and disappeared to the loft guest bedroom, with liquor, ice and glasses. Michael suggested that we retire for the evening. I made a pitcher of Hennessey, ice and Coca Cola, and grabbed several blunts from my office stash. After taking a shower with Michael; I locked my bedroom door, put the vanilla gown back on and got into bed. Michael seeing the stripper pole in my bedroom; decided to do a strip tease for me. I turned off the lights and lit candles. I was really becoming turned on as he gyrated, and did his dance near the pole. I saw yet another side of Michael and again I was impressed. Michael danced for me for about 15 minutes. I then motioned for him to join me in bed and when he did; I positioned myself on top of Michael and began to give him a superlative blow job as he satisfied me orally also. Just as he was about to climax I stopped, repositioned myself, let him enter me and began to make love to Michael fiercely in an attempt to make this day a memory that I would soon forget. I must have been hurting or either scaring Michael by my hard and heavy sexual movements because he raised me off of him, laid me down in the bed and began to kiss me all over. "Baby, calm down. Like I told you before, it's gonna be okay; you can't shake this in one night. I want you to lie here and let me take care of you. I promise, I'm gonna protect you and keep you safe." Michael then began exploring my body using his tongue. I put him back inside of me again and by the time we reached our climax point again; my mind was in a state of sheer ecstasy and I was now in seventh heaven. I believe my sexual moaning probably could've been heard over in Canada. I was glad that my room was soundproof and that my guests were on a different floor on the other side of the condo; because Michael took me to heaven and back sexually. Michael and I climaxed at the same time. He got up and entered the bathroom. I decided then to call Shavonne. She was still crying uncontrollably. I tried to calm her down, but to no avail. She told me she had full blown AIDS; and that she was on a mission to raise a hundred thousand dollars or more. I told her that she could count on two grand from me. She thanked me but said she was getting this money from men only. She was on a mission to make anything male suffer. She asked if I wanted to buy her house or any of the belongings she had because she was retiring, leaving town and moving to Texas to live with Sharondelle. With DeJuana and Pastor dead and no church, she really had no reason to remain in Michigan. I suggested that she rent the house out, which would bring in some money; but she said she didn't want anything that would remind her of Pastor or Detroit. I once again thought about Pastor and all the lives destroyed and people that had died because of their affiliation with him. I began to get angry, but thought about what Michael said and began to pray silently.

*"Lord I ask that you forgive me for the way I am thinking now, but thank you for the things you've given me. Thank you for sparing my life; and for everything else. It could have been worse. Lord, thank you for sending Michael., I'm not ready for marriage yet, but I am giving this to you. I know you'll show me the way." Amen.*

My bathroom door opened suddenly and Michael stood there holding my favorite liquid body wash in his hand. "Put the phone down and come here please." He requested. I told Shavonne that I was glad she was okay; turned the phone off and joined Michael in the bathroom. He had filled the garden tub with bubble bath and had lit candles. After we finished bathing together, Michael assisted me in changing the linen and we got back in bed. He found a gangster movie on TV; we drank, made love again, and then fell asleep in each other's arms.

\* \* \* \* \*

Monday morning I was awakened by Michael who was standing over me holding a tray. The tray contained a single red rose, and a breakfast consisting of scrambled eggs, hash browns, toast, turkey bacon, orange juice, a glass of champagne containing a single strawberry, and a diamond necklace that matched the ring that he'd previously given me. I looked at the clock, it was 9 a.m. I ate, showered, dressed and then I realized that I had no job to go to. As Michael showered, I met Alessandra and Debonair in the kitchen. I told them that they were going to have to run interference for me with Michael. I called Uncle DeArthur and explained that I needed to meet with Monticello and I needed him to come watch my back. That way I wouldn't be totally lying to Michael. He asked for details and agreed right away. That is what I loved most about Uncle DeArthur, he went along with almost everything me or Debonair got involved in. I guess it came from him not having children. He over compensated through Debonair and me. When Michael came out of the bathroom he asked me what I had planned for today. I told him that I had to meet with Uncle DeArthur one on one and that Debonair would keep him company until I returned. I thought he was going to object at first but he told me to just make sure that I kept my cell phone on. I felt bad about lying to him but I knew that I was going to say goodbye to Monticello for good today.

\* \* \* \* \*

Debonair went home for a minute to check on things and took Michael with him. Alessandra left and I took that opportunity to contact the Sullivan triplets and explain everything that happened at the church. I left out the part about Michael when I spoke on my rescue. I put Alessandra in that spot; so the triplets told me that they were each sending her a 2 carat diamond bracelet. I put the triplets on hold and called Alessandra. She giggled like a school girl when I told her she was about to receive some jewelry. I figured it would make her feel better seeing as how I was rocking a 7 carat diamond. I finished talking with the triplets and told them I'd call them again later.

* * * * *

While Michael was gone with Debonair; I packed a mini suitcase with a negligee, and products I needed and put it in the trunk of my car. I locked the diamond ring Michael gave me in my floor safe. I dressed myself in all black and headed downtown. I took my mini suitcase with me as I entered The Foxy Lady restaurant. I was greeted by Monticello and boy did he look good. He was wearing a peach colored shirt with a lion design on it and matching pants and alligator shoes. As he hugged me, I detected the fragrance of Giorgio Armani Cologne. He had a table set up once again with flowers, balloons and a bottle of Moet Black. We ate a quail dish with salad, bread and sweet tea. As I looked around the restaurant; I saw a distinguished gentleman sitting at the bar dressed to the nines in a deep purple silk suit, matching gators, small squared sanglasses; and a matching stingy brim hat. He was making small talk with two cute lady bartenders. It was Uncle DeArthur. Every now and then he would glance over at the table that we were sitting at. After seeing him I smiled and because I now felt at ease; I began to talk a little more to Monticello. We discussed the bombing at the church yesterday and me being out of touch with him for a while. I told him that I had been working at the church for three years without a vacation and finally decided to take my vacation weeks all at once. I stayed as vague as possible; although I could tell by the way the conversation was going that he really wanted to ask a lot more questions; but didn't want to come off as being too demanding. I knew he remembered what I'd previously told him. As we continued talking, he told me that he was going to lose his task force because most of the cases had been solved and because the majority of the major conspirators no longer existed therefore; only Minister Marvin, some of the Freeman brothers and Leonardo DeGraffenreid could be prosecuted. He said that now over 2,000 bodies had been found, including Marion Stevenson and Denise Bellman along with her son. I told him I'd heard about Denise and her son on the news. He said that the rescue teams had been working overtime pulling bodies from the rubble. When he said that; I began to feel queasy again. After lunch ended he asked me if I wanted to join him in his suite at Aces High Hotel. He said that the surprise he had for me was there. I was reluctant about going, but me being greedy, I decided to take him up on his offer. I excused myself and went to the ladies room. A moment later the lady bartenders entered and spoke. I told them where I was headed.

They left and relayed the message to my uncle. As we walked through the tunnel to the hotel; I watched as Monticello took out the hotel keycard from his pants pocket. I memorized the room number and while we were still walking, I sent a text to Uncle DeArthur. He texted me back "okay," and assured me that he would book the room next to it.

\* \* \* \* \*

As I entered the room, I received a text from Debonair stating that he was on his way to the airport with Michael. Michael had received a call from Caesars' in Las Vegas. There was an emergency meeting back in Las Vegas that he had to attend regarding his job and he would be gone for 2 days. He would be back Wednesday afternoon and wanted me to come pick him up at the airport. I texted back that I understood and it would not be a problem. Debonair sent a second text letting me know that Michael was about to call, and for me to find some privacy so that I would be able to talk to him. I texted back that I would get situated; and thanked Debonair for looking out for me. Michael called and I quickly disappeared into the bathroom. The call only lasted for a few minutes, but I managed to convince Michael that everything was okay because I was still with Uncle DeArthur. Michael said that when he returned he wanted to meet the remainder of my family. I said that would be fine; I would have a dinner at my house and he hung up. Monticello asked me who was it that was continually texting and calling me. I told him that it was my father and my uncles. I said that they were thinking about expanding their clothing store and wanted me involved in it. He bought my story. I gave him a look which said "*You are fucking up asking me questions.*" He knew what it meant because he quickly apologized for questioning me. Knowing that Michael would be on the private jet for a couple of hours calmed me down. After that Monticello and I had drinks we snuggled up with each other on the bed and made small talk. I waited for Monticello to *try something,* seeing as how we were lying next to each other in bed. I would look at him and he would look away and stare into the TV screen. I asked if everything was all right and finally he told me that he wanted me really bad; but didn't want to mess things up by moving too fast. I told him everything would be okay and he began to rub and kiss me, making my temperature rise with each kiss. After about an hour; we had sex but it wasn't what I expected it to be. True enough his package was on point but he didn't know what to do with it. I then realized that he was sexually inept. That was why he didn't have anyone special. He probably was trainable; but I just wasn't ready to put in the work. I knew then that this was going to end quickly or so I thought. I entered the bathroom and thought to myself. "What the hell was I thinking?" When I came out; Monticello was standing there holding a ring box. I opened it and inside was a 2 carat diamond. He then told me he wanted us to become exclusive, and he wanted me to meet his mother; who he said was hounding him to get married. I didn't say anything because I remembered that he had previously told me that his mother was dead. I decided to buy some time and told him that I needed to discuss it with my family and I would let him know something soon. I then hugged him and let him sex me again; hoping it would take his mind elsewhere. This time the session seemed to be better seeing as though he was kind of angry now. After showering, we went down to the casino floor and gambled until midnight. When we returned to the room, Monticello fell asleep; I erased my number from his cell phone, slipped the ring back into the duffle bag he already had in the room; kissed Monticello goodbye and left; hoping that I would never see him again.

\* \* \* \* \*

When I arrived home, I called Uncle DeArthur and told him that I was safe and back in Lathrup Village. He told me that he was entertaining the two female bartenders in his room; and that my father was with them. I told him to let his brothers know that we were going to have a family dinner at my house on Wednesday night. After I finished talking to him, Debonair rang my doorbell. He had driven through the subdivision and saw my lights on. "How did things go?" He asked. "Monticello wanted to be exclusive, but I knew that wasn't gonna work. I would be out cheating in a heartbeat. He doesn't hold my interest in anything; especially sex. I would never date a policeman anyway; most of them have psychological problems. You see how he acted before. I fucked up because I slept with him. At first I thought that would make him go away; but I was wrong. He spoke on his mother and how she is hounding him to get married. He told me she was dead when we first met." I said. "Damn Natalie, Why did you do that? He's really gonna be looking for you now." Debonair said. "I think you might have something worthwhile with Michael. If I were you, I'd really look into it. You need to straighten up." He said; continuing the conversation. "I know; but I am not ready to settle down. I'll straighten up later on. I'm only 25. I need to hang out for a while longer." I replied. "And truthfully Debonair, you and I both know that I am not marriage material. I'm a Champion, and you see what happened to my daddy and yours. I'm not gonna act right, just like them and you. I will get bored and it will start again; me running around. Although I am a female Champion, I still have the Champion genes, DNA or whatever it's called. I like the challenge of the chase, money, sex and my freedom way too much; plus Michael seems like he could be somewhat possessive." "Well cousin just don't let life pass you by; get serious before it's too late." Debonair replied. We hugged and I reminded him about the upcoming dinner. "Bring one of your classier women; I will be trying to impress Michael." He laughed and said. "No problem. I will be bringing your favorite female, Alessandra. She's gonna come over Tuesday and help you with whatever you need. You know it's gonna rain all day, so I'll be over later; keep Tuesday open." I knew what he meant, but I never had male company at the house anyway.

* * * * *

Tuesday morning rolled around and I decided that I was going to get a caterer to do my desserts, cornbread, and homemade rolls. I would do everything else. I knew that one of Uncle DeArthur's girlfriends had a sister that was a caterer, so, I told him to have her call me. An hour later Penelope called and we discussed her making several desserts and sending them over. I offered her extra money because I knew it was on short notice; but she declined and said that she would do it for a small fee so that her sister could score some extra points with Uncle DeArthur. I cleaned up around the condo, called Debonair and had him come over and put the extender on my dining room table to make it longer. After Debonair left, I made a quick trip to the salon and had Trina do my hair. I left and got my nails and toes done. After I came in I talked on the phone with Lady Monica and then Frenchee B. who finally decided to have a private service for Claude even though he'd been cremated. I picked out the dress that Frenchee B. had given me and decided that I would wear that and the shoes to the sit down part of dinner. I then talked with the Sullivan triplets who begged and pleaded with me to come back to Las Vegas.

* * * * *

Tuesday evening came around bringing with it a hideous rainstorm, loud thunder, excessive lightning and high winds. I took that opportunity to prepare some of my signature dishes. I got everything together for potato salad, collard greens, macaroni and cheese, candied yams, fried corn and other dishes. I put everything together so that I would only have to put the finishing touches on them on Wednesday. Alessandra came over to keep me company and prepared several fruit and vegetable trays. As I was getting my ribs seasoned my phone rang and Michael was on the other end. "How are you my beauty? I am glad to be talking to you, I miss you and I'm sorry I had to leave so abruptly, but I will be seeing you before you know it." He said. "Well baby, it's raining like crazy here." I heard a slight bit of laughter in the background. "I'm here with Alessandra we are getting things together for tomorrow. We'll have good weather tomorrow; so we are gonna have an old fashion cookout, along with a sit down dinner. "Everybody's coming. I already know my family is gonna love you. Are you gonna call me from the airport?" I inquired. At that moment my doorbell began to ring. "Michael someone is at my door; it's probably the delivery guy from the liquor store, do you want to hold on or shall I call you back?" "I'll wait." He said. I put the phone down and checked my pocket for the twenty dollar bill that Debonair had given me to give the delivery guy. I opened the door, and the delivery guy stood there holding a huge box filled with different liquors, beer, wine and mixers. He said, "My tip has already been taken care of." Alessandra came out of the kitchen and instructed him where to put the box. He left and as soon as I closed the door I heard a knock. I re-opened the door and there stood a slightly wet Debonair. "Natalie, I picked up something personal for you." He stated. I walked away and returned to my phone. The call had turned into a dial tone. "Damn," I replied. "That's no way for a lady to speak," I heard a voice behind me say. When I turned around, there stood Michael (also slightly wet) holding several suitcases. I dropped my phone ran to him and hugged him like it was my first time seeing him. Even though it was raining like crazy, the day seemed to get better by the minute. After Debonair helped Michael put away the suitcases, and Michael changed clothes; my doorbell rang again and my father entered along with both of my uncles. All were carrying bags of ingredients for dishes to be served at the dinner along with pots, pans, and serving dishes. They were then introduced to Michael. My father and my uncles took turns looking at the 7 carat diamond that I was wearing. Uncle DeAngelo and Uncle DeArthur smiled immediately. It took

a little longer for my father; but Michael whispered something to the three of them, and my father finally warmed up and let a smile take over his face. The men then kicked Alessandra and I out of the kitchen and began chopping, mixing and preparing food. The male bonding started and Michael was fitting right in. I could tell that everything was going to be just fine. Alessandra and I decided to play billiards and about 5 minutes later Michael brought us a large pitcher of Hennessey and Coke, along with chips and dip. I waited about 30 minutes and made an attempt to enter the kitchen but was stopped at the door by my father. I could hear laughter and talking and from what little I did see, the men were having an

SINNING & SANCTIFIED

all-around good time. Alessandra began to tease me by saying, "I better be maid of honor or else we are gonna have a big problem." I began to laugh and for a split second I imagined myself in a beautiful Italian lace wedding gown surrounded by bridesmaids and the whole nine yards. "Think you might do it?" Alessandra asked as she stared at my ring. "I don't know; I'm gonna pray hard and between God, and my family I know the right answer will come. I am feeling Michael; and I know he definitely is feeling me. There is one minor issue that we will have to discuss; but I know that everything should be all right." I replied. "What's that?" she asked. "He can be kind of overprotective. Don't get me wrong, it's okay to a certain extent, but I just don't want it to get out of control. After I speak on it; I believe Michael will calm down." I answered. "Well I hope so; I'm ready for something good to happen. Maybe some of the good trickles down my way." She replied. "Good things are already happening for you kiddo; you will have 3 diamond bracelets from the Sullivan triplets tomorrow; but don't mention them in front of Michael. You can tell Debonair, but I think he already knows." I said. "I won't say anything; I got your back because you had mine. I can't wait to get my diamonds." Alessandra stated as she smiled. "My newest diva, I know that you will look fabulous in them." I replied. We both laughed and gave each other a high five.

\* \* \* \* \*

Michael and the family came out of the kitchen carrying trays of meat, cheese, olives and crackers along with several pitchers of drinks. Michael and my father quickly set up my dining room table buffet style. "Everything is basically ready now. We'll put the finishing touches on tomorrow." Uncle DeArthur said."

\* \* \* \* \*

Everyone poured themselves a drink, and we each walked around the table and fixed ourselves a plate of snacks. My father began to speak. "Natalie Jenelle Champion, Michael asked me for your hand in marriage and wants my blessing, along with the rest of the family. After speaking with him, he let me know that his main priority is your happiness, for your financial future to be secure, and for you to be the best person that you can be; and that he is willing to accept you as you are. Michael also stated that he will love you unconditionally, protect you, provide for you, always profess his love for you, and always put you first. After careful consideration, I told him that I will give him an answer after dinner tomorrow." At that point, my uncles and Debonair agreed. Michael spoke next. "Mr. Champion I look forward to your decision tomorrow." "Call me DeAndre," my father said. Michael shook hands with all the men, and then he hugged Alessandra, hugged me; and planted a kiss on my lips which caused a round of applause from everyone. I knew that I was going to have to be up at the crack of dawn, so around 10:00 o'clock, I asked everyone to leave and get some rest so that we could start early. My father and his brothers ignored me and finally left after watching the 11:00 news. I think my father was trying to see where Michael was going to sleep. Michael left with Debonair, and Alessandra pretended that she was spending the night and disappeared to my loft guest bedroom. After I was sure that my father was not going to return to my house, I called Debonair and told him to come and get Alessandra and bring Michael back. I wound up going to bed at 12:30. Michael was understanding about the whole situation and told me that he would make me smile again when we woke up in the morning. I tried to get a quickie but Michael told me to go to sleep. I didn't take no for an answer and we wound up making each other smile anyway.

\* \* \* \* \*

Wednesday morning, I got up around 7:30, after sexing Michael again. We showered and dressed. I inspected my ribs, steaks, and chicken and other meats; while Michael prepared the 3 barbeque pits. Alessandra and Debonair arrived at 8:00 am. Alessandra joined me in the kitchen as Michael and Debonair manned the barbecue pits. Alessandra was wearing her three diamond bracelets from the Sullivan triplets. I complimented her on them and she blushed and giggled. Around 10:00 a.m. I heard a horn blow, several car doors closing and knew that my father and his brothers were here. My father had his apron and his puffy chef hat in his hand, a cooler and several cases of beer. Michael went to assist him and transported everything into the kitchen area. Uncle DeArthur had Chanterelle with him; and several bottles of champagne. Uncle DeAngelo had a cute chocolate colored female with him who I had never seen before. She was introduced to everyone as Maxine. She looked similar to the singer "Lil Kim." They brought several fifths of Hennessey and Remy. I found out that Maxine was a lady Disc Jockey and she asked if she could provide the music. She informed me that her equipment was in the trunk of her car that was in my driveway. I agreed but told her not to go overboard because it was a weekday and I didn't want any problems from the neighbors. My father also brought a cute petite female that I didn't know. She was introduced as Taffi, who I later found out was another one of the lady bartenders from The Foxy Lady. After finding out that my dishes were completed and the kitchen was now available. My uncles and father entered the kitchen and put the finishing touches on their dishes, in between socializing with the women. Around 4:00 I received a phone call from Penelope stating that my desserts and breads were ready. I informed Uncle DeArthur who told me he would meet her at Evergreen and 696. I relayed the message to Penelope and she agreed. I gave him her fee and a tip. He left and returned about 15 minutes later and gave me the tip back. After all of the cooking was finished, I excused myself, took a shower and decided to change into a cute casual outfit since we'd all agreed to picnic outside instead of having the sit down dinner inside. Uncle DeAngelo's friend set up her equipment, Michael and Debonair set up tables and chairs on the deck, and set up an area for the food and drinks, and the party began. As I walked around, I could see that everyone was having a great time. The food was excellent, the weather co-operated, and everybody was eating, dancing and drinking. We even held an impromptu talent show. Alessandra acted as MC, Maxine provided the background music. I did a comedy act, my uncles, along with Debonair, sang a song by Gladys Knight and the Pips, with Taffi pretending to be Gladys. Michael sang a song by Kem and I caught myself feeling love for him again. Even my father let his hair down and told a funny story about his glory days. He seemed to be enjoying himself too. Michael announced that he really wanted to be a part of our family and that he was in the process of getting his family together to meet all of us. I realized that he was serious about this marriage thing and I began to get nervous. Alessandra and Debonair noticed it and so did my father; but my father reached me first. "What are you gonna do about this, little girl? And what do you want my answer to be?" He inquired. I went straight into my little child act. "Daddy I care about Michael deeply; but I'm not ready for marriage, can you stall for me?" I begged. "I know what to do little girl. Get yourself a drink and calm down." He answered. We hugged and I disappeared and rejoined Michael.

\* \* \* \* \*

Later that evening, in front of everyone; my father told Michael, "Son I had reached my decision regarding you and my daughter; but I don't feel that it is fair to say anything yet. Son you expressed that you wanted both families to meet and I think it would be better to make my decision known along with your family being included and present. I think that both families should meet and this time let's really have a sit down dinner." Again, both of my uncles and Debonair shook their heads and gave thumbs up in agreement. "That's fair, Mr. Champion; I mean, DeAndre," Michael answered, facing my father with his back to me. I winked at my father and breathed a sigh of relief, knowing that he had bought me some extra time. I silently prayed that I wouldn't blow it with Michael; and once again put it in God's hand; but I knew that I probably wouldn't be ready for marriage for at least another 5 years. As the night wound down, Maxine started playing slower love songs as we all slowed danced. Around midnight; the ladies along with Alessandra and I cleared away all the leftover food as the men put away the tables and chairs. Michael hosed down the deck and assisted Debonair in loading Maxine's DJ equipment into her vehicle. Uncle DeArthur approached me and said. "Natalie, I like Michael; and even though you've only known him for a short period of time; from talking with him; he seems to have your best interest at heart. Are you ready for marriage?" I smiled, looked at him but did not answer. I then gave him a long hug, kissed him on the cheek and said. "I love you Uncle DeArthur; you are my favorite uncle. I'll talk to you in the morning." I thanked all the ladies for coming as Michael and I escorted everyone to their vehicles. I hugged my Uncle DeAngelo, told him I loved him and asked him to have his brothers meet me tomorrow. My father was the last to leave again. I told him, "I am so glad that you are my father. I love you, respect you, and appreciate you." Debonair and Alessandra were still in the backyard. I told them that Michael and I were going to bed and they were welcome to stay in the guest room again because they both had been drinking heavily; and I didn't want to see anyone in trouble for drunk driving. They agreed. Michael and I said goodnight and disappeared for a night of discussion and sexual enjoyment.

\* \* \* \* \*

Michael and I showered and hopped into bed. "Natalie, I know you are nervous about getting married, but I promise you if we get married, you won't regret it. I'm not saying that we have to do it right away, but I do want to be married to you." He said. I didn't want to hurt Michael so I quietly agreed and told him that we would discuss it further in the morning. We had several drinks, made love and both slipped into a coma like sleep. As I slept, I began to have the strangest dream. I dreamed that I'd met Michael's parents, brothers, grandparents and several other family members. We were at a large restaurant along with my family having an elegant sit down dinner. Everyone was dressed in white. Michael's father called me away from the crowd and offered me a check for $750,000 not to marry Michael. He said if I didn't accept the check that he would have me encased in cement and buried alive. He also said that he didn't have anything against me personally; it was that he had someone else picked out for Michael. I began to cry and ran toward Debonair and my Uncle DeArthur for comfort. The dream was so realistic that I began to whimper which woke Michael. "Baby what's wrong? Why are you crying?" he asked. "I was having a bad dream, but can't remember what it was." I answered. Before morning came, I'd had the same exact dream four times.

* * * * *

The next morning I woke up before Michael. I went downstairs and got on my house telephone. I dialed my father and he contacted my uncles and Debonair (who was still in my house). All four of them were now on the phone. "It is mandatory that I see the four of you today. We will meet at the business at high noon." I then hung up and turned around to find Michael standing there. "We're starting today off on the wrong foot. Baby without trust, we have nothing; now please; I beg of you to tell me what's wrong." He said. "There are just some fears that I need to face head on." I replied. "I will prepare myself, and go onto the battlefield soon. No need to be concerned Michael, I'll be fine." "Well if you are going into battle, I am going with you." He answered back. "I'm letting this go for now; but, trust me, I am gonna get to the bottom of this." He kissed me on the neck and forehead and ran back upstairs and into the bathroom. I followed and sat on the side of my bed contemplating what I was going to do next. I went to the other shower, got in and bathed, in anticipation of meeting with my father and uncles. I thought about what I would say to them. I already knew that I was going to tell them about the dream; and I wondered what their reactions were going to be.

* * * * *

When I returned to my bedroom to get dressed; Michael was standing in front of my full length mirror. "I have to return to Las Vegas tomorrow; but I will be back on Saturday night. I think yesterday went extremely well; how do you feel about it?" he asked. "I think so too." Will you be contacting your family while you are in Vegas?" "Yes, my brother Massimo is in New York and Vittori is here in Michigan. My father is in Vegas so I will be talking to all of them. Baby I want you to be comfortable, so where do you want to have this dinner? I am willing to fly all of you out to Vegas if you want or we can have the dinner in New York, or here in Michigan. Think about it and when I call you later, you can give me an answer." "What about your mother and sisters?" I asked. "I only have the two brothers; they both are single but have girlfriends; and my mother passed away 3 years ago from breast cancer." I hugged him and said. "I'm sorry to hear that Michael. I would consider going to New York, but I will discuss it with the family and let you know. I have a meeting at noon with my uncles, did you want to stay here or go with Debonair?" "I'll hang with Debonair; he said he has some collections to do." Michael answered. I hoped that his seeing all of Debonair's girlfriends wouldn't give him the impression that I was similar, seeing as how I carried the Champion genes. My doorbell rang and Debonair was standing there with keys in hand. "Tell Michael to come on." He said. Michael kissed me and told me he'd be back soon. I got dressed and left headed to Southfield to meet with my family.

\* \* \* \* \*

I pulled into the strip mall on 15 mile and Lahser Road at 11:55. I saw my father's Cadillac turning on 15 mile. Before I could exit my vehicle; my Uncle DeAngelo pulled up next to me in his Cadillac. Uncle DeArthur's Cadillac was parked on the side of the building because he had opened up the business this morning. We all hugged and entered the building. As I looked around, I was impressed by the vast array of suits, accessories and shoes that adorned the racks and walls. I had to say that the buyer for the store was earning his money. We all entered the office and sat down. I waited as my father closed the door. "I want to thank everyone for coming, and this will not take long. I care for Michael deeply and I want to be his wife; but not right away. He is willing to wait, but not for long. I am also concerned about his family, I don't know if they know about me, and I am concerned because of the dream I had last night." I proceeded to tell everyone about the dream. "I wouldn't worry about that, it was only a dream." Uncle DeArthur said; in an attempt to console me. "This may be true, but I have to wonder if that is a sign that I need to proceed with caution. I need everyone's input; we have a choice of where we can meet Michael's family. The dinner can be either here in Michigan, New York or Las Vegas. Michael is willing to fly all of us out to Vegas or New York if need be. I think I want to go to back to Vegas." I said. "Let's take a vote."

\* \* \* \* \*

I called Debonair, and when he answered, I asked him where he was. He told me he was at the Mercedes dealership waiting to pick up some money from Alessandra. I asked where Michael was and he said that he was on the other side of the building; looking at vehicles on the showroom floor. "We are taking a vote on where we are gonna have the sit down dinner with Michael's family. The choices are New York, Michigan or Las

Vegas. What is your vote?" I asked. Debonair said, "I'm voting with you, I really can go anywhere; but cast my vote for the same place that you choose. Here comes Michael, do you want to say something or should I just hang up?" "Hang up." I said quickly. "Well gentlemen where are we going?" I inquired. My father and his brothers wrote their choices on a sheet of paper, and placed them in a large martini shaped glass that was sitting on the center of the conference table. I wrote my answer along with Debonair's, and placed them in the glass. My father emptied the glass and began to unfold the pieces of paper. He then revealed that the vote was unanimous. We would be meeting the family in Las Vegas. I thanked everyone for their time and left. My father and Uncle DeAngelo remained behind to work a couple hours at the store. I decided that since I was out, I would stop at Aces High Casino and play for a while. After arriving, I played until 3:00. I stopped to visit with several of the bartenders and waitresses that I'd become familiar with. I won $1400.00 (after spending $40) and headed home. On my way home I decided to tell Michael that we all would pay our own airfare. I didn't want his family thinking we were a group of freeloaders.

\* \* \* \* \*

Debonair and Michael were in my game room playing pool when I arrived home. I told Michael that the family had voted to meet in Las Vegas. He said that would be fine and he would have one of the private jets from Las Vegas pick everyone up at the airport. I told him that my family was willing to handle their own airfare and travel arrangements, but he insisted that it would not be necessary. "The Cavelleto family has got this. The only thing you guys need to do is pack. I just need to know how many will be coming, everyone will be bringing dates I hope?" "Yes, there will be nine" … "ten" (Michael interrupted me). "I will be with you guys; and you and I will be renewing our membership in the mile high club." He licked his lips and smiled. "You are soooo nasty." I replied. "I know; that is why you love me." Michael said and winked at me. I excused myself, entered the kitchen and prepared the breakfast nook area so that we could have a light dinner consisting of the leftovers from yesterday. Around 6:30 Debonair's girlfriend Donna came over (by taxicab). When she noticed my ring, she squealed with excitement. She wanted to know when the big day was. I told her we had not set a date yet. As she and Debonair began a new game of billiards; Michael pulled me to the side and said. "There is nothing wrong with being a playboy; Hugh Hefner has done it for years. It's a good fit for some, but not for others." After eating and playing a few more games of pool, Debonair stated that he was taking Donna home and they left. I watched as Michael did laundry and packed for his flight back to Vegas. He told me that he would set everything up and the dinner would be held on next Friday night. He guaranteed that I would be impressed. After we made love twice; Michael fell asleep in my arms as I laid there still concerned about the dream. I finally shook it off and fell asleep hours later.

\* \* \* \* \*

The next day, Debonair, Donna and I drove Michael to Metropolitan Airport for his flight back to Las Vegas. I walked Michael to the boarding area while Donna and Debonair remained in the car. I kissed Michael goodbye and Michael told me he'd call me when the plane touched down. He also told me to let everyone know to get packed that we would be leaving for Las Vegas Sunday night at midnight. I could hardly wait because I was going to shop like crazy. I didn't want to expose Debonair by telling Donna about Las Vegas because I already knew Debonair was taking Alessandra. I called everyone and told them to pack that we would be leaving at midnight Sunday. As I walked back to my vehicle, I got an eerie feeling as I saw a man in the crowd that I could have sworn was Pastor Hunter. The face was different; but the walk, mannerism, height and body structure was the same. I knew that he was dead from the explosion; so I shrugged it off, got in my vehicle and drove back to Lathrup Village.

\* \* \* \* \*

Several hours later, I received a call from Michael as I was completing my packing. He told me everything was ready on his end and his family couldn't wait to meet me and my family. Everything had been arranged, we would be staying for one week. We would be attending several shows; we would go shopping and sightseeing and have a sit down dinner at one of the most elegant restaurants in Las Vegas along with a small intimate meet and greet at his father's home along with a picnic; if the weather cooperated. After we finished talking, I called everyone to let them know the Vegas agenda so that they could pack properly. I made sure to pack several of the gowns I'd gotten from the triplets. I called and made an appointment for Saturday, to get a complete treatment consisting of hair, nails, waxing etc. Donna kept calling me asking me if Debonair was going with me. I hated to lie but, told her no. I said that I was leaving town with my father. I called Debonair to let him know that Donna was in her investigative mode and suggested that he disappear until Sunday because she was more than likely following him around. He thanked me for looking out for him and said he knew what to do.

* * * * *

Saturday, I cleaned my condo, went to the gym for several hours; kept my appointment for my spa treatments, hair and nails, secured my documents and travelers checks and tried to the best of my ability to dodge Donna, who had been constantly calling me to find out where Debonair was. He had given her the slip and was hiding out at my father's house in Sterling Heights. Alessandra had given Donna the slip also and had been staying downtown at Royal Flush Hotel. I spoke briefly to Lady Monica who told me that she and Anthony had just come back from down south (Tennessee) looking at property. They'd found a baby mansion and would be moving soon. Anthony hadn't heard about her sleeping with Pastor and she was going to keep that a secret. She also said that she was having nightmares about Pastor standing over her; but his face was different. She claimed that she could feel his presence; but when she woke up no one would be there. I began to experience a frantic feeling upon hearing this. She said that she was also was anxious to move; and that she was packing every day and could hardly wait until the papers were signed at the end of the week. She mentioned that she had also secured a position as organist for Tennessee National Baptist; a local church; and would make her debut on the first Sunday. She said that while she was walking through the airport she ran into First Lady Hunter. Her ex-brother in law L.H. was heading back to Ohio to prepare his house for First Lady to move in. The Hunter house had been sold to an Evangelist that was new in town; and First Lady was moving to Ohio on Friday. I told her that I was leaving for Las Vegas with my father and uncles; and I was hoping to have some good news when I returned. After that I spoke to Shavonne who told me she had also sold her house and was leaving for Texas at the end of the month. I spoke to Frenchee B. who told me that Julius was about to expand the funeral home and move in with her. Julius had made so much money doing memorial services for a lot of the membership that he had enough to do some expansions and renovations. Frenchee B. also told me that she'd sold the house on Lodge Drive and was moving into a small mansion on Strathcona in the Palmer Park area so that Julius would be closer to the funeral home. She was going to keep the real estate business for one more year and then find a buyer. I realized at that moment that everyone was moving forward and that I needed to do likewise. I called Alessandra and told her I was glad she was coming to Las Vegas with us and that we were

*G Street Chronicles* / 181

going to turn Las Vegas on its ear. I then called the Sullivan triplets on three-way; so that Alessandra could thank them for her bracelets; but did not tell them I was coming back to Vegas. After Alessandra hung up; the triplets and I talked until midnight and I fell asleep.

# Chapter 21

*Secluded Area in Northern Michigan*

At a private hospital, hidden away in a wooded suburban location, a doctor and his team of surgeons who had recently performed facial surgery were consulting with one of their patients by telephone. They were all conversing by way of the speakerphone feature.

"How are you doing so far? What's going on with you?" The doctor inquired.

"Not much, I secured a house, and I did get my people together. I am going to be doing something similar to what I used to do; only I am gonna revise it some. This time it will have a lot more flair." The patient replied.

"That's good, son, because you are gonna be all right; no one should ever know your truth. I do great work and there will be minimal scarring. Just stay out of the sun and try not to put stress on the muscles; use a soft soap for now. Get as much rest as you can; and keep up with you medication. Also stay away from dust and dirt; and please wear the mask for a while longer. It's only been a couple of weeks. I want to see you in my office again in two weeks for a follow up."

"I will follow your orders to the letter; and thank you so much for everything you did for me. I will get my flight booked now. I am going to send you a bonus for taking care of me so quickly. Keep an eye on your private checking account for a $10,000 deposit." The person on the other end of the line said.

"I will be looking forward to it," Dr. Nicholson replied.

"Oh, and if you know of anyone who needs my services; please let me know; but they must be discreet; and really should be a member of the organization; if possible."

"Will do," the voice responded.

The call was then disconnected.

# Chapter 22

*Lathrup Village, Michigan*

Sunday came quicker than I thought it would. I woke up ready to attend church; but realized again that I had no church to go to. I decided to go to breakfast with my father and his brothers. We all met at Bob Evans near 696 and Dequindre. Debonair was still in hiding but did attend the breakfast. I was told at breakfast to be ready at 9 pm because Uncle DeArthur had rented a Cadillac Escalade stretch limo; and was picking up everyone for the drive to the airport. After breakfast I went home and paid bills online, cleaned the refrigerator and took a nap so that I would be fresh for tonight.

About 7:00 pm. I got up showered and got dressed. Finally I got the call that Uncle DeArthur was in route. I checked to make sure that I had everything and watched as Uncle DeArthur pulled up in the Escalade. Inside was Debonair, my father, Maxine, Taffi, Chanterelle, and Uncle DeAngelo.

After leaving my house, we headed downtown, picked up Alessandra and headed for the airport. When we arrived at Metropolitan Airport we were escorted to a private jet and inside; along with the pilot and flight attendant was Michael. We all hugged each other and said a travel prayer.

After the flight took off; my father and uncles each entertained their lady friends, but still my father watched me and Michael like a hawk. It was like he knew we were up to something…*which we were.*

Several times we tried to disappear to the bathroom, but were stopped by my father who would usher us back to our seats. After about 2 hours into the flight my father fell asleep so Michael and I finally got the chance to re-new our membership in the mile high club. I asked Michael if my father had installed a GPS tracking device on him and we both laughed at the joke.

# Chapter 23

*Las Vegas, Nevada*

Our flight touched down in Las Vegas and we were escorted to a private area where we met Michael's father and brothers; Vittori and Massimo. Michael's father Salvatore appeared to be in his early 50's; and Salvatore looked like back in the day actor Caesar Romero. He was around 6'4. His son Vittori, 6'0, age 26 and his other son, Massimo, 6'0, age 30. I knew if Michael and I ever had kids they would be gorgeous. Between the Champion genes and the Cavelleto genes there was going to be some pretty children. Everyone was introduced and the luggage was then loaded into a black super-stretch Hummer limousine. I was then presented with boxes from Tiffany jewelers. The box Michael's father gave me held a 5 carat ruby and diamond tennis bracelet with my name spelled out in rubies. He then disappeared into a separate limousine with his sons, after they presented me with their gifts. The box that Vittori gave me had a pair of heart shaped, five-carat diamond and ruby earrings and the box that Massimo gave me held a five-carat diamond and ruby necklace that matched the tennis bracelet. I could see sparks of jealousy coming from Maxine, but Taffi, Alessandra and Chanterelle seemed fine.

\* \* \* \* \*

After about 45 minutes of driving we pulled up in front of a place that looked like a palace. It was gated, had a fountain in the middle of the circular driveway and took up almost 3 city blocks. When the limo came to a complete stop, servants and valets rushed to retrieve luggage and help the ladies from the vehicle. We were escorted into the mansion and I have to say it was breathtaking. It looked like something out of an Italian movie. There was a winding spiral staircase, exquisite artwork and statues etc. Several extremely gorgeous females descended the stairs and surrounded Michael's father, who was already there and now dressed in a black and white smoking jacket with black satin pants, holding a large cigar. The ladies looked like Las Vegas showgirls, and were exquisitely dressed in long sequin gowns, fur wraps, stilettos; and iced out in diamonds. Salvatore introduced his companions as Carlotta, Stefania, Vannia, Lolita and Starletta. Carlotta and Starletta were African American. He explained that these were some of his ladies. My uncles, and to my surprise even my father all smiled and gave him a high five using their eyes. At that moment I nudged Chanterelle so that she could take a picture of them. Salvatore hugged everyone and looked at my engagement ring and told Michael. "Yes, son I think I taught you well." I was nervous at first, but it was beginning to subside. Actually seeing Salvatore and now knowing he was a player just like my family members seemed to ease my nervousness. And God this man was so fine; all I could say was "Damn, Damn, Damn." Vittori and Massimo told everyone that we would meet their lady companions later. We were all escorted to our bedrooms. I was given a bedroom by myself and was told by the maid that I could slip into Michael's room later. I asked the maid how many rooms were in this mansion and she informed me that it had 25 bedrooms and 10 bathrooms. She also told me that 10 of the bedrooms had built in floor Jacuzzis.

* * * * *

The bedroom given to me was decorated in purple and gold. It was beautifully furnished. It also held a super king sized bed. After getting settled we all were taken on a tour of the mansion and given the history of it. When we went outside the rear looked like a location in Rome, Italy. I decided right then that my wedding would take place in this location. There was a roman balcony, a cobblestone road, a long winding canal, an outside Jacuzzi, a swimming pool, tennis court, basketball court, a stone gazebo large enough to seat 30 people and a small bridge, crossing over a stream. Massimo came over as I was standing with Michael and said. "I hope you had a good flight, I've heard so much about you; it's good to finally meet you; I believe you will be good for my brother, I already see a change in him and I think it's because of you." Just hearing him say that made me feel a little more relaxed. After Massimo walked away, Michael escorted me back inside and down a long hallway and opened a door to a room. "This was my bedroom when we were kids. As you can see, I'm a face of racing. I always attend the NASCAR every year. This year you will be going with me I hope. I looked around and there were miniature race cars, posters of Michael and Mario Andretti, Dale Earnhardt Jr., and other NASCAR sports memorabilia. There were beautiful oil paintings and portraits of Michael and his brothers and a portrait of Michael by himself, and a portrait of a woman who resembled Barbara Eden. I found out that it was Michael's late mother. "The artist that did these still lives here in Vegas." Michael said. "He will do ours after we get married if that is okay with you?" I nodded and quickly changed the subject. "What a large bed; did you have this custom made?" I asked. "Yes; me and my brothers would hang out in here and play; and I've always liked my space." He answered. "I wanted to show you this so you will know how to get down here later." I giggled and said. "I would like it better if you came to me." Michael hugged me and said. "Your wish is my command. That's why your father is on the other side of the house." We both laughed and proceeded downstairs.

* * * * *

Everyone gathered outside for snacks beside the winding canal. Vittori came up to me and asked me what part of Michigan I resided in and if I ever visited the Eastern Market District in Detroit. I answered. "Yes." I told him that I usually came to the market on Saturday's and that I had bought produce from his company on several occasions." I also told him I lived in Lathrup Village in my own condo that was paid for. He must have thought he'd offended me by the tone of my voice when I spoke; because he quickly apologized and told me that he lived in Mount Clemens. He told me that he was glad to meet me and that he felt that I would be good for his brother but not to rush things. As he continued talking, a young lady approached us and introduced herself as Vittori's girlfriend, Maya. I was kind of shocked, but was also happy. We all walked around and chatted for a while. Maya let me know that she was an up and coming fashion designer and told me that she would be happy to assist me in any way regarding wedding apparel. I thanked her and told her that I would let her know if I needed her. Vittori called for one of the maids who escorted Maya away. "She always comes over here unannounced. She is one of my girlfriends, but she is kind of bossy; so I only deal with her part time. You will meet the love of my life tonight." He replied. Vittori kissed me on the cheek and walked away. I thought to myself, "sounds like Molina." As Vittori left; Michael approached and put his arm around me. "Is everything okay beautiful?" I nodded and we joined the others on the terrace.

* * * * *

That night we all went sightseeing again via limousine. Michael's father took pride in telling stories regarding several landmarks we ventured upon. Several of the sites I'd seen before when I was with the triplets and each time we came upon one Debonair and I would look at each other and smile. All during the sightseeing I kept staring at Salvatore; this man was just too fine for words. When we reached the Palazzo Casino, we met Vittori's love of his life. She was a Vegas showgirl name Darcelle. She was very tall; tanned skinned and looked like Tyra Banks. We all had dinner at the casino, watched a show and were introduced to one of the female entertainers name Bobbi. She was the fiancée of Massimo. They would be getting married next year. He confided in me by saying, "I want my cake and ice cream too." I smiled; when he said. "I never had a sister; but I think if I could have had one, I would have wanted it to be you or someone like you." Both Bobbi and Darcelle were very friendly and receptive when they found out who I was. They continually brought drinks for everyone. Maxine seemed to have an attitude and began talking ghetto-ish, pointing her fingers and staring at the both of them. They were a bit overfriendly toward the males, but I sized it up to just attempting to be nice to visitors.

* * * * *

My Uncle DeAngelo excused himself from the table taking a resisting Maxine with him. He evidently chastised Maxine because when they returned to the table; she remained quiet the rest of the night. I noticed Salvatore, and Massimo wink at my Uncle DeAngelo like they were saying; "that's right keep her in check." When we arrived back at the mansion that night Uncle DeAngelo announced that Maxine would be catching a flight back to Detroit first thing in the morning. That night I overheard Maxine attempting to apologize; but to no avail; Uncle DeAngelo wasn't having it. Michael came to my room and we drank a bottle of champagne, made love like two porn stars and fell asleep until the sun began to rise. He left in the nick of time, because about five minutes later; my father knocked on my door to say good morning and would not leave until he came inside of the room and told me how nicely decorated it was. He then insisted that I see the inside of his room. I knew he was looking to catch Michael but he didn't. As we walked to his room; I kept giggling and he gave me a dirty look; but finally smiled and kissed me on my forehead.

# Chapter 24

*Las Vegas, Nevada/ New York, New York*

L ater that morning when we met in the spacious dining room for breakfast; Maxine was gone. Uncle DeAngelo gave her plane fare and dismissed her. She did get a ride to the airport in one of Salvatore's limos. My Uncle DeAngelo apologized for last night and asked that the Cavelleto family not hold this against us. Salvatore stated that we were all human and prone to sometimes made incorrect choices. I was really gaining much respect for Michael's father. I thought he was a class act; and the way the women catered to him each knowing about the other; and no dissention amongst them; all I could say was "Wow." This man's game was definitely on point. Salvatore asked my Uncle DeAngelo if there was anyone he wanted to send for. Uncle DeAngelo thanked him and told him that if it was okay; he would like to have an afternoon or night out and he would be open to meeting some Vegas ladies. Salvatore smiled and said that would be fine. Salvatore then stated that the men would be going to his friends' haberdashery to get suits and accessories; while the ladies would be shopping and having spa treatments. Everyone changed clothes and left via two different limousines. My father poked his tongue out at me, mocking me because Michael would be riding in the limo with the men. I thumbed my nose at my father and started laughing. Michael kept calling me while we were out. We were basically having phone sex; especially the way he was whispering into the phone.

\* \* \* \* \*

While we were out shopping, I received a call from the Luxor Casino/ Hotel to attend an interview for the position of Chief Executive Banquet Director-Coordinator. I had applied for the position when I was visiting with the Sullivan triplets. I put my purchases in the limo; had the driver drop me off at the hotel, where I also changed clothes, and I met with the Chief Operations Officer along with the Food and Beverage Director, casino owner and several others. I dazzled them all from the time I entered the office. I was immediately told the job was mine; and that I would start the beginning of the next month, which was a couple of weeks away. The company would pay for my relocation.

After the interview, I rejoined Taffi, Chanterelle, Salvatore's ladies and Alessandra. We laughed and talked about Maxine and her attitude.

"Yeah, she was cute but she had an attitude, she acted like she wasn't used to having anything, and she acted ghetto to top it off." Taffi said.

"I truly think that she over-reacted; the ladies were just trying to be nice. I don't think they would disrespect their men right in front of their faces." Alessandra said.

"Well, you know that we as women have to be careful; if we are too friendly, we are accused of trying to be slick, sneaky and seductive; if we are not friendly enough, we are accused of being bitches." Chanterelle stated.

Salvatore's ladies apologized for the misunderstanding and explained that Bobbi and Darcelle were just being hospitable. At that moment, we all began to bond. We were enjoying each other and before late afternoon we were loaded down with bags of clothes, and had enjoyed much laughter, conversation, eyeballing the men and good food. We all watched as Taffi obtain several numbers from men. Chanterelle said she was going to behave and so did Alessandra. Salvatore's ladies told them what happens in Vegas stays in Vegas and Alessandra and I shook our heads in agreement. They talked with a few men but didn't accept any numbers or give theirs out. The 7 carat diamond ring I was wearing acted as a keep away. Several men spoke to me but did not pursue me after eyeing the rock. I smiled and kept on moving.

Alessandra called me to the side and said, "We have to be careful where we go; don't forget the Sullivan triplets are here in Vegas. I don't want you to get into something you can't get out of."

I thanked her for reminding me; because I had gotten all caught up in Michael and his family that I forgot that the Sullivan triplets basically were all over the place.

\* \* \* \* \*

That evening we all dressed elegantly, the men were in tuxedo's and the ladies were in evening gowns, as we flew to New York to see one of Salvatore's and Massimo's favorite plays. I was glad we'd left town; I didn't have to worry about running into the triplets that night. As we entered the theatre, my Uncle DeAngelo had no trouble meeting women.

Before the intermission; he had a fist full of numbers and a companion sitting with him. Salvatore introduced everyone to several of his theatre friends, including Dominic and Sophia Locceri of Manhattan. Dominic Locceri was fine as hell. He resembled back in the day actor John Saxon. He appeared to be the same age as Uncle DeArthur and Salvatore. His wife Sophia resembled actress Rachel Welch. Alessandra kept staring at him and he stared back at her. It was like she was mesmerized by him; and I could understand why. Like I said; he was fine. I couldn't wait to find out what was up. I smelled a secret between the two of them.

The Locceris insisted that everyone spend the night at the Waldorf Astoria Hotel and they would foot the bill. Everyone would have breakfast the next morning to celebrate Michael's pre-engagement to me. We all were then transported via limousine to the hotel. Luckily there were several shops in the area so everyone bought what they needed so that they would have a change of clothes for the breakfast.

Once again as a crowd of people passed by, I could have sworn that a man that walked by quickly was Pastor Hunter. He had that same swagger in his walk and body type and height that Pastor had but his face was different. This man looked like a Blair Underwood wannabe. I convinced myself that I was just tripping' and let it go.

* * * * *

When we all arrived at the hotel, my father insisted that I get a room next to his.

Michael and I giggled as Salvatore told him. "She's grown, DeAndre, let it go."

From the look on my father's face, I thought he was about to go off on Salvatore and I'd lose Michael forever. But to my surprise; my father smiled and said. "Man I am just having fun."

But deep down inside, I, being of the Champion regime, knew better. I winked at Michael, pointed at my phone and walked away.

About three in the morning; I texted Michael; who was in a room down the hall. He came to my room and it was on with us again.

# Chapter 25

*New York, New York*

The next morning, we had breakfast with Salvatore's friends and went on a mini-shopping trip. Sophia seemed to be intrigued by my father and kept staring at him. She also winked at him a couple of times. I noticed *Dominic hitting her on the arm several times to get her attention.*

After the Locceris left, Massimo and his lady, Bobbi, took all of the ladies to the garment district where we purchased several purses and other items. Most of the vendors knew him and we all got massive discounts on our purchases. I bought more purses than the others because I was going to make some money off of them when I got back to Detroit. I called Charlene, Darlene, and Marlene and told then I was shipping the purses to their house and they said okay. That evening we boarded the plane back to Vegas. Massimo and his lady stayed behind but promised to be at the dinner on Friday.

As I boarded the plane Massimo whispered in my ear. "I really enjoyed you guys; see you on Friday…..soon to be sister-in-law."

I began to cry tears of joy. I rushed to the bathroom on the plane and composed myself before getting seated. When I sat down, Michael was staring at me really hard. "Did someone upset you my beauty? He asked. It appears that you've been crying recently."

"No baby, those were tears of joy." I then repeated what Massimo told me before I boarded.

Michael replied. "I knew they would love you, because I do."

\* \* \* \* \*

That eerie feeling overtook my body for a split second and went away. I don't think Michael noticed it, but Debonair sure did because he started walking toward us. I waved him off and he made a U-turn and headed back to Alessandra and sat down. Michael and I made it to the bathroom on the plane again and did the mile high club thing again because my father was busy entertaining Taffi. We stayed in the bathroom so long that when we did come out; I had a cramp in my leg. For the rest of the flight Michael sat next to me rubbing my leg. My father noticed just as the plane was touching down. Salvatore had noticed the second we came out of the bathroom. He kept looking over at Michael and me and snickering.

# Chapter 26

*Las Vegas, Nevada*

For the remainder of the week, we traveled around from casino to casino. Salvatore knew a lot of people in Vegas. I found out that in his early days he'd held several positions of Headlining Entertainer at many of the casinos, and he knew many of Las Vegas' elite, New York's elite and had friends that were movers and shakers in New York, Atlantic City, Las Vegas and even Monte Carlo. Now he held massive stock in many of the casinos and other businesses. I was kind of bored with the casino scene but kept quiet, because my father and uncles were having a good time gambling and running around town with Salvatore and the ladies. I convinced Michael to sneak off with me and we would go make love. Michael had to go back to work for a couple of days so Alessandra, Debonair, Vittori, Darcelle and I hung out between Salvatore's mansion and Caesar's Palace Casino. I had to limit where I went so that I wouldn't run into the Sullivan triplets. We mostly stayed in the villa at Caesars' Palace drinking and smoking blunts. Debonair and Alessandra understood what I was doing so they would stay in when I didn't want to go out. I think Vittori knew also, but never said anything, because he would stay in with us and have room service or have Darcelle retrieve whatever we wanted.

\* \* \* \* \*

Thursday night before the dinner, we were introduced to the remainder of the Cavelleto family. I met Michael's grandfather Luciano and his wife Maria both 75. (Salvatore's parents). They had been married for almost 60 years. You could tell that both of them were gorgeous back in their younger days. Luciano looked like the singer Tony Bennett and Maria looked like a now older Farrah Fawcett. Luciano and the Champion men hit it off right away. Luciano kept telling Michael that I was gorgeous. Maria opened up the kitchen which was huge; and we had an old fashion Italian cooking session, where everyone participated and I felt the uniting of the families once again. By the time the food was finished it was enough to feed at least 30 people. There was a multitude of Italian dishes and Massimo retrieved several bottles of vintage wine from the wine cellar. Massimo and Bobbi had flown in early and joined everyone in the festivities. That night we ate, drank, danced and again there was an impromptu show given by both families. Salvatore and his ladies performed a number from when he was an entertainer. My uncles did a routine, my father told some stories, and Michael sang a song again, Alessandra and Debonair performed. I did my comedy routine and Luciano and Maria told stories about the old country. Maria was kind of distant toward me at first. I was guessing because of Luciano but before the night ended she'd warmed up to me and gave me a long beautiful white Italian lace scarf. She told me that she'd be happy if I were to become Michael's wife. I tried to hold back the tears but once again lost that battle. After looking at the scarf, I decided that with some alterations and additions this would be my wedding veil when the time came. The top part of my dress would match the scarf.

\* \* \* \* \*

The festivities ended around two o'clock and the announcement was made that the sit down dinner would be held at the Joel Robuchon Restaurant, at 7 p.m., which was a five-star restaurant in the heart of Las Vegas. It would be a six course meal, with every luxury imaginable. There would also be limousines sent to transport everyone to the restaurant. Before I went to bed I picked out several outfits that I thought might be appropriate for the dinner. I knew I had to be 100% on point because I was going to be the star; and I wanted all eyes on me.

\* \* \* \* \*

Friday morning I woke up and asked God for a sign letting me know what I should do. Everyone met for breakfast which the staff had prepared. I tried not to eat much because I wanted to enjoy dinner. I slipped out and made a trip over to the villa at Caesars' because Trina was there with all of her stylists; participating in the annual Hair Show. After she did my hair, I left and got my toes and nails done. I returned back to Salvatore's and began to prepare for the evening. That afternoon; I looked over my outfits again and started with the shoes and purse. I then checked with the rest of the ladies. After seeing Taffi's evening gown, Alessandra's outfit and finding out that Chanterelle would be wearing a Chanel linen pantsuit, I decided on a pair of black satin heels from Valentino along with a long, black and silver evening gown by Kay Unger. I was also adorned in long diamond earrings, diamond tennis bracelet and necklace with diamond ankle bracelet. I would carry my black Judith Leiber small, beaded purse and I would also wear my fur muff that Michael had bought me.

\* \* \* \* \*

Later that evening when we all gathered to be transported to the restaurant; everyone was looking very elegant. The Champion men were all dressed to the nines. They were wearing a vast array of silk suits, animal orientated shoes; and designer hats. Salvatore and his sons were also dressed to the nines in suits that were made of material I had never seen before. I made it my business to be the last person to come down the staircase. When I made my descent; I looked into Michael's face and he was in possession of the sexiest smile. I knew then that wedding would be sooner than I thought.

\* \* \* \* \*

As we entered the restaurant; I overhead some people talking and one of them said. "You can't keep doing the same thing and expect different results." At that moment I realized then it was time to start making some different moves in life. I hoped for the best from his father; and my father. We were seated and I kept getting compliments from my family and Michael's and even from patrons in the restaurant regarding my appearance. I felt once again like a movie star with her own entourage. We all dined on a six course meal consisting of many fine French food dishes too numerous to mention. Michael took me out on the balcony before the fourth course was served and got down on one knee and asked me to be his wife. In the proposal he clarified that we would set the date later. I accepted and he hugged me and we both almost cried. When we rejoined the others; my father gave his blessing and so did my uncles and Debonair. After hearing my father's decision, Michael presented me with another ring more beautiful that the seven carat. This one was ten carats and was a marquee cut. Michael said he bought this one because he knew my favorite cut was the marquee. Salvatore asked me to take a walk with him and I became fearful because I thought about the dream. When we were alone he told me that he felt I would be good for Michael and that I had his blessing the moment I walked into his house.

\* \* \* \* \*

We returned to the table and he made his official announcement; along with a champagne toast, welcoming me and my family into their family. My father followed with a similar toast. Michael got down on one knee once again and proposed again as he'd done previously on the balcony. He repeated everything verbatim. I said "yes;" then Michael and I kissed. The families proceeded to hug one another and the restaurant gave Michael and me a standing ovation; and the restaurant sent over several bottles of champagne. Everyone cheered especially when they saw the ten carat diamond I was now wearing on my finger. I looked over and Uncle DeArthur was wiping tears from his eyes. I ran to him and hugged him because I didn't want him to seem weak in front of his female companion. He whispered in my ear, "good looking out."

\* \* \* \* \*

Later that evening we returned to Salvatore's mansion. The staff had decorated and had food and drinks set out; and an extravagant party was given in honor of Michael and me. We both changed clothes and this time I wore a one of the beautiful cream colored sequin gowns by Yves Saint Laurent that I'd received from the triplets. I met many more of Salvatore's friends and many of the staff that Michael was in charge of at Caesar's Palace. Everything turned out fabulously. There was plenty of food, drinks, music and dancing. I was already full from the dinner; so I only ate a few finger foods, but I did get my drink on. Michael and I slipped away for about 20 minutes and got a quickie in before Salvatore and my father came looking for us. The Champion men were having the time of their lives. They were all surrounded by females; in addition to their dates. Salvatore had so many beautiful women on the premises; for a minute I thought I was in Hugh Hefner's Playboy mansion. Massimo and Vittori were surrounded by females. There were also quite a few married couples there. I saw Sophia Locceri looking for her husband, Dominic. When she couldn't find him, she started following my father around. He gave her the slip and wound up at the swimming pool with Taffi and about eight other females.

\* \* \* \* \*

Alessandra had slipped off from Debonair, who was also being entertained by several women. I figured that Alessandra had disappeared somewhere in the mansion and was having sex with Dominic Locceri. I had made it my mission to find out about those two when we touched down in Detroit. The party lasted until dawn. After the party ended, Michael and I, along with Salvatore and Stefania, thanked everyone for coming and as the staff began to clean up, Michael and I disappeared to the far side of the house, took a shower, and retired to his bedroom. My father was having such a good time, that he didn't even come looking for me; which gave me and Michael a chance to really do some porno type sexing. I knew that we all were leaving the next afternoon and I wanted to get my freak on. Michael asked me when would I be selling my condo and moving out to Vegas. I told him that we would discuss everything in detail when he joined me in Detroit on Wednesday night. I realized that I needed to make some type of moves because I had nothing major going on in Detroit; but I did have something lined up in Vegas. It wouldn't be starting until the first of the month. I asked Michael if I could have three weeks and he agreed.

\* \* \* \* \*

Saturday night everyone said their goodbyes and my family and I were chauffeured via limo to McCarran Airport. We all boarded flight 526 back to Detroit at 11:00 pm. As I attempted to board the private jet; Michael held on to me like a drowning man going under for the last time. I had to tell him that it wasn't going to be that long before we saw each other again. I was going to surprise him and let him know that I had been offered a high end position of Chief Executive *Banquet* Director-Coordinator at the Luxor Casino/Hotel. I would also oversee operations at the Bellagio, MGM Grand and the Wynn. While on the plane as everyone was sleeping, I decided that I would lease out my condo to Charlene, Marlene, and Darlene. Those ladies were obsessively clean and would take care of my place. The money I'd receive from them would pay the taxes and association fees for the condo; plus give me something to put in one of my many accounts. This arrangement would also give me a safety net; just in case I would ever have to return to Michigan. I also felt like the condo would still be in the family.

\* \* \* \* \*

Debonair woke up about 5 hours into the flight and I told him of my plans. At that very moment, he decided to let Uncle DeArthur's ladies, Chanterelle and Trixie, lease his condo. He told me that the radio station had called him back because the gentleman that they had chosen for the new spot had received an offer of employment elsewhere. Debonair would be getting a primetime spot; along with several major sponsors. I had to cover my mouth to keep from screaming with joy. I asked him what he was going to do about his women. He said that he was now considering asking Alessandra for her hand in marriage and bide his time. He also said that he did not want to overshadow me regarding my impending nuptials.

We ordered a bottle of champagne and toasted both our good news as everyone else slept. He woke Alessandra up and asked her to marry him right there on the plane. She said yes on the spot; and they disappeared to become members of the mile high club. He had bought her a 5 carat diamond and platinum ring. We ordered another bottle of champagne; (on me); and the three of us agreed that we would let everyone else know about our good news in a couple of days. I hadn't been this happy and filled with enthusiasm for a long time, and I definitely welcomed the change.

# Chapter 27

*Lathrup Village, Michigan*

When we arrived back in Detroit, Sunday morning, I was hyped up to the one hundredth degree. I could hardly wait to talk to my fathers' ladies about the condo. I slept until 11a.m. and I called them and arranged to meet with them on Wednesday.

I also called the moving and storage company to get things set up so that I could store my furniture and other items until I decided what to do with them long term. It was going to be hard to tell my father and uncles that I would be leaving town. Once again I asked God if I was doing the right thing. I looked up as if he was going to give me an answer right then, but he didn't.

I called Frenchee B. and she told me that she was in the middle of helping the movers and Julius move into their new digs on Strathcona.

Next I called Lady Monica who said she was glad to hear from me and that she and Anthony would be moving south on Friday. She was having a party on Tuesday night and wanted me there. She also told me to let my family know. It was going to be held at Shadiki's in Greektown. I now had something to do.

Then I unpacked everything and took several bundles of clothing to the 7 day cleaners and retrieved the ones I had carried in previously. I sent text messages to the family about the party and everyone said even though they were still tired that they would go because we all loved Lady Monica. We all decided that we would get her and Anthony a going away present. My father and uncles said that they were going to custom design a suit, shirt, tie and matching shoes for Anthony, and give Lady Monica a $2,000 gift certificate to Lord and Taylor.

After hanging up, I sent Michael several sexy text messages, made a trip to the gym, exercised for several hours, returned home and went to bed around 11:30 p.m.

\* \* \* \* \*

Monday, I slept until around 10:30. After showering and getting dressed; I searched through my wardrobe and decided that I would wear the dress that Frenchee B gave me along with the shoes. I felt like black and gold. I spoke with Shavonne for a brief moment. She told me that she would be moving to Texas on Saturday. Sharondelle was here helping her pack for the cross country movers; and they were going to fly back together; because she was really feeling the effects of the disease and now needed someone with her most of the time.

Alessandra came by flashing her ring and bracelets from the triplets again. She told me to come with her so that we could get our hair and nails done. She said she was footing the bill because she was celebrating her engagement.

I said, "That's cool," and we left.

While we were both under the dryer at Trina's shop; Alessandra told me what I had been wondering about for a while. She admitted that several years ago she had held a job in New York at a semi high end night club as an exotic dancer and that Dominic Locceri had spent a lot of money on her. He also paid off some delinquent bills that she had acquired. She also admitted that she slipped off and slept with him in Salvatore's house. She begged me not to say anything to Debonair.

I responded by saying; "That is between you, Dominic and God."

As we headed to our favorite restaurant; I asked. "Did you enjoy yourself, was the sex good, the money right; and did you get what you needed?"

She shook her head and said, "Yes, Yes, Yes."

We both laughed and gave each other a high five as we entered Red Lobster for some cheese biscuits, Lobster with pasta and drinks.

# Chapter 28

*Southfield, Michigan*

News reporter Vincent Arbetello sat in the lunch room of the Channel 7 news building, which was located in Southfield. He was looking through an itinerary that had arrived by Federal Express regarding an up and coming Dog Show that was going to be held at the Houston Convention Center. First prize for the poodle and beagle categories would be $250,000. Although Vincent had worked for Channel 7 for over 20 years; his major income came from participating in Dog Shows, which was his number one hobby, and investing in the stock market. He had acquired over 100 gold ribbons and championship trophies; and his bank accounts held several million dollars from his involvement with these shows. His main breed of dogs was the poodle and the beagle. Even though Vincent had clocked major dollars; through the shows and his investments, he still held on to his job at Channel 7. He said he didn't want his degree in Broadcast Journalism to go to waste or become stagnant. Vincent was 45 years old, 6'4, 190lbs; with deep dark brown hair. He possessed the facial features of actor Charlie Sheen; and the personality of a playboy. Vincent also dressed very dapper, yet conservatively. You never saw him without a full suit of clothes on. He took care of his body by working out three to four times a week. Many of his suits were custom made and he also shopped at *"Dress like a Champion,"* especially for his alligator and crocodile footwear. When he did order suits, ties and shoes; his bill would never be less than $75,000; and he placed an order at least 3 times a year. Women flocked to Vincent like bees to honey. He possessed a sexy, yet powerful voice which was made for public speaking. Everyone obsessed over his physical appearance, personality; and his money. Vincent drove a 2012 black on black supped up Chevrolet Corvette convertible similar to the one Debonair owned. As he continued to browse his itinerary; he smiled in the fact that he would soon be traveling to Houston to once again pursue his main hobby, the Dog Show.

\* \* \* \* \*

After his break was over, Vincent Arbetello returned to his cubicle to prepare his reports for the evening news. As he unlocked his computer, a message flashed across the screen; "General Manager needs to see you in his office." Vincent re-locked his computer and walked down the hall to the office and knocked on the door. "Come in." stated the General Manager, Edgar Hamilton. "Vincent, I will get to the point and not waste your time. You are a great news reporter but your ratings have been falling off the last quarter and this quarter also. I think you may be losing your fan base. I hate to say it but you haven't really been connected to anything extraordinary for a while. The top brass here at the station are considering not renewing your contract next season. Vincent you and I have worked together for years. I respect and admire you, but you really need to give us something that will blow this station off the map. I know you are attending the Dog Show in Houston soon. Maybe you can come up with something there. Off the record, Vincent, do whatever you can to pull a rabbit out of your hat; because personally I don't want to see you go." Vincent stood there for a minute with a look of shock on his face, and whispered to himself, "After all I have done for this station. After all these years of hard work I've put in. I am the one responsible for turning this station into the number one news station in Detroit. All of the charity events I started, sponsored, and gave donations to. All the families of Detroit I've helped; and all of the other things I've been a part of; and they are talking about not wanting to renew my contract. I'll show these bastards. Shit; Detroit loves me. Especially in the hood; because I am down to earth and will hang with them in a heartbeat. I have helped convicts turn their lives around. I have kept people out of jail. I have helped unwed mothers get jobs. I have stood up for the innocent, when they tried to prosecute them. They want something that will blow them away; then that is what they'll get. By the time I am through; I will own this station." He then turned around and began his journey back to his office. Once inside he screamed. "This is not over. They are not gonna just boot me out of here. I will leave on my own accord. Watch out, world; here I come again, here comes Vincent Arbetello in a blaze of glory."

## Detroit, Michigan

About ten minutes after the leasing company picked up First Lady's car and drove away, The 53' footer Allied Van Lines moving truck pulled up to the soon to be former Hunter mansion in Palmer Park. First Lady Hunter opened the door and introduced herself. After a brief survey of the house, the movers confirmed that it would take the crew about eight hours to have everything removed from the house. They also told First Lady that they would have her belongings in Ohio on Saturday afternoon. She agreed and gave them the house key along with instructions to drop the key off at the real estate company on Grand River after they had emptied the house. She then proceeded to load several suitcases into an awaiting cab for her ride to the Marriott Hotel in Southfield where she would be staying until her flight to Ohio on Friday afternoon. As the cab pulled away; she blew a kiss toward the house and quietly said "I hope whoever gets you now has better luck than I did. Thank you for the good times and the bad. I am stronger now and I am leaving the old behind and embracing the new. Goodbye house, I am no longer First Lady Hunter; I will now be known as Charisse Kelly soon to be Hutchinson."

* * * * *

Monday, mid-morning, at Shadiki's in Greektown, the banquet staff held a meeting regarding the upcoming party settings for the Davenports party. Uncle DeArthur called me from the clothing store and asked me to contact Lady Monica on three-way so that he could find out Anthony's favorite colors and if he'd mentioned anything to her about any suit or shoes in particular that he might be interested in. After talking with them for about 15 minutes, Uncle DeArthur had all of the information he needed so that he and his brothers could custom design a suit, and shoes for Anthony's going away present. I realized that I hadn't gotten the gift certificate for them to give to Lady Monica. I called back to the clothing store and told Uncle DeArthur that I would be there in an hour to pick the check for the certificate. He told me that he would be waiting on me and to stop and pick up his lunch order from the restaurant around the corner from the store.

## Lathrup Village, Michigan

At 12:35 p.m. I walked into "Dress like a Champion." I had a large bag of food containing fried chicken, coleslaw, biscuits, mashed potatoes and sweet tea. My uncle told me to have a seat and invited me to have lunch with him. "I just wanted to let you know that I had a great time in Vegas. Have you thought anymore about the wedding date?" he asked. I replied;

"Let's talk about something else; what are you wearing to Lady Monica's party?" "I don't know yet, but I guarantee you that I will be on point." We both laughed, as he handed me a check for two grand, plus $200.00 cash. We hugged and I left, in route to Lord and Taylor to obtain the gift certificate. After that I stopped at Wesley Berry florist and arranged to have a custom bouquet of flowers delivered to Shadiki's for Lady Monica, from the Champion men.

\* \* \* \* \*

Tuesday morning I awoke, showered, dressed and made a special trip to the gym, and stopped by Trina's to get a touchup on my hair. When I finally arrived back home, I prepared the gift certificate for Lady Monica by placing it in a decorative envelope. I also custom made a small card on my computer that I would have my father and uncles sign. I also packed myself a just in case bag, and put it in my trunk; because I was attending the party solo and wanted to be prepared just in case I met someone that I might be interested in for the moment.

\* \* \* \* \*

Later that night, the atmosphere at Shadiki's was spectacular. People young and old were in attendance to say goodbye to Anthony and Lady Monica. The banquet staff had decorated using flowers, banners, special lights, balloons, streamers, satin tablecloths, crystal glasses and they had even set up several VIP tables' right in front of the special table for Anthony and Lady Monica. They had also set up a table that was exclusively for gifts only; and another for food. All of the liquor was included and was on a portable bar. As Alessandra, Debonair and I entered the restaurant; we were stopped by one of the waitresses and asked our names. After we told her; we were escorted to one of the VIP tables. About five minutes later my father and his brothers along with their dates entered and joined us at the table. I had the men sign the card and placed it on the gift table along with the certificate. I saw a large box on the table already. It had a familiar label on it; therefore I knew it was from my family. As I sat down, I looked around the table to see that all of us were looking fabulous. The Champion men once again were on point, (especially Uncle DeArthur) all of them were wearing either silk or linen suits, and alligator shoes; (in an array of different colors). Alessandra had on a cute navy blue sequined asymmetrical skirt that reached several inches below her knee, with matching top and navy blue heels with rhinestones around the ankles. Plus she was rocking her 3 bracelets from the triplets, and her engagement ring.

I wore the black and gold sequined dress given to me by Frenchee B. along with my matching shoes; and my new engagement ring along with a few other diamonds.

\* \* \* \* \*

About ten minutes later, the restaurant was filled to capacity. Anthony and Lady Monica came over and spoke to all of us as the DJ began playing music. As we were talking, a tall brown skinned gorgeous man I'd never seen before asked me to dance, as he spoke to Lady Monica and Anthony. He introduced himself. He stated his name was Alonzo Kenneth Crawford. After my family got up to dance, Lady Monica asked me to join her and Anthony at the main table after I finished dancing. I agreed and walked to the dance floor with Alonzo. The DJ kept playing good music and each time I would try to walk away Alonzo would grab my arm. As we continued to dance; I learned that Alonzo knew Lady Monica because she and his mother, Yvette *(who was on the dance floor)* were friends and that she also gave Alonzo piano lessons when he was a child. Alonzo was sexy as hell. He was dressed in all black and iced out in diamonds. He was around 6'2", 28 years old, and well-built. He held me in his arms while we slow danced to a song by Luther Vandross. I was feeling kind of good, even though I had only scratched the surface in getting my drink on. Alonzo kept complimenting me on how good I looked. After finding out that my last name was Champion; he kept saying that I was a definite winner. Alonzo had a smooth, calming effect about him and I had even forgotten that I didn't have a date. Debonair came over and cut in while I was still dancing with Alonzo. I asked Alonzo not to wander off too far and he told me he wouldn't.

\* \* \* \* \*

As I danced with Debonair he reminded me that Michael was due back on Wednesday and he told me to try and stay out of trouble because of the fact that I had the Champion DNA. I laughed and assured him that I had planned on behaving like a lady because I would see Michael tomorrow. I joined Anthony and Lady Monica at their table and was introduced to many of their friends and also friends of Anthony. People were there from Michigan and from out of town. Charisse Kelly even attended. L.H. was with her and they announced they were expecting a child, their getting married in one week; and that they were leaving in the morning for Ohio. Lady Monica and Anthony were dressed to the nines. Both of them had on white and gold. They looked more like a couple that were getting married.

We talked and drank champagne for about 30 minutes. The DJ then played a song by Charlie Wilson and I felt someone grab my hand. Once again it was Alonzo; who said "let's go." I accepted and we stepped onto the dance floor again.

\* \* \* \* \*

I noticed that this time as we danced; time seemed to stand still and it was like we matched each other move for move. We were totally in sync dancing to the music. As everyone cheered us on, I began to wonder how he would stack up in bed. He was someone I definitely wouldn't mind hanging with for a while. I could tell by the imprint in his pants, by his movements, and the way he would occasionally lick his lips that I would not be disappointed if I decided to take on the challenge. And last but not least he wasn't that bad to look at either. He could actually be considered as "eye candy."

\* \* \* \* \*

The DJ saw that Alonzo and I were feeling each other on the dance floor and played another song. This time Alonzo got as close to me as he could and expressed his desire to sex me up later. He told me that he didn't mean to come off as cocky; but guaranteed me that he could make me call out his name and beg him not to stop; if I only gave him the chance. He told me he lived in Rochester Hills, but had booked a room at Aces High Casino/Hotel across the street because he was planning on getting his drink on and did not want to get in trouble for attempting to drive home after the party. I told him that I would take his invitation under consideration and that I was engaged. He responded by saying he was, as well, to the daughter of a wealthy businessman and he was getting his "variety is the spice of life" thing out of his system because he was going to try to be faithful when he got married. He continued by saying there was no guarantee because being faithful was not in his DNA. I was actually flattered that he asked for a session, and told me the truth. I was seriously thinking about taking him up on his offer. Debonair danced back over to me and whispered in my ear; "I can tell that you are gonna get wild tonight; just make sure that you charge your phone so that you'll be ready when Michael calls. Cousin Natalie; I love you; don't get into trouble. Let Uncle DeArthur know where you'll be."

I shook my head in agreement and pushed him back toward Alessandra as she continued to dance. Alonzo asked me who was that as the music ended; and I told him that was my cousin Debonair.

"I am impressed that your family is close. My family is the same way." He said.

\* \* \* \* \*

After a few more dances, we joined Anthony and Lady Monica at their table. We ate and watched as they opened their gifts and gave acknowledgements to the gift givers. During the party, Shavonne Swanson, Frenchee B. Henderson, along with Julius Fitzpatrick and several others called to express their love and best wishes to Anthony and Lady Monica and were put on loud speaker so that the partygoers could hear them talk. Ex-First Lady Charisse and I got a chance to talk also. She told me that she was upset with me at first for concealing Pastors extracurricular activities; but had to respect me for not wanting to get in the middle of a marriage. She also told me that she had seen a man in the airport that reminded her of him but he had a different face. She then quickly changed the subject and told everyone goodbye as she and L.H. prepared to leave the party. After bidding farewell to Lady Monica, *who cried and did not want to stop hugging me*, I made my exit from Shadiki's restaurant with Alonzo. We walked through the tunnel and entered room 2775 of the hotel.

\* \* \* \* \*

Alonzo and I both were already buzzed from drinking at Lady Monica's celebration, but decided to smoke a few blunts, and have a few more drinks. We had also brought some food from the party and we nibbled on it. I changed clothes in the bathroom and texted Uncle DeArthur to let him know where I was. He texted me back; stating that he had booked the room across the hall and was in route to the room. Alonzo and I got naked and sexed each other like porn stars for hours. I passed out several times from the pleasure and several times had to wipe tears of ecstasy from my eyes. I had my "A" game on because Alonzo wept silently several times also. Alonzo definitely kept his promise about me calling out his name and begging him not to stop. And I begged several times. I must say that I had never in life been sexed like that before; and I have had my share of mind boggling sex. For a minute I wondered if I had gotten involved with a master playa. The man was definitely experienced in woman pleasing. I knew that I would have to get an encore from him. When the sun came up I received a text from Debonair stating that Michael was leaving Las Vegas at 8:00 a.m. I showered and got dressed; I woke Alonzo up and told him that I had to leave. He asked me if I'd enjoyed myself and told me he held much respect for me. He stated that I was definitely a worthy adversary; and had given him a challenge sexually. He then reached in his pocket and handed me three grand and his business card. We ordered a quick breakfast and said goodbye. Alonzo was in the printing and graphics business. He was the owner of 5 franchises in Southfield, Troy, Madison Heights, Clinton Township and Oak Park. Alonzo sent me a text stating that he needed to see me again and I agreed.

* * * * *

As I was walking out of the hotel elevator, I received another text. This time it was from Uncle DeArthur who suggested that I go home. I texted back and told him that I was on my way. He said that he wanted to speak with me and would be at my house at 11am. I agreed and headed home. Around 11:05 Uncle DeArthur pulled up into my driveway and exited his vehicle. I had prepared lunch and invited him in to join me. As we ate; he asked me if I enjoyed myself last night. I said yes and thanked him for having my back. He then asked for a strong drink and the look on his face scared me because I had not seen him look so serious in quite a while. He told me that a strange man showed up at Lady Monica's party last night about 15 minutes after I'd left. He said that he had a weird feeling about the man. It was like he knew him from somewhere but couldn't put his finger on it. As I listened I began to feel strange and started shaking. He then said "I didn't mean to upset you my beauty; but I just thought you should know." He said that Lady Monica got real antsy when she saw him also; but Anthony calmed her down and told her not to worry then he decided at that moment that they would leave town tonight instead of Friday. They would just have to stay in a hotel until the furniture got there on Saturday. He then changed the subject and asked when Michael would be returning. I told him later this evening; that he was on the jet as we spoke. I called my father's ladies Charlene, Darlene and Marlene and told them that I was on my way to finalize the plans about the condo with them.

* * * * *

Thirty five minutes later, Uncle DeArthur and I pulled up to the condo where the Rosemond triplets resided. Charlene opened the door and hugged me tightly. As we walked in; I smelled a familiar fragrance. It was the triplets' southern fried chicken and peach cobbler. As we all sat at the table; I decided that I would move out on the last Saturday in the month. They promised me that they would take care of my place and each wrote a check which would keep my taxes paid up to the year 2017. They also each gave me another check for $2,000. I called the moving company back and arranged to have my belongings picked up in 2 weeks. Uncle DeArthur told me that he would pay for the moving and pay the storage fees for 1 year. The company sent a representative and Uncle DeArthur presented him with the check and I signed all of the paperwork. Uncle DeArthur, the triplets and I then had a celebration toast, and Charlene packed us some chicken and cobbler.

\* \* \* \* \*

Uncle DeArthur drove me to the bank and waited for me as I made deposits of the checks given to me. As he drove me back to my condo, Uncle DeArthur asked me how I was going to break the news to the rest of the family. I told him that we would have a family potluck dinner on Friday night and I would let them know at that time. When we reached my condo Uncle DeArthur eyes started filling up with tears. I told him to be strong and that I had a feeling that things were going to work out where the family would still be together regardless. He hugged me tightly as I thanked him for everything; and reminded him once again that he was my favorite uncle, and then he drove away.

\* \* \* \* \*

I looked around the condo and decided to take as many clothes as I could to the cleaners. I dropped them off, paying for them in advance, and headed to Kroger to buy the last groceries I would ever buy in Michigan. When I reached the checkout, I realized that I had forgotten some of my cash. I told the cashier "I truly apologize, but I will have to return at another time." As I started to walk away I heard the words "I am paying for that; bag it up and give it to her." I turned around and a hand was reaching in my direction; waiting to be shaken. "Hello, my name is Vincent Arbetello from Channel 7 Action News." He said as he shook my hand and at the same time handed the cashier five one hundred dollar bills. "Thank you Vincent, I thought I recognized you from TV." I said. "I don't like to see damsels in distress; and I can tell by the way you carry yourself that you are worthy of an act of chivalry. I also shop at your family's clothing store." He replied. "Thank you again." I said. "I hope you will excuse my manners; my name is Natalie, Natalie Champion." "I kinda thought you were; I can see the family resemblance." He replied. "Vincent, I always watch you on the news. I know this might sound common but I would like to have an autographed picture of you. I am leaving town for good in two weeks." I stated, batting my long eyelashes at him. He gave me his business card and I told him that I would send him his money. As we loaded the groceries into my car; I noticed that he looked troubled. "Vincent, what's wrong?" I asked. He shrugged his shoulders and looked down at the ground. For some reason I felt sorry for him and said. "Let me go home and put up these groceries. I want you to meet me at Trumpps on 8 mile, we are gonna talk this out and I will bring your money also. Vincent, you are my favorite Channel 7 Action News personality; and if you need a shoulder to cry on; let it be mine." Then it hit me. Vincent had come to my rescue some years ago. I was 17 at the time, wild and rebellious. I was learning to commit jewelry store and fur store break-ins, and about to wind up in jail if I wasn't careful. Vincent talked to me sincerely, showed up at court; spoke in my behalf, and kept me from going to jail. (*The arrest and case was dismissed and all paperwork destroyed*). He never exposed me to my family. I knew then that I had to help him if I could. "Let's say Trumpp's in one hour, okay?" I stated. "Okay, Natalie," He agreed, and we both drove off in opposite directions.

* * * * *

After arriving home; I raced through the condo like I was in a marathon. After putting away my groceries, I showered, changed into a calf length brown suede skirt and jacket set, flat ironed my hair, grabbed a thousand dollars from my safe, a pack of cigarettes and left for the club to meet Vincent. When I arrived he was sitting in a booth drinking a boiler maker (shot and a beer). I sat across from him and ordered a drink for the both of us as I took his hand and placed five one hundred dollar bills into it. When the barmaid returned, I handed her a twenty; which Vincent quickly grabbed from her and placed back in front of me. He then paid her and as she walked away; he began to tell me what his General Manager had previously told him regarding his future at Channel 7. After that he told me about his love of dogs and his affiliations with the Dog Shows. He then changed the subject and wanted to know about me and how my family was doing. He once again mentioned that he shopped at the family business and asked if they had their new stock in yet. I told him I wasn't sure and suggested that he call the store later. We resumed talking about Channel 7 not renewing his contract; and him needing to get a great story.

* * * * *

Then it hit me like a bolt of lightning. I said; "Vincent, remember several months ago when you did a segment on people faking their death?" He answered that he did. "I have a funny feeling that someone everyone thinks died might have faked his." I replied. He then inquired. "Why do you say that?" As he ordered another round of drinks for us; I began to tell my story. "Vincent, a couple of weeks ago, when Journey Toward Christ church exploded into bits, it was said that the Pastor was found in the rubble along with many others; but I am now beginning to believe it was not him. I was the Administrative Assistant to that Pastor. Several people have told me that they think they have seen him in different states and other locations, they say that his face is different, but he has the same walk, body frame and mannerisms. I have witnessed the same thing they were talking about. For the last couple of weeks I have been in Vegas, New York and back to Michigan. I witnessed this person several times in airports, and on the streets, but thought nothing of it until I heard the same thing from others. My uncle said he saw a strange man at a party on Tuesday; and the guest of honor also saw this person and became quite uncomfortable." Vincent then said to me. "You say this person was a Pastor before?" "Yes, and he admitted to some very vile things right before the explosion. He was also the beneficiary to several older congregation members that had no family left." I added. "I remember that incident, because I covered part of it on the news." Vincent replied. "You know you might have something worth looking into. If this is true he could now be travelling around with a new identity and a new or similar occupation; like a Traveling Salesman, Evangelist, or something else that involves being near a multitude of people. Tell me more." He said, really becoming even more interested in our conversation. I answered by saying "Well, Vincent from what I have heard, the house he once lived in was recently purchased by, a new Evangelist which nobody has actually seen. Do you think he could be one in the same? Evangelists do travel a lot; that might be worth looking into huh?" I eagerly inquired. I wrote down the address to the house along with the name of the Real Estate Company that had handled the sale of the house and passed it to him. Vincent made several phone calls as I left to go to the ladies room.

\* \* \* \* \*

When I returned, he said. "You will never believe this. I am scheduled to go to Houston to a Dog Show at the Convention Center soon; and I just found out that there is a big revival booked on the same day on the other side of the Convention Center. It is a faith healing revival with an evangelist by the name of Ramall Turner. I think I will check it out. I also just found out through two of my colleagues who are now on vacation hunting; about a previously closed surgery center in a secluded area that has now reopened. I think I'm gonna meet them up there and do some poking around before I leave for Houston." Vincent began to write notes in a small notebook that he'd taken from his suit jacket pocket. Being the reporter he was; Vincent continued to ask me questions as he ordered more drinks. At that time, I told him about Shavonne, Frenchee B; Lady Monica, Minister Marvin, and I decided to send text messages to a few of them getting permission for Vincent to contact them. "Tell me something else about this supposedly dead Pastor. What was his name and tell me something that he did or would do that only you and others close to him would know about. How does the man you say you and the others saw, look like now?" I told Vincent that his name was Terrell Lamar Hunter and described how he looked then and how he looked now, and the habit of him switching hands when he ate. (*He would eat his meat using his left hand; using a fork and eat his vegetables using his right hand; using a different fork*). After filling Vincent in with the information he asked for, we changed subjects again and began to talk about the upcoming Dog Show and my impending marriage. Vincent looked at my ring and said "I know the Champion family, your family and I go way back. I remember you Natalie." "I remember you too Vincent." I replied. Vincent asked me if Michael liked dogs and I told him I was not sure. He then said that if he did, that he was going to give us one of his prized poodles or beagles that no longer participated in the shows. He explained that there was nothing wrong with the dogs, he just wanted them to have a good home and if Michael had no objections; the dog would be ours as a wedding present from him. I explained that the wedding would be coming soon and would be held in Las Vegas. I wrote down his home address, programmed his telephone numbers into my cell phone and told him that he would be receiving an invitation in the near future. He then told me that he would be leaving and would be in Houston by the end of the week; but first he was gonna make an impromptu trip to meet up with his hunting colleagues. He also told me that he would call me as soon as he found out anything.

* * * * *

As I finished my drink and prepared to leave, Vincent stood up, hugged me tightly, grabbed my hand, placed the 500 dollars into it, and winked at me. I looked at Vincent and he now had a look of enthusiasm on his face. The somber attitude had disappeared. He kissed me on the cheek and quickly walked away. He was on a mission and I knew deep down inside that he was about to blow some things out of the water and regain his crown of top news reporter for Channel 7 Action News.

\* \* \* \* \*

The valet pulled my car around and, as I fastened my seatbelt, my cell phone began to ring. I looked at my vehicle's clock, which read 4:15 p.m. Debonair was on the other end. "Natalie, please forgive me for telling you that Michael was heading for Detroit at 8:00 this morning; he is leaving Las Vegas at 8:00 p.m. When I called you this morning, I made a mistake. I think I'm losing it. This engagement thing is tearing me apart. I am not ready to get married, either. I am only 28 and my biggest fear is commitment to one person. I just talked to Michael and he is about to call you. As a matter of fact, where are you and are you by yourself?" "I am just leaving Trumpps on 8 mile. I had drinks with Channel 7 news reporter Vincent Arbetello and I am on my way home. I was with Uncle DeArthur and the Rosemond triplets earlier; I am about to return home and get ready for Michael because if he's leaving tonight, he should be here no later than 4:00 a.m. I can clean the condo, cook something light and get some sleep, so that I will be ready when he touches down," I replied.

# Chapter 29

*Secluded area in Northern Michigan*

As darkness began to approach, Dr. Monroe Nicholson, plastic surgeon, and his team of surgeons prepared to depart from the secluded hospital in the woods. Reaching for the door handle on his 2012 Range Rover, the doctor realized that he'd forgotten his wallet in his locker. He waved goodbye to the others as they drove away.

"See you guys next week," he yelled.

He turned around and re-entered the clinic. As he flicked on the office light, a shadow appeared and quickly flicked off the lights.

"I know that you told me to come back in two weeks, but I realized that I have too much to lose if what you did for me would ever get out," the intruder said. "I am sorry that things are gonna have to end this way, but I cannot afford to have you around."

Dr. Nicholson said, "Son, is there any way we can work this out? Just let me live; you can keep the bonus money. Son, this really isn't necessary."

The intruder grabbed the doctor and struggled with him briefly, rendering him unconscious. The intruder ransacked the office, looking for any evidence of his ever being there, but found nothing. After a few minutes, the doctor awakened. He was blindfolded, with his hands and feet bound to a chair and his mouth taped. The intruder removed the tape when the doctor regained consciousness. He then physically forced a pint of bitter liquid down the doctor's throat by yanking his head backward, holding his nose, and making him swallow.

\* \* \* \* \*

After 30 minutes, Dr. Nicholson was deceased from the ingested poison. The intruder untied the doctor, who fell to the floor. A flash drive fell underneath him from his lab coat pocket, but the intruder didn't notice. The intruder wiped the excess liquid from the doctor's mouth and then silently disappeared as quickly as he'd appeared.

As he made his way through the woods, he made several calls on his cell phone.

"Is everything set for Houston?" he asked.

After receiving his answer, he stated, "Good, I'll be on the plane in a couple of hours. Make sure that my hotel suite is in the rear of the hotel. I don't need to come in contact with a lot of people yet. Also, make sure that all of my meals are sent to my room."

# Chapter 30

*Houston, Texas*

In Houston, Texas, Sharondelle Swanson was in the process of making dinner for her and her mother. Since moving to Texas, Shavonne had rapidly deteriorated from her disease. The plane ride had really taken its toll on her physically. She now looked like she had aged 20 years. Sharondelle had taken her to the salon and had her hair cut because it was falling out. Shavonne was now wearing an extremely short, blonde haircut. The money that she'd collected from her high rollers was dwindling down because, due to her retiring from the bank, her insurance had been cancelled and any accumulated bill payments were coming out of her pocket along with her medications. She was going to be completely broke by year's end. She had also taken a loss on the selling of her house. As she lounged on the sofa, a blinding pain overtook her body and she screamed out. Sharondelle, who was in the kitchen, came running to her side.

"Mother, are you okay? Do you think we need to call the doctor again?" She asked.

"No, baby, just get me some water and my medication," Shavonne answered.

Sharondelle quickly disappeared to the bathroom and returned with a handful of pills and a small bottle of sparkling water. She handed them to Shavonne who quickly popped the pills in her mouth and took a long swallow of the water. Shavonne then pointed to the 60-inch TV that was bolted on the wall of the living room. Sharondelle turned on the TV and handed the remote to Shavonne who began flipping through the channels. She stopped when she reached the religious channel. She became intrigued with a white man dressed in a white suit. He was an evangelist named Cecil Plummer. He was placing his hands on different people who were proclaiming that they were being healed by his very touch. The crowd in the background was cheering, throwing money and struggling to get touched by this man. When the commercial came on and as the announcer began to speak, Shavonne sat up, grabbed a pen and paper, and began to write down the information. The announcer spoke with power and an attention grabbing voice.

"Ladies and gentleman: Evangelist Cecil Plummer is introducing his new protégé, formerly from the Wolverine state; come out and meet Evangelist Ramall Turner at the Touch and be Healed Revival. Are you ill, suffering from financial difficulties, want a better life, want to be healthy, have bad habits you want to break, need a new job, house, car, husband, wife? Do you need to get control of your children, get off drugs or alcohol, or any other type of problem? If so, The George R. Brown Convention Center is the place you will need to be. New and powerful Evangelist, Healer Ramall Turner is coming to town. Three days only, two services per day at 11 a.m. and 6 p.m. Seating is limited to 20,000 each service. Come on down and receive your healing. Admission is free. Parking is free. George R. Brown Convention Center: Friday, Saturday, and Sunday only. Come on down and be a part of The Touch and be Healed Revival."

Shavonne wrote all the information and placed it in her purse next to the tray table. She continued to watch the faith healing show as the white suited evangelist went from person to person, laying hands on them. Some of them fainted and were carried off by the evangelist's assistants. Some of them jumped up and down, some cried and some testified to how great he was. At that very moment, Shavonne decided that she was going to give God one more chance. She was going to the Saturday evening show to be healed. Unbeknownst to the public, this new evangelist was trading on the name of Cecil Plummer and they didn't know each other. By the time Evangelist Plummer would find out, it would be too late.

# Chapter 31

*Secluded area in Northern Michigan*

After riding by the former residence of the Hunter family and now new home to Evangelist Ramall Turner, Vincent found a shirt on the fence in the rear of the residence. He tagged and bagged it and left it with Michelle Gregory's cousin at the crime lab. Later that night, he left for the woods. As daybreak introduced a new day, Vincent Arbetello pulled up to the cabin in a rented Range Rover and was greeted by his colleagues, Ron Tuttleman and Roger Woodhaven. The two men were rugged looking.. Both were tall with long, grayish hair and long beards. "We are glad you decided to come up, Vincent, but we have bad news. Roger's wife has taken ill and we have to leave right away," Ron stated. "That's okay, guys; I need to have some peace and quiet before I leave for the Houston Dog Show. We'll make up for it up later," Vincent replied. As Roger and Ron loaded the last suitcase in their pickup, each of them expressed to Vincent how they felt about his situation with Channel 7 and wished him well. After they were gone, Vincent unpacked, took a shower and checked the computer. After confirming his reservations for the Dog Show and eating a small meal, he fell into a coma-like sleep and slept until the next morning.

\* \* \* \* \*

At 5:00 a.m., he was awakened by the sound of a dog or wolf howling. He washed his face, dressed in his camouflage gear, grabbed his gun with silencer, a pair of gloves, a GPS tracking device, his video recorder, several cell phones (one being untraceable), and some other necessities. He began walking through the woods, following the sound of the howling. After walking for about 45 minutes, he stumbled upon a building in a secluded area of the woods. He saw a wolf run off into the woods and the howling ceased. As he looked around the building, he saw a vehicle and wrote down the license plate number. He opened the door to the vehicle and, after looking through papers, discovered the vehicle belonged to a Dr. Monroe Nicholson, Plastic Surgeon. He also found papers stating that Nicholson's medical license had been suspended for unethical practices. Vincent knocked on the building door and several windows. When no one answered, he picked the lock using a tool given to him by an ex-burglar whom he had helped to get acquitted. At the time of acquittal, the ex-burglar was a 17-year old named Natalie Champion, who Vincent talked to with love and wisdom. His words made her cry, yet think. Vincent Arbetello was a contributing factor in Natalie's returning to school and getting her life back on track. He entered the building and called out, but got no response. As he looked around, he realized that the building had been converted into a clinic/hospital and had a surgery room and a pharmacy, along with very expensive equipment and various medications.

\* \* \* \* \*

Vincent went into reporter mode and began to videotape everything. As he wandered up and down the halls videotaping and talking, he began to smell the odor of death. Being a news reporter, he'd smelled that odor before. As he walked, the scent became stronger. Vincent turned down a long hallway and when he reached the end, he saw an office with the door ajar. He looked in and saw a body lying face down. Vincent carefully turned the body over and realized that it was Dr. Nicholson. After looking at his body, Vincent realized that he was a victim of cyanide poisoning. He took a second look and discovered a flash drive that had been lodged under the body. He quickly retrieved it and placed it in his pocket. Vincent looked around and found several other flash drives. He figured that they contained medical information on clients that had used the doctor's services. Vincent used the untraceable cell phone to contact the police as an anonymous caller and left the premises before they arrived.

\* \* \* \* \*

Vincent called Michelle Gregory at Channel 7 and told her about his discovery of Dr. Nicholson. He convinced her to keep the story under wraps for a least a week, if possible. He said that he needed a couple of days and after that, he would have a complete story that was going to blow everyone out of the water. She wished him luck and asked if she could be the one he'd celebrate with when this was over. He agreed and told her that if everything worked out, he would give her a celebration that she would never forget. Vincent arrived back at the cabin and removed the flash drive that he'd found under the doctor and placed it in his laptop. He discovered exactly what he had hoped it would reveal. There was medical history on Terrell Lamar Hunter along with before, during, and after surgery pictures. Along with the pictures, was the price of the surgery, payment schedules, times for follow up appointments, copies of prescriptions for medications to be taken, and other vital details. There was also a videotaped interview of Dr. Nicholson and his patient eating lunch and discussing surgery procedures. Vincent watched that part closely and discovered what Natalie Champion had said about Pastor switching hands while eating. That was a habit he still held on to. Vincent then watched the other flash drives, which were also about the surgery. Vincent jumped for joy and began preparing videotapes and written reports. He devised a plan to follow and observe the new evangelist in Houston while at the Dog Show. Eight hours later, Vincent had completed phase one of his mission and was packing up, heading to the airport for his flight to Houston, Texas.

# Chapter 32

*Lathrup Village, Michigan*

I had turned in early and my sleep pattern was on the verge of re-adjusting itself. Unfortunately, around 5:15 a.m., I woke up at the sound of my house phone ringing.

Angry about my sleep being disrupted, I angrily answered. "Who is calling me at this hour of the morning? This better be important."

"Natalie, baby, I am sorry, get up and get things together, I am at the airport and I am picking Michael up. We should be at your place in about 30 minutes," Debonair said.

"Thanks for looking out. I am so sorry about my tone; please accept my apology," I replied.

"Just have some coffee and a light breakfast ready, if possible," Debonair requested.

"No problem," I replied and disconnected.

I quickly prepared scrambled eggs, hash browns, cinnamon toast, turkey bacon and coffee. I placed the food in the oven's warming tray and went back to bed. Forty-five minutes later, I heard Debonair opening my door. A few minutes later, I heard Debonair putting food on a plate. Michael came directly to my bedroom, quickly undressed, kissed me, told me how much he loved me, got into bed and was asleep within 10 minutes.

Debonair sent a text to my phone from the kitchen thanking me for the food and saying that he was going to eat and go to sleep in my loft guest room until noon.

Three minutes after that, I received a message from Vincent Arbetello. The message read: "I am on my mission to find out everything I can about what we talked about. I have completed phase one and you are not gonna believe what is going on. This is gonna be an across the state lines story when I'm finished. I am en route to Houston now; I may need you to fly down here this weekend. I will keep you posted and will pay for your trip. I think I am gonna need you to play a role for me. Talk to you soon.

Vincent."

I snuggled up next to Michael and went back to sleep.

# Chapter 33

*Houston, Texas*

Vincent Arbetello's plane touched down at Bush Intercontinental Airport in Houston. The time was 7:00 a.m. He had eaten breakfast on the plane, so he wasn't hungry. After retrieving his luggage from baggage claim, he spotted Evangelist Ramall Turner being escorted to an awaiting limousine accompanied by several others. Vincent postponed picking up his rental car. Instead, he hailed a cab and followed the limousine to the nearby Houston Marriott hotel. He stood back as the clerk checked Evangelist Turner into a luxury suite on the top floor. *I got to find a way to get on that floor*, Vincent thought to himself, as the evangelist and his entourage walked away with the hotel concierge, Judith McMillen. Vincent realized that he knew the concierge and decided to have a seat in the lobby. When she returned and spotted Vincent, she approached him and they hugged. "What are you doing in Houston?" she inquired. "I'm here for the Championship Dog Show, plus, I think I might have a story brewing. Do you think you can get me a room on the top floor where that evangelist is?" Judith nodded her head and motioned for him to follow her. Five minutes later, Vincent had a room directly across from Evangelist Turner. As Judith was leaving Vincent's room, she invited herself to have dinner with him and he agreed to 8:00. Judith McMillen was a tall, homely looking lady around 42. She had attended the same high school as Vincent and often assisted him with his homework because, back then, she was considered a nerd who knew everything. She had always liked Vincent, but he only saw her as a classmate. Vincent turned down the covers, did a review of the story he was working on, and called the kennel to make sure that his dogs had arrived safely. He then reviewed the Dog Show itinerary and soon drifted off to sleep.

\* \* \* \* \*

Around noon, he was startled out of his sleep by the sound of a heated argument coming from the room across the hall. He realized that it was the room of the evangelist. Vincent jumped into reporter mode and decided to eavesdrop. He grabbed his audio/video recorder and quietly made his way to the door. As he leaned on the door, he heard a deep voice say, "Why are you trying to back out now? This is going to be one of the biggest paydays yet. I need your part of the money so we can get this going. I really need you to trust me; you need to be thinking thousands, not hundreds. If we do this right, we can be on the pathway of being set for life. I don't need you getting a case of the good conscious now." The second voice replied, "You can't keep scamming people like you are doing. It does catch up to you, trust me. And don't forget about all of those people you let die like sacrificial lambs in Detroit. I let you talk me into this, but I am having second thoughts. I have gone as far as I am going with you. I am gonna take this money I have and walk. Good luck, but I am out of here." The evangelist's voice replied, "Well, you can leave, but you know I have connects everywhere. Try to enjoy your money because you won't be around long, Mr. Kenneth 'Po Boy' Chatman. I refuse to let you fuck my money up or try to take me down. I thought you wanted a better life, but I guess I was wrong. You are destined to be broke all of your life. I was trying to let you have something when I rescued you from the streets of Chicago along with Billy, but I see you are content living the life of a bum." Vincent smiled, knowing that he had some more information to go with the story.

\* \* \* \* \*

Vincent then heard footsteps and several sounds like someone was being punched and kicked. He then heard a loud scream. Vincent retreated back to his room and positioned himself and his video recording device so that he could get a look at whomever was about to leave. A few seconds later, a man came stumbling out of the room. He was bloody and battered; his clothes were also partially torn. Vincent videotaped him as he staggered down the hall and collapsed at the elevator. Vincent called 911 and five minutes later, they were on the scene asking the victim what happened. Vincent overheard them saying that they would be transporting the patient to Memorial Hermann Hospital. He made a mental note to make a trip and interview the victim.

\* \* \* \* \*

Vincent closed his hotel door in the nick of time because Evangelist Turner and his entourage came out of the room and made their exit through the doors at the end of the hallway. Vincent also heard the evangelist state that room service was to deliver all of his meals. Vincent knew what his next move would be. He would set things in motion that would result in the evangelist having to exit his room to eat.

\* \* \* \* \*

After showering, getting his video recording equipment together, and adding some dialogue to his report, Vincent put on a toupee, some old clothing and shoes, a hat and a pair of sanglasses. Two hours later, Vincent entered Memorial Hermann Hospital in search of patient Kenneth Chatman. After questioning the clerk at the desk, Vincent was told that Mr. Chatman had been pronounced dead from internal bleeding because of numerous stab wounds. "Damn, damn, I need to find that weapon," Vincent whispered, as he proceeded back to his rental vehicle. As he drove back toward the hotel, Vincent spotted the evangelist and several of his entourage entering a restaurant off the freeway. He parked several blocks away and retrieved a small recording device from the back seat of the vehicle. He entered the restaurant and found a seat where he could see every move of the evangelist. He ordered a plate of food and coffee as he watched the evangelist order food for everyone at his table. They were engaged in deep conversation, but he couldn't hear what they were saying. He positioned his undetectable video recording device next to his coffee cup and was shocked when the waitress brought silverware to the table and handed two forks directly to the evangelist.

\* \* \* \* \*

Vincent watched and recorded as the evangelist ate his steak with his fork using his left hand and after about 15 minutes, he requested that his vegetables be replaced with hot ones. After receiving them, he ate them with a different fork, using his right hand. Vincent then placed his recording device in his jacket pocket, his sheer handkerchief barely covering it and continued to record the evangelist. Vincent paid the waitress, ordered an extra-large cup of iced coffee to go, stood up and proceeded to walk by the table where the evangelist was seated. As Vincent reached the table, he forced himself to trip and spilled coffee all over the light colored suit the evangelist was wearing. He made sure to drench the shirt so that it would have to be immediately removed. Vincent apologized and proceeded to assist the evangelist in disrobing. "I will be more than happy to pay for your dry cleaning, sir; just let me know where you will be staying and I will send you some cash," Vincent said. "That is not necessary; it was an honest mistake," replied the evangelist, not knowing that Vincent was secretly videotaping as they spoke. The waitress had brought over several towels and Vincent saw surgical scars as the armor bearers wiped the neck, face and chest of the evangelist. One of the men quickly returned to the restaurant with a new shirt and suit. The evangelist headed to the bathroom to change.

\* \* \* \* \*

Vincent followed behind him and once inside of the bathroom, apologized again and offered to pay for dry cleaning again, still videotaping and now getting a better look at the surgical scarring. The evangelist once again refused Vincent's offer to pay, but requested that he come to one of his shows. Vincent agreed to come to the Sunday show and left without introducing himself. Vincent now had 75 percent of his story. Sunday would be the icing on the cake.

\* \* \* \* \*

Several hours later, Vincent slipped out of the hotel and headed for the Convention Center to secure things for the Dog Show, which was to begin on Friday also. He walked around, speaking with other contestants; he checked his poodles and beagles, picked up his paperwork, paid all necessary fees, and played with the dogs. He then inquired about the revival that was going to be held on the other side of the Convention Center and made sure that there was no way that he could possibly run into the evangelist by mistake. He devised an escape route just in case. After securing everything, he made a trip back to the hotel to prepare for his date with Judith McMillen. He really didn't want to be seen in public with her, so he decided that he would take her to a dark, unpopular bar and grill near the airport. He would also talk her into getting into the room across the hall so that he could search for the weapon because everyone was empty handed when they left earlier. Vincent then watched from the peephole as once again, the evangelist and his crew left the room. Vincent decided after they'd left that he was going to find the weapon without Judith's help. He took a chance of using his keycard to enter the room. He was shocked when the door popped open. Propping the door open with a chair, Vincent looked around and when he saw a brown paper bag, he looked inside and saw an eight-inch carving knife wrapped in cellophane with blood on it. He quickly retrieved it and left the room, undetected.

\* \* \* \* \*

He called Michelle Gregory back in Detroit, told her that he was sending her something special delivery, and explained the situation, including the death of the doctor in the woods and Kenneth Chatman of Chicago. He told her to get the evidence to her people at the crime lab and keep it under wraps; but he would need DNA information by Sunday afternoon. He then prepared the package for delivery. After disappearing through the rear of the hotel, Vincent made his way to the UPS down the street and had the package shipped back to Detroit, with instructions for the recipient to contact him on his cell phone when the package arrived.

\* \* \* \* \*

Vincent returned to the hotel, showered, changed clothes and waited for Judith McMillen. When Judith arrived at his room, Vincent requested that he be moved to another room on a different floor. Judith helped him move his belonging, and he smiled when he received another keycard, which was completely different from the one he originally had. That night, Judith and Vincent started their date at the dark bar by the airport, but wound up traveling to several other bars. Vincent even watched as Judith McMillen let her hair down and rode a mechanical bull at a country and western bar. They even sang a duet on a karaoke song. Around 3:00 a.m., they returned to the hotel and Vincent, now highly intoxicated, wound up having sex with Judith in her room. When he awoke the next morning, realizing what he'd done, he quickly and quietly got dressed, retrieved the used condom from the bed, and double checked to make sure no holes were in it. He went back to his room, threw up, and then stood looking in the bathroom mirror, questioning his sanity.

"Thank God I used protection. Michelle can never find out about this. She is the one I am gonna marry. I've got to cut down on drinking before I get into something I can't get out of," he said, aloud.

# Chapter 34

*Lathrup Village, Michigan*

Friday morning, I woke up when I smelled the aroma of French Roast coffee, homemade biscuits, grits and salmon croquettes. I jumped from my bed and entered the shower. As I exited the bathroom, realized I had company and came down to find my father, Uncle DeArthur and Michael preparing breakfast and setting up the breakfast nook with dishes and glasses. Five minutes later, Uncle DeAngelo arrived with Debonair. After we all ate, I cleaned up the area accompanied by Michael and we all left in my father's car en route to Kroger in Lathrup Village. After shopping for dinner items, we arrived back at my house where the men began to prepare the food for tonight's feast. I changed clothes, called Trina and headed to her shop. She had a booth waiting and within two hours, I had been given a relaxer, trim, a deep chocolate color and a flat ironed style. I then stopped and got my nails and toes done along with some eyelashes and an eyebrow arch, and picked up my dry cleaning. I sent Vincent a text stating that I was glad things were going well and for him to keep me posted. I returned home and was told that the dinner would be held at 7:30 and that everyone was anxiously awaiting my announcement.

\* \* \* \* \*

The day went quickly and before I knew it, evening had set in. I changed clothes and my father, uncles and Michael did the same and put the finishing touches on the meal. Around 6:45, the dates for my father and uncles arrived, along with Debonair and Alessandra. As we dined on Italian cuisine, I announced that I had gotten a high-end job at the Luxor Casino/Hotel and that I would be moving at the end of the month. I also told Michael that the Luxor Casino/Hotel was putting me up in a corporate suite off site and that I would be staying there because I refused to live with him until we were legally married. I told him he would be welcomed to come over spend nights if he wanted. I also told him to give me 90 days on the new job and after that, we would contact a realtor and start looking for a house. He seemed shocked to hear it, but after looking in my father's face, he chose to accept it and leave it alone. We then set the wedding date for New Year's Eve.

* * * * *

After I made my announcement, Debonair made an announcement about his new job with the radio station in Las Vegas and that he and Alessandra might get married in Vegas on or around Christmas. That way, her family could come out. As everyone celebrated and toasted with champagne, Debonair and I slipped away and he told me that he was going to prolong marriage as long as possible, even if he had to go into seclusion.

I laughed and said, "Don't worry, it will work itself out. You know I feel the same way."

We hugged and rejoined the others who were now in my recreation room shooting pool. For the remainder of the night, Michael stuck to me like glue and Alessandra did the same to Debonair. Uncle DeAngelo shook his head because he could tell that both Debonair and I were feeling smothered. Uncle DeArthur stared at the both of us all night and barely said anything. I could tell by the way he hugged me goodbye that he knew that I was not very comfortable. Debonair, Alessandra and I drank quite a bit and by 11:30, he and Alessandra had disappeared and were passed out in my loft guest bedroom.

After my family left, Michael and I found an old movie, The Untouch-ables, that I thought I'd misplaced in the house and watched it until I fell asleep at the foot of my bed.

# Chapter 35

*Houston, Texas*

Back at the George R. Brown Convention Center, Friday night had been a good night for Vincent Arbetello, who was in heaven as he led his prized show dogs around the track. Vincent was dressed to the nines in a black silk tuxedo with tails. The dogs were photographed, measured, graded for their poise, tricks, physical appearance, breed and other attributes. Vincent won several ribbons that night and was invited back for the trophy ceremonies and presenting of the money on Saturday. Once again, he'd won the top prize for his dogs' categories. All he had to do was pick up his prizes on Saturday afternoon. As the show ended, Vincent felt extremely proud and was surprised to see that Judith McMillen had attended to cheer him on. "I didn't know that you were a fan of the Dog Show," Vincent said, as she approached him and the trainers that were loading the dogs into the carriers. Judith replied, "I am not really, but I had such a good time with you last night that I had to come and see you once again." Vincent thanked her for coming, told her that he had other business and that he would see her later. Vincent dismissed himself from her and followed the trainers to make sure that his dogs would be attended to and properly shipped to their kennels back to Michigan. Judith stood there on the arena floor with a look of disappointment on her face.

\* \* \* \* \*

At the home of Sharondelle Swanson, the usual Saturday morning cleaning ritual was taking place.

"Mother, I am gonna take you to the revival on Sunday evening if that's okay with you," Sharondelle stated. "I have too much to do today and tomorrow I have to play the organ for morning services. I promise, I will come straight home from church, take a nap and be fresh."

Shavonne, who was lounging on the sofa, agreed and struggled to lift herself from the sofa. She stood up and walked slowly into her bedroom where she began to sort through clothes looking to choose an outfit to wear. She realized that all of her clothes were now too large. Shavonne had lost over 50 pounds. She immediately requested that Sharondelle stop at a boutique and purchase her a skirt and jacket. Sharondelle agreed and left 10 minutes later. After an hour of searching, Sharondelle found a designer denim skirt and jacket for her mother and returned to the house. She assisted Shavonne in trying on the outfit and, after seeing how well it fit, she washed and ironed it and placed it in Shavonne's closet for Sunday.

* * * * *

Saturday afternoon, Vincent Arbetello was being photographed and smiling as he proudly accepted the gold ribbons, trophy and a check for $250,000 as the top prizewinner of the 2011 International Dog Show in the Poodle and Beagle categories. After accepting, Vincent shook hands and talked with several people before leaving to go to UPS to have everything shipped back to Michigan. He deposited the check and sent a text message to Natalie Champion asking her to call him because he had an assignment for her and would be paid if she accepted, along with a free trip to Houston. No sooner than he pushed send on his phone, Judith McMillen approached him and asked him to go to dinner with her again tonight. Judith was at UPS sending her mother a pakage. Vincent explained that he would have dinner with Judith, but was unable to stay out late. Judith was disappointed, but agreed to meet Vincent at 7:00. In anticipation of their second date, at 6:45 p.m., Judith knocked on Vincent's hotel room door. Getting no response she knocked harder. She turned the knob, opened the door, only to find the room empty. Vincent had already checked out and was now staying at The Crowne Plaza Hotel near Bush Intercontinental Airport.

# Chapter 36

*Lathrup Village, Michigan*

S aturday afternoon, while picnicking with Alessandra, Debonair and Michael at Belle Isle in Detroit, I received a text message asking me to contact Vincent Arbetello ASAP. I excused myself, stood next to Alessandra's SUV and returned his call. Vincent answered on the second ring. "Hi, Vincent, Natalie here; what's up?" I asked. "I need you to come to Houston right away; I have an assignment for you. I really can't explain things on the phone. How soon can you be ready; because I need you here no later than noon tomorrow. I can have a private jet at City Airport in the morning at 9 a.m.; that way, you will get here by 11 am. Is that doable for you?" I could tell by the tone of his voice that something major was about to take place. I answered, "No problem." He told me to bring Michael and Debonair for support. He also told me he had talked to Lady Monica and Frenchee B. He requested that they watch the revival on TV tomorrow at 6 p.m. He then told me about the winning of the Dog Show, which reminded me to ask Michael about the dog. I motioned for Michael and Debonair who walked over to the truck. I told them I had to go to Houston to help Vincent, while Alessandra was still flipping ribs on the grill. They both agreed to go with me and I asked Michael about the dog; he said he liked both poodles and beagles. I then knew what we would be getting from Vincent for a wedding present. I told Vincent to be ready on New Year's Eve.

\* \* \* \* \*

Several hours later, around 11 p.m., after enjoying the picnic, Michael, Debonair, Alessandra and I were headed back toward Lathrup Village, riding in Alessandra's Mercedes SUV. I believe that Alessandra knew that something was up with Debonair because while she was driving, she kept insisting that he spend the night with her at her place. He started an argument with her about needing some by himself time as Alessandra pulled into our subdivision. Debonair jumped out of the truck along with Michael. I tried to console Alessandra by telling her that he was just buzzed from drinking, but she wasn't buying it and after I got out of her vehicle, she drove away in tears. I started to talk to him about it, but he waved his hand and I decided to leave it alone. Debonair went inside of his condo and Michael and I walked around to mine. Michael asked me, "What just happened? Everything was fine with them a few hours ago." I shook my head, we entered the condo, packed for Houston, and fell asleep.

\* \* \* \* \*

Sunday morning, 6 a.m., I heard Michael talking to someone on his cell phone as I entered the kitchen. "It's almost ready now, come on over. Yeah, she is up, I hear her walking," Michael said. Michael turned around from the stove, facing me and said, "Debonair is on his way over for breakfast. Grab a shower and come back down so that we can eat." I must have really been wiped out because I did not even hear or feel him get out of bed. I made a mental note to be checked out by my doctor. I took a 15-minute shower, and returned to find breakfast on the table. Debonair and Michael were in the process of making themselves a plate of bacon, eggs, toast, hash browns, and orange juice. My cell phone rang and Vincent was on the line. "Good morning, Natalie, I just called to let you guys know that the plane will be waiting at City Airport and you guys will be picked up at Bush Intercontinental. I am staying at the Crowne Plaza in Houston; the limo will bring you here. Oh, and do me a favor, bring your makeup and if you have a long wig, bring it, too. And bring a silver outfit that can be worn at a church event," he said. I replied, "Vincent I don't have a wig." "That's okay; I will have one waiting for you. The limo will be at your house at 8:15; hope you guys will be ready." "We are all here; having breakfast and will see you soon," I said. Vincent then disconnected the call.

\* \* \* \* \*

As I finished the last of my orange juice, my house phone rang and it was Alessandra. She asked to speak to Debonair. I pointed at him and laid the phone on the counter. I walked him into the dining room and said, "You really need to handle this. She is about to become your wife and you should just be truthful about things." Debonair looked at me, looked at the phone, picked it up, and disconnected the call. I ran back upstairs, grabbed my silver skirt and jacket set, and placed it in my suitcase. An hour and five minutes later, a white stretch Lincoln limo pulled up and loaded our bags into the trunk. Ten minutes later, we were en route to City Airport.

# Chapter 37

*Houston, Texas*

Back in Houston, Vincent made a trip to a costume shop and purchased a platinum shoulder length wig, some lightly tinted sunglasses and a pair of matching platinum gloves. He hurried back to his room, made a call to the Embassy Suites and asked for Michelle Gregory. When she answered, he asked if she'd received the paperwork and if she had the Channel 7 Houston affiliates in place. She answered that she did and that she had all of the DNA evidence reports that he'd previously asked for. She told him that the camera crews were ready and everything was a go for the 6:00 p.m. event. Vincent then instructed Michelle to meet him at the Crowne Plaza Hotel Conference Room at 5:00 p.m., along with everyone else, so that we all could be briefed on our duties. Vincent then called the affiliates and informed them as he prepared his video recording devices, including the letter that would be read and his closing statements that he would need to complete his mission.

Vincent's phone vibrated and when he looked, Frenchee B. Henderson and Lady Monica Davenport had both left messages saying, "Headed to Houston. Flight lands at 5:00. See you at the Convention Center. We know whatever you have going on is gonna be big; hope you are right about everything; just wanted to be a part of it. See you tonight, good luck and bless you."

"Thanks ladies for having my back," Vincent said, aloud as he closed the cover on his phone.

\* \* \* \* \*

Sharondelle Swanson kissed her sleeping mother on the forehead as she prepared to leave the house for 11:00 church services. Shavonne got of bed and showered after hearing Sharondelle pull out of the driveway. Even though she had been extremely sick and weak, today she felt stronger than she had felt in a long time. After exiting the shower, Shavonne looked into the full-length mirror on the back of the bathroom door and saw a person that she hardly recognized. The disease had really taken her body through some major changes. Shavonne's face no longer had the look of beauty and radiance. She looked as though she'd aged 20 years. Her eyes were yellowish, her face was sunken in, and her weight was down to a mere 100 pounds. Her once full breasts were sagging and her long, luscious hair was now a thing of the past. She almost cried, but managed to hold it together as she dried herself off and put lotion on her body. After that, she took her medications, entered the kitchen, retrieved the breakfast Sharondelle had left for her, and ate as much as she could. After rinsing the dishes and placing them in the dishwasher, she found her favorite Gucci purse and placed a thousand dollars into it along with a .357 handgun, some tissues, her wallet, a small bible, and a handwritten note. She then retrieved her outfit from the closet and laid it across the chair in her bedroom. "Damn, I am tired; I have to sit down for a minute," she said. After making it to the sofa, Shavonne turned on the TV and started watching Evangelist Cecil Plummer as he conducted another healing revival from a sports arena in Washington, D.C. As people shouted, ran up and down aisles, threw money at him, cried and rolled around on the floor; Shavonne looked on with the hopes that later this evening she would be one of those people healed after Evangelist Ramall Turner laid hands on her at the George R. Brown Convention Center Revival.

\* \* \* \* \*

After several hours, private flight number 231 touched down at Bush Intercontinental Airport. After retrieving our luggage, Debonair, Michael and I were escorted to an awaiting MetroCars limo and driven to the Crowne Plaza Hotel in Houston. We entered the lobby and were asked to wait five minutes and then escorted to a suite at the top of the Hotel to room 3400 where Vincent Arbetello answered the door and greeted us with a big smile. Vincent gave me a hug, which lasted a bit too long according to the look on Michael's face. We all sat down and Vincent apologized for not offering us drinks, but said that he needed everyone to be focused and that we would celebrate later back in Michigan. Vincent then escorted me into an adjacent room. As Vincent explained what everybody's role would be, he handed me a small suitcase containing the wig, gloves, sunglasses and the note I was supposed to read. Vincent had friends who worked at the Convention Center that were going to make sure that he was one of the people chosen to be healed and seen by millions. The show was going to be televised. After explaining my part of the plan, Vincent showed us to our room across the hall. He asked me if I would meet with him and his crew at 5:00 in the conference room and I agreed. He said that we would all ride to the Convention Center together. Vincent was still vague on what was about to go down, but I could tell from his enthusiasm that it was going to be something that would be remembered for a long time.

* * * * *

We all unpacked our things and went to lunch in the hotel restaurant. It was now 2:30. Michael and I window shopped in the hotel gift shop as Debonair talked to several of his girlfriends on his cell phone. At 4:15 p.m., we returned to the room so that I could read over the note and perfect my act. Vincent called once again and asked me to be dressed and at the meeting at 5:00. I took a quick shower, got dressed and was walking into the hotel Conference room at 4:55 pm. As Debonair and Michael sat in the hotel lobby, Vincent and his crew entered and the meeting began. Vincent went over the plan one last time and the meeting adjourned. Vincent then introduced me to Michelle Gregory. I had seen her on TV, but she was more beautiful in person. She was around 6'0, slim, age 42, with long hair. As everyone started leaving, the affiliates from Houston and Michelle left in a separate limo. The technical crew followed in the news truck.

* * * * *

Vincent, Debonair, Michael and I followed in a second limo. Vincent and I were both in disguises. Vincent was in a cheap navy blue suit and white shirt with some fake Cartier glasses on and fake alligator shoes. I was not used to seeing him dressed in anything but the best, but I knew it was just part of his disguise. I was dressed in my silver short skirt and jacket outfit, heavy makeup, with a shoulder length platinum wig, matching stilettos, small, silver clutch purse with black fishnet stockings and the gloves. I looked like a cheap hooker. I think my disguise was turning Michael on because he kept staring at me and saying that he was going to have to ask me for forgiveness later on that night. I told him to stop flirting because I had to focus, but I promised him that I would allow him to do whatever it was he needed to do that would require his asking for forgiveness. Debonair and Vincent laughed at our interaction as we pulled into the special parking area for limousines at the Convention Center.

* * * * *

Dominique Hunter had come to Houston to attend a weekend with several friends who had previously graduated from Spelman College.

The fun weekend of partying had come to an end. Dominique had been dropped off back at the Holiday Inn so that she could pack and get ready for her flight back to Atlanta. After the destruction of Journey Toward Christ, Dominique, grateful to still be alive, had begun reading her bible and had taken on a small interest in religion. Just as she placed the last article of clothing into her suitcase, her cell phone rang and she answered. "Hello, Ms. Hunter, this is Delta Airlines calling. Due to the overbooking of your flight, we had to bump several people and you are one of them. We are sorry for the inconvenience and if you agree to fly out tomorrow, we will give you 100 dollars back, pay for your hotel and give you a voucher to fly anywhere in the U.S., which is good for one year." "Well, it appears that I have no choice, but I will take the offer." After receiving her information and having the hotel concierge prepare paperwork so that she could keep her room for an extra night, Dominique unpacked a few things and turned on the TV that was in her room. The advertisement for the revival came on. Dominique then said, "I might as well go to the revival since the Convention Center is only a few blocks away. It will pass the time and after it's over, I can come back here, get some sleep, and leave for Atlanta in the morning." She changed clothes, grabbed her bible and headed out of the hotel for the short walk to the Convention Center.

\* \* \* \* \*

Sharondelle Swanson opened the door to her Cadillac Escalade and motioned for her mother to get in. Sharondelle retrieved a small step stool and proceeded to assist her mother in an effort to get her inside of the truck. Sharondelle said, "Mother, it would be easier to get you into the truck if you would hand me your purse." "No, I will handle my own purse; nobody touches this," Shavonne screamed, as she struggled to reach the seat. Finally, after getting situated, Sharondelle locked her mother's seatbelt in place and they drove away. Sharondelle complimented her mother on how nice she looked. She mentioned the suit and that the stylist had done a nice job on her hair. Shavonne moaned and told her daughter to just hurry up, drive, and get them there safely and on time. Sharondelle was already aware of her mother's mood swings resulting from the disease and medications that she was taking, so she shrugged it off and continued to drive.

\* \* \* \* \*

Sharondelle entered the freeway and within 20 minutes, was pulling into the parking lot of the Convention Center. "I am gonna let you out here in front of the door, Mother, and I will find a parking spot and then we can walk in together," Sharondelle said. Sharondelle assisted her mother out of the vehicle and sat her on a bench that was inside of the main entrance. Sharondelle returned to her truck and took off in search of a prime parking space. She got lucky because about five rows over, someone who had changed their mind about attending the revival was pulling out. Sharondelle parked the Escalade and within minutes, was walking back toward the main entrance to join her mother. When she arrived, Shavonne was discarding an empty water bottle into the trash. "I see that you took your meds; are you ready to go in?" Sharondelle inquired. "I'm as ready as I'll ever be," Shavonne responded.

\* \* \* \* \*

Two ladies exited separate limos and greeted each other with a long hug and an air kiss to each side of the face. Both ladies were dressed in white suits with exquisite headwear and designer shoes and bags. As the limos pulled away, the two began the walk to the entrance of the George R. Brown Convention Center. Frenchee B. Fitzpatrick extended her hand showing off her newly acquired seven-carat diamond wedding ring. She'd gotten married to Julius at the Christian L. Yarborough building the day of Lady Monica's party. "It's nice to see you again," she said. "I heard about the going away party, people said it turned out really well. Did you and Anthony get our gift?" Lady Monica Davenport responded by saying, "Yes, we received the gift and it was beautiful. Anthony can't stop talking about it." Frenchee B. then said, "Well, I'm glad you both liked it. I thought you and I should try to make an effort to be nicer to one another; for a long time, we were like rivals. It's not over, though. Why do you think I called you out of the church to ride with me? I don't need your money to save my son, Marvin. I have money of my own. I wanted you around so I could rub my success in your face whenever I needed something to do." Frenchee B. then changed the subject. Flashing her ring in Lady Monica's face again, she said. "I know about you and Julius sleeping together, but that's okay, he's mine now." She flashed the ring again as she continued speaking. "Julius and I got married in a private ceremony the day you and Anthony had the party. Oh, by the way, how do you like Tennessee and your little organ playing job?"

\* \* \* \* \*

Before Lady Monica could answer, Frenchee B. walked away. Lady Monica was stunned by the statements of Frenchee B. She dropped her head in total shock from the news of Frenchee's marriage to Julius and her knowing about them sleeping together. She was also upset about Frenchee B. slipping back into her bitch mode. Lady Monica shook her head and mumbled under her breath, "That's okay, bitch, you won this round; but, it's not over yet. Don't judge my abilities by your inabilities. I'm not the pushover that you may think I am." She then entered the Convention Center in anticipation of finding a prime seat for the evening.

\* \* \* \* \*

Our limo driver pulled up to the VIP entrance and assisted me in getting out of the limo. Exiting the limo, Vincent gave thumbs up as the limo chauffeuring Michelle Gregory and the affiliates approached, along with the Channel 7 news vehicle. Michael, Debonair and Vincent followed me as I walked toward the entrance. After being escorted into a special seating area of the Convention Center revival floor, Vincent and I took our seats. Debonair and Michael were escorted to seats behind us. After securing his seat, Michael came over to me, kissed me and wished Vincent and I good luck in whatever we were about to do. He also told Vincent, "I trust you with her life, Vincent; return her to me safely." Vincent swore to Michael on his life that I would be fine, nothing was going to happen to me and that I would be back in his arms before he knew I was ever gone. The Convention Center continued to fill with people. As I glanced at my watch, I realized that we only had about 12 minutes before the show started. I looked around at the crowd and all I could see was a multitude of faces of all races, genders, and ages. Then, I spotted a lady who looked familiar, yet unfamiliar. After staring for several minutes, I realized it was Shavonne Swanson. The disease had really taken its toll; she definitely did not look the same. The days of glitz and glamour for her had reached the end of its road. Seeing her looking the way she looked now was tearing me apart inside. I began to remember how she looked back in the day and tears began to form in my eyes. Vincent noticed and asked me if everything was all right. He then told me that the show was about to start and he needed me to be focused. I remembered the old saying "sometimes you just have to play through the pain." I dabbed my eyes with a Kleenex and discarded it in the basket at the end of the row we were sitting in. When I returned to my seat next to Vincent, he held my hand and we both prayed that things would go as planned. Five minutes later, the lights went down in the Convention Center and music began to play. The curtain rose and a 200-voiced choir stepped forward. Vincent held my hand tighter and looked into my eyes. At the same time, we both whispered, "It's show time…"